"Will y??? ?"

At her failure to respond, he shook her lightly. "I'm not going to let you go until you do." Slowly she turned her head.

Unlike his other kisses which had been intended more to establish his mastery than arouse her, this one was meant to be deliberate, skillful seduction. He held her gently, restraining his hands from exerting any pressure on her slender trembling body until he sensed her willingness to remain in his arms. Slowly he drew her down onto the bed without interrupting the kiss. Moving his lips downward to the pulse that pounded in her throat, he felt his own desire mount.

"If you don't want this pretty dress ruined, sweetheart, we'd better take it off," he whispered tersely. As she stiffened slightly, he kissed her again, this time forcing his tongue past her soft lips before he pulled away slowly. "Please, Anne, help me unfasten your dress."

"I'll do it," she murmured shakily. Had anyone told her a half hour earlier that she'd be removing the clothes that she'd donned so carefully as a protection against this man, she'd have laughed in derision. But here she was doing just that—and swiftly too—because he'd kissed her . . .

The Lady Anne

Elizabeth Evelyn Allen

WARNER BOOKS

A Warner Communications Company

WARNER BOOKS EDITION

Warner Books, Inc.
666 Fifth Avenue
New York, N.Y. 10103

 A Warner Communications Company

Printed in the United States of America

First Printing: April, 1985

10 9 8 7 6 5 4 3 2 1

Chapter 1

IN general the Reverend Myles Thompson approved of arranged marriages; in particular he fervently hoped that the one he had promised to bless in a few weeks would end his eighteen years of irritation with the reluctant bride-to-be. Almost from the moment of her conception, this young girl had posed a problem of no minor magnitude for the curate, since her mother had adamantly refused to be a bride at all.

Had the woman been of common stock, the scandal would have caused no more than a ripple of excitement among the members of his East Midlands parish. Clandestine dalliances between randy young aristocrats and servant girls had always been an accepted fact of life in rural England, and the children born from such fleeting unions could be found in most villages and hamlets, their beginnings sensibly forgotten by the humble folk with whom they lived. Reverend Thompson had often performed his Christian duty in such cases by securing a small payment from the responsible father and then locating a needy farmer in a neighboring parish to wed the unfortunate mother-to-be.

But alas for his peace of mind, no such practical solution had been possible in this case, because the principals involved were each the only child of the two wealthiest and most powerful families in the parish. Their romance had been a delight originally to the pastor, and he had confidently expected to officiate in the ceremony to unite the two families in the felicitous wedding of the son and daughter. Summoned to

1

Grayhaven, the country estate of Lord Gerald Gray, on a
November day of 1822, Thompson had arrived cheerfully
prepared to post the banns. Instead he was greeted somberly
by Lady Margaret Gray, the sister of Lord Gerald, and asked
to counsel her niece, Lady Mary Gray. In the subsequent half
hour with the beautiful young woman, the shocked church-
man learned that there would be a child but no wedding.

Even after eighteen years he could still remember the
coldly defiant words of the slender nineteen-year-old heiress
when he had importuned her to reconsider the marriage.

"I no longer love the mawkish clod," she'd declared.

"And what of the child?" he'd demanded sternly.

An impatient shrug had accompanied her reply. "Since I
am unable to rid myself of it, I'll remain here with Aunt
Margaret until it is born."

"And afterwards?" he'd asked, unpleasantly aware that the
scandal was being laid on his doorstep.

Again the indifferent shrug. "I'll return to London."

"And the child?"

"Let its father decide. After all, it's his problem."

During the ensuing months Reverend Thompson had of
course heard numerous rumors about Lady Mary's riding
wildly around Grayhaven acres, about her screaming tantrums,
and about the arrival of a midwife from London; but not until
the following August was he once more summoned to the
Grays' estate. Greeted again by Lady Margaret, he learned
that Lady Mary had done precisely as she'd promised, with
one small deviation. A month after the birth of her child,
whom she'd refused to look at even once, she had departed in
the company of a Cambridge student and arrived in London
some four weeks later. As Lady Margaret led him into the
formal drawing room, she announced that his presence had
been requested by her brother and that she would like such
matters as might be discussed to remain confidential.

Never had the reverend faced a more antagonistic assortment of aristocrats, all of whom he'd known for years. The
only unfamiliar occupant of the room Lady Margaret intro-

duced as her solicitor, John Peabody of London. By the end of the conference that ensued, the lives of eight people had been permanently altered, including that of the minister himself.

Having precipitated this crisis, Lord Gray began the "discussions" with a strident demand that Margaret quit being a "damned fool" and give the "unwanted brat" to the parson for placement in a church orphanage or any place else where both the child and the year-long scandal would be forgotten. No one interrupted his harangue except Lady Alvina, Lord Gray's plump wife, who interposed a tearful plea: "Please let our Mary forget her one youthful indiscretion."

Although Reverend Thompson resented the callous attitude of Lord Gray—the child was one of God's creatures, however shamefully it had been conceived, he had thoroughly concurred with the proposed disposal. But what followed was a horror that rendered him speechless. In the dispassionate voice of legal authority, John Peabody served as spokesman for Lady Margaret and the other three people assembled. The reverend gazed at these three with unspoken sympathy. Sir Geoffrey Ashton, the child's father, who had desperately pleaded with Lady Mary to marry him until the day of her departure, sat quietly next to his father and mother, Lord Stanley Ashton and Lady Caroline. Nothing in their handsome, disciplined faces revealed the turmoil they must have experienced while listening to Lord Gray.

Momentarily lost in his own thoughts concerning the problems involved in arranging for the child's future, the reverend almost missed the impact of the lawyer's request that Lord and Lady Gray sign the release relinquishing all claims on the child for themselves and their daughter.

"A common procedure," he informed them, "to prevent all future legal entanglements." With a speed that bespoke of intense relief, both signed. The next paper Peabody handed them, however, aroused renewed cries of outrage. It announced the adoption of the child by Lady Margaret Gray, who would share guardianship with the young father, Sir Geoffrey Ashton.

Only when Gerald Gray's angry denunciation of his sister ended did he receive the third paper, a copy of Lady Margaret's will naming the child as her heir. Her brother's explosion this time was a snort of contempt. "Heir to what?" In answer to this ill-advised question, John Peabody produced a document affixed with the colorful seals of two Cambridgeshire officials and three London ones.

"This," he explained dryly, "is the final division of Lord Albert Gray's estate as dictated by his will of 1815, but delayed in execution by Lady Margaret Gray, his daughter and co-heir, because of family considerations. In light of her newly acquired responsibilities, she decided to exercise that option two months ago at the time of the adoption. Kindly note, Lord Gray, that your sister retains her ten percent ownership of Gray's Shipping and the right to monitor the company books that she maintained for the last fifteen years of your father's lifetime, a right you denied her when you assumed ownership. In addition, Lady Margaret is now sole owner of the manor house and acres of the estate known as Grayhaven, as well as all funds remaining from Lord Albert Gray's estate now on deposit in the two specified London banks."

Gerald Gray's face had assumed a sickly pallor, and his voice had lost some of its earlier bluster. "Be damned to her!" he shouted. "I'll instruct my solicitors to sue."

"You're welcome to consult your solicitors, of course," Peabody had agreed imperturbably, "but both the will and the division of properties have already been established in court, and the deed to this estate and the bank funds have already been legally placed in Lady Margaret's name."

A week after this unpleasantly divisive conference, Reverend Thompson had instructed his congregation to appear at the christening of the child who had already become the center of controversy. Having been erroneously informed that the nursling was a lad and having heard nothing to the contrary during the whole of the conference, he was discomfited at the start of the ceremony to discover a pink-ribboned infant girl in the small litter placed before him. In that moment of brief viewing as the wide-eyed child submitted to his ministrations without a whimper, he experienced a strange antipathy that had increased over the years. Had she been the lad he'd expected, he often speculated, she would not have aroused such an uncharitable emotion in him. Or had she been petite and brunette like her mother, she would have been far easier to conceal. But in appearance the small creature who had been placed into his spiritual keeping was a faithful replica of her six-foot-two-inch father with his bright blue eyes and indeterminate light brown hair. Anne Margaret Gray, however, had not inherited her father's mild disposition or obliging nature. She had instead, the reverend reflected sourly as he sat in the quiet dignity of Grosvenor House in London seventeen years later, become the most notorious child in his parish by the time she was twelve and a source of constant irritation to him personally.

Not even the miracle of this hopefully forthcoming marriage could erase his resentment; in fact, it had rather added to it. In the circumscribed world of British aristocracy in the nineteenth century, an illegitimate child had no right to disrupt the established order. Yet this marriage that Sir Geoffrey Ashton had arranged for his daughter had done just that. It would allow Anne Gray to become a legal part of a family whose heraldic entitlement reached back to the battle of Agincourt in the fifteenth century. The idea that Lord Harold Anthony Brownwell, a leading member of the House of Lords whose name appeared no fewer than four times monthly in *The Times* and whose two oldest sons were already recorded peers, should consent to a union between his youngest son, Gilbert Anthony Brownwell, and a girl with Anne Gray's imperfect background was appalling. The reverend sipped his hot mulled wine and sought a better word, one that would express his disapproval, yet not diminish his sense of Christian charity. "Gratuitous," he decided, best described the unearned good fortune being offered Anne Gray by the Brownwell family. Not, he pursed his lips in silent censure, that she had the humility to appreciate the gift. When he had attempted to inform her of the illustrious Brownwell history, she had only mocked him with that theatrical voice of hers.

"Every family produces discards," she had scoffed. "I wonder what kind Gilbert is—reprobate or half-wit?"

Frowning at the memory of those words, Myles Thompson accepted another cup of hot wine to ward off the chill of the April air and settled back to await the arrival of Lord Ashton, Sir Geoffrey, and the more notable Brownwells.

Across the room a less pretentious man had been watching the reverend's florid, complacent face with a cynical amusement. "The hypocrite sermonizes even when he doesn't have an audience," Padric Neill mused sardonically, remembering the first time he'd met the man. Neill had been working as Anne Gray's tutor only a few months when the officious minister had called at Grayhaven to protest the employment of an Irish Catholic to teach a young Anglican child. Incredibly Thompson had requested that Neill remain in the room.

"There is nothing personal in my criticism," the minister had insisted piously, "but I am the spiritual guardian of my parishioners as well as their religious leader. Dear lady," he'd implored Lady Margaret, "consider the damage to the child's soul if she should become tainted by a papist. Anne is already outside the pale of society. We don't want her to become a religious outcast as well."

Neill, who had not been in Ireland for twenty years and whose religious convictions ranked saints on the same level of believability as leprechauns, had waited tensely for Lady Margaret's reaction, since he had been without employment for several years prior to gaining this humble position. But the blunt reply had changed her from employer into trusted friend.

"I consider Padric a teacher rather than a Catholic, Myles. After all, he did teach at Harrow school for twenty years without being accused of corrupting Anglican English youth."

"Ah, but he was dismissed from that post," Thompson had pounced; and Neill had been impressed by the efficient news gathering in a rural England so far removed from London.

"He was dismissed only because he dared correct the erroneous Irish history a fellow teacher was imparting to the pupils," Lady Margaret had explained blandly. "I'm certain that you have also heard that Padric was an outstanding scholar at Trinity College in Dublin, which surpasses our English universities in many areas of classical learning."

"Just so, dear lady, but a classical education is unfortunately inappropriate for a young girl, especially one in the position of your ward. She should be disciplined by an English governess in subjects more suited to her station." Absorbed as he was in his own righteous convictions, Thompson had failed to note the glint in Lady Margaret's eye; but her words of dismissal had sent him scurrying from the house in a huffy anger.

"Anne's 'station' in life is my responsibility, Myles, and her education is Padric Neill's. You may concern yourself with her welfare only while she is at church."

Immediately upon the minister's departure, Margaret had opened the door leading to the rear hallway and called out, "All right, Miss Big Ears, you can come in now."

Unabashed, the tall child had challenged her tutor. "Paddy, did that man mean an outcast like Robinson Crusoe or like—"

"Robinson Crusoe was a castaway, Anne."

"Or like the King Charles the Roundheads drove out?"

Even at that age, which was still some months under seven, Anne Gray had amazed him. Having learned to read fluently sometime before his arrival, she had been allowed the unsupervised use of Lady Margaret's hotchpotch library and had already developed the definite eclectic preferences of adventure stories, history, and geography. In the following nine years of day-long study, she had added only two additional favorites, language and mathematics. In the one she had acquired a skill that soon matched Padric's in vocabulary and usage, but in mathematics she had quickly surpassed him in ability. Gratefully he had yielded much of this instruction to Lady Margaret, whose numerous account books were maintained with meticulous accuracy and who had taught Anne the skill before the child was fourteen. Two other Grayhaven people had also contributed to Anne's unusual education: Mac Dougall, the estate handyman, who had tolerantly imparted to her an appreciation of the function and value of tools; and Emily, the family seamstress, who had taught her practical sewing.

Padric often speculated that Anne's fierce interest in these pursuits stemmed from her dependency on the three people who had been the only reliable companions in her peculiarly isolated life prior to his own arrival. Although her father and grandfather had been regular visitors, they had never really shared their lives with her. After Sir Geoffrey's marriage to the self-centered Lady Elizabeth Cavendish, even that limited companionship had been drastically curtailed for a critical four years. With a rankling bitterness, Padric glanced once again at Myles Thompson, now dozing comfortably in front of the fire, and remembered the part the minister had played in excluding Anne from sharing even a small part in her father's life.

The reverend had called at Grayhaven soon after the christening of the newest Ashton, an infant girl Lady Elizabeth had produced in the first year of the marriage. He was, he had insisted, on this mission at the behest of the Lady Elizabeth, who had complained to him that the Ashton pew in his church was now too crowded to accommodate Anne any longer.

"I agree with her, dear lady," the pompous ass had informed Margaret, "especially with the probability of another child in the not-too-distant future. It would be better, dear lady, if you and your ward remained apart from the Ashtons at church."

Margaret's retort had been icy. "Kindly inform Lady Elizabeth that she is welcome to use the Gray pew at any time in the event of future overcrowding in the Ashton one. Anne and I will not be using it again.''

Not even Lord Stanley Ashton's fury with his daughter-in-law had altered Margaret's decision; but for the next few months the angry old aristocrat had spent his Sunday mornings with Anne at Grayhaven. How the ten-year-old girl had loved those long hours alone with her grandfather and how hurt she'd been when he, too, was finally "excluded" from Ashton Manor and moved to London with Lady Caroline.

During this period of unhappy adjustment, Anne had learned the meaning of the words *bastard, by-blow,* and *illegitimate,* not as part of a vocabulary lesson but as the epithets hurled at her one day by a drunken tenant farmer Margaret had evicted from Grayhaven. She had listened to her aunt's agonized explanation and nodded. Returning to the classroom, she had calmly announced, "Paddy, I'm not like other people." Not a complaint, but a statement of fact! However, her attitude toward study had changed abruptly from lighthearted play into a determination to excel. With no one to compete against, she had concentrated on speed in working a problem or memorizing a passage from Virgil's *Eclogues.* Even her recreation hours had reflected this new drive to succeed. She stopped racing her pony with careless exhilaration and began to follow the rules her aunt had tried to teach her earlier, and she now played cards and chess games to win.

Recalling those months of change, Padric realized that Anne's sudden aggressiveness had been more a refusal to accept responsibility for her own illegitimacy than it had been open defiance. But at the time it hadn't been easy for him or Lady Margaret to accept her sharpened tongue or defensiveness. The public trouble had started when Reverend Thompson arrived for his weekly visit to impart religious training to a child he considered lamentably godless. During such earlier lessons, Anne had been politely inattentive; but now she understood his not-too-subtle allusions about her unconventional status.

At his first mention of her "special need to be humble," she had asked sharply, "You mean because I'm a bastard?"

Aghast because he'd rarely heard a man articulate that forbidden word, and never a young girl, Thompson was preparing a fiery rebuke when Margaret had interrupted.

"Anne, that is not a word we ever say!"

"But it's what he thinks every time he looks at me," the child had scoffed, "so tell him to stop thinking it."

Whether or not the reverend had reported that incident as widely as Padric suspected, the fact remained that a few weeks later a youth, several years older than Anne but shorter by inches, had called her "Bastard" on the street in Ramsey. Her face alight with battle, she had picked up a handful of mud and smeared it on his face.

"That is not a word we use in public," she'd said primly and walked away, leaving the furious lad to face the unkind ridicule of his friends. His squire father had been outraged by what he'd called "the bastard's unprovoked assault." The second incident had involved the same group of "young gentlemen" from the Allerton Academy for Young Gentlemen, which catered to the sons of the local gentry too unimportant to qualify for Eton or Harrow. A friend of the first youth had struck Anne with a large soft lump of mud, and she'd retaliated by pushing him into the small creek that flowed through Ramsey. While the others had stood on the bank and jeered, partly at Anne and partly at the lad floundering in the muddy water, she'd climbed down the bank and pulled him out.

"Don't ever throw mud at me again," she'd warned him calmly.

Padric had watched the exchange from some distance away and had rushed to the scene, his heart pounding in fear for his pupil; but he'd quickly joined the other watchers in laughter as Anne performed her "rescue." However, during the next few weeks the entire situation had ceased to be amusing, except perhaps for the student body of "young gentlemen," who'd found a suitable target for their youthful derision.

When a delegation led by the headmaster of the academy and Reverend Thompson had advised Lady Margaret to keep Anne at Grayhaven, the furious woman had sent for her London solicitor, John Peabody; Lord Ashton; and Sir Geoffrey. The arrival of all three men had wrought still another change in the girl's life. While the lawyer had visited the academy and the fathers whose complaints had been the loudest, Lord Ashton had remained at Grayhaven to renew his friendship with "the gel who's more Ashton than the pack of them (Elizabeth's two daughters and one son) and a saucy minx to boot." The old gentleman could think of no higher praise to express his complete approval for Anne's courageous actions. Sir Geoffrey, on the other hand, had reacted with the belated responsibility of fatherhood. He'd begun to ride across the four miles separating the two estates on a daily basis, more often than not interrupting Anne's regimen of study to counsel her on the need for more ladylike behavior. Padric had been bemused at first; the father's advice had seemed as ridiculous as telling a greyhound trained for racing to act like a lapdog. He knew that his pupil had enjoyed the fights as much as the impudent lads, and she was often able to make her father laugh at his own pretentiousness. Over the months Sir Geoffrey had developed a deep appreciation for this oldest child who resembled him physically, but whose wit and willpower dwarfed his own. He'd also developed an ambition which would be lifelong to make her into a lady who would never again be subjected to cruel prejudice. To this end he'd enrolled her in the Allerton Academy for Young Ladies, the counterpart of the one for young gentlemen. Padric suspected that a large donation of funds had accompanied her acceptance into that institution, one of the kind the tutor abominated. Such schools, he knew by experience, offered little in scholarship but excelled in the art of making haughty, arrogant women out of ignorant young girls.

During her four years there on a one-day-a-week attendance, Anne had mastered the elegant mannerisms of snobbery and the art of dancing gracefully with young men shorter than herself. Padric chuckled at the memory of the other abilities she'd acquired during those "young lady" years, when she'd learned to return the subtlest of insults with malicious humor and to imitate Dame Allerton and the more affected of the girls with devastating accuracy. But she'd also developed a sense of clothing which flattered her slender maturity and made her height less objectionable. Upon her "graduation" a few weeks before her sixteenth birthday, Sir Geoffrey had decided to celebrate both events by giving a week-long party for her at Ashton Manor. The invitations had been received with shocked surprise by Grayhaven residents, since Lady Elizabeth's antagonism toward her husband's oldest child had remained a constant force over the years.

Padric never learned what happened at that party, but a grim-faced Margaret and Anne had returned three days later and retired behind a wall of silence. In the process of seeking a new position himself, since he'd completed his nine-year assignment here, Padric was unprepared when Anne had emerged from her room with the inspired idea to turn Grayhaven into a school which, she announced, would keep "Paddy employed and put an end to Father's ridiculous plans for me." A relieved Margaret had heartily endorsed the project; and in under two years Grayhaven had become a respected academy, and Anne had proved herself an excellent teacher.

Padric Neill sighed with regret and resignation. Sir Geoffrey had persisted until he'd finally arranged this preposterous marriage between Anne and some young aristocrat whom Padric was convinced would prove worthless, even if he didn't turn out to be a witless young scapegrace. The only note of cheer the headmaster of Grayhaven found in the dismal situation was the rumor that the young couple would live abroad. Away from rule-bound England, Anne might find the respect she deserved and some creative outlet for her driving energy. Although the fifty-five-year-old Padric would never admit it even to himself, he was close to tears at the thought of bidding farewell to the young girl he loved with a fierce, protective pride, a girl who was leaving him the legacy of happy memories and a permanent home.

In a somber office in the drab judicial area of London, John Peabody was also reviewing the life of Anne Gray. Although he had never actually seen this ward of his most affluent client, he had been involved in her life since she was a week old when he had arranged for her adoption in spite of his own disapproval of a spinster lady becoming a surrogate mother at the age of forty-two. But thorough lawyer that he was, he had researched the child's background with scrupulous care and had kept his files current. Her mother, Lady Mary Gray, had a scandalous record since she'd been sixteen with one hushed-up escapade after another, several involving men. Even after her desertion of Anne she'd had two affairs that were public knowledge. Ironically, though, she'd married the respected though impoverished Robert Palmer, a member of the powerful Palmer family, produced a son named Scott, and now lived respectably abroad with her diplomat husband. Damned unfair, the solicitor reflected, for the guilty mother to escape so easily leaving her aunt burdened with the scandal of an illegitimate child. Peabody had been little better impressed with the character of Lady Elizabeth Cavendish, about whom his source of information had said, "She's as iron-willed as Lady Macbeth and as ambitious as Julius Caesar." She seemed to have lived up to this description as Sir Geoffrey Ashton's wife, especially in her cruel avoidance of the child the father had been decent enough to claim publicly.

It had been Lady Margaret's and Peabody's own efforts that had made Anne Gray's life bearable. He had secured financial security for her and her aunt by removing control of Margaret's wealth from her selfish brother, and he'd made certain that Lord Gerald Gray had paid every pound that Margaret's ten percent of Gray's Shipping had earned in the eighteen years since. He had helped his client turn six hundred fallow acres at Grayhaven into a productive farm by locating two excellent tenant farmers and by making sure the East Midlands Hunt Club did not ravage those acres with their annual insanities.

He had secured the service of an excellent teacher for the child, although he privately would have preferred a less educated governess.

Seven years ago he'd rushed down to Grayhaven to resolve a nasty problem dealing with some doltish country squires who'd encouraged their sons to plague the girl. That was the first insight he'd gained into the character of Anne Gray, whom he'd found to possess some unfortunate tendencies toward violence. So unimpressed had he been, that five years later he had tried to stop Lady Margaret from indulging her ward in the foolish expense of creating a school. But he'd been wrong; even that impossible school was thriving, as did every business venture his client had undertaken.

Abruptly Peabody returned his attention to the urgent business at hand. A month ago Lady Margaret had arrived at his office in painful agitation over the marriage that Lord Ashton and Sir Geoffrey had arranged for Anne. As a realist the solicitor knew that marriages between aristocratic families were often based on financial considerations, so he had tried to persuade her to accept the inevitable.

"Your niece is handicapped in a variety of ways, not alone by birth. You've described her height and her independence. Perhaps this marriage—"

"Don't be such a fool, John. I know my niece's handicaps better than you do. What I want to know is why a man as important as Harold Brownwell would accept her as a daughter-in-law. Find out about this son of his. I'm willing to wager he'll prove to be a scoundrel or worse."

As usual Lady Margaret had been right. Gilbert Anthony Brownwell had a dismal record of failure and debauchery, which made him even less desirable than a successful scoundrel. He was the son of Lord Brownwell's second wife, a woman described as totally unscrupulous. Her son Gilbert had been involved in a shocking scandal with the daughter of a Yorkshire landowner when he was nineteen, the year he'd been expelled from Oxford after only six weeks of attendance. He'd been cashiered out of the Royal British Navy for shipboard brawling and gambling after two years of service. In the past three years he had resided in a suite of expensive rooms near Piccadilly Circus and gambled steadily, losing thousands of pounds over the gaming tables. One source reputed that he had lost twenty thousand pounds in one year. Until some weeks ago he had been living with the notorious wife of a professional gambler, a woman he'd been involved with at the time he'd agreed to marry Anne Gray.

Lady Margaret's reaction to the dossier had been characteristic. "I'd have preferred that the young fool had two heads! And to think that the Ashtons plan to send Anne abroad in the care of an immoral wastrel who isn't even a good gambler. Well, at least I can decide the place they will live. If the young man was cashiered out of the navy, that means he was an officer, since common seamen are brigged and not dismissed. Possibly he has the brains to know a little something about ships. In that case I'll need to acquire part ownership of a shipbuilding company. Don't look at me, John, as if I've taken leave of my senses. I did know that he had been in the navy, so the idea is not new. I prefer not to invest in French companies, so that leaves Canada or America. What I want you to do is to locate a shipping firm from one of those countries that is seeking British investment capital. Find out what it will cost me to buy a substantial percentage of the ownership. I'll also want to know something about the owners and their operation."

"Lady Margaret, I am very afraid that you will lose a good deal of money on a gamble like this."

"Nonsense. Anne is as good a bookkeeper as I am. She can watch out for my investment."

In the next busy week Peabody had found an American company whose owners were currently in Liverpool. In front of him now was their answer to his letter of inquiry; but the amount they were asking for a one-third ownership was staggering—forty thousand pounds. Despite the excellent reputation of the two men, Thomas Perkins and Paul Bouvier, the lawyer was convinced that Lady Margaret would be a fool not to investigate them at great length before dealing with them. But he knew his client and her abrupt way of making business decisions, and he dreaded the trip he would most probably have to make to Liverpool.

He consulted the clock and hastily reread the second letter he must deliver to his client. It was from a police official who had promised to check into the rumor that Gilbert Brownwell had been arrested three weeks ago, following a disturbance in his flat. According to the official, the man had been arrested but the records of the arrest had been removed from the police files. However, the reports of his earlier two arrests for drunken brawling were intact. Both times he had been fined heavily. Peabody sighed and summoned his driver; he wanted to reach Lady Margaret at Grosvenor House before the Brownwell family arrived.

In his London townhouse on Grosvenor Place, Lord Stanley Ashton was also rereading a letter he had received two hours earlier from an exhausted rider who'd identified himself as one of Lord Brownwell's grooms. In it Lord Brownwell stated that he'd gone to Dover to meet his wife and sons, who were supposed to return from France together. Only his wife had been aboard; Gilbert had sent a message requesting that the meeting with the Ashtons be held in Le Havre instead of London. "Stanley," the letter continued, "I know this is a damned imposition; but as I warned you, my youngest son tends to be an inconsiderate young whelp. However, I do confess to some puzzlement in the matter; my older sons also request that you and your family accompany my wife and me to France. The captain of the *Dover Princess* has agreed to hold the ship at Dover until your arrival."

After a brief consultation with his son, Stanley Ashton had written a note of agreement to the change in plans and asked the groom to deliver it to his employer after both he and his horse had rested for the night. While Geoffrey admitted to a growing doubt about Gilbert Brownwell, Lady Caroline was cynically negative.

"I warned you that the Brownwells would reconsider and refuse your offer," she snapped.

"This isn't a refusal, m'dear," Lord Ashton assured her mildly, "it's merely an inconvenience. I suggest you order your maid to start packing."

"I'm sorry, Stanley, I'm not going. I have been against this marriage from the beginning. I find it very distasteful that you two men have risked the family reputation with your ridiculous determination to marry Anne to a man so far beyond her in social rank. I agree with Elizabeth that you'll just expose the unfortunate girl to even more ridicule, and I certainly agree with her that you had no right to spend such a fortune on Anne when there are three other children to consider."

"What my son and I spend on Anne is none of Elizabeth's business," Lord Ashton snorted. "God knows she was pauper enough when she joined the family."

"She has been an excellent wife to our son, and she has never caused a shred of scandal. I know, Geoffrey dear, you feel that she should have welcomed Anne into your home; but the one time she tried proved to be a disaster."

"That was her fault, Mother, not Anne's."

"Elizabeth was merely trying to preserve the family's reputation."

"What happened?" Lord Stanley demanded.

Geoffrey shrugged. "I decided to give Anne a party for her sixteenth birthday, and it turned out badly."

"Why?"

"Because," Caroline snapped, "Geoffrey tried to force people to accept his daughter. Just as he is doing now and just as he has always done. I often feel that everyone's life would have been much simpler, had he given her up completely in the beginning. Perhaps he might have felt differently about Elizabeth's children."

"Why should I need to feel differently, since I love them the same as I do Anne?"

"No, you don't, son. You've never gotten over the infatuation you had for Mary Gray, and you've always been fonder of her child than your legitimate, proper children."

"If he has, m'dear," Lord Stanley blustered, "it's because that moral prig he married has made a pair of peacocks out of those two prissies of hers. Not a brain between them. I hope to God Geoffrey has the sense to raise my grandson himself."

"Elizabeth and Caroline are charming little girls, Stanley."

"Then you save yourself for their weddings. This one for Anne is mine and I wouldn't miss it. Take care of yourself, m'dear; don't know when we'll be back."

On the short walk to the hotel, Lord Stanley attempted to explain Caroline's attitude to his son. "She's a proud woman, lad, and it's been hard on her, especially with that wife of yours demanding Caroline's complete loyalty. What happened at Anne's birthday party?" he demanded abruptly.

"Anne attracted the attention of a Cambridge student Elizabeth's cousin had invited and—"

"Roger Cavendish? Didn't know that fat pipsqueak had any friends."

"A young man named David Langdon."

"That'll be Viscount Haverly's heir."

Geoffrey smiled; his father's knowledge about the aristocracy was encyclopedic. "David seemed quite smitten and he and Anne danced the whole evening together. Next day she helped him with a mathematics assignment, and he couldn't praise her enough."

"What happened?"

"While Anne and I were giving the children a pony ride, Elizabeth told the lad about Anne's background. Later she insisted that we owed it to David's family to protect him from an 'embarrassing romance.'"

"The bitch, the damned jealous bitch! So that was why she came bleating to London for a month to enlist your mother's help in bringing you around."

Geoffrey nodded glumly.

"I suppose the young Cambridge pup skulked away without a word of apology to Anne. I hope you had the sense to give your wife what for and tell her that Ashton Manor is as much Anne's home as it is hers."

"Anne · and Lady Margaret won't even come near the place."

"Don't blame them, but that tempest does explain why Anne's so set against this marriage. Best let me handle the minx tonight. She's got an artful knack of plaguing you into saying things you don't mean."

Only Lady Margaret and Reverend Thompson were at the hotel to greet the Ashton men on their arrival. Geoffrey cut the reverend's fulsome speech of welcome off abruptly.

"Where's Anne, Margaret?"

"She's saying good-bye to Paddy. He came down to London to see her and to hire a teacher to replace her."

"Have the fellow stay for dinner, Margaret, I always enjoy his company," Lord Ashton suggested.

"The 'fellow' "—she smiled caustically—"has already declined the honor on the basis that he enjoys reading medieval history but not being a part of it. As I do, he feels that forcing a girl to marry against her will is as barbaric as slavery."

"You've a sharp tongue, Margaret."

"That I have, Stanley. Where are the Brownwells?"

Upon hearing the explanation, she looked at the two Ashtons with unsmiling cynicism. "It should be a lovely voyage for Anne," she murmured. "Lord and Lady Brownwell will have four days to make their inspection. How thoughtful of them to protect their son in case Anne falls short of their expectations."

"That's nonsense, Margaret," Lord Stanley protested. "Harold Brownwell is a decent—" But Margaret had ceased to listen; John Peabody had just entered the room and was looking for her.

"Excuse me, gentlemen, my solicitor has arrived; and if you don't mind, I shall ask him to dine with us." She had taken only a few steps when she heard the stir of movement among the men gathered near the entrance, and she glanced up toward the stairway. Anne was making the dramatic entrance she'd promised she would, and Margaret smiled in malicious anticipation of John Peabody's reaction. From his condescending attitude whenever she had attempted to describe Anne, she knew he expected an awkward and unattractive girl. She would have been doubly pleased had she known that the balding solicitor was actually waxing poetic over the young woman descending the stairs.

John Peabody's first impression of her as she'd stood poised at the top landing was that she must be an actress or other celebrity, since her posture was so regal and her sweeping survey of the men watching her from below was so haughty. With her light brown hair falling in loose curls around her shoulders, her bright blue eyes commanding in intensity, and the faint smile of challenge softening the well-marked features of her face, she looked like a Valkyrie handmaiden on her way to a Viking battleground. Her costume, too—for such he thought her brilliant cerise gown was—made the illusion of watching a stage play complete. It was as different from the pallid-colored, crinoline-shaped dresses the other women wore as the plumage of a flamingo was from the dull feathers of an English sparrow. Unrelieved by so much as a flounce of lace, the fitted bodice ended in a bold stand-up collar that framed her face, while the long full sleeves were tightly banded at the wrist. Only the wide skirt adhered to current fashion, allowing the wearer to move with graceful freedom down the stairs.

Not until she was halfway down the long flight did Peabody notice her height and become startlingly aware of her identity. This beautiful young woman was Anne Margaret Gray, the girl he'd grown to pity over the years. Without a quiver of disappointment, she accepted the news that her bridegroom was even more reluctant than she; and the lawyer's admiration for her grew as he listened to the bantering quality of her low voice.

"It would seem, Father,"—she grinned impudently at Sir Geoffrey—"that you and I have quarreled needlessly for this past month. Gilbert Brownwell may not be the fool I thought him; at least he had the good sense to know when he's not wanted."

Surveying his granddaughter with obvious pleasure, Lord Stanley returned her grin and answered for his son. "He's waiting for you in France, you saucy minx, and we're leaving tomorrow morning to join him there."

The lawyer held his breath as he watched Anne's broad smile shrink to the challenging one she'd worn before. Turning toward her aunt, whose expression was grimly angry, the young girl asked lightly, "Aunt Margaret, when your father tried to force you to marry a man you didn't like, how did you escape?"

For a moment the older woman stared at her niece in confusion and then laughed. "It wouldn't work in today's world, unfortunately; people have become too enlightened."

"What was it?"

"I told the wretched man I dabbled in witchcraft, and he promptly departed for South Africa."

Anne pursed her lips thoughtfully and looked back at her grandfather. "I think I'll try insanity," she said. "There's no doubt it runs in the family."

Chapter 2

THE *Dover Princess* was a proud luxury ship which in the twenty years of its existence had transported many of the wealthiest members of the British elite to the resort ports of the continent. Its specialty was the reverent elegance it offered ladies of quality, both in service and appointments. Even the goods carried in the hold were feminine, delicate English wools on outbound trips and expensive French perfumes on homeward ones. Often the target of ridicule by the crews of saltier ships that plied the channel waters in good weather and foul on established schedules, the *Princess* was operated on the fair-weather principle that wealthy women expected even the elements to be subservient to their whims. Thus it had remained snugged up to its dock in the port of Dover until the last of the storm clouds dissipated. Now with his ship polished to gleaming perfection, Captain Newland waited for the last five passengers to arrive before he sailed on the evening tide for the four-day voyage to Le Havre.

Having been asked to accommodate these latecomers only two days ago by Lord Brownwell, whose family members were frequent passengers aboard the *Princess*, Newland had taken the precaution of researching their unfamiliar names in his book on British peerage. To his satisfaction both Ashtons were bonafide and solvent, while Lady Gray was part owner in Gray's Shipping. The Anglican minister, too, was a welcome addition to this or any ship about to embark on the uncertain waters of the English Channel. But as he watched these personages dismount from the carriage that had just arrived on the dock, he was disconcerted to discover that they had brought no servants with them. Furthermore, he noted with distaste, they had obviously been caught in the storm as it moved inland. The three men and the younger woman had mud streaks on their wet cloaks and their boots. Quickly the captain dispatched a seaman to cover the freshly honed decks with protective mats; mud was never allowed to befoul the immaculate beauty of his ship.

Perferring to greet his guests more formally at dinner, Captain Newland turned his attention to the mechanics of ship's business and so missed the confrontation that took place minutes later in the opulent main salon. Had he been present, he would have been most provoked; despite his precautions both the polished deck and handsome rugs were tracked with mud and dampened with dripping moisture. Having followed her aunt up the gangplank, Anne expected to be led to the same cabin; but a polite steward had guided her in the opposite direction and into the main salon where a dozen people were already assembled for tea.

Anne's eyes instantly riveted on the smiling woman whose gracefully gesturing hand summoned her closer. Never had the inexperienced young girl seen a more impressively beautiful human being than the woman who was addressed by the steward as Lady Brownwell. Her pale blond hair was arranged in a softly flattering coiffeur, framing a face that retained an almost girl-like appeal. The expressive light brown eyes studied the newcomer from beneath heavy fringes of long gold-flecked eyelashes, and a smile curved the sculptured lips into a lovely arc of welcome. Draped in folds that bespoke years of expert posturing, the rose velvet gown spread softly around the chair. But it was the quality of the voice that arrested Anne's attention; she'd heard those cultured, arrogant tones too often not to recognize the assumed authority of aristocracy.

"I'm Suzanne Brownwell, Gilbert's mother, and you must be Anne. You look very different from what I was led to expect."

Straightening from the curtsy that had been her automatic response to the first of Lady Suzanne's greeting, Anne was dismally aware of her disheveled appearance. Twice in the past hours she and Margaret had been forced to stand in the rain while the bemired coach was pulled out of the mud; the third time she'd helped push it out of a deep rut in the soggy road. Both her hair and her blue wool cloak were soaked, and her shoes were covered with mud. Resentful of the enforced inspection she was undergoing, she reverted to the bravado that had salvaged her pride during the four miserable years of pretense she'd spent under the once-a-week domination of Dame Allerton. Parting her lips in the smile that had so irritated that worthy dame, Anne waited for her present inquisitor to continue. Neither the sentiments expressed nor the sharpened voice surprised her.

"I really didn't expect you and your family to come, under the circumstances; I know I wouldn't have been as tolerant as you if a young man had postponed an engagement with me.

Please do sit down, Anne; you're much too tall to remain standing while we talk.''

In a voice that stopped just short of insolence, Anne declined the request. "I wouldn't dare, Lady Brownwell. I've already ruined the carpet by standing here; I don't want to risk spoiling a beautiful chair as well. Do you mind if we postpone this conversation until later? I'd like to go to my cabin.''

"Would you like me to send one of my maids to help you dress? Your journey here must have been frightful.''

"It was, Lady Brownwell, but I won't deprive you of your maid's services. Excuse me, please." Inclining her head in the direction of the several people who were watching her, Anne turned and strode across the room to the companionway where the steward waited silently. She had only the barest glimpse of the tall man whose gray eyes held a twinkle of amusement as she brushed past.

Inside the cabin Anne found her aunt bundled up in a warm wool bed robe, sipping a small glass of brandy.

"Where in the world have you been, Anne?''

"Meeting Lady Brownwell.''

"Good Lord, how did you manage that?''

"I didn't. She did the managing.''

"Oh, dear, and you look so bedraggled.''

"That was the idea. Your steward brought you straight here, mine took me into the main salon to stand dripping all over the floor like a drowned cat while her royal highness inspected me.''

"How dreadful!''

"Why didn't you tell me that she'd be aboard?''

"I didn't want to make our miserable trip here any worse. Was she difficult?''

"She didn't even want us to come. Aunt Margaret, when are you going to tell me what you know about the Brownwells? The only thing Father will say is that they're a fine old family, and Grandfather keeps repeating that this son is good-looking and tall.''

Margaret sighed wearily. "Get those wet clothes off, dear. The little I know can wait until you're comfortable." Leaning back in her chair, she closed her eyes in frustration. What was she to tell Anne? That both of the Ashton men were determined to persist in this insanity despite their knowledge of Gilbert Brownwell's unsavory past? When she and John Peabody had showed the two the dossier, Stanley Ashton had merely snorted.

"Wild oats, Margaret. His father already told me about most of this. With a wife like Anne, the young pup will settle down."

Geoffrey had been only slightly less optimistic. "I don't like the navy thing particularly, but most young bloods are reckless at that time of life."

Disgusted with the pair of them, Margaret had instructed her patient solicitor to contact the Americans in Liverpool and accept their offer on a provisional basis. If for some reason Anne was not forced to marry, Margaret would reimburse the two owners for the expense of bringing their ship to Le Havre in early May.

"But I want you there before that time, John, if it's possible," she'd insisted after they'd completed a difficult hour of planning. She wished that he were aboard ship at the moment; people usually acted less rashly in the presence of lawyers. With Lady Brownwell already living up to her reputation of being a possessive, unprincipled mother, and with Anne becoming more and more reckless with that scathing impudence of hers, Margaret dreaded the next few days. Determined to remain as cheerful as possible, she opened her eyes and smiled.

"How would you like to live in Boston, Anne?"

"Why do I have to live any place but Grayhaven?"

"Because your young man has indicated that he'd like to live abroad for a year or so."

"He's not my young man, but Boston would be better than France. At least his mother would not be able to get there as easily."

"Did you dislike her that much?"

"Wait until you meet her. Aunt Margaret, how much is my father paying for this marriage?"

"All young ladies are given dowries."

"You mean their husbands are, and I'm no young lady. I've known exactly what I am since I was ten years old. Sometimes I wish my father had never claimed me; then you and I could have lived alone somewhere and I could marry whomever I liked, even someone without money."

Since Margaret had often wished the same thing, she nodded in understanding, but with the reservations she'd always had about poor men who pursued potentially wealthy young women. Her own youthful experiences with such suitors had been unpleasant, and there had been that young teacher at Grayhaven who had boasted to Paddy that he planned to marry Anne.

"How well did you like Ian Shaw, Anne?" she asked cautiously.

Anne looked at her aunt and frowned. "The little man preferred to be called John, and why did you ask?"

"He was interested enough in you to request my permission to marry you."

Anne stared at her aunt and then broke into laughter. "The only thing John Shaw was interested in was replacing Paddy as headmaster and getting control of enough money to be secure for life. I'd already told him he was too old for me and three inches too short. Did my father know?"

"I believe that Ian approached your father, too."

"So that explains all this rush to get me married off. Father would despise having an Irishman in his family. Aunt Margaret," she exclaimed suddenly, "the ship's moving!"

"It has been for some minutes. Why don't you go on deck and watch?"

"Come with me?"

"No, I'm not very fond of standing on a rolling deck. I plan to take a two-hour nap before dinner. But you go, you'll find it an exciting sight."

Reminded that this was her first time aboard a ship, Anne hastily donned a dry cloak before she left the cabin and raced along the companionway and onto the windswept deck. For a moment she stood in the protected lee, lost in the wonder of seeing the shoreline recede, and then she impulsively walked toward the rear of the ship. Gripping the polished oak taffrail, she leaned seaward for a better view of the white cliffs of Dover that seemed to rise from the sea like huge ghostly monoliths.

"I never tire of looking at them," a deep masculine voice sounded next to her; and Anne turned to meet the gray eyes of a man she judged to be almost as ancient as her grandfather. His warm smile gained her instant trust.

"For once the poets didn't exaggerate," she agreed happily. "They really do look like chalk. And there's the remains of the old Saxon castle that used to guard the port during the fourth century. I don't understand how men thought they could keep enemy ships from landing when they were stuck in a fort almost four hundred feet above. Arrows wouldn't go that far in those days and catapults weren't very accurate. Do you suppose they just used the castle for a lookout tower?"

The man smothered a smile and asked, "How much else do you know about Dover, young lady?"

"I know that some historians claim it's the oldest defended port in England, at least it was when Julius Caesar tried to land in fifty-four B.C. Even the ancient druids or Britons who lived here then defended it successfully. I suppose the reason everyone worried about Dover is the fact that it's only eighteen miles from the continent."

"How many times have you visited Dover to learn all that?"

"Never." She laughed. "Until a month ago I'd never been more than ten miles from my home. The only things I know about any place else comes from books. Look over there," she cried suddenly, pointing to what seemed like an impenetrable mountain range of dull gray stone. "Is that a fog bank?"

"A very dense one." He nodded. "We'll be in the middle of it in less than an hour."

"I'd hate to be lost in it without a compass. We could sail around in circles for weeks."

"You don't have to worry about Captain Newland. He knows how to handle this ship in all the tricky weather conditions of the channel."

"Oh, I wasn't frightened. It might even be fun, and it would take us that much longer to reach France."

The man's smile faded as he looked at her "Aren't you looking forward to seeing France?"

"I don't expect to see much of it," she answered more cautiously, suddenly reminded that she was talking to a stranger.

"Tell me, young lady, if you had your freedom of choice, what would you want to do with your life?"

"Work with mathematics," she answered promptly.

For a moment the startled man stared at her in disbelief before he commented lamely, "That's an odd choice for a woman."

Her laughter rang out across the water. "That's what every man says, and I'll never understand why. It's the easiest subject of all to learn. Numbers don't change and the rules don't change, so there's only one correct answer possible."

Recalling the hundreds of columns he'd added inaccurately during his lifetime, the man chuckled. "What in the world do you plan to do with it?"

"I haven't decided yet exactly, but I will!" she declared confidently.

Regarding her with less condescension now, he probed gently, "Isn't marriage supposed to be everything a young woman thinks about?" His sharp eyes didn't miss the slight tensing of her shoulders or the sudden change in her smile.

"It's supposed to be," she answered slowly, "but it never is. I just don't want to waste my life doing the silly things most women do."

Lord Brownwell was still thinking about the remarkably

articulate girl he'd just left and the shock that was in store for his youngest son when he entered his wife's cabin. With an intense distaste, he sat down to watch the routine of preparation that had preceded Suzanne's every public appearance for all of the twenty-five years of their marriage, a marriage he had regretted within months. She was, he thought dispassionately, the most self-centered woman he'd ever known. Sitting with her face covered by a heavy layer of cream and her two maids hovering over her, performing the rites of beautification, she looked more like a serpentine basilisk than a pretty woman. But it had been that flawless face and her charming mannerisms that had lured him into an ill-considered marriage two years after the death of his first wife, Eleanor. At that time Suzanne was the childless widow of one of Eleanor's cousins, and he'd actually believed that she would help him rear his two young sons.

Thank God she hadn't even tried, and they'd both turned out to be fine men; but she'd ruined the son she'd produced from this marriage. Lord Brownwell had tried to gain control, but Suzanne had proved the stronger influence; and Gilbert had acquired her selfish duplicity and her irresponsible extravagance. His mother had lied for him, shielded him, and excused his every failure, until at twenty-four this youngest son was a bounder—a damned expensive bounder! Irritably Lord Brownwell suppressed his momentary guilt about foisting such a failure onto the slim shoulders of Anne Gray and turned his attention to the more pressing problem of speaking privately to his wife. Using the only effective technique he'd learned over the years, he announced abruptly, "I paid back the fifteen thousand pounds you borrowed from your Birmingham friend."

As he'd expected, her response was instantaneous; she dismissed her maids and turned furiously to face him. "When are you going to learn," she snapped, "not to talk in front of servants?"

"When you quit using them to hide behind, madam. Why

did you borrow money when I told you six months ago that I had none to spare?''

She shrugged indifferently. ''How did you find out?''

''The scoundrel demanded collateral from me. He wanted the deeds to Brownsville and the London townhouse.''

''Edward is a gentleman and not a scoundrel.''

''You're a gullible fool, madam, if you think that. He has his fingers in every criminal pie in Birmingham.''

''If you could pay that debt, Harold, why did you tell me that you had no funds?''

''Because it was and is the brutal truth.''

''What about my own fortune?''

He laughed harshly. ''You squandered every pound you received from your father and first husband years ago, and since then you've squandered most of mine. Edward Doncaster will never be fool enough again to lend you as much as a shilling.''

''In that case, Harold,'' she said calmly, ''you will have to keep me better supplied.''

''Madam, by law the only things I have to supply you are board and room, and that's all you're going to receive. We'll live at Brownsville with Harold, and the only entertaining you'll do will be for the locals. If you dare invite Doncaster or his kind there, I'll put you under restraint with a keeper.'' Abruptly he changed to a new line of attack. ''How much of that money did you use to pay Gilbert's debts?''

He could see her facial muscles stiffen even under the heavy cream, and he braced himself for her evasions. ''Very little of it. Most of it paid for my own clothing. Why do you always suspect him?''

''Because he's usually guilty. Three months ago he swore he was free from debts when he agreed to marry Geoffrey Ashton's daughter. If he lied to me, I'll find out. And now, madam, I want to know why he refused to come to London to meet her and why he has suddenly decided to live abroad. God knows I've wanted to ship him off to Australia ever since he disgraced himself in the navy.''

At these harsh words Suzanne's brown eyes sparked with fury and her words gushed out with a reckless lack of restraint. "Because Gilbert doesn't want to marry this scarecrow you picked out for him and because he can no longer tolerate the injustice of being the only Brownwell man in four without a title. When you paid for his navy commission, I begged you to purchase a title for him instead."

"Titles, madam, are not that easily acquired."

"You made certain that both your other sons acquired them."

"By law, not by chicanery. Harold is my legal heir, and Arthur was named heir to an uncle in his mother's family."

"I know all about his mother's family. I was part of that sanctimonious clan for five years. It should have been Gilbert who was chosen."

"The Feltons are not fools; your son has proved an embarrassment to both families."

"He is your son, too."

"A circumstance I have regretted increasingly over the years. Was what you said about his refusal to marry this girl another of your lies or a fact?"

"It was a mutual decision."

"And a damned poor one. Lord Ashton is a good friend of mine."

Her shrug was eloquently indifferent. "Then let one of your own sons marry the girl."

Harold Brownwell's sudden frown was more speculative than angry. "I might do just that. But keep in mind, madam, that without her dowry, Gilbert will be a total pauper."

"He can live at Brownsville with me."

"No, he cannot—not there or on any other of my properties."

Suzanne glared at her husband, and her eyes narrowed with a shrewd, catlike intensity. "Harold is years too old for her, and Arthur is involved in a ridiculous pursuit of Lord Radbourn's widow."

Her husband's bark of laughter was without humor. "So Gilbert's not so reluctant after all?"

"What other choice do you give him?" she asked bitterly. "Now please leave my cabin and allow me to finish dressing."

"No one would miss you if you didn't show for dinner at all. How much did you pay that sniveling steward to arrange the insulting reception you gave Anne today? Well, she made you look the fool. So tonight, if I were you, I'd put a leash on that poisonous tongue of yours and try to act like a lady, which you damned well are not. And one last word of advice, madam, before you call anyone else a scarecrow, I suggest you look in your own mirror."

Having delivered this one last acrimonious taunt, Lord Brownwell cheerfully made his way to the small salon reserved for gentlemen card playing and joined Lord Ashton in a spirited game of piquet until the dinner hour. Only when his fellow peer questioned him about his conversation with Anne was Brownwell's conscience joggled by another twinge of guilt.

"Saw you talking to my granddaughter a while ago. What did you think of her?"

"Is she really the scholar she seems?"

"According to her tutor fellow, she's like a terrier with a bone when she wants to learn something."

"She doesn't seem too pleased about the marriage."

"She's not. Hasn't had enough experience with men to know what she wants. But your lad looks like he can turn a girl's head once he decides she's worth the chase."

Brownwell nodded glumly. Gilbert had turned the heads of a dozen eligible young women in the last two years alone, but he hadn't bothered to complete the chase with a one of them. It was the thought of Anne as an unhappy bride that depressed him until he watched her walk across the room with her aunt. Then his smile of greeting broadened into a chuckle. In that cherry-colored dress she had on, she looked lively enough to challenge any man. His chuckle turned into laughter at her reaction when she heard his name.

"That was very unfair of you not to give me warning, Lord

Brownwell, but at least now I won't have to treat you with prim and proper respect.''

"Don't feel put out, Harold," Geoffrey cautioned lightly as he joined the group. "My daughter rarely treats anyone with prim and proper respect unless it suits her purpose. It's good to see you smile again, Anne. I was beginning to think you'd declared war against me."

Stretching the few inches it took to kiss his cheek, she scoffed, "Since when has that ever kept us from being friends? But you don't have to worry about me tonight. I promised Aunt Margaret that I'd be sedate and modest during dinner."

Whether her promise had been a serious one or not, Anne was constrained to keep it after the same steward she'd met earlier led her to a place at the dining table between Lady Brownwell and Reverend Thompson. From Lord Brownwell's hiss of irritation, she knew his wife had done the arranging—and done it well; three stolidly impassive strangers were seated opposite while all friendlier faces were far removed. Even Captain Newland was missing from his customary place at the head of the table. The thick channel fog had completely enveloped the ship, and the lonely sound of fog horns could be heard above the human ones of conversation. Lighted only by the swinging lanterns suspended above the table, the faces of the eighteen diners had an eerie look as they faded in and out of the pools of light. Moving to and from the table were four silent seamen, looking almost shadelike as they served a twelve-course dinner with the four accompanying wines.

Even before the aperitif wineglasses were removed, Suzanne began the subtle probing with an experienced skill. "You seem older than your eighteen years, Anne, especially in the ... unusual choice of color and the ... interesting design of your gown."

Struggling to maintain an expression of youthful respect and to respond to the slur with diplomatic language, Anne was pleasantly surprised to hear the reverend clear his throat.

"I can assure you, dear lady," he spoke soothingly, "Anne

is not quite eighteen; I officiated at her christening myself. But I do agree with you that young girls should wear the more modest colors of white and pink. Anne, I regret to say, has been given a wide latitude in the choice of her own clothing and in many other things as well.''

With soft bell-like tones, Lady Brownwell took up the challenge. "And what would these other things be, Reverend Thompson? During our chat this afternoon, you expressed some displeasure about her education.''

Anne winced slightly in disgust; with the instinct of a homing pigeon, the reverend had already ingratiated himself with the only other spiteful person aboard the *Dover Princess*. She listened intently to his explanation, which she knew would be a malicious criticism of Paddy.

"A most unfortunate education, dear lady," he confided as he leaned forward and sideways as if to eliminate Anne's unnecessary presence. Obligingly she leaned back in her chair to allow him unobstructed viewing of the lovely face turned avidly toward his. "I'm afraid Sir Geoffrey ignored my suggestion that she be trained by a proper nanny or a governess.''

A delicate eyebrow lifted in surprise. "She has had no formal training, then?''

"Not a suitable one, but she has been instructed by an Irish tutor whom I believe had some slight experience in teaching. As Anne herself can tell you, he insisted she learn a number of inappropriate subjects. She is, I believe, quite proficient in languages, several of which will be entirely useless to her.''

Inclining her head toward the girl who had taken no part in the conversation, Lady Suzanne asked, "What languages have you studied, Anne?''

"French, Latin, Greek, and Gaelic, Lady Brownwell," Anne murmured.

"How odd.''

For a moment or two the conversation lagged, and Anne was able to eat a few bites of the delicately sautéed fish; but she laid her fork down when the reverend leaned forward again.

"Dear lady, I'm certain that Anne would be interested in hearing something about your son, as indeed I would. You mentioned earlier that he had attended Oxford. Did he complete his training there?"

As brief as her career in teaching had been, Anne could detect the defensiveness of the older woman's response. "Gilbert found the academic atmosphere there too confining."

"Does he have a profession, Lady Brownwell?" Anne asked quietly.

The brown eyes that turned sharply toward the girl held a glint of anger. "Gilbert did not attend college to become a tradesman. Gentlemen rarely do."

"My father studied mathematics and natural science at Trinity College in Cambridge in order to make the Ashton estate more productive; so some gentlemen do learn a profession in college." Anne regretted her impassioned words instantly when Lady Brownwell's eyes traveled down the table to rest with sour contempt on Geoffrey Ashton.

"Gilbert had no such need. One of his older brothers manages the Brownwell estate, while the other manages the one in Essex. But Gilbert is very different from his brothers. For one thing he is far too sensitive to tolerate the tedious restrictions of the country now that he has adjusted to the more challenging life in London. Naturally, as a child on our Yorkshire farm, he enjoyed riding and swimming and all of the outdoor activities. But at present he prefers the more gentlemanly pursuits."

"If he likes London so much, why is he planning to live abroad?" Again Anne regretted speaking, because Suzanne Brownwell was looking at her husband with ill-concealed anger.

"Because, Miss Ashton," the older woman snapped, "he is presently at odds with his father." So intent was she on her own resentment, Suzanne Brownwell failed to notice the

stunned expressions on the faces of both of her companions.
It was the flustered reverend who sought to rectify the error.

"I beg your pardon, dear lady, but I'm afraid you're
laboring under a misconception. While Anne is Sir Geoffrey's
daughter, she is unfortunately not an Ashton."

The silence that followed his revelation was agonizing for
Anne; she couldn't believe that her father had not explained
that circumstance. But as she watched Lady Brownwell's face
tighten with shocked fury, she knew the disclosure had been
unexpected.

"I thought you knew," Anne mumbled.

"I most certainly did not," the woman rasped.

"I'm sure Lord Brownwell knows."

"Of course he does. It's just the kind of churlish revenge
he'd take on my poor Gilbert. He has always hated the fact
that my son was better-looking and more popular than his two
dullards. I will not endure his foisting off a nameless foundling on my son."

Aghast at the virulence of the woman's speech, Myles
Thompson protested helplessly, "I assure you Anne is not a
nameless foundling. Her father and mother are members of
two fine families, and she has been carefully reared by Lady
Margaret Gray."

"She is a social outcast regardless of the fools that spawned
her. And my husband has deliberately schemed to make
Gilbert as much an outcast as she. How dare he degrade my
son by marrying him to an illegitimate pariah who will ruin
his life!"

Anne had listened to this deluge of abuse in mute horror,
but the final words released her pent-up anger. Unlike Suzanne
Brownwell, however, Anne had learned to control that anger
enough to deliver her verbal reprisals in a deceptively sweet
voice that was deadly in its effectiveness.

"I agree, Lady Brownwell," she purred. "Your son doesn't
need anyone else to ruin his life; I imagine you've already
done the job thoroughly. I wouldn't think of depriving you of
his exclusive custody. Excuse me, Reverend Thompson, I'm

sure you and your friend will enjoy each other's company more if I'm not here.''

In one fluid movement she pushed her chair away from the table and rose gracefully, pausing only long enough to smile faintly at the three strangers across the table, who had lost all sign of their earlier boredom. Once inside her cabin, she pulled on her hooded cloak and quickly left the small room that threatened to smother her. Feeling her way along the darkened companionway and across the fog-enshrouded deck, she reached the taffrail at the aft of the ship and clung to the sturdy barrier as a drowning man clings to a piece of flotsam. Her terrified father found her there twenty minutes later. He was breathing hard as he put his arm around her.

''My God, Anne, you might have fallen overboard.''

''How diplomatic you are, Father, but I had no intention of jumping into the English Channel.''

''What happened, Anne?''

''She called me Miss Ashton until Reverend Thompson explained with his usual delicacy. Then she called me any number of less attractive names. I told her she could keep her precious son.''

''Anne, you didn't.''

''Oh, but I did; and now I'm telling you. I wouldn't marry that woman's pampered offspring even if my only other choice were your hunchbacked stable sweeper.''

''You're more polite than I would have been about my wife, Anne,'' the familiar voice of Lord Brownwell sounded in the dark. ''And I don't blame you for your low opinion of my son. He is, as you have correctly guessed, a bounder. Now let's get off this slippery deck; it's no place for inexperienced landlubbers. Take my arm and your father's and we'll walk back together. The next time you feel the need to cool off, young lady, I suggest you put your head into a basin of cold water in your cabin. You frightened a number of people, including the captain and his crew. Here's your cabin, Anne. Your Aunt Margaret and the dinner you didn't eat are waiting for you. Don't let what my wife said bother you again, she won't repeat those insults; and you won't be forced to do anything against your will. Geoffrey, I want to talk to you and your father tonight.''

Unable to add anything of a private nature to the other man's sweeping declaration, Geoffrey kissed his daughter and held her for a few seconds before he turned her over to Margaret and departed with Lord Brownwell. Still shaken by the terrible fear that had gripped him until he'd found Anne safe, Geoffrey was not in his usual agreeable mood. Twice the Brownwells had insulted her, first by not appearing at the earlier appointment and now by embarrassing her in front of strangers. God knows she'd suffered enough from public censure all her life—the worst from a member of his own family. His wife had hated Anne from the first; and in spite of all Elizabeth's charming denials, he'd always known why. Not because of the illegitimacy, but because he'd loved Anne's mother. Elizabeth had never been able to accept the fact that she was second choice, and she'd taken her resentment out on a defenseless girl. Tonight Suzanne Brownwell had done the same thing even more outrageously.

If he could have walked away from his commitment at that moment, he would have felt justified, despite the danger his daughter faced of marrying some security-seeking teacher like that Irish upstart, John Shaw. Geoffrey had been furious the day that odious little foreigner had confronted him with his insolent proposal. By comparison, Gilbert Brownwell had seemed an excellent prospect, even though his father had admitted that he had no money and his former navy captain had given him a generally negative report.

''Brownwell was a devil with the wives of other officers and a violent hotspur when he was gambling and drinking. If he had been able to accept discipline, he might have made a good fighting man. He was a fine navigator and the best swimmer in the navy—saved two seamen during a storm at sea. But for the most part, he was a failure.''

Thinking about that report now and the information Margaret's lawyer had uncovered, Geoffrey frowned. What gave the mother of such a man the right to scorn Anne? He knew the answer, of course; like Elizabeth, Suzanne Brownwell believed herself to be above reproach even for a degrading display of malicious temper. His bitter reflections were disturbed by the sight of Lord Brownwell speaking quietly to the ship's passengers not involved with the causes of the unpleasant scene at dinner. That he lived up to his reputation as peacemaker in the House of Lords was obvious when one of the men who had heard the entirety of Lady Brownwell's tirade spoke to Geoffrey.

"Your daughter's a lady regardless, Sir Geoffrey. Took an hour of abuse without a flicker; but when she used that pretty voice of hers, she cut the pair of them down with one stroke."

Mollified to an extent, Geoffrey listened as his own father took a subdued Reverend Thompson to task. "Parson, you were brought along to perform a wedding, not to play the toady to a new member of your pack of yapping bitches—my damned daughter-in-law included. You level your spite against our gel once more, and I'll see you defrocked."

Within minutes after the scene in the gracious salon had reverted to the more usual rituals, with the ladies sipping delicate Madeira wine and the gentlemen their brandy, Lord Brownwell signaled the Ashtons to join him in the card room. His opening words stunned Geoffrey.

"Gentlemen, I will not attempt to apologize for my wife. Suffice to say she acted without my permission and, I regret to say, with her usual lack of prudence. Since I do not want you or Anne or her aunt subjected to any more abuse at the hands of my family, I wish to extend an offer to you. I have an older son who might be more than willing to offer Anne the protection of his name, should she be receptive to the idea."

Geoffrey's glow of relief was cut short by his father's good-natured refusal. "That's a generous offer, Harold, but our gel's too headstrong to be yoked to a man who's already set in his ways. She'd just play hob with his life. I don't think we should count your young whippersnapper out until he's had a chance to speak for himself. Once all of us old fools stop interfering in their lives, he and Anne might make a lively couple.''

To Geoffrey's intense disappointment, Brownwell nodded in agreement. ''You could be right. I suggest we let Anne do her own choosing. I imagine that after tonight she's going to demand that right anyway.''

Cabin-bound until late the next morning, Anne had spent a restless night reassessing her life and coming to a decision far different from any she had made before. She was, she concluded, the most overprotected girl in England. Last night Aunt Margaret had almost promised her a safe return to Grayhaven, where she could be protected from any further attacks by people like Suzanne Brownwell. But Grayhaven no longer seemed the exciting place it once had. The ''independence'' Anne believed she'd had there no longer seemed real; Aunt Margaret and Paddy had, in reality, been her loving, gentle keepers, allowing her only the illusion of freedom. And if she returned to Grayhaven, she would continue to be under the domination of her father and grandfather as well. Anne smiled ruefully; these four older people who loved her would continue as they always had to compensate for her ''misfortune'' and to enforce their own decisions about her future. Even the one original change in her life that she had initiated herself had been carried out by Aunt Margaret, leaving Anne only the one task of teaching the few students Paddy had deemed her capable of handling.

By contrast, life in Boston—in a country where there were no aristocrats, no caste system, and where no one knew the history of Anne Gray—seemed suddenly very attractive. Compared to the number of people who dictated her life at present, one young husband would be a far less formidable opponent. As much as she despised Lady Brownwell, she felt a recurring tingle of victory—the woman would be three thousand miles away. And if the son proved to be the coddled weakling Anne suspected he would, he should be easy to manage. She'd had no problem managing John Shaw; she'd simply laughed and pushed him away when he'd attempted to embrace her. Since Gilbert Brownwell didn't want this marriage any more than she did, he probably wouldn't even pay much attention to her. The prospect intrigued her; according to reference books, common people in America were able to work at what they chose—some of the poorest people there had become generals and admirals and presidents. If that freedom were also extended to women, she knew of a number of exciting things she wanted to try.

Fortified by this philosophical acceptance of marriage as a means to escape any more domination, Anne rejoined her family in the main salon, prepared to withstand the polite contempt of the strangers aboard, who by this time knew all the sordid details of her life. But when several of them smiled in a friendly fashion as she entered the area, she knew that the combined power of Lord Ashton and Lord Brownwell had smoothed even those troubled waters. Had she not been completely absorbed in her own thoughts, she might have wondered about another odd change in human relationships. Her father and aunt were chatting together in perfect harmony, an abrupt contrast to the caustic animosity that had existed between them for months. Had she known the reason behind this mutual felicity, her own decision might have undergone another reversal. The pair had enthusiastically agreed to sponsor the older Brownwell son, should he appear interested. Sir Geoffrey was delighted by the prospect of Anne equaling Elizabeth in rank and in her becoming the titled superior of every Cavendish in Yorkshire county, including Elizabeth's disdainful mother. Margaret's approval was less vindictive; her beloved niece would remain in England, under the protection of an older, more stable man who would discourage Anne's wild, impulsive tendencies. At Lord Ashton's insistence, both of these guardians had promised not to discuss the matter with Anne.

That day and the next two passed without any reference to the events of the first night aboard or to the possible marriage.

As the fog lifted and the sun turned the dull gray waters to a sparkling blue, the more adventuresome of the passengers deserted the card tables for games of quoits on the deck, in which the three oldest men quickly established their supremacy in tossing their rope rings over the pegs. Anne watched these men play and enjoyed her grandfather's and Lord Brownwell's relaxed conversation. At one point, when the ship was becalmed, she learned that her father had been a member of the Cambridge rowing team; for two hours he joined the seamen in the small boats and helped pull the ship back into the path of the wind.

This pleasant holiday mood was destroyed on the fourth morning by Lady Brownwell's emergence from the seclusion of her cabin. Resplendently garbed in a soft lambskin cape, dyed the color of her hair, she swept into the main salon during the breakfast hour. Disdainful of the hearty English fare of kidney pie and kippers, she ordered a *petite déjeuner* for two and graciously asked Anne to join her at a private table. Both Lord Brownwell and Lady Margaret stiffened defensively, but Anne smiled reassuringly at them and accepted the invitation. Still smiling, she watched her hostess pour the rich black coffee into delicate china cups and uncover the plate of hot buttered croissants.

"I believe we should clear up our slight misunderstanding, Anne," Lady Suzanne began the conversation. "Had you not taken me by surprise the other night, we would never have gotten off to a poor start. I have decided to withdraw my objections and welcome you into my family."

Anne almost dropped the flaky croissant she was about to eat. "Why would you?" she asked bluntly. "I have the same drawbacks I had the other night—I'm too tall for a woman, my education is unfeminine, and I'm still a social outcast."

Lady Suzanne's disciplined face remained serene, revealing not a hint of her fervent desire to tell this impudent chit that she wouldn't qualify as a kitchen slavey if conditions were as they should be. But the ugly specter of an impoverished Gilbert forced to seek menial labor had haunted her for two days, ever since a churlish husband had informed her that Harold was also available. Carefully she chose her words of explanation.

"Anne, I'm sure you're too mature to believe in fairy tales, so I'll speak frankly. You have many fine qualities and will undoubtedly make Gilbert a good wife, but I'm a romantic. I would have preferred him to make the choice himself."

"Why didn't he, Lady Brownwell?"

"He hadn't yet found a girl who appealed to him."

"But he will accept me?"

"It is necessary that he marry at this time. He has suffered some financial reverses recently. His . . . investments have been unwise and perhaps even foolish, but with the help of your . . ."

Anne's small smile was firmly in place and her tone of voice was light as she completed the older woman's thought. "My dowry will keep him solvent. Father's offer must have been very generous to have accomplished that miracle."

Momentarily stung by Anne's blunt words, Suzanne's face hardened perceptibly, but she controlled her impulse to slap the impudent face opposite her. "Dowries are always a part of marriage contracts, so there is nothing unusual about yours." She leaned forward and smiled suddenly. "Anne, I want us to be friends for the rest of this voyage, especially since you'll become my daughter-in-law in a few days. You and Gilbert will be able to become friends more quickly if you and I are civil to each other."

Unwilling to risk the fragile peace with another rude rejoinder, Anne spent the next dreary hours being regaled with stories about Gilbert's success in athletics, his popularity with the young ladies who had pursued him, and his remarkable courage in an emergency. Twice Margaret joined them and unsuccessfully attempted to change the topic of conversation, returning to her cabin each time to seek relief from boredom. Anne nodded, smiled, murmured inanities, and envied the men playing quoits on deck. Not until Lady Brownwell decided it was time to dress for dinner could Anne escape her stultifying domination.

Aunt Margaret's comment when her niece entered the cabin was sardonic. "I believe I liked her better when she was screeching like a fishwife. Did you learn anything of value about that paragon son of hers?"

"Before she decided that she and I should be friends, I learned he was marrying me for my dowry and that he lost all of his own money in bad investments."

"That's an interesting definition for gambling."

"You mean at cards?"

"Among other things."

"How stupid!"

"Worse than that, I'm afraid. Did the woman say why she'd changed her mind about you?"

Anne's smile matched her aunt's in cynicism. "Yes indeed, I have fine qualities and I'll make a good wife. Aunt Margaret, if she ever comes to Boston, there's going to be a second Tea Party, because if I can, I'll shove her into the water."

Margaret regarded the girl thoughtfully. "What made you change your mind about this marriage?"

"Because next time Father might choose someone even worse. Besides, I like Lord Brownwell very much."

"He likes you, too, Anne."

Unaccountably, the next morning Anne awakened in a state of acute nervousness. Since she'd never experienced such a condition before, she attempted to analyze the possible cause logically. At Grosvenor House in London when she'd first expected to meet the Brownwells, she'd been poised, confident, and defiant. And yesterday her only emotional response to Lady Suzanne's absurd preoccupation with her son had been disbelief and boredom. But there was no mistaking the symptoms this morning; her hands felt clammy, she tripped three times over the same piece of luggage, and she spilled the coffee the steward had delivered to the cabin. It was, she decided hopefully, only the unusual circumstances of arriving at her first foreign port so early in the morning. Once all the last-minute preparations were completed and she was stationed at her favorite railside position on deck, she would regain her customary self-assurance. Rushing to don the bright blue velvet suit she and Emily had designed for the occasion, she felt the unbelievable sting of tears when one of the buttons fell off and she was forced to sew it back on. Sympathizing with Anne's agitation, Margaret gently pushed her out of the cabin.

"I'll finish the packing, dear. You go on deck and watch the landing. It'll be a spectacular sight."

Having entered the great half-moon bay carved by the Seine River sometime during the predawn hours, the *Dover Princess* was being carried swiftly on the incoming tide into the inner port of Le Havre. As Anne scanned the approaching shoreline, her nervousness increased and she jerked when Lord Brownwell's voice sounded by her side.

"It's not as beautiful as Dover, but it's one of the greatest ports on the continent. You look very lovely this morning, Anne," he said reassuringly.

Smiling in appreciation at his effort to ease her unreasoning fear, Anne knew with the logical part of her brain that the fitted jacket and the wide full skirt were flattering to someone her height, but she wished that for the next few hours she could be five inches shorter.

"Remember what I told you, Anne," her companion continued. "You're not going to be forced into any marriage you don't want. The decision will be completely yours. But if you do decide to become a Brownwell, I'll welcome you as a daughter." Leaning toward this kindly man who more than anyone else understood her dilemma, she kissed him lightly on the cheek.

When the ship was still a hundred feet away from the shore, he pointed to the three men standing together on the dock. "Those are my sons. It's the first time I've seen them all together in years. The one who looks like me is Harold, the dark-haired one is Arthur, and the other is Gilbert."

Anne didn't need his identification to recognize the youngest son. Slightly taller than his brothers, he was the masculine edition of his beautiful mother with the same gleaming blond hair, the faintly tanned complexion, and the golden-brown eyes. In dress, too, he was the more flamboyant, almost Beau Brummel in the dramatic cut of his burgundy-colored jacket and cream-tan trousers, which tucked into polished cordovan boots. Whereas the other two men wore the conventional dark gray suits with snowy-white linen stocks and ties, Gilbert Brownwell's looked to be ruffled cream silk. Just before her eyes focused on his, Anne thought irrelevantly that financial reverses hadn't taught him much about economy. He was more expensively garbed than Queen Victoria's princely husband, whom Anne had glimpsed on the balcony of Buckingham Palace.

But at that moment Gilbert smiled at her, a warm smile that invited her response, an appealing smile that marked him, at least in small part, his father's son. Her remaining logic fled, and her whole being was suffused with a joyous relief that made her eyes luminous with emotion and curved her lips into a tremulous smile. Without volition, she moved along the railing toward the gangplank that now connected the *Dover Princess* to the dock, her eyes fastened on the blond man striding toward that same ramp. Still thirty feet from her goal, she stopped with a jolting abruptness to watch a scene unfolding that filled her with a sick revulsion. The golden man hadn't been rushing to greet Anne Gray, but someone far more important to him—his mother, whose emotional excitement was obvious even to the most disinterested observer. In her flowing gold fur cape over a silk burgundy-colored dress, Lady Suzanne looked a match for the handsome man smiling up at her as she struggled down the gangplank, almost upsetting Reverend Thompson and Lord Ashton, who were escorting her.

With the powerful emotion of a moment ago replaced by a disillusioned sanity, Anne watched the reunion of the mother and son as they moved along the dock oblivious to anyone else. With an almost dispassionate objectivity, she noticed the way the two blond heads inclined in the same graceful manner as the pair engaged in an absorbing conversation, and she noted again the expensive elegance of their clothing. Her smile now the smaller one of defiance, Anne looked away toward the spot where the remaining Brownwell sons stood. As her eyes met the gray ones watching her with sympathetic understanding, her smile broadened into a mocking grin of self-deprecation. Squaring her shoulders with unconscious challenge, she nodded her head in a salute to the man she knew was Sir Harold Brownwell.

Chapter 3

HAD Anne been able to overhear the several conversations among the Brownwell brothers as they waited dockside for the arriving *Dover Princess*, she would have suffered fewer pangs of jealous anger and none of joyous anticipation. She would have been too busy formulating a speech of denunciation and refusal in addition to some pungent taunts aimed at the prettily dressed popinjay still under his mother's doting domination. But none of the separate dialogues had been intended for her ears.

The two older men had arrived half an hour before the youngest to engage three carriages and a dray wagon from among the dozens lined up along the stone-paved embarcadero. Experienced by years of travel in French ports, they hired the four most aggressive dockhands to carry the trunks from the ship's cabins. English seamen were never allowed on French docks except as visitors. Watching the ship still many minutes away, Sir Harold Brownwell spoke lightly to his brother.

"Do you want to take care of the greeting or the luggage?"

"You're the diplomat of the family. At the moment I'd rather meet the devil than her majesty. How many trunks do you suppose the damn woman brought with her this time?"

"Four times more than she needs."

"I wish to God she were going as far abroad as our brother."

"I've wished that and worse since the day she joined our family."

"Why the hell would you want her at Brownsville? Why didn't you let her stay in the London townhouse?"

"Because I've already leased it out from under her."

"Are we that far in debt?"

"Farther. If I hadn't been able to sell off one of the vineyards, we might not even be allowed to leave France. She ran up two thousand pounds of bills while she was in Paris the last time."

"What a bitch! Are we clear now?"

"Hardly. Last year Father was forced to mortgage Brownsville and the Birmingham property to pay Gilbert's debts. Sorry, Arthur, but it looks as if you'll have to postpone your wedding."

"God, don't call him Gilbert like his mama does. I can just barely stand using the name Tony."

"Tony, then. I'm sorry about your wedding, Arthur."

"Don't be. Vivian has agreed to live in the Feldwood Park cottage for two years, so we'll be married quietly next month. Thank the Lord I have good tenants for the big house; I'll need the lease money to get the farm started. I'm not going to let my wife support me, although she wouldn't mind."

"You're a lucky man; Vivian's a fine woman. I wonder what kind Tony's getting?"

"Whatever kind, she'll be too good for him. Do you suppose he'll even show up to meet her?"

"No, Arthur, but he'll come to meet his mother; our Tony hasn't enjoyed having to live economically these past weeks."

"Didn't you tell the fool that she hasn't a pound left, Harold?"

"Many times, but why should he believe me when she's always been able to keep him supplied—at our expense. He'll show at the last minute after all of the work is done. There he comes now. By God, look at his suit! I expect it cost three times one of ours." Harold's eyes held a bitter cynicism as he watched his youngest brother's studied approach, and his greeting was caustic. "You look like a bridegroom. What is it? Parisian?"

Gilbert Anthony Brownwell scowled at the speaker and shrugged. "The suit? I suppose it is; it's one of those Mother had made for me. So take your complaints to her. God, I'll be glad when this is over."

"You don't have long to wait," Arthur promised maliciously. "This time next week, you'll be able to chase your own wife around the bedroom instead of someone else's. And if I'm not mistaken, there she is."

"Where?"

"Use your eyes! She's standing right next to our father at the railing."

"My God, she's as tall as he is and she looks like something out of a German opera."

Harold had been watching the girl for the past minutes with far more perceptive eyes than either of his brothers. He'd noted the graceful way she'd kissed his father's cheek and the animated glow on her face. She looked young, even vulnerable, but her eyes held a promise of excitement; and he experienced a reaction to a woman he hadn't felt in years.

"You're wrong, Tony," he said quietly. "She's beautiful. You don't deserve her."

"I sure don't. What the devil am I going to do with her? I'd have to be drunk to get near her in the bedroom."

"How would you know?" Harold asked with contempt. "The only women you've been in the bedroom with are whores—both married and unmarried."

Even as he was arranging a practiced smile of charm on his

face, Gilbert managed another taunt. "At least they weren't circus freaks like this one."

"No, they were sluts. Speaking of which, there's your mama being convoyed down the gangplank—first off, as usual. She'll expect you to meet her. I'll take care of Anne Gray," he added softly, smiling with subtle irony as he watched Suzanne clasp her son and kiss him with an ardor that sickened the older brother.

Equally disgusted with the dramatic reunion but more outspoken, Arthur muttered, "My God, they look like a pair of stage lovers. I don't envy you having to explain that scene to any woman, much less to a young girl who expected to meet her bridegroom. If she has any sense, she won't even get off the ship. Well, I'd better get the luggage off before anything else happens."

Nodding in agreement, Harold looked up toward Anne, flinching as he noted her stricken face and her gloved hands clutching the railing. But as he watched, she looked away from the gangplank and met his eyes. He sucked in his breath with startled surprise. This was no naive country girl, not with that taunting smile; this was a sensitive, spirited woman. Impatiently now, he moved toward the gangplank to await her, standing to one side as the other passengers crowded off and forced Suzanne and her son farther down the dock. He spoke to Lord Ashton, whom he knew, and acknowledged the introductions to Sir Geoffrey Ashton and Lady Margaret Gray with an automatic courtesy; but his awareness remained centered on the young girl who had as yet made no move to disembark.

On the empty deck, Lord Brownwell finally took Anne's arm and led her toward the gangplank. "I think we'd better leave and give the ship back to the captain." He smiled; but his jaw was rigid as he guided her to the dock. That damned young fool, he cursed silently, and the bitch who whelped him. His good humor was restored, though, as he noted the expression on the face of his oldest son. Not all of his sons were blind, he reflected with satisfaction, realizing with a shock that this was the first time Harold had showed an interest in any woman since his wife's death three years before. Lord Brownwell's smile broadened as he watched his oldest son tuck Anne's arm in his and escort the entire party of guests toward the carriages, amused by Harold's careful distribution of the Ashtons and the reverend into one, and himself, Lady Margaret, and Anne into the second. His smile lasted only until the carriage had been driven off, and then he turned his attention toward the remaining members of his family.

Harold's arrangement had not been entirely his own idea, although he approved of it enthusiastically. While they had been waiting for Anne, Lady Margaret had pulled him aside and said bluntly, "Sir Harold, I want my niece away from here as quickly as possible. Can you arrange a carriage for us? Her father will see to our luggage."

"That's all taken care of, Lady Margaret, and I'd be delighted to escort you and your niece to the inn." By the time Anne did descend, the need for such an immediate departure had become more urgent; his damned stepmother was talking rapidly to Gilbert and gesturing dramatically toward the ship's deck. Not for anything would Harold let that pair of fools insult this girl again. He was relieved that Anne did not glance in their direction even when the carriage began to move, but he was disturbed by her withdrawn silence. Except for a conventional murmur when they were introduced, she had not spoken, nor was she smiling. Mercifully, the need for him to initiate a strained conversation did not arise; Lady Margaret was as aware as he was of the awkward situation.

"Has your brother been separated from his mother a long time?" she asked abruptly.

"About three weeks," he responded promptly with deliberate irony. "But Tony and Suzanne have always had a special attachment for each other."

"I thought the young man's name was Gilbert."

"It is, but Arthur and I have always preferred Tony."

"I shouldn't wonder," she murmured.

Emboldened by Lady Margaret's tacit disapproval of his brother, Harold turned toward Anne. "Miss Gray, I would like to impose upon your good nature for a special favor. I have several horses stabled at the inn, and the mare is in need of exercise. If your aunt will give her permission, will you go riding with me this morning?"

"That's the best idea I've heard in days," Margaret exclaimed before Anne could answer. "She has been in the company of old people long enough. As soon as our luggage arrives, she can change into her riding clothes."

"Knowing Arthur, your trunks will be in your rooms before you are."

"Good, then there's nothing to delay Anne exercising that mare and my getting some sleep on a bed that doesn't pitch and roll."

Having been preoccupied with her gloomy thoughts and with the strangely aching hurt she'd felt since the moment Gilbert had deliberately ignored her, Anne had paid scant attention to the earlier conversation. But the prospect of escaping any further embarrassment appealed to her sense of reckless daring; a horseback ride could last for hours.

"I would be delighted, Sir Harold"—she smiled suddenly— "and I hope your mare is as tired of being cooped up as I am. Do you suppose we can get away without seeing anyone?"

"I'll make sure we do," he promised. An hour later they were mounted on two of the most magnificent thoroughbreds Anne had ever seen and riding at full gallop down the dusty country roads. She exulted in the smooth gait of the mare and in the wild spirit it exhibited as it stretched out to race the gelding Sir Harold rode. Mile after mile the two riders paced their mounts until the man pulled to a stop in front of a weathered cluster of buildings identified only by the crudely lettered word *Auberge*.

"Lunchtime," he announced as he helped her dismount and turned the horses over to the farmhand waiting for them. "This is one of the oldest rural inns in France," he told Anne as he led her inside the rustic, kitchen-style room, where steaming pots of food bubbled on their spits over the hot coals in the open fireplace. Standing behind a huge old iron stove, a large woman called out a greeting to Sir Harold.

"That's Alette," he whispered. "I've known her since my mother first brought me here when I was a small lad. This is wine country and most of her customers are people who've come to the area to restock their cellars. Our family owns four small vineyards near here which I'm obliged to visit. After we eat I'll take you to see the closest one, if you're not in any hurry to get back."

Anne shook her head vigorously, her mouth watering as she surveyed the tureen of thick green soup Alette was ladling into individual bowls. Halfway through the rich fish stew that followed, Harold lifted his glass of golden wine in a toast. "May the remainder of your stay in France be happier than this morning was, Anne. Do you mind my calling you Anne?"

"Of course not."

"Then I want you to stop treating me as you would your grandfather. Even though I'm thirty-seven years old and a widower, I still prefer to be called Harold by a pretty young lady. There now, I've revealed my worst secrets, so I expect to hear some of yours in return."

Momentarily startled, Anne gasped and then broke into soft laughter. Harold was very much like his father, she thought, with the same relaxed way of talking and the same friendly attitude toward other people.

"I was merely trying to impress you with my best behavior, which I rarely use with my grandfather. He calls me a saucy witch, among other things."

"In that case, perhaps you'd better treat me as you do him. I think I'd prefer a saucy witch to your best behavior. What other secrets do you have, Anne?"

"I didn't want to leave the ship this morning."

"Are you sorry you did?"

"No, and I want to see your vineyard. I've never even seen a grapevine before."

With the restraint that had existed between them broken, the next few hours rushed by with a bemused Harold listening to the exuberant young girl speaking excellent French to the farm workers as she walked past the rows of verdant vines. During the leisurely ride back to the inn, they stopped several times; and Harold found himself talking more freely than he had in years. He was intrigued by this girl who had no conception of her own power to attract a man.

While they were exploring the countryside, the other members of the party were engaged in quite different activities. From a casual remark by Geoffrey that Margaret had turned the fallow Grayhaven acres into a productive farm in a year's time, the discussion had evolved into a pencil-and-paper plotting of the two Brownwell estates. Seated around one of the tables in the public room of the inn, Lord Brownwell and Arthur had coerced Margaret and Geoffrey into an acre-by-acre revision of their own unproductive properties. Lord Ashton escaped enlistment by insisting that he'd retired from farming. "Haven't worried about an acre yield of anything since my son took over; and you'll find he just follows Margaret's advice. Come on, Parson, let's you and me play cards before they get started on sheep. Can't stand even to talk about the smelly creatures."

For the other two occupants of the room the entire day had been a disaster. Gilbert Anthony had been publicly blistered on the dock by his furiously scornful father. "You infernal numbskull, you left the girl standing on the deck while you cuddled up to your mother like an infant taking suck. If I didn't know you to be a damned lecher with women, I'd think you a mincing fop incapable of performing like a man. You agreed to this marriage, and at that time you were told everything about this girl. But if you've changed your mind, just let me know; and we'll get your problems solved in a few days."

Stupidly Gilbert had resorted to insolence. "I don't think I'm your only son with problems. Harold thinks that giant you brought here for me is attractive. How do you like the idea of your favorite son saddled with her?''

Lord Brownwell gazed at his youngest son with pity. ''Gilbert, I hope for your sake that you listen to this final warning. You have received your last money from anyone in the Brownwell family. If your mother has promised you any more support, she was lying. She doesn't have a shilling to her name. Ask her where she got the money that paid off your last gambling debts. Your only hope was the young lady you just insulted, but if Harold finds her attractive, I will give him my unqualified blessing.''

It was this final statement that had shocked Gilbert into a belated search for Anne Gray—a futile one, as it turned out. When he discovered that she'd gone riding with his brother, he'd mounted his brother's third thoroughbred and wasted two hours riding trying to locate the missing couple. Returning to the inn in a stormy rage, he compounded his earlier omission in good manners by attempting to flatter the girl's aunt, only to find her an adversary who held him in contempt. Smiling with the youthful appeal that had proved effective with most of the old ladies he had wanted favors from in the past, he approached her with a studied degree of polite diffidence.

''I'm worried about your niece, Lady Margaret. I don't like the idea of her riding in a strange country.''

''Anne's an excellent horsewoman.''

''I don't doubt it, but she is out with a stranger and has been for hours.''

''Nonsense. I found your brother a charming gentleman.''

''You approved of her accepting his invitation?''

''Anne didn't accept anything. I accepted for her. Since you were not available, I was delighted when Sir Harold was.''

Gilbert's eyes narrowed in controlled anger as he tried one more appeal. ''I think I should have been consulted about the choice of her companionship for the day.''

Margaret smiled frostily. ''Young man, as a gambler you should know when you do not hold winning cards.''

"I am not a gambler, Lady Margaret, I merely play cards with other gentlemen."

"I think it only fair to warn you, Mr. Brownwell, that my solicitor has given me a thorough report on all your activities. I found very little in his report that was favorable. Now perhaps you can understand why I find your brother more trustworthy."

Sir Geoffrey Ashton gave him an even colder reception when Gilbert attempted an explanation for his behavior on the dock.

"I'm sorry about this morning, Sir Geoffrey. I fully intended to meet your daughter, but my mother required my attention for a few minutes, and I—"

"I am very content that you did not, Mr. Brownwell. Your brother handled the situation admirably."

Stung by the cold contempt in the older man's voice, Gilbert blurted, "Since I agreed to marry your daughter, I think I should be the one—"

Again he was mercilessly cut off. "You may have agreed, but I consider your actions this morning a breach of that agreement."

"My God, Harold is twenty years older than she is."

The answering shrug was eloquently effective. "But eminently suitable in my estimation. Good day, sir."

Not even Lord Ashton's kindly-meant intervention blunted Gilbert's sharp realization that he was no longer being pursued.

"Leaves a lump in the craw to be snubbed, don't it?" The old man chuckled. "Always want to bash the other fellow myself. You're going after this thing the wrong way, son. We'll overlook that foolishness on the dock this morning. You were just flummoxed by the idea of being trapped. The thing to do now is to go after the gel, if you think she's worth the chase."

"I don't think her aunt or father will let me near her."

Lord Ashton's chuckle broadened into laughter. "Those two have been trying to curb Anne's spirit without much success since she was born. She does her own deciding, but don't make the mistake of underestimating her; she's not a gullible chit. But then I imagine a lad like you knows how to turn a pretty head in his direction, if you've a mind to. All I ask, son, is that you play the game honestly."

Gilbert knew the words were intended to encourage him, but the truth was he'd never pursued a woman in his life. And he rarely felt more than a fleeting attraction for the ones who pursued him. How the hell was he to convince a headstrong giantess whom he found repugnant? If he hadn't revealed that opinion so obviously this morning, he might have survived with simple attendance and polite talk. But now he'd have to pretend to be a smitten fool, and the thought galled him. It didn't help matters to find his mother waiting for him in his room.

"What did your father say to you this morning?"

"What you damn well should have. He told me that he approved of Harold marrying that damned girl."

"He'd told me the same thing."

"He also suggested that I ask you where you got the money to pay off those debts."

"That's hardly important now."

"I think it is. Where did you?"

"I borrowed it from a friend."

"Who?"

"A gentleman named Edward Doncaster."

Gilbert stared at his mother in disbelief. He knew the name and the reputation that went with it; furthermore, his informants had been the worst scum of London. The thoughts that crowded his head now were the ugly ones of suspicion. Had his beautiful, vain mother become one of the bored, middle-aged women who wallowed in the slime of promiscuous infidelity? How else would she be able to borrow money from a man like Edward Doncaster?

"How well do you know this man, Mother?"

"Don't be impertinent, Gilbert. He is merely a friend, nothing more. Besides, your father has repaid him."

"With what? Harold has been haranguing me for weeks

about the threat of bankruptcy. According to him there's no money left."

"So your father keeps saying."

"And you really don't have any money left?"

"I'm afraid not."

"Yet you still spent a bloody fortune on more clothes for us?"

Her delicate shrug was uncaring. "I refuse to dress like a pauper. They can raise the money if they want."

"But I can't. If I want to survive, I'll have to marry Anne Gray. Why in hell didn't you warn me this morning?"

"Kindly do not blame me for what happened this morning. You wanted no part of her; and if I remember rightly, you even insisted that Harold could have her. I did try to warn you, if you recall."

"Not very hard, you didn't."

"That was because I believe that there could be other, more suitable girls for you since you found this one unbearable."

"Where? Do you know anyone who will pay twenty thousand pounds for me at the moment?"

"Given time I might. If you will give up this odd notion of yours to live abroad, I'm sure—"

"Don't be an idiot, Mother," he interrupted rudely, "just get out of here and let me dress. Much as I hate it, I'd better show up for tea."

Eventually he had gone downstairs, but he hadn't joined the others; instead he'd ordered wine and isolated himself in front of one of the mullioned windows overlooking the courtyard. Where the hell were Harold and the girl? They'd been gone for almost eight hours. How the devil could anyone ride for that length of time? Restlessly he looked over at his mother, seated alone now and staring moodily into the fire. She was beginning to look her age, he reflected without pity; there was no sparkle left in the masklike face, only petulance. She looked up as he sat down next to her.

"When they return, Gilbert, I advise you to show a little enthusiasm. Keep in mind that Harold is more experienced than you in getting his own way. Not that he had to work for it; his father always made sure that he received the lion's share of everything, while you've been left out. Arthur has been favored over you almost as much. When I think of how much they've been given and how much they've hated and resented you . . ."

Gilbert stared at her with a sudden enlightened cynicism. He'd heard the same complaints for years and always believed them, but now he heard only the whine in her voice and the deliberate untruths of her words. God, what a mess she'd made of the Brownwell family, and what a mess he'd made of his own life.

"I hear their horses, Gilbert," his mother whispered sharply. "Go outside and meet them."

He'd reached the entry when he heard the laughter and the muffled sounds of good-natured bantering outside the door. Hastily he ran up the stairs leading to the private rooms and stationed himself in the darkened hallway from where he could see the entry. He had only a brief glimpse of wind-blown hair and a woman's green habit before his brother's broad shoulders obscured his view. But he heard her throaty chuckle and her low-pitched musical voice exclaim, "It was a glorious ride, Harold. I've never ridden so far before or so fast."

Gilbert raised his eyebrow at her familiar use of the first name, but the voice itself was more than bearable. At least she didn't screech like a shrew. He strained to hear his brother's reply and felt a renewal of anger when he did.

"Will you ride with me again tomorrow morning, Anne?"

"Before breakfast?"

"If you like. Alette bakes fresh bread every day, and even the horses run faster when they get scent of it. Will you come?"

"I'd love to, Harold. And thank you for today, I had a wonderful time."

As his brother moved aside to allow her to mount the stairs, the watching man had his first real look at her face.

He'd been too far away when she'd been on the ship. But how the devil had Harold known she was beautiful? Not alluringly beautiful, but there was a radiance; and the hair he'd thought drab had sun-burned glints of gold in it and looked silky to the touch. The blue eyes were compellingly bright and the lips inviting enough to be kissable. He'd been wrong about her body, too; she was slender, but certainly not bony, with breasts that looked shapely even under the wool cloth of her jacket. What a damned fool he'd been not to take a better look this morning.

When she was still six feet away, he stepped from the shadows and said softly, "You've been gone a long time, Anne." He watched as her expression changed to surprised caution and then to guarded recognition.

"You startled me, Mr. Brownwell." Her low voice had lost the warmth it had held for Harold.

"I didn't mean to, Anne."

"I prefer you call me Miss Gray. Did you wish to see me about something in particular?"

Damn her cool self-control! "Yes, as a matter of fact I do. Since you and I are to be married, I think you'd better limit—"

"That is by no means a certainty."

"The devil it isn't. I've already signed all the agreements."

"But I haven't, Mr. Brownwell. Furthermore, your mother informed me about your reasons for signing. You'll pardon me if I'm not flattered that the only reason you agreed to marry me was your current need of money."

Why the hell had his mother told her that? Disconcerted by Anne's directness, he lowered his voice to a more intimate level. "Anne, will you spend tomorrow with me after you return from your ride?"

"That may be quite late, I'm afraid, but perhaps I'll see you at lunch. Now, if you'll excuse me . . ."

The goddamned arrogant chit, dismissing him as if he were an unwanted peddler! He stared at the door she'd closed in his face with such a swift finality.

Inside the room Anne was leaning against that same door, her heart beating as erratically as a captured bird's. She wished she'd never seen him and that he'd leave her alone as he had on the dock. She'd had a good time with Harold and hadn't been bothered by any of these uncomfortable palpitations. What was the matter with her that she'd let someone who looked like the detested Suzanne Brownwell disturb her almost to the point of blushing? She was polishing her dusty boots with unwonted vigor when Margaret arrived, followed by two husky workers carrying large containers of steaming hot water.

"You have just enough time to wash and dry your hair before dinner," her aunt announced briskly while the men emptied the water into the small tub secreted behind a screen. "And I want you to wear that pretty dress you've been saving for a special occasion; everyone could stand a little cheering up.

"How was your ride with Sir Harold?" she asked after the men had gone.

"He's very nice."

"Did you see the other one?"

"I haven't met Sir Arthur yet."

"Don't be tiresome, Anne, I meant the young scamp."

"He spoke to me in the hall."

"I thought he might. What did he want?"

"To see me tomorrow, but I told him I was going riding again with his brother."

"Good." Margaret was smiling with satisfaction as she left the room.

Gilbert Brownwell fully intended to be waiting at the foot of the stairs when Anne came down for dinner. Since he had to play the besotted swain, he was determined to play it for public viewing. Unfortunately his brother and Sir Geoffrey were already there, and Gilbert retreated angrily back into the public room, where he was forced to stand in ignominious silence as Anne swept by. Unaware that he did so, he whistled soundlessly when he saw her gown. Of blue-purple velvet, it made her look as dramatically beautiful as the actresses he'd admired on the stages at Drury Lane and Covent Garden. He wondered if she realized what a daring dress it was or how tempting it made her look.

While Anne might have denied the second adjective, she'd been in a daring mood the day she'd forced two reluctant London seamstresses to remake the gown, one of the three Margaret had insisted be sewn professionally.

"I refuse to look like a fat statue or a pouter pigeon," Anne had declared in disgust at the original design. Stubbornly she'd insisted they remove every bit of the offensive crinoline and every scrap of excess fabric. The result was a lowered bodice that fit her slender waistline with snug reverence and revealed most of her shoulders and a hint of her rounded breasts before it billowed into a voluminous skirt. Anne's determination to create her own style in dresses did not stem from a wayward desire to be vulgar. Having been made painfully aware of her unusual height when she first matured, she had compensated by refusing to wear the fashions that were becoming to shorter girls. By choosing uncluttered lines and vivid colors, she had developed a bold style that ignored current trends. As her crowning achievement, tonight's dress was everything she'd hoped it would be; and indeed it did cause quite a stir among the other members of the party. She grinned impudently at her father's raised eyebrow and her grandfather's chuckle; and she was delighted when Lady Suzanne's mouth remained unattractively open a second too long. Even Reverend Thompson greeted her with a grudging smile of appreciation.

Seated between Harold and Gilbert as a result of Lord Ashton's subtle rearranging, Anne lost all trace of her ship-board decorum and became a lively respondent to her grandfather's sly humor and Harold's more sedate contributions. Only once was Gilbert jarred out of his generally dour mood, when he retrieved Anne's napkin from the floor and returned it to her lap, managing in the process to caress her leg lightly and whisper the word "Tomorrow" in her ear. Not a question, but a statement! Noting her heightened color, he smiled with satisfaction.

That his "tomorrow" did not materialize as he planned was due more to an accident than to any deliberate avoidance on her part. On their way home from breakfast at Alette's, the mare threw a shoe; and Anne and Harold were forced to walk their horses the five miles back to the inn. Because boots designed for riding made painful walking shoes, they had rested frequently along the way and did not arrive at the inn until midafternoon. A furious half-drunk Gilbert met the exhausted pair, and only Harold's cold authority prevented an ugly scene of recriminations. Pacifying the irate man with a promise to join him for tea, Anne retired to her room for a bath and hopefully a nap; but she was rudely disturbed by a pounding on her door after what seemed like only moments of sleep.

"You've kept me waiting long enough," Gilbert stormed, refusing to leave until she accompanied him downstairs. Resentfully she brushed her still damp hair and changed from her bed robe into a dress behind the screen.

"My father will be very angry at your presumption, Mr. Brownwell."

"He isn't here, nor are any of the others. They're spending the day at the port master's home; so for once your guardians won't be here to protect you."

Harold was there, however, relentlessly there. He'd seen his brother drunk too often to allow him alone with any young girl, much less with Anne. Even though Gilbert had sobered considerably, tea was a desultory hour of stilted talk followed by four even drearier hours. Continuing exhaustion dulled Harold's and Anne's wits, and Gilbert's main contribution was a repeated insistence that he would accompany them on all future outings.

"You're more than welcome, Tony," his older brother assured him, "but tomorrow you'll be bored because we're going to the château. However, I'd appreciate you showing

Anne the ruins if you do come, since I'll have to spend the day working.''

During only one moment of that endless day did Anne experience the emotional reaction to Gilbert she was beginning to hate when he escorted her to her room after a late dinner. Angered because she eluded his offered embrace, his promise was more a threat than an invitation. ''Tomorrow you'll be with me, not with my brother.'' She spent a restless night torn between resentment and anticipation.

The following morning she and Harold waited half an hour until the innkeeper informed them that Monsieur Gilbert was asleep and very difficult to awaken.

''Do you still want to go with me, Anne?'' Harold asked.

Mutely she nodded her head; but for the first hour of riding on a strange road, she was morosely silent. Not until they crossed the mighty Seine River on a poled ferryboat did she take an interest in the beautiful countryside; although actually it was her first sight of the gray-stone château with two medieval towers still standing that dissipated the remainder of her gloom. The château, Harold explained, had become a part of the Brownwell estate upon the death of his mother's uncle, the last surviving member of the ancient de Vernay family. Since much of the sprawling structure was no longer maintained, Harold insisted on accompanying her into the oldest parts where crumbling stone stairs made any extensive exploration dangerous.

''When I was young, I spent most summers with my uncle; and I used to dream of restoring the castle and living in medieval splendor,'' he admitted.

''I don't think that medieval splendor was very comfortable,'' Anne argued. ''The walls were always damp and people suffered from chilblains and ague.''

His laughter echoed against the stone walls of the great hall they were standing in. ''There were also armies of vermin that spread the other diseases, but at least in this part of France there was enough wine to deaden the more unpleasant realities. You're right, though, Anne, I didn't fulfill that youthful dream.''

A short time later in a small outbuilding, she discovered a second of Harold's discarded dreams. Inside the heavily windowed room were dozens of artist's easels with a variety of pictures still fastened to the frames.

''I didn't become a painter, either.'' He smiled.

Anne, whose own experience with art was limited to unsuccessful attempts to draw the anatomy of a frog, was impressed with the excellence of his work, especially with the portrait face of a serenely beautiful young woman.

''That's a picture of my wife, Bess,'' he said quietly. ''She loved this château as much as I did.''

Uncomfortably aware of the sadness in his voice and of her own lack of acquaintance with death, Anne remained silent during the walk to the estate office, while her companion talked about his wife—not mawkishly with raw grief, but sentimentally with remembered happiness. Unaccountably Anne wondered if Gilbert had ever loved any women the way Harold had his wife.

Noticing her distraction, he murmured gently, ''Enough about my life. What of your young dreams, Anne?''

She shook her head; even the nebulous ones she'd formulated aboard the *Dover Princess* seemed unhappily remote now. ''I don't know,'' she answered reluctantly. ''Something like Aunt Margaret's, I suppose. At least I've already started learning all of hers.''

''That sounds like a dull future for a young girl.''

''No, it's not, really. I enjoy everything except the farming part. May I watch you work this afternoon?''

''You'd probably have a better time in the library, but you're very welcome to keep me company after we have lunch.''

Once settled in the office, though, Anne's period of inactive observation lasted only a few minutes; within half an hour she was absorbed in the books and ledgers that the estate manager, Felipe Verge, carried from the dusty shelves. Amazed by the intricacies involved in the calculation of the varying amounts of wine produced from different harvest years, she was soon concentrating on the columns of figures, completely unaware of the odd expression on Sir Harold's face. Long before her interest waned, the job was completed; and the manager poured three glasses of wine from a bottle he handled with ceremonial respect.

"A special salute, Monsieur Brownwell, to our so excellent helper. We are through in half the time today. And now one more thing before you and Mademoiselle Anne return to Le Havre. While we were working, Madame Verge made some of her bonbons for you to take to your family. She remembered how you and your brothers enjoyed them when you were younger."

As she and Harold rode back to the inn in companionable silence punctuated only by their laughter as they sampled several of the rich buttery confections, Anne reflected that it had been an almost perfect day. The angry hurt she'd sustained when Gilbert had failed to join them as he'd promised had faded into a vague sense of defeat, which deepened sharply when he failed to greet them on their return at dusk. Lady Brownwell was the first to remind the young girl of her son's absence.

"I'm afraid Gilbert finds your idea of entertainment too tedious to tolerate. He has other friends who're not as self-centered as his brother."

Lord Brownwell's irritated response spared Anne the necessity of defending herself or Harold. "Madam, the only thing your son can't tolerate is the idea of the honest work his brother performs."

Despite her resolve not to think about the blond-haired man who'd disturbed her equanimity for the three days she'd known him, Anne was acutely conscious of the empty place at the dinner table. Even though she took a lively part in the conversation, she felt depressed, a mental state her grandfather quickly noted and commented on as he bid her good night.

"Best admit to yourself that you're attracted to the young man, Anne, and talk to him. Don't waste your breath denying what we both know is true. I've watched your face and I've spoken to the lad. The two of you are as prickly as burrs. He did promise to wed you, and I'm thinking you aren't really opposed to the notion."

"He's nothing but a conceited, arrogant, self-centered—"

"That he is and probably more, but talk to him anyway. You'll have no excuse tomorrow; Harold and his father will be gone all morning."

Contrarily Anne refused to take Lord Ashton's advice. Even earlier than on the previous three days, she was mounted on the mare, riding swiftly down the road leading to the small country inn she'd visited twice with Harold. She was almost there when she pulled to a halt and surrendered to the inevitable; she had been unable to outrun either her own turbulent thoughts or her grandfather's advice. Tethering her horse by the small stream that flowed alongside the road, she settled down on the grassy bank to analyze the unfamiliar emotions that disrupted her peace of mind. Frustratingly, as the uncounted minutes passed, no matter how logical her explanations were, she achieved neither understanding nor acceptance of her emotional turmoil. She almost welcomed the sounds of a human intrusion with relief until she recognized the angry intruder as the man who was causing her distress.

"I've been searching for hours," Gilbert blurted. "What the devil do you think you're doing?"

Hating the flush that reddened her face, Anne snapped, "Nothing that need concern you, Mr. Brownwell."

"Tell that to your grandfather, he's the one who's worried."

"He hasn't worried about me in ten years."

"You ungrateful brat, you've been gone four hours and you're more than six miles from the inn."

Stung by the epithet he'd called her, she sputtered, "I wish it had been four days and that I was back in England."

"So do I. Then maybe we could all have some peace.

What makes you think that you're safer than any other stupid girl would be riding alone on a country road where any damned French peasant could assault you?"

"No one else has, Mr. Brownwell. You were the only one with that degree of rudeness."

During this angry exchange, they had remained facing each other some ten feet apart, shouting in voices loud enough to be heard twenty yards away. Anne was the first to find any humor in the situation.

"I think my grandfather tricked you into riding after me." She smiled impishly. "He wanted to make certain we had the conversation he thought we should."

Gilbert returned her smile sheepishly. "Do you want to talk?"

"I can't think of anything to say, Mr. Brownwell."

"You could start by calling me Gilbert."

Recalling the tedious number of times she'd listened to his mother pronounce that name with the loving emphasis of adoration, Anne shook her head. "I prefer the name your brothers use."

"Call me Tony, then." He laughed as he walked toward her. "Now that we've been formally introduced, I suggest we sit down. We must have looked a pair of fools a minute ago."

"Why were you so angry when you found me?"

"I was worried about you."

"No, you weren't, it wasn't that kind of anger. Why were you?"

"Because you've been avoiding me for days."

"I wasn't yesterday; besides, you started it."

"Then we're even."

Unwilling to concede such an easy victory, since hers had been the deeper hurt, Anne remained silent, tensely aware that his arm had circled her waist and was forcing her closer to him. She felt his warm breath on her cheek and averted her head still more.

"Are you afraid of me, Anne?" She heard the lazy assurance in his voice and stiffened, wishing desperately that she'd had enough experience with men to treat him with an equal degree of amused condescension.

"No," she lied shakily, "and I don't think this is what Grandfather had in mind."

The easy laughter that greeted her words caused a thrill of fear to travel down her spine, even while a strange inertia gripped her.

"Sometimes talking is a waste of time," he murmured with his lips against her ear.

Anne felt the rush of hot blood that suffused her body and heard the frantic pounding of her heart. Unprepared for her own paralyzing physical reaction to a man's touch, she recoiled away from him and struggled to her feet. Gilbert reached her as she prepared to mount her horse.

"What's the matter with you?" he muttered, subduing her easily with strong hands that held her captive against him despite her efforts to escape the close physical contact of their bodies. His lips ground into hers without tenderness until her agitation subsided, and then his kiss became a slow seductive caress as he felt the stirrings of passion in her response. His pleasant sense of triumph continued to build as her body molded itself to his and her lips ceased to be passive, returning his pressure with a warmth that should have warned him. Instead it lulled him into an arousal that shocked him with its abrupt intensity. Hastily he released her and moved aside, remembering only at the last moment to appear reluctant. But what the devil! She'd pretended to be an innocent, yet no untried virgin he'd ever kissed possessed that kind of fire. Angrily he wondered how much of it his saintly brother had taught her during their day-long excursions together, and his lips curved into a cynical smile as he stroked her flushed cheek lightly.

"We'd better get back before someone else sends out a search party."

Unwilling to end the enchantment, she nodded mutely, vaguely confused by his sudden reversal from impassioned lover to impatient escort. His following words, though, ended

that confusion and turned the enchantment into something
shameful.

"Next time, fondling, we'll find another spot. This one, I
suspect, belongs more to Harold than to me."

Momentarily Anne heard only the resentful flippancy in his
voice, and she remained motionless until the ugly implication
of the words cooled her fevered brain like a shower of icy
water. The realization that he believed she had invited Harold
to kiss her jarred her into action, and for once she blessed her
height. In one swift movement she had mounted and turned
her horse toward the road; in another moment the mare was in
full gallop.

Taken by surprise, Gilbert cursed the stupidity of his
careless accusation. He couldn't remember why he'd said it;
and certainly she hadn't known what he was referring to at
first. Damn the hot temper that had gotten him into trouble all
of his life! He'd had the game won, why hadn't he just
flattered the sensitive bitch? What difference did it make what
she was or how many men she'd known as long as Harold
hadn't been one of them?

Gilbert wasn't worried about overtaking Anne; the mare
was fast but no match for a powerful gelding. It was the need
to devise a convincing apology that had him flummoxed; and
for someone with her ability to twist words, it would have to
be damned logical. Ironically it was another explosion of his
temper and his furious words after he'd pulled his horse
abreast of hers that forced her to listen. When the damned
chit ignored his command to slow down, he was forced to
grapple the reins from her hands; and she'd struck him
furiously with her crop in the process. By the time he
managed to halt the frightened mare, his arm felt torn from its
socket, and his self-control was in a blazing shambles.

"You addle-brained idiot, you almost killed a good horse.
Just because I made a fool of myself doesn't give you the
right to abuse a fine animal."

"I wasn't hurting it," Anne shouted back.

"The hell you weren't. This is a thoroughbred, not a plow

horse. Now walk it until it cools off, or damn it, you'll be doing the walking.''

Having ridden only the heavier breeds of horses at Grayhaven, Anne was uncertain about the stamina of this more highly bred type of horse. "I don't think you're right, but I'll slow down," she conceded, "providing you stop glaring at me as if I were guilty of deliberate cruelty."

His anger, however, was not to be so easily assuaged. Driven by the dismal knowledge that marriage to this exasperating girl was his only chance to avoid a bleak future, he continued his rash tirade.

"I don't know what you're guilty of, but you're an impossible person to talk to."

Anne regarded him curiously. "That's because you make unfounded accusations. Why did you?"

"Why did I what?"

"Consider it necessary to insult your brother?"

"I don't like having to compete against him when he has everything to offer."

"What are you talking about?"

"Don't playact like a naive twit. He has a title, a beautiful home, and the approval of everyone including your father and your aunt."

"But that's stupid. He isn't even competing."

"The devil he isn't!"

Anne was silent for the next mile; the idea that Harold was anything but a friend had never occurred to her. Still, such a possibility would explain Aunt Margaret's peculiar advice of the last few days and her father's odd attitude, and even Lord Brownwell's oblique insinuation: "Either way, you'll be my daughter-in-law." But they were all wrong! Harold had indicated no such interest in her, and yesterday he'd expressed a love for his dead wife that still persisted three years after death. He'd called his Bess a gentle, unassuming woman— two qualities Anne lacked completely. Why would Harold even consider her as a replacement? Anne paused in her reflections; she knew she'd never be content as a replacement for anyone else, especially not for someone who'd been highly successful as a wife. She realized something else, too—she didn't want another placid, settled life in rural England with still another older person in control. Besides, she'd experienced none of the physical excitement for Harold that she felt for this pampered, unpredictable man she was with now. As ignorant as she was about marriage, she suspected that those wild emotions were a necessary ingredient. Why submit to the ridiculous restraint of marriage if the man and woman were merely going to remain friends? Impatiently she glanced over at her companion, hoping he might be in a more conciliatory frame of mind or that he might at least agree to speed up the restless horses.

Although Gilbert's mood had undergone changes during the past half hour, they were not necessarily an improvement. His rage had been replaced with an ill-humored petulance— his arm smarted from the stinging blows she'd given him when he'd stopped her horse, and she hadn't even had the decency to apologize. Furthermore, his plaguing doubts had deepened into certainty; what woman wouldn't choose an established aristocrat over a man without prospects? One additional annoyance weighted his already burdened mind— what the hell had happened to him when he'd kissed her? He'd been with dozens of women, many of them far more agreeable than this one, and never experienced much of any reaction on a single kiss. But with her he'd acted like a rutting bull. And it wasn't just woman hunger; he'd spent the night before with an attractive widowed farm woman whose appetites in bed were unrestrained. Marriage to this sharp-tongued Anne Gray would be bad enough without the complications of a physical attraction. Remembering that his goal of marriage was by no means certain, he studied the girl next to him from beneath lowered eyelids. She sat a horse with graceful ease, guiding the animal expertly even while she was engrossed in thought. She wasn't really beautiful, he decided; but her face was arresting in its facile ability to mirror her changing moods and emotions. And her eyes had the power to disconcert him as surely as her slender body had aroused him. Why either attribute affected him, he was at a loss to explain. He'd always preferred brown-eyed women, and this girl was too damned tall for any man. Trapped in this uncomplimentary perusal when she looked in his direction, he smiled uncertainly.

"I was wrong about that remark I made, Anne, but I'm not going to apologize for kissing you."

Her breathing once again impeded by emotion, Anne mumbled, "I wasn't angry about that, Mr. Brown—Tony."

The quality of his smile changed subtly. He hadn't been the only one affected by that kiss; and if he guarded himself against any emotional involvement in the future, he could replace his brother in her affection without much more than a flattering attendance. There was still the hurdle, however, of convincing her two watchdog guardians.

"Will you have tea alone with me today, Anne?"

Reminded suddenly that she'd eaten only the hard roll she'd taken with her on the morning ride, she answered with a considerably stronger voice. "If we can have it right away. I meant to have lunch at Alette's, but I forgot."

"Alette's?"

"It's a—"

"Another of your and Harold's special places?"

Her brief euphoria vanished, Anne kicked her horse gently into a canter, refusing to answer the sarcastic question or to glance at her companion until she pulled to a stop in the inn courtyard. Dismounting as quickly as she could, she was still not swift enough to avoid Gilbert's arms.

"You've a hot temper, Anne Gray," he chided her as he bent to kiss her set lips. She didn't respond, not even when he kissed her the second time; there was no enchantment to either kiss, only a professional charm similar to that displayed by the doorman of Grosvenor House, who had smiled the same way for every guest.

From the darkened interior of a room overlooking the courtyard, a quiet man had watched the scene taking place below, his eyes focused on the flushed face of the girl. Not once in all the hours he'd spent with her, Harold Brownwell mused sadly, had she offered anything more than a warm platonic friendship. With him, she'd been relaxed and playful, even frivolous, without feeling one pulse beat of the chimerical magic of love.

"She treated me like a second grandfather, Bess," he said softly to the woman who was never far from the surface of his consciousness, "yet I felt younger with her than I have since you left me. She seemed so much a part of my life, I almost kissed her yesterday. Perhaps that is all it would have taken to win her loyalty, now it's too late for even that. She is still attracted to Tony, although she knows that he's just a childish weakling. He can't give her happiness, Bess, not the kind we had."

He looked down at his brother, accurately assessing the possessive triumph reflected in that handsome face, and sighed. Anne deserved better. Even a marriage without love would be preferable to the spiteful insecurity of a life with a man who had never accepted responsibility in his spoiled life. But Harold knew that such a marriage would be lacking for himself; he was no stripling to be satisfied with less than the capacity for passionate love he'd sensed in Anne from the moment he'd seen her on the deck of the ship. The sensitive quickness of her understanding, the proud lift of her head, and her intense desire to master the world around her—all of that glorious, unawakened potential wasted on such a man as his brother.

Long after Anne and Tony had vanished from the courtyard, Harold stood motionless, contemplating the courses of action he could take. He knew that he was Sir Geoffrey's and Lady Margaret's choice and that his own father would approve of his marriage to Anne. He smiled suddenly with a mocking honesty. She would never submit to him or to any man unless it was what she wanted to do. Resolutely he turned toward the table in his room and hastily wrote two brief letters before leaving for a quiet talk with his father.

Lord Brownwell's terse announcement at dinner that Harold had sailed for England on the evening tide to take care of business affairs at home met with differing reactions. Anne felt a pervasive sadness at the thought of losing another of the few friends she had known in her short life. Her father and aunt exchanged grim looks of bitter disappointment, unhappily aware of Lady Brownwell's brief smile of satisfaction. But it was Gilbert's audible whisper to Anne that expressed all of their thoughts. "That leaves just you and me, Anne."

"Where does that leave us, Mr. Brown—Tony?" she asked, her eyes filled with less than joyous doubt.

The answer to her probing question was instantaneous; Gilbert had already determined the rules of the courtship he embarked on even during that unhappy dinner. Anne became the target of a blatantly public pursuit which left her vaguely discontented. He escorted her relentlessly about the inn, hovering over her at meals and in the company of others, his conversation a flattering solicitude for her needs. Gilbert was chivalry personified in the chaste kisses he bestowed on her at the foot of the stairs each time they parted. In his invitations to take her shopping in Le Havre he generally included Margaret; and these excursions became another opportunity for displayed gallantry. Each morning he rode with her for an hour of brisk cantering without dismounting along the lonely stretches of roadway. The only hours he wasn't in attendance were the three between those rides and lunch when he would disappear, leaving her with a shadowy memory of the one kiss that had made her feel alive. As the days passed without any dramatic resolution to her dilemma, Anne became increasingly irritable with the reassurances given her by the members of her own family. While not perfect, they now claimed, Gilbert was at least becoming acceptable.

Since this was not the reassurance she wanted or needed, she began to take lonely walks away from the inn along the beaches that flanked the harbor. Seated on a foam-sprayed rock, she stared out over the gentle breakers lapping the rocky shore and admitted her frustration with the man who now dominated her thoughts. Upon returning to the inn, she submitted ever more unwillingly to the display of his affection, which she knew was a spurious sham. She would have welcomed a return even of the temperamentally abusive man he'd been before; this charming, handsome replacement aroused only her distrust.

On her third such walk Anne noticed what she thought must be a dolphin swimming far away from shore. Only when she studied the pattern of the steady progress across the water did she realize that the performer was a man. Fascinated because she'd never observed anyone swim, she envied the skill that made such a feat possible. After watching the distant figure stroke rapidly back and forth in a line parallel with the beach and then finally head inland, she gasped when she recognized the blond head of the swimmer. Experiencing an illogical pride in his accomplishment, she remained motionless as he strode out of the water some eighty feet from where she was sitting.

When he joined her there some minutes later, he was dressed in the heavy jacket of a common seaman rather than in one of the dandified suits he usually wore, and his facial expression was somber.

"Hello, Anne."

"Hello, Tony. Where did you learn to swim like that?"

"In the river near our home in England."

"You do it well."

"I enjoy it."

"Why are you dressed in those clothes, Tony?"

For a moment he regarded her soberly. "Because I was trying to find the courage to apply for a berth aboard some ship headed for Australia."

Anne sucked in her breath sharply, relaxing only when he smiled at her with the careless charm she hated and said lightly, "But I changed my mind and decided to marry you instead. Come on, fondling, let's go back and tell our families the good news."

As he kissed her lightly on her forehead, she shoved him

furiously away. "Don't do that," she cried sharply, "we're not on display now. At least when we're alone, I'd appreciate your being honest even if you show only your contempt for me."

His eyes were glittery as he yanked her angrily toward him and put his arms roughly around her.

"Honesty isn't very wise in our case," he muttered, his mouth lowering to hers with a violent pressure that swept her breath away. When she responded with the pent-up hunger of a long week of discontent, her fierce emotion equaled his. He was the first to pull away, but he didn't release her; nor did he offer any resistance when her arms tightened around him.

"I warned you that this wouldn't be very wise," he said thickly. "Unless you know what you're doing, I think we'd better leave; and I think we'd better be married before we come here again. Will you marry me, Anne Gray?"

"Yes," she whispered and then added with a faint giggle, "if you'll kiss me again like you just did."

He stared at her a moment before his laughter joined hers. "You're becoming a wayward hussy."

She grinned back at him. "I think I must be, because I feel so alive again." He kissed her then, but carefully—she was almost too alive.

Chapter 4

Two mornings later in the Protestant church of Le Havre, a relieved Reverend Thompson officiated in uniting Anne Gray to Gilbert Brownwell in holy wedlock, rendered less than reverent by a curious impatience on the part of the groom's mother. When Margaret had tried to insist that Anne needed a wedding dress, Suzanne Brownwell had murmured, "Nonsense," and gone through the bride's limited wardrobe, selecting a vivid leaf-green linen dress.

"This will do splendidly," she exclaimed. "I have an Alençon lace scarf that she may use as a veil." Suzanne was equally resourceful about the rings when Gilbert attempted to consult his father about their purchase. "No need," she interrupted briskly, "I have an excellent pair she may have." Neither of the proffered rings compared to the several that graced Suzanne's own fingers, neither of them was a traditional wedding band, and the fact that they fit Anne's finger at all was an unimportant coincidence.

Reverend Thompson also contributed to the unseemly haste by scheduling the ceremony for an early morning hour almost before the disgruntled bridegroom was fully awake. "We don't want our bride to become nervous," the minister had chirped brightly when Margaret protested. "We don't want her to change her mind now that she has finally decided to become an obedient wife," he added. "I think, dear lady, that she has kept all of us in suspense long enough. I for one must return to England to resume my duties, and I imagine that other members of the party are equally impatient."

Having just arrived from England, John Peabody looked up from the marriage contracts he was preparing for the bride's father and commented dryly, "I suggest, then, Reverend, that you cancel your proposed trip to Paris and reschedule the wedding for a later hour tomorrow. I will need the extra time to complete these documents."

Myles Thompson glared at the solicitor in protest at his interference. "It is a matter of some importance to my parishioners that I visit Paris while I'm in France. The ladies will expect a complete report. Moreover, the church will be occupied during the later hours with another wedding and a funeral."

Of all the wedding party, only Lord Ashton retained a sense of humor. When he and his son met Anne as she walked nervously down the stairs, he handed her a bridal bouquet that brought a wan smile to her tense lips. Buried in the center of a sheaf of white roses were a dozen brilliant red ones.

"Marriage is often like the War of Roses, granddaughter, and since you're a red Lancastrian and your husband a white Yorkist, I predict there'll be battles aplenty. You're a rebel, Anne; but if you work to make this thing a success, you'll soon bring your husband to heel. Remember, gel, a little obedience won't crush your spirit."

Anne clutched the symbolic bouquet all the way to the church, deeply touched by her grandfather's perceptive understanding of her nature. Walking proudly between her two tall Ashton men, she stopped abruptly at the sight of Gilbert and his mother standing together near the altar. Once again they were dressed in their matching burgundy-and-cream outfits, and once again Anne felt like an alien outsider—a feeling that persisted throughout the ceremony. Even as she and her new husband sat side by side in the carriage on the return trip to the inn, his mother dominated the conversation from the opposite seat. Anne quietly removed the filmy scarf she'd worn as a veil and returned it to Suzanne, murmuring her thanks with an ironic inflection. No one paid the slightest attention to her words; Suzanne accepted the scarf without a break in her enthusiastic harangue about Gilbert's social future in London. Had she dared, Anne would also have returned the rings to her mother-in-law; they felt like unwanted slave chains on her fingers. Only three times did she pay any attention to the other three occupants; twice when her husband squeezed her hand, she smiled at him. And once when her father asked where she wanted to live, she answered, "Boston," with a vindictive emphasis. The idea of shoving Suzanne Brownwell into a deep pit of water was no longer an amusing flash of humor.

John Peabody, who'd remained behind to complete the marriage contracts, met the entire party ceremoniously in the private dining room which the innkeeper had decorated with bridal splendor. Myles Thompson smiled importantly as he signed the papers and then handed the quill first to Sir Geoffrey, then to Lord Brownwell, and finally to Gilbert and Anne.

"Now that the legal folderol is finished, let's get on with the business of celebrating," Lord Ashton prompted as he distributed brimming glasses of champagne to the guests before he raised his in the first toast, "To my favorite gel and her new husband."

"May the marriage be a happy one," Geoffrey said quietly.

Anne giggled as her grandfather led the innkeeper and the two serving girls bearing the festive plates of food past her. In the middle of the creamy white cake was a mound of red strawberries, and circling the large omelet were dozens of red radishes. Lord Ashton winked at her as she raised her glass in a private salute to the War of Roses; she was going to miss his irreverent sense of humor.

Her smile faltered slightly at her new brother-in-law's toast. "To Anne and Gilbert Brownwell; welcome to the family, Anne," Arthur said warmly. The new name shocked her into the realization that Anne Gray no longer existed; she felt an odd twinge of regret as her husband led her to the place of honor at the table and seated her with courtly gallantry. But the next hour was not to be her time of triumph!

From Gilbert's other side, Suzanne Brownwell raised her glass with a dramatic flourish. "Now that my son is married," she announced in a bell-like voice that quavered with excitement, "and in charge of the dowry money, he and I will live in our London townhouse. His wife may live there, too, unless she prefers to return to her aunt."

With a smile of scornful contempt, Suzanne brandished her glass in her husband's direction. "I warned you, Harold, that I would not abide being buried at Brownsville. Gilbert can well afford to support me in London now."

Only a tense silence greeted these taunting words for a few seconds until Lord Brownwell addressed his youngest son in quiet, firm tones. "Is this your mother's idea, or did you and she plan it together?"

Gilbert shook his head vigorously. "I don't even intend to return to London."

"You couldn't anyway, son, not to the townhouse. It's been leased to a member of Parliament for the next four years."

"How dare you!" Suzanne shouted at her husband. "Then Gilbert and I will just lease a house of our own."

Studiously her husband ignored her. "Where do you and Anne intend to live, Gilbert?"

"Abroad someplace."

"Gilbert," his mother pleaded, "if you don't like London, we could live somewhere in the south of England or even here in the north of France."

"I wondered," Lord Brownwell now addressed his wife coldly, "why you suddenly became so agreeable about this marriage. You believed that it would return the control of your son's life back to you. He is a married man now, madam, and that privilege belongs exclusively to his wife."

Arthur Brownwell cleared his throat nervously. "Suzanne, Tony can't live anyplace in England or the continent for the next five years."

This time the silence was of a long duration, broken once again by Lord Brownwell's quiet voice. "I think you'd better explain, Arthur."

"Tony was arrested in London and accused of attempted murder."

"My God! What happened?" The father's face was ashen.

"A man broke into his flat and attacked Tony. Tony defended himself with a sword cane."

"But that's self-defense!" Lord Ashton exclaimed.

"Not if the woman involved was the man's wife," John Peabody reasoned. "Then it can be interpreted as a defense of the sanctity of the home on the part of the attacker, especially if the woman claimed that she'd been held against her will. Was that the case?"

Arthur nodded. "Yes, it was; but she and the man had a record of previous such entrapments."

"Who was the man?" Peabody persisted.

"The same gambler Tony owed twelve thousand pounds to. Harold and I paid that debt with the money Suzanne gave us; the rest we used to pay the hospital expenses for the man and the fines."

"Did Chadwick help you?" Lord Brownwell asked.

"The police wouldn't even talk to us without a family solicitor present."

"Why wasn't I notified?"

"If we'd told you, Tony would still be in jail. The only reason the police let him go was the criminal record of the other man, but what they did was illegal. They would never have risked exposure to a member of Parliament. As it was, they gave us just one day to get our brother out of England, so we left London aboard a dirty fishing vessel. Tony's just lucky that the inspector in charge of the case was a reasonable man and not a martinet."

"You make me ill, Arthur," Suzanne raged. "You make my son sound like a criminal when he isn't guilty of anything. I insist that we all return and clear Gilbert's name, and then he can stay where he belongs."

Peabody shook his head. "Such a move would be very foolish. For the past year, your son has been involved with some very criminal people, and the woman he lived with was notorious. But I understand on good authority that she is very beautiful and an expert on the witness stand. If a jury believed her claim, your son could be accused of more than attempted murder."

"It was only self-defense, Mr. Peabody," Gilbert insisted tiredly. "Both Becker and the henchman he brought with him were armed with knives, and even—even the damned woman attacked me. But by the time the police arrived, the other man had disappeared."

Lady Brownwell moved closer to her son and glared at her husband. "It's all your fault, Harold. If you'd given me the money when I first asked for it, none of this would have happened.''

''Madam, the money I repaid the scoundrel you borrowed from was not mine. It was part of Anne's dowry, the fifteen thousand pounds Lord Ashton gave for his granddaughter's marriage.''

Anne's gasp of shock was drowned out by Suzanne's angry voice. ''Is that all the money Gilbert is to receive? You told me the dowry was considerably more.''

''Madam''—Lord Brownwell's voice rasped with anger— ''dowry monies are intended for the support of both the husband and wife. It does not belong to the husband alone.''

Suzanne's head moved impatiently as if to ward off an annoying insect. ''Was that all there was?''

''No, there is still the twenty thousand pounds her father has offered.''

''Good''—her jaw clamped strongly over her words—''Arthur, can Gilbert live in Scotland or Ireland?''

Smiling maliciously at his stepmother's single-minded persistence, Arthur shook his head. ''Not Wales, either, Suzanne. The closest you can be to Tony during the next five years would be Iceland or Greenland.''

''Don't be a fool. I have no intention of deserting my son. I will go into exile with him.''

''You'd find it a miserable existence, madam,'' Lord Brownwell scoffed. ''Sir Geoffrey has agreed to my terms that the dowry money be paid in annual installments of two thousand pounds.''

Aroused from the sullen mood he'd been in since the discussion began, Gilbert jerked to sudden attention when he heard these terms. ''How the hell can I live on two thousand pounds a year?'' he demanded hotly.

''You'll work for a living like the rest of us,'' his father snapped coldly.

''The devil I will! That wasn't what I agreed to when this whole damn thing started. There wasn't any mention of installments then, only the whole amount. And that's what I want. I don't appreciate being lied to or cheated."

"I would be careful about calling other people liars or cheaters, Gilbert," his father thundered. "You lied to me about being free of debt, and God knows you've cheated all of your life."

Had either the father or son been alert at that moment, they would have noticed that the bride had not looked up from her plate since the Brownwells's argument had begun. Her mind was reeling from the revelations she'd heard; and her heart was thudding so painfully she felt smothered. The cold mathematics of her marriage were brutal facts; her father and grandfather had paid thirty-five thousand pounds to buy her a husband. For that amount, she realized bitterly, she could have been a repugnant, crippled hag and the purchased husband a paragon of virtues instead of this sulky man sitting next to her. When her aunt had talked about his gambling, Anne had envisioned him losing a few pounds at cards. But he'd lost fifteen thousand pounds and seemingly felt no compunction. That he'd had other women she'd known instinctively; but that his mistress had been a notorious harlot was an ugly mortification for a virgin bride. A bride who now faced five years of exile because her husband had been judged too violent a criminal to be allowed in England!

Twisting the hated rings that burned her finger, Anne considered the other facts she'd learned at her bridal breakfast. Her mother-in-law's approval had been given only to regain possession of her son, and not once had that son protested the possession. He hadn't even remembered he had a wife when his mother had announced that she and Gilbert would live together in London. But it was his reaction to the payment of the second part of the dowry that had crushed Anne's remaining hopes. "I," he'd said, not "we"—"How can I live?" and "I don't appreciate being cheated." The champagne she'd sipped during the earlier toasts to a happy marriage churned uneasily in her stomach. Imperceptibly she flinched at the strain in her aunt's voice.

"I think I may have a solution to this problem of money," Lady Margaret disclosed cautiously. "In a few days I am becoming a partner in a Boston shipping firm. Since Gilbert has had experience with ships, I'm certain he can be of use to the company. To that end, I've made certain provisions with the other owners who will arrive in Le Havre in a few days. It is my hope that Anne and Gilbert will find Boston a comfortable place in which to live."

Anne winced; her aunt, too, had contributed to the purchase price of the husband! She'd bought him employment that would be guaranteed no matter what his performance was. The demoralized bride listened to the sharp hiss of Suzanne's reaction to Margaret's plan.

"Is the home you've arranged for my son a proper place, Lady Margaret?"

"I've arranged only for your son to find work, Lady Brownwell. He and Anne can take care of their own housing."

"How can he on the pittance he's being given? I've heard that Boston has some lovely neighborhoods. I would think that you would want your niece to have the protection of a suitable home, one that could accommodate their guests from England."

Anne smiled faintly at her aunt's tart rejoinder: "Guests from England are the last things Anne and Gilbert will need. If I remember my American history correctly, Bostonians are not too receptive of British visitors."

"Nonsense. Provincials always welcome titled aristocrats. Therefore Gilbert and Anne will most definitely need an attractive home."

"Since I have no intention of buying them one, I suggest we return to the subject of Gilbert's employment," Margaret said tiredly.

"My son is not a tradesman."

"I don't imagine he has either the skill or training to be one, but it is my understanding that he does know ships. I imagine he can be useful to the owners."

"From what you promised earlier, at least he'll be your agent there."

"No, he won't. Anne will be my agent because she does have a trade, Lady Brownwell. She is an excellent bookkeeper."

"Then what will be my son's position?"

"That will depend on what he can do. But with his school record in mathematics and other things, it will most certainly not be in the area of money management." Anne smiled again; her successful aunt held few things in life more sacred than the profitable management of money. "However," Margaret continued, "there will undoubtedly be other jobs he's qualified to learn, such as . . ."

"Such as carpentry or manual labor? Margaret Gray, I will not countenance any more of your insults. Obviously you have had little experience with gentlemen, otherwise you'd realize that Gilbert will never submit to your spiteful interference in his life." In her fury, Suzanne pushed her chair backward, upsetting it in the process, and stood up, leaning heavily on the table to gain a better position for her shrill attack. "Since your niece is such a good bookkeeper, let her earn the living. In that way she might be of some conceivable use to my son. As it is now, she is nothing except a miserable millstone around his neck."

Anne was the only one who did not react violently to these vitriolic words; she remained immobile in her chair as if she were turned into stone. She heard her husband mutter, "Oh, my God!"; her father command John Peabody to begin annulment proceedings; and Arthur Brownwell whisper sibilantly, "Once a bitch, always a bitch."

Only Lord Brownwell had the courage to stoop to his wife's level. "Madam, you sound more like a gutter-born fishwife than a lady. If you say one more word, I will silence you physically. As for you, Gilbert," he admonished his son, "if you have any sense left after all the years you've been pampered by your foolish and vicious mother, you'll accept the opportunity Lady Margaret has offered. I doubt if anyone else will hire you. And just in case you still have any illusions about your future, I am going to be very specific. If your wife is made to suffer through any negligence on your part or any cruelty, I will disinherit you and leave the property in trust for her.''

Turning once again to his wife, now staring open-mouthed at him, Lord Brownwell announced coldly, "You're to go to your room and pack your trunks—you, not your maids. I dismissed both of them this morning. In two hours, whether you're packed or not, you'll be aboard the *Dover Princess* in the cabin I have reserved. If he wishes to, your son may help you. But not another word, madam, to any of these people here. You have disgraced my name and my family's honor for the last time.''

Ignoring his white-faced wife, Lord Brownwell addressed Sir Geoffrey. "I am entirely in sympathy with your desire to annul this marriage. If such a thing is possible, I will assuredly support your petition.''

An agitated Reverend Thompson leapt to his feet. "This marriage is holy. It was performed in the sight of God in a place of worship, and only God can dissolve it.''

"Mr. Peabody?'' Lord Brownwell raised his eyebrow in question.

"I'm afraid the reverend is right. All of Gilbert's actions took place prior to the wedding, and we knew about most of the charges in advance. At the moment, an annulment is impossible, and there is little I can do to reclaim the contracted dowry funds.''

Lord Brownwell sighed and walked over toward Anne, who had remained motionless throughout the entire scene, offering no response to anyone's efforts to console her.

"Let's you and me go for a walk, Anne,'' her father-in-law said briskly as he drew her to her feet and linked his arm through hers. "There's nothing I can say that will ease the hurt you've suffered this morning. Just remember, though, if you ever need me, I'll do everything in my power to help you.''

Anne stared at him blankly for a brief moment before her

self-control broke. With a wrenching sob that shook her slender frame, she fled from all the faces watching her with deep sympathy and ran blindly up the stairs to her room. There she vomited repeatedly until the upheaval subsided and she felt empty of all feeling. When Margaret came to her a few minutes later, Anne had regained her composure and was changing into her riding habit. The older woman noted the two wedding rings lying on the table and wisely let the distraught girl leave without a word.

Mounted on the mare, Anne rode slowly down the road she'd taken with Harold more than a week before. She experienced no exhilaration and no relief from the hollow void that made her feel more dead than alive. Oddly enough, her thoughts reverted to the portrait Harold had painted of his wife. She wondered if this were the way he'd felt when his beautiful Bess had died, as if there were no future and as if memories hurt too much to recall consciously. Dismounting from her horse, she stood on the bank of the Seine River looking down on the ferryboat she and Harold had used to cross the swift currents. Had Harold really wanted to marry her? With him, her future would have been serene and dignified; with the man she'd chosen, there might not even be a future.

In the distance she could see a ship with its sails furled being pulled by small boats toward the mouth of the river. As the ship hove into sight, Anne could see the faces of the seamen straining at the oars of the long boats linked by strong hawsers to the sailing vessel. When one of the men noticed the lone girl seated on the bank, he shouted a greeting which she recognized as an oddly pronounced "Hello." Anne returned his broad smile and waved, and she soon was returning the smiles of the thirty men who lined up along the deck of the ship, waving at her. Not until she saw the flag at the ship's aft did she realize that she'd just glimpsed her first Americans. They were, she thought, the friendliest people she'd ever seen, and soon she would be living among them. With or without her problem-plagued husband, Anne Gray was going to America. Not until she was almost back at the inn did she remember that her new name was Anne Brownwell.

Three nervous, worried men were waiting for her, but her husband was nowhere in sight. As she smiled cheerfully at them, the men relaxed visibly and led her back to the table where they'd been sipping wine and talking. When Lord Brownwell poured a glass for her, she giggled. "I think you'd better order me some food, since I've forgotten to eat any today, and I don't think a drunken bride would add much dignity to the situation."

As she ate the small meat pie placed before her, Sir Geoffrey asked her seriously, "What do you intend to do, Anne?"

"Go to America, Father. It seems like a wonderful country."

Lord Ashton guffawed. "Told you, Geoffrey, that our gel would be all right. Takes more than a tongue-drubbing to throw her off stride."

"Are you sure, Anne?" her father persevered.

"About America? Absolutely."

"What about my son, Anne?" Lord Brownwell questioned her, his pleasant face lined with strain. "Will you be able to put up with him?"

"I don't know, it depends on him. But I'll survive either way."

"One thing I can promise you, Anne, Gilbert's mother will never come to Boston to upset you again."

She grinned at Lord Brownwell's serious expression. "Tell her it wouldn't be entirely safe. Gilbert isn't the only one with a propensity for self-defense; I've been known on occasion to forget my father's counsel that ladies should be delicate, gentle creatures. Stop laughing, Grandfather, or my father-in-law will be convinced that Reverend Thompson is correct in his estimation of my character."

During the hour she spent with the three men now bound together by a marriage of uncertain future, Anne maintained a light raillery, not once betraying her inner sadness at the prospect of their sailing out of her life on the evening tide.

The older two were the first to depart, each man leaving her with a sealed envelope. The one from her grandfather contained a letter of credit which she knew would be honored at any bank in the world. In the one from Lord Bromwell was a letter from his oldest son. Harold had left her and Gilbert the three thoroughbred horses as a wedding gift. Anne's eyes were moist as she handed the envelopes to her father.

"I'm sorry you didn't marry the older one," Geoffrey said slowly. "If you had, you'd be in England where we could see each other from time to time. Don't forget your grandfather and me, Anne."

"How could I ever?" She smiled, suppressing the dull ache of incipient loneliness. "All I have to do is look in a mirror to see both of your faces. And when I return, neither you nor I will ever have to apologize for my birth again."

"If that's the only reason you've decided to stay with that reprobate husband of yours, I'm not letting you do it. You'll return to England with me; and if it's your desire, I'll force Elizabeth to welcome you into my household."

She stared at him in horror. "I'd be so miserable there, Father, your wife would be justified in putting arsenic into my tea. You and Aunt Margaret and Grandfather have been wonderful to me, but you've controlled my life almost as much as Lady Brownwell has Gilbert's. Now I want to make my own decisions and my own mistakes. Even if he turns out to be a very bad husband, I want to live my own life. And I want you to go back to England and live yours without worrying about me anymore."

Her father nodded slowly and kissed her good-bye; but Anne knew better than to expect miracles. Geoffrey Ashton would continue to feel responsible for her until the day she returned to England, and even then he wouldn't consider her mature enough to function without the guidance of a man. Anne took a deep breath and hoped the husband she was about to search out now would prove manageable.

Chapter 5

OPENING the door to her room, Anne was startled to find all of her trunks gone and her clothes missing. Uneasy because in her protected life she'd never been really alone before, she turned back into the hall only to come face-to-face with her husband. He was leaning against the wall watching her. Her heart pounded with an odd mixture of relief and apprehension as he led her down the hall and into a large bedroom that overlooked the harbor. Without a word he opened one of the two doors cut into the wall opposite the balcony. Inside one of the small rooms, he pointed to her trunks piled beside his own. Then, taking her arm, he escorted her over to the table before the fireplace and seated her. The cheerful fire spread a golden glow over the room and made the wineglasses sparkle on the table graciously laid out for dining. With practiced ease he poured two glasses and handed her one.

"Well, Anne?" He raised his glass in a toast.

"Well, Gilbert?"

"What happened to Tony?"

Anne answered slowly, "I think he left with Harold." His smile disappeared, replaced with the pinched look of long-standing jealousy.

"And is my elusive wife sorry that she didn't leave with Harold, too?"

"No." She looked at the beautiful face of her husband,

remembered momentarily the stronger one of his brother, and added, "Not particularly."

In the awkward silence that followed, he refilled the glasses, although hers had scarcely been touched, walked to her chair, and bent to kiss her cheek and whisper in her ear, "I've ordered our dinner to be served up here. Let's be friends, Anne?"

"Oh, we can be friends, Gilbert. It's just that I've already eaten." Her voice was still remote and cool.

He pulled away from her sharply. "A bit unusual, isn't it, eating your wedding supper without your husband?"

"It's been an unusual day."

"That it has. For four hours I waited for you while you were out riding all by yourself in a strange country like some wild gypsy. Very unusual, wouldn't you say?"

"I'm used to riding by myself."

"Not anymore. From now on you'll ride only with me."

"Is there to be a 'now on,' Gilbert?"

"That's a stupid question. You're my wife."

"From what you said earlier, I wasn't sure."

He groaned. "You mean that one slip of the tongue? Believe me, it will never happen again, if for no other reason than to avoid being ridiculed by everyone from your Aunt Margaret to your Aunt Margaret's lawyer." Anne made no response, she had none to make; how could she really describe her hurt? So she sipped her wine and continued to watch him with the usual faint smile curving her lips. It was he who fidgeted. "Tell me, Anne, was today the first time you'd heard about my evil character?" Her smile remained intact as she studied his face; his inflection on the word *evil* made it sound like *naughty* or *mischievous*.

"I knew something about your gambling but nothing else." She shrugged.

"Well, there wasn't much else. None of that other was my fault, and you can't blame me for what my mother said. But how is it you didn't know all about it? Your aunt paid that legal minion of hers to pry into every bit of my private business."

"That wasn't very hard; your 'private business' sounded very public to me."

His eyes narrowed to angry slits. "All right, Mrs. Brownwell, if that's your opinion, our future life will be completely secret. We'll go to Australia and no one else will be told where in Australia we settle."

"How can we when the ship we'll be sailing on goes to Boston?"

Gilbert glared at her. "Your confidence in me is over-whelming. You sound as smug as your aunt and as understand-ing as my father. Well, I've had enough inquisition for one day. Since you won't join me for dinner, I'll have mine alone downstairs. And since you obviously don't want my company, I'll bid you good night now." He slammed his glass down on the table, making an ugly splotch of red wine on the white tablecloth, and banged the door shut as he strode out of the room.

Fighting the anger she felt for both her husband and herself and hating the fact that she wanted to cry, Anne moved restlessly out onto the balcony. It was lonelier there and colder. In unhappy desperation she walked to her aunt's room and knocked. Margaret looked up from a table cluttered with the remains of dinner and two large open ledgers. She studied her niece's face and asked, "Are you all right? I've been worried."

"I'm fine now."

"I wouldn't blame you if you remained sick for a month after that scene this morning. Where is your husband? Not that I don't wish he were on the other side of the world, but it appears you are married to him."

"He's downstairs someplace."

Margaret hesitated. "Anne, are you afraid to be alone with him? It's not unusual, dear. All young brides have a certain amount of fear about being alone with their husbands for the first time." And for Anne, the dam broke! All day long she had been driven by many fears, but not once by this one. She threw back her head and laughed.

"No, Aunt Margaret, I'm not afraid of being alone with my husband because of that. Why should I be? Paddy gave me two books to read before we left Grayhaven."

"Paddy did what? Well, that meddling old Irishman. I wasn't even aware that he knew too much about it himself." Margaret joined Anne in laughter. "Anne, you're amazing. I swear that you were born a hundred years old."

On the way back to the room she was supposed to be sharing with a new husband, Anne remembered those two books of Paddy's again. One was a scientific anatomy book with obfuscating words that all but eliminated the meaning, while the other was a well-thumbed little booklet issued to adolescent boys in better-class Irish schools. And her laughter pealed out again. An old-maid aunt, a bachelor tutor, and a booklet that referred to women's "parts"! She didn't know a thing, not a single thing about what that ugly little book called "the intimacies of marriage."

Staring about the empty room, Anne was acutely aware that this was her wedding night, a wedding night without a husband. Not quite, she thought with a burst of humor. She did have a husband, an expensive one, whom she would join for dinner. Hastily she unpacked the filmy heather-blue dress she'd saved for this occasion; but while she was searching for the three matching petticoats, she lost her courage. Her husband was capable of blunt language, and her ego was bruised enough for one day. Sadly she donned instead her bridal nightgown of soft silk and the velvet robe she'd made herself in the London hotel room. She brushed her long hair until her scalp tingled and, with a shrug, settled down to reading Henry Fielding's *Tom Jones*, one of Paddy's last gifts to her. She was still reading when Gilbert stumbled through the door, drunk and argumentative.

The only other men Anne had seen in so advanced a state of inebriation had been villagers who had looked only slightly more sullen than they usually did. But her husband's normally handsome face was completely changed; his eyes were badly focused, his lips were loose, and his expression that of a cruel child. She was sickened by his slurred-together words and by the crude meaning of those words. "Virgin bastard. Cold virgin bastard. Had to get drunk to go to bed with you. Had to get drunk to sleep with a tall skinny bastard."

With her heart pounding, Anne stood up and braced herself as he grabbed her shoulders and jerked her toward him. She twisted her elbows in front of her and shoved them into his chest, but his arms were strong and his fingers bit deeply into her flesh as he dragged her back. Almost by instinct she stretched a leg around one of his and kicked the back of his calf with all the power she could muster. He stumbled just enough for her to pull loose and retreat across the room. Cursing now, he lurched toward her with his hand raised. She dodged to one side and put her foot out as he lunged. With a relieved satisfaction she watched him fall heavily, facedown to the floor, where he lay as if he'd been sledgehammered. When he didn't stir, she knelt down and rolled him over. He was sleeping with his mouth open, and his fetid, wine-sour breath whistled from his throat.

With ungentle hands and a sense of revulsion, she pulled his clothes off of him and dragged him naked to the bed. At that moment his whole being affronted her sensibilities. It took all of her strength to pull him up on the bed. Dropping the covers on top of his inert body, Anne looked at the man she had promised to obey for life and shuddered. She thought with a deep regret of what their wedding night might have been.

Listening to his snores and gurglings, Anne calmly removed her velvet robe, took out a needle and thread, and stitched up a torn shoulder seam. When she'd finished, she blew out the candles; and because there was no other place, she climbed into bed beside her husband. In the morning she awakened first and turned her head to look at his face; it was still mottled and unpleasant. Without bothering to move quietly, she washed herself and donned her riding habit; and in the cool chill of the dawn, she raced down country roads and breathed the fresh air that helped erase the memory of the previous night's ugly reality.

Hours later, when she returned to the room, her bridal suite, she found her husband sitting at the table eating breakfast. He was elegantly dressed and groomed, smiling with a cool contempt as he glanced at her windblown hair.

"Did you enjoy your ride, wife?"

"As a matter of fact, I did"—her lip curled—"husband."

"Did you enjoy your sleep, too, wife?"

"More than you did, I expect." She shrugged.

He had stopped smiling during this exchange, but his voice remained deceptively mild as he rose from his chair and extended a hand toward her. "Come over here, I want to show you something." She let him take her hand and lead her over to the bed. "You, Anne Gray, are as much a whore as your mother was."

In consternation she tried to pull her hand away, but his fingers gripped hers with a steely strength. She stared at him blankly as he flung the bedcovers back from her side of the bed. "Look at the sheets, bitch! Not only did I have a bastard foisted on me, but a secondhand one as well." She still looked at him in uncomprehending confusion; she had no idea what he was talking about. He jerked her arm roughly. "Don't tell me she's also an ignorant one? A virgin, my soiled wife, bleeds when she's first bedded by a man. But there's not a drop on your sheet, is there? Not one drop to help you protest your innocence."

Understanding flooded her brain like hot water from a teakettle, and she threw back her windblown hair and laughed. She laughed until her eyes were suffused with tears and her voice choked. "You drunken oaf, you strutting cock, you conceited little mama's boy, you were so drunk last night, you fell flat on your face on the floor and went to sleep. I undressed you and dragged you to bed where you snored peacefully all night. Not once did you touch me. Not even once." Her laughter rang out once more. "And furthermore, you whoreson"—she had learned far more from *Tom Jones* than Paddy would have appreciated—"how dare you talk to me about being secondhand when you've been sleeping with women since you were sixteen. Maybe I should have you checked for the pox before I ever climb into bed with you again.''

Gilbert's elegant, aristocratic, beautiful face had once more acquired the blotchy red fury of a street brawler. He glared at her and his fingers itched to strangle the laughter in her throat. Then, with the same theatrical presence his mother could command, he rearranged his facial features, swung gracefully around, and walked dramatically from the room. Still laughing, Anne sat down at the table and ate the remains of his breakfast, picked up the copy of *Tom Jones,* and finished her reading. It turned out to be a far better instructor about "the intimacies of marriage" than the other two books Paddy had given her.

Much earlier than he had the night before, Gilbert returned to the room carrying two bottles of wine and swaying drunkenly on his feet. Anne was sitting propped up in bed writing in her leather-bound diary. She watched her husband as he set the bottles on the table with the meticulous care of an intoxicated man who believes his physical dexterity unimpaired. Her amusement ended as he turned to her. With now frantic haste she tried to climb out from the other side of the bed; but besotted or not, he moved with a heavy efficiency and dropped down on the bed, almost crushing her leg. With owl-eyed concentration he removed his coat and then his boots. Wildly she twisted away from him to roll over toward the edge. Each time a heavy hand descended and pulled her back. After a gymnastic exhibition, he held up his breeches for her approval. She struggled on. He finally succeeded in removing the stock from around his neck and sat peering down at his ruffled shirt. He looked over at Anne and decided to leave it on. Pushing himself off the bed, he lifted the covers and climbed in, anchoring his floundering wife firmly. As soon as he had subdued her flailing arms and kicking legs, he grabbed a handful of her nightgown and jerked. But the beautiful soft silk and carefully sewn seams held firm. Frustrated he pulled the yards of fabric up around her waist where they bunched in wadded rolls. Ruefully Anne remembered the pride with which she had created this gown and wished that she'd had the foresight to wear one of her ancient flannels instead.

Early during this determined claiming of his conjugal right, Gilbert remembered that he was an adroit lover. His wet kisses smeared a trail across her chin, cheek, forehead, and occasionally her lips. His convulsing hand located one of her breasts and squeezed spasmodically with the mechanical skill of a dairy farmer. When he finally penetrated her virginal barrier, Anne jerked. Nothing in any of the books had warned her about this pain suffered by a woman. Dry, unprepared, and shocked, she experienced not one pleasurable sensation during the entire demeaning subjugation of a disobedient wife. After what seemed an hour of torture, he gave one last convulsive shudder, relaxed with a satisfied grunt, and fell asleep still on and in her. She waited for another minute, then pushed his flaccid weight off her in disgust.

To her credit Anne did not shed a single tear. She spent the next hour cataloging his faults and cursed her bad luck of falling in love with an overgrown, self-centered, arrogant child. Then, still true to her disciplined training, she reached over the inert body of a snoring husband and extinguished the candles on his nightstand. Her last waking thought was a fervent desire to redesign the human anatomy so that men had fewer of the advantages and more of the indignity.

Arising silently at dawn, she scrubbed herself with unusual thoroughness in cold water and once more donned her riding habit. Just as she was about to leave the dressing room, she paused and returned to rummage around in a trunk of school supplies. With an angry satisfaction she located a piece of tapered charcoal, marched over to her side of the bed, and flipped the covers back. Swiftly she circled the ample smears of blood with a heavy black line and wrote, "Is this proof enough, husband?"

While walking stiffly down the stairs, she began to chuckle at what the landlord's daughters would think when they changed the bed. All humor ended, however, when she remembered the night just passed; and she wondered how often other young brides suffered the same degrading experience.

At the stables she found all the gates shut and barred. After minutes of pounding on one of the doors, she was rewarded by the sight of a disgruntled groom peering out at her. Without a word he shoved a sealed envelope into her face. Bewildered, she studied the missive which had "Madame Brownwell" scrawled across it. But her bewilderment changed to wild fury as she read the enclosed note: "Since you have consistently refused to obey me about riding alone, I was forced to sell your mare. The other two horses will not be available unless I am present. Perhaps the two of us can enjoy a companionable ride together later in the day." It was signed "Your loving husband."

Had he been standing in front of her at that moment, she'd have driven a pitchfork through him. Blindly stalking out of the yard into the street in front, she contemplated walking down to the waterfront and boarding a ship, any ship at all, which would take her far away from this place. But common sense, a riding skirt unsuitable for walking, and a dull pain left over from the night before dissuaded her; and she returned to the empty public rooms of the inn.

Standing indecisively in the entry, Anne contemplated the limited opportunities available to a fugitive wife who'd been denied her usual means of escape. To seek sanctuary with Aunt Margaret would mean having to answer probing questions, but to return to an arrogant, self-centered, dictatorial husband and admit defeat was unthinkable. Neither did she wish to encounter the innkeeper, who most probably knew all about the unhappy course of her marriage. Turning to leave the inn once more, she was halted by a voice greeting her from the stairs.

"Why aren't you out riding?" John Peabody asked.

This was the fourth person she hadn't wanted to meet this morning. "I thought I might have breakfast first," she muttered.

"They don't start serving here for another hour; but if you'd care to join me, there's a small café several blocks away."

"I'm not really dressed for the street, Mr. Peabody."

"No one will notice this early, and I would enjoy your company."

Trapped because she could think of no additional excuse, she nodded compliance; and within minutes she was seated in a picturesque stone restaurant which connected with the bakery next door. With brusque efficiency her companion ordered a substantial breakfast as they were being escorted to a table, and already cups of steaming hot coffee had been served.

"Do you want to talk, Mrs. Brownwell?"

"Please call me Anne. I'm not used to the other name yet."

"Was it the horse Sir Harold left for you that your husband sold yesterday?" Peabody asked her abruptly.

"Yes," she answered unwillingly. "How did you know?"

"I overheard the transaction and I spoke to your husband about it last evening."

"It must have been early in the evening," she said bitterly.

"It was, but he was already drinking fairly heavily."

"Does Aunt Margaret know about any of this?"

"I haven't told her, but I imagine she knows part of it. Anne, are you still determined to remain with him?"

"I told my father that I was."

"May I give you some advice?"

"I'm certainly not doing very well on my own."

"I think your husband is afraid of you." At her burst of derisive laughter, he explained, "I believe he is just beginning to realize the shock you sustained when you first learned of his record. He hadn't felt much in the way of guilt before that, but now he is more defensive; and you are a very intimidating young woman."

"Is that why he sold my horse?"

"No, I think he was afraid you'd ride off and not return. Would you have?"

Anne smiled ruefully. "I might have been tempted to this morning."

Peabody nodded. "Then you need some practical advice. Your only chance for a successful marriage is to get as far away from both your families as you can. To do that, you'll have to overlook some of his indulgences."

"Like his drinking?" she asked scornfully.

"I think he's drinking to gain the courage to face you. He told me that you refused to eat your wedding supper with him. If so, that action hurt his pride."

Anne was thoughtful throughout the remainder of that lengthy breakfast and during the short walk back to the inn. After a brief stop at the kitchen to order bathwater, she avoided meeting anyone else by taking the rear stairway to her room. Mercifully sometime during her absence her husband had departed, and she had the space to herself for a leisurely bath. Not wanting to be seen until she was attractively dressed, Anne took the precaution of bracing the door to the necessary room shut with a chair placed beneath the knob. Just before she finished drying her hair and completing her grooming, she heard sounds in the bedroom and knew her husband had returned. Her heart pounded with a sudden panic and all of her carefully laid plans to confront him calmly dissolved. Taking a deep breath, she left the haven of the bathroom, intending to leave the bedroom immediately; but a smiling husband intercepted her. Frantically she turned toward the balcony and almost reached it before he stopped her determined flight.

"Were you planning to jump off?" he derided her gently as he locked his arms firmly around her. "I owe you an apology, Anne. I read the message you left for me this morning."

With a flash of temper she remembered the note he'd written her. "You owe me two apologies, Mr. Brownwell. Why did you sell my mare?"

"Because I didn't want to spend a week looking for you at Alette's or the château or any other of your hiding places."

"I doubt you would have even bothered, Mr. Brownwell."

"You call me that again and I'm going to shake you until you show some sense. I spent two hours searching for you this morning."

She jerked in dismay. "I hope you didn't bother my aunt."

"Of course I did. That was the first place I looked."

"But why?"

"I was a brute last night and you had every reason to be afraid."

"I hope you didn't tell her that, because I wasn't afraid of you."

"If you weren't afraid, why did you fight me so hard?" When she didn't answer, he tightened his hold on her and pressed his lips against her ear. "It doesn't have to be like that, Anne," he murmured.

"I wouldn't know." She shrugged lightly.

"Yes, you do know. On the beach that day you said you'd marry me, you wanted me as much as I did you." She hated the blush that reddened her face and impaired her breathing, but she wasn't unhappy that he was also having trouble. "Will you kiss me now, Anne?" At her failure to respond, he shook her lightly. "I'm not going to let you go until you do." Slowly she turned her head.

Unlike his other kisses, which had been intended more to establish his mastery than to arouse her, this one was meant to be a deliberate, skillful seduction. He held her gently, restraining his hands from exerting any pressure on her slender, trembling body until he sensed her willingness to remain in his arms. Slowly he drew her down onto the bed without interrupting the kiss. Half sitting, half reclining, he freed one hand to caress her firm young breasts, wishing he'd had the foresight to undress her first. Moving his lips downward to the pulse that pounded in her throat, he felt his own desire mount to an uncomfortable level.

"If you don't want this pretty dress ruined, sweetheart,

we'd better take it off," he whispered tersely. As she stiffened slightly, he kissed her again, this time forcing his tongue past her soft lips before he pulled away slowly. "Please, Anne, help me unfasten your dress."

"I'll do it," she murmured shakily. Had anyone told her half an hour earlier that she'd be removing the clothes that she'd donned so carefully as a protection against this man, she'd have laughed in derision. But here she was doing just that because he'd kissed her, and doing it swiftly, too. Even so, he had his robe on and was helping her before she finished. She knew he was an expert at the task by the way his fingers unfastened the ties to her petticoats and shift and rolled the stockings from her legs, but her vanity was salvaged by the fact that his hands weren't at all steady and the smile he gave her was as tremulous as her own.

Gilbert was having trouble with his breathing as well. He'd known since the moment he'd seen her in the purple dress that had made her look like an actress that she had a proud carriage. But the sight of the long, slender thighs, which were feminine without the soft plumpness of shorter women, had almost unmanned him. She had the beautiful muscled body of an athlete, lacking only the vain awareness such women usually had of their power to arouse men. He cursed his own stupidity at having violated her the night before without attempting to give her pleasure, because he wasn't at all sure he had enough self-control to make this coupling any better for her. Relieved that her eyes were tightly closed when he removed his robe and joined her in bed, he kept his ready body apart as he reached out to caress her. Counting on the fiery passion he knew she possessed, he kissed her slowly, moving his tongue against hers with a tentative exploration, prepared to withdraw should she reject this untried intimacy. His heart pounded at her eager response, and he moved his hand gently over her firm breasts, pausing to fondle each taut nipple before he trailed his hand down to the triangle of silky curls between her slim thighs. Her taut muscles relaxed and allowed his questing fingers to stroke her warm, moist passage with a sensuous caress.

Ever more conscious of his own urgent need, Gilbert positioned himself above her and pushed her legs apart with the light pressure of one knee. Entering her as slowly as his throbbing impatience would allow, he willed himself to remain motionless as he renewed the intensity of his kisses. Perspiration coursed from his face and his body trembled with the effort; but not until she pressed her hips convulsively against his did he begin the rhythmic thrusting in and out. Stunned at first by the powerful surge of sensation that transfixed her, Anne's participation was delayed until the instinct of mating replaced her mental control and drove her relentlessly toward an unknown goal. She didn't hear his groan of frustrated suppression; her consciousness floated somewhere outside her straining body, returning only when she felt the hot rush of fire that exploded from her lover's body and he collapsed on her as he had the night before. But this time her arms welcomed him, and she held him tightly until he kissed her and rolled away.

As he wiped the perspiration from their faces, Gilbert embraced her impulsively and chuckled lazily into her ear. "Do you learn all your lessons that quickly, Anne Brownwell?"

Although she smiled at him, she didn't answer because she couldn't; she was still dazed by the violence of her emotional upheaval. Not until her breathing quieted did she remember anything so sensible as the fact that it was still midday or that her aunt would be worried about her.

"I should tell Aunt Margaret that I'm no longer missing," she whispered.

"She knows already, fondling."

"How? I haven't seen her for two days, and after your disturbing her this morning—"

"I expect Mr. Peabody has told her that you're all right."

A cold premonition gripped her. "When did you talk to him?"

"I saw him downstairs when I was having breakfast."

"What did you talk about?" she asked lightly, but the magic of the moments just past was rapidly dissipating.

He laughed complacently as he remembered the lawyer's sharp warning: "Any more of your drunken brutality, I'll see that Anne returns with her aunt to England where I'll use every available law to rid her legally of your unwelcome encumbrance." Gilbert turned confidently toward his wife. "I didn't say more than two words to him, sweetheart, he did all the talking."

Anne asked the question dully, but she already knew the answer. "What did he tell you?"

"To stop acting the fool." Her guess had been accurate; even this beautiful reunion with her errant husband had been "arranged." Everything he'd said and done had been in obedience to John Peabody's command "to earn the dowry money by at least treating her decently."

"We'd better get dressed," she murmured flatly, "before someone starts looking for us."

"No one will." He grinned at her. "The door is locked and bolted, and our meals and baths will be delivered on the schedule I gave the innkeeper this morning."

She shoved herself to a sitting position and stared over at the door. "Then I've been nothing but a prisoner for the last three hours."

Shaken into the unpleasant realization that she was angry at him, Gilbert roused himself to protest, "I only locked the door to keep you from running away until after we talked."

"We finished that talk some time ago, and the key still isn't in the lock," she observed coldly.

"And it won't be," he snapped, "until you've learned to act like a wife and not some independent—"

"I've been a wife for more than two days, and this is the first time you've remembered unless you were reeling from too much wine."

"I spent most of those days waiting for you to return from racing all over the countryside like a damned hussar," he flashed, "or listening to you insult me with that asp's tongue of yours. And while we're on the subject, where'd you go this morning? Unless you stole a horse, you couldn't have been riding; but you weren't anyplace around here."

"I was having breakfast elsewhere in town," she replied icily.

"Then how the hell did Peabody know you'd be in our room?"

Sitting naked in bed with a husband who was glaring at her, and feeling as vulnerable as a plucked chicken, Anne snatched up one of her petticoats, wriggled it over her head, and anchored it firmly over her exposed breasts. Still not answering his last suspicious question, she swung her long legs over the side of the bed and walked swiftly toward the necessary room. Neither as modest as his wife nor as securely in control of his temper, Gilbert lunged out of bed and caught a handful of petticoat before she could reach her targeted sanctuary. Thrown off-balance by his angry jerk, she stumbled backward, knocking them both to the floor in a spot uncarpeted by so much as a thin mat, and landed squarely on his lap.

"That's the second time you've tried to kill me," he gasped peevishly after he'd caught his breath. "Damn it, get off my legs before they're in worse shape than my arm was when you almost beat it into a crippled pulp."

"Let go of my petticoat, then. As for your arm, I struck it only to make you loose my horse. I don't like being held against my will." Bracing her hand against his leg, she pushed herself to her feet, turned around, and pulled him to a standing position. This time it was he who headed toward the bathroom, turning his back on her with stiff dignity. Anne noticed the two large red blotches on his buttocks and giggled. It was too much to retain an angry vexation against a husband with a bruised posterior.

"If you'll lie down, I'll rub you with salve," she offered.

Not deigning to reply, he continued into the necessary room, closing the door with a harsh click. She blushed profusely when she heard the sounds of his relieving himself at the commode; she was rapidly losing the last remnants of her modesty and innocence. When he emerged, he was carrying the chair she'd used earlier to prop the door shut.

"Get your salve," he ordered, "and don't ever try to keep me out of that room again." She watched him limp across the room and smiled with a sharpened humor. He reminded her of one of her obstreperous pupils who'd always claimed to have a sore thumb whenever there was a writing assignment. Like the pampered youth, her husband was making certain she didn't forget his injury. Taking her time in the bathroom, she scrubbed herself thoroughly for the third time in a single day, reflecting with wry amusement that wives required a good deal more washing than maiden ladies.

Gilbert was lying facedown in the center of the bed when she approached and sat down beside him. Timidly, since it was the first time she'd ever initiated contact with his body, she began to apply the soft lanolin salve with gingerly strokes, scarcely daring to look at his beautifully proportioned physique. But as he relaxed under her gentle touch, she gained the courage to ply her strong hands with soothing effectiveness. Expecting him to fall asleep under her ministrations, she learned another valuable lesson in the relationship between a man and a woman when she attempted to leave the bed ten minutes later. Her husband turned over with one convulsive movement and pinioned her in his strong arms, dragging her down beside him. Anne flushed a fiery crimson when she saw the state of his arousal; it was one thing to have felt the evidence during a moment of passion, quite another to view it without the concealment of blankets. But that the end would be the same, he allowed her no doubt.

Roughly he tore the protective petticoat from her body and gripped her resisting buttocks moving her hips at will over his throbbing body. His lips ground against hers briefly and then traveled expertly downward to encircle the nipple of one breast, not softly but with a demanding harshness. Without any of the consideration he'd displayed earlier, he explored her body with consuming passion, his mouth moving relentlessly from one sensitive spot to another while his hands manipulated her body to satisfy his own need for physical contact. Anne gasped in shock before the torrid flood drowned out all thought except a fierce concentration on the new sensations he was arousing in her. Panting with an uninhibited desire that made her feel boneless, she tried to signal her readiness; but he persisted with an implacable thoroughness to arouse her to a state that bordered on frenzy. She dug her fingers into the taut muscles of his back, and her lips sought whatever purchase they could gain on his exposed neck. Her legs opened instinctively when the man made his plunging entry into her body, his face sharpened by a look of savage ferity that made him seem a stranger to her. But Anne was answering his thrusts with a savagery of her own; she was experiencing the full reach of sensuous cataclysm for the first time. She wasn't aware that she cried out before his lips descended on hers, and his hand grasped her hips to keep them bound to his in the final moments of a pounding ecstasy.

As he collapsed on her and their perspiration mingled together freely, she clung to him tenaciously, unwilling to end what had been a shattering revelation. Anne Gray, who'd always prided herself on emotional control and physical restraint, had just revealed a complete lack of either quality. Furthermore, she felt not an iota of shame for her abandon, only a feline satisfaction—a sense of having successfully withstood not merely domination by the passionate lover who now lay torpidly inert on top of her, but also the more subtle control of the family solicitor. Not by any stretch of the imagination could John Peabody have counseled her husband to treat her as he just had. The earlier seduction, which had been a politely controlled one compared to this sensual violence, might well have resulted from a bland suggestion "to court her gently as befits an innocent young girl." But never in his lifetime would the cautious lawyer ever counsel any man to ravage a woman. Anne smiled with a very private glee—as a replacement for her lost innocence, she had gained a wide sweep of knowledge about the emotional motivations of men.

Rousing himself sluggishly at the sound coming from beneath him, Gilbert opened his eyes to peer at what he expected to be a tearful, hysterical woman. Her muted giggles made him blink with incomprehension; he'd never handled even an experienced partner with that degree of ferocity. But he'd been blindly angry at his almost virgin wife. After being treated with gentle gallantry, she had ungratefully turned on him and destroyed his dignity with her usual biting sarcasm. To add insult to the injury she'd caused when she'd fallen on him, she'd giggled like some idiot child dismembering an insect. But it'd been the slow, insidious intimacy of her hands massaging his flesh that had destroyed his self-control. All of his good intentions had been obliterated by a blind passion to possess her and to crush that independent spirit of hers. Not even when he'd been drinking had he ever used so much strength on a woman; yet this one had responded with an almost equal power and with as great a passion. Disconcerted by her bubbling laughter, he moved to separate himself from her; but her arms still held him firmly and they remained joined together, facing each other side by side.

His delayed question—"Are you all right?"—elicited only another soft chuckle and shockingly a softer kiss on his moving lips. Staring into her wide-opened blue eyes, which held an expression of warmth he couldn't fathom, Gilbert felt a sudden rush of admiration. Life with her was not going to be the dull routine he'd feared. Affectionately he kissed her eyelids shut and closed his own.

Hours later he was awakened by a discreet knocking at the door. As he groped for the woman he expected to be by his side, he heard her low voice across the room saying, *"Un moment, s'il vous plaît."* Hastily he arose from the bed, which was no longer rumpled, to find his bed robe neatly laid across the smoothed-out comforter. Stepping aside as Anne brushed past him to complete the task of making the bed, he donned his robe and ran his fingers through his tousled hair.

For the following moments he remained stationary, watching his wife move gracefully toward the door. Her hair was neatly groomed into loose curls and she wore a graceful blue velvet garment buttoned modestly to her neck and flaring to the floor in unrestrained fullness. His appreciative smile faded, however, when she unbolted the door and unlocked it with the key he'd placed in the pocket of his coat for safekeeping. More speculative now, he studied her as she admitted the waiter into the room and helped him arrange the dinner bowls and plates on the candlelit table. Listening to her chat amiably with the servant in the French vernacular of the region, he wondered about the extent of her education. This was her first trip to France, yet she spoke the language fluently.

In the bathroom where he'd gone after the waiter had departed, Gilbert found the tub emptied and an ewer of hot water awaiting him. His wife had been even busier than he'd thought.

"What were you and that man talking about?" he asked as he seated her at the festive table and poured her wine.

"He told me that his wife was beautiful but that he was worried about her health," she responded with a wide smile.

"He said nothing of the kind. The pretty compliments he paid were for my wife, not his; and the person who is worried is your aunt. Anne, I've spoken French all of my life," he said sternly.

"I know you have." She grinned at him. "You even mutter it in your sleep."

Ignoring the gibe, he continued the reprimand. "So I would appreciate your telling me the truth in the future. After dinner we'll go together to see Aunt Margaret and tell her that I'm the one with all the bruises. That should please her and keep the lectures at a minimum."

"We don't have to. I've already sent her a note explaining that you hurt yourself in a fall and will be in bed for a few days. Now we don't have to listen to advice from anyone."

"In that case I'll take the key to our room back, if you

don't mind. I think, my beautiful young wife, you're a bit too resourceful to be trusted with it.''

Repressed laughter gurgled in her throat. ''You already have it back, Tony. I slipped it into your pocket when you were pouring the wine.''

He regarded her silently through half-closed eyes, but a smile twitched at the corners of his lips. ''One more question, Anne,'' he said softly, ''one that you neglected to answer earlier. When did you see Peabody this morning?''

''I ate breakfast with him,'' she responded promptly, ''and he wasted an hour enumerating all the merits of my becoming an obedient wife.''

Smiling with all the elegant charm he possessed, Gilbert raised his glass in a silent toast to her. In several more days of pleasant isolation, she might just become one.

Chapter 6

Six days after Anne's wedding, Margaret Gray was still engaged in pursuing the same goal she had for eighteen years—ensuring the protection of the niece she had raised. Long before Suzanne Brownwell had made a fool of herself at that disastrous breakfast, Margaret had entertained few hopes for a successful marriage. She had been bitterly disappointed when the older brother had returned to England, leaving the field clear for the sullen popinjay whom she had detested on sight and who had almost ruined his chances himself when he had snubbed Anne on the first day. Had Stanley Ashton not protested, she and Geoffrey would have taken her home. Instead they had gambled on her making the wiser choice of

Harold Brownwell, and of course she hadn't. The foolish girl
had chosen the more difficult man.

Only on two occasions had Margaret had a glimmer of
respect for the self-centered young fop, and both times he had
destroyed that respect. When Anne had run away from her
wedding breakfast after an hour of torture, Gilbert had started
after her. But his tearful mother had stopped him at the door,
and the fool had gone with Suzanne instead. Margaret had
been the one to attempt giving comfort to the disturbed bride,
but Anne had elected to fight her own battles, just as she
always did. However, the visit to Anne's room had not been
entirely wasted; Margaret had taken the two wedding rings
for safekeeping and the three blue silk petticoats that matched
the most expensive gown in her niece's wardrobe. In her own
room she had painstakingly stitched her wedding gift to the
young couple into the hems of those petticoats, but now the
one thousand pounds' worth of small gold coins would be for
Anne's benefit alone. Any bridegroom who still said "I"
rather than "we" could not be trusted to share even a pound
with his wife. The innkeeper's daughter, who cleaned the
bridal suite daily, had returned the altered petticoats to Anne's
trunk without anyone being the wiser, but the rings could not
be entrusted to a stranger. Margaret had returned them privately
to Anne at dinner last night when the newly married pair had
finally emerged from the seclusion of their room.

"I was hoping someone had stolen them," Anne muttered as
she shoved the glittery rings into her pocket before turning to
smile at her husband and John Peabody. For a moment the older
woman was worried that Gilbert might have witnessed the
transaction, but his tolerant expression of affection for his wife
did not change. It was that expression of tender possession that
had renewed the aunt's hopes. He seemed genuinely in love
with her niece. Margaret sighed with relief, and the first hour
of the dinner party was delightfully free of all undercurrents of
discontent. Only when Peabody asked Gilbert to accompany
him to the waterfront the following morning to meet the two
American captains was there any hint of resentment.

"I won't be free tomorrow," Gilbert said. "Anne and I are going riding."

"I strongly recommend you reconsider, Mr. Brownwell," the lawyer urged. "Americans tend to be very sensitive about Englishmen, especially about those they plan to employ in their business."

"Sorry to disappoint you, Mr. Peabody, but I have no intention of making any permanent plans at the moment. Anne and I might not even be going all the way to Boston."

"Of course we are, darling," his wife declared. "I've promised to look out for Aunt Margaret's investment there."

Gilbert's fleeting frown had been quickly replaced by a smile. "All right, fondling, we'll go to Boston; but don't expect me to become a colonial rustic. I'd feel like a fool in buckskins."

Margaret's brief optimism vanished and her cynicism returned in full; Anne's husband was still an indolent wastrel who expected to be maintained in luxury. Until late that night she revised the provisions of the documents and contracts she and her solicitor had prepared during the previous four days. But now even more meticulous care and planning were necessary to assure Anne's security. Gilbert Brownwell had no intention of supporting himself or his wife; furthermore, he was a reckless gambler and a violent man when he was thwarted. Margaret realized that she herself was gambling by investing forty thousand pounds in a firm already in financial difficulty in spite of the excellent reputations of the two owners. However, her only other alternative was to send funds to America on a regular schedule, funds that would be readily available to the husband; and she was too much of a businesswoman to attempt supporting a fifteen-thousand-pound-a-year gambling habit.

Bitterly she deleted the first provision of the proposed contract; the Americans would not have to supply Gilbert with employment. The monetary provisions she rewrote with a vindictive intention of keeping as much money as possible from his control. He would receive the first payment of the dowry only after he left the ship, and he would have no access to the additional ten thousand pounds Margaret was sending to America. She had intended that this money be used to purchase a home, but now it would be placed in a Boston bank to be released only on her signature or Anne's. Only the Americans were to know about the gold coins in the petticoats; and only in the case of two emergencies should Anne be told about them prior to landing in Boston. If there should be a disaster at sea or if Gilbert should insist on taking his wife from the ship at a port other than Boston, the partners should make certain Anne had the gold with her and knew of its existence.

Carefully Margaret reread the dossier of Gilbert Anthony Brownwell, more complete now with the additional information she'd learned at the ill-fated wedding breakfast. His proclivity toward explosive violence was too consistent for her to ignore. Prudently she decided to make her American partners responsible for Anne's physical safety as well as for her financial security. They were to keep her under surveillance as much as possible aboard ship. If they were forced to separate her from her husband, they were to do so without regard for his rights. If he deserted her at any time either in a foreign port or in Boston, they were to offer her a home until an escort could arrive from England. Margaret sighed heavily, wishing she had someone else with whom she could share the awesome responsibility of sending a young girl abroad with a husband who at best was little more than a charming scoundrel. For five years Anne would be under his domination with only the scant supervision of two men who might prove as culpable as Gilbert when it came to the temptation of money.

She'd slept but little before she and John Peabody were driven to the docks to await the *Boston Queen*. As the vessel drew close, Margaret was impressed by the way it rode in the water. Unlike trimmer ships, it was not built for speed, but its wide beam and high freeboard meant greater stability during a storm. Margaret also noted with satisfaction that the *Boston Queen* was being docked by an expert. Under partially reefed sails the ship was jockeyed close enough to the sea wall for ship's lines to be thrown to waiting dockworkers.

She was to meet that expert an hour later in the person of

Captain Thomas Perkins. Everything she knew about his career at sea indicated an excellent record. He had been with Commodore Oliver Hazard Perry for six years and cited for his contribution to naval victories against the Barbary pirates and the British thirty years earlier. It was this part of Perkins's record that gave Margaret her greatest comfort. Any man who had faced both pirates and the British must be fearless. If anyone could get her niece safely across an ocean, he could. Margaret's love of the sea was strictly limited to shipping profits, not to ships or sea travel.

As soon as she had met Thomas Perkins, she breathed even more easily. He was a man her own age whose eyes were shrewd and direct. Although he was short, his body was muscular and trim; and he wore his uniform with the practiced ease of years. His hair was a wiry, grizzled mixture of black and white and fitted neatly to his head with windproof discipline. But it was his expression of untroubled self-confidence that Margaret trusted the most.

Just as she was pleased by Thomas Perkins, so was she disturbed by his partner, Paul Bouvier. Both his age and appearance startled her. Twenty years younger than Perkins, he looked thirty instead of forty. He was a tall, slim Frenchman whose dark face was full of Gallic charm. Since he'd been in America for ten years, she'd expected him to look American; instead he remained typically French in appearance and attitude. Even his straightforward answers and excellent record failed to eliminate all of her prejudice against handsome men of his nationality.

It was surprising, then, in view of her distrust that it was the Frenchman who first accepted the conditions of Margaret's propositions and broke down his partner's objections. From the onset, Perkins was against the proposal. It lacked, he explained, the "cards-on-the-table dealings" his Yankee ethics demanded. Even though he disapproved of a paid-for husband, he refused to come between a husband and his wife. After reading the dossier on Brownwell, he objected to having a man with such a record of violence on his ship at all. And he was adamant about having a woman employed in the shipyards under any circumstances. As for the gold coins, he bluntly told Margaret that he would not be responsible for money that was not locked in the ship's strongbox. Secretly he thought Margaret a foolish old maid who was trying to run her niece's life.

John Peabody tried legal tactics of persuasion and failed to win a point. The lawyer insisted that similar conditions existed in many English negotiations. That particular argument elicited the disdainful response from Perkins that "unlike Englishmen, Yankee traders deal in products, not personalities and people."

At this point in the deadlock, Margaret was discouraged; she had anticipated none of these objections. But since her main objective was Anne's safety and not the business deal itself, she would not compromise her demands. It was then that Paul Bouvier entered the discussion.

"My partner," he apologized, "does not understand the European custom of arranged marriages. In America such things exist, but not so openly, nor so widely accepted, I think. In my own case a marriage was arranged, but not a happy one. So fifteen years ago my wife disappeared while I was at sea. Even so, divorce is impossible in France. Today I am more happily married—not so legally, perhaps, but more happily. Myself, my Lynette, and our two children live with Captain Perkins and his wife in Boston. My children are illegitimate, but in America that condition is not so important as in Europe. Forgive my asking, Madame Gray, but is not your niece likewise unfortunate?"

The Frenchman's keen perception caught Margaret completely by surprise. No mention about Anne's status appeared in any of the papers she'd given to the Americans; she had wanted Anne to be free of the stigma in America at least. But now Margaret faced a dilemma: if she admitted the fact, Anne would be exposed; on the other hand, this business alliance was the only one that could protect her niece. Once again Margaret gambled. "Unfortunately, she is," she confessed.

Paul Bouvier beamed. "Now we have no problem, I think.

This explains why Madame Gray has made conditions and why the husband is not so good a one." He turned toward his partner. *"Mon ami,* we have been through much worse together. I think perhaps this niece needs our protection, too. As for the husband, he is one against many. It is our ship, *mon ami,* and we have our little means."

While he was talking, Captain Perkins had been watching Margaret's face and the hope it held. Slowly he nodded. "I stand corrected, madam. We would be delighted to stand in for you by protecting your niece as long as she is with us."

Thus, over a glass of excellent port the American shipping firm of Perkins and Bouvier became Perkins, Bouvier and Gray. With the contracts signed and the money safely locked in the ship's strongbox, Margaret could return to the inn and continue a lonely vigil over the young couple of lovers who may or may not have appreciated her actions had they known. But she herself felt no qualms at interfering in their future.

Chapter 7

ANNE and Gilbert Brownwell boarded the *Boston Queen* on the sixteenth day of their marriage, May 22, 1841. Anne's laughter as she negotiated the wooden ramp was a tribute to her husband's skill in preventing an overly sentimental farewell scene between his wife and her aunt. For three days he had used his charm on both the women to keep them from depressing thoughts of separation. Margaret had been included in their shopping tours and their meals at the inn with such an airy graciousness that even she had become slightly more hopeful for the marriage. With his wife, Gilbert had been particularly solicitous. He had taken her on daily rides, and after the last one insisted that she help him rub the horses down before they were placed in their stalls aboard the *Queen*. Because of his efforts the last three days in France had passed swiftly, and Margaret had been grateful for his light touch. But now, as she stood on the dock waving to the young couple waving back at her from the ship's railing, she felt her sixty years and a deep sadness at being parted from the girl who had been the center of her life for the past eighteen of those years.

Anne waved back at the lonely figure until the ship began to move slowly away from shore, towed by the strong-armed seamen manning the oars of three small boats. Minutes later she felt the great ship shudder as the outgoing tide exerted its powerful pull and the wind filled the towering sails. She and her husband stood together and watched the miracle of a lumbering wood vessel become a graceful thing of beauty on the open sea.

For Gilbert this had always been the finest moment of sailing, because for a brief time he held the illusion of leaving all his problems ashore. The illusion had never lasted beyond the first card game or a sharp disciplinary command by the captain, but this time he smiled with confidence as he held his wife close beside him. So far she'd exceeded his limited expectations to such an extent that he felt more and more content with life. His earlier fears of her proving repulsive in bed seemed ridiculous now; he had found her slender, muscular strength more exciting than the plump softness of any woman he had ever known. He smiled as he contemplated the wild abandon of her responses and the unmistakable love she held for him, and he felt a warm glow of possession.

Looking down on the young couple from the elevated wheelhouse, Thomas Perkins and Paul Bouvier exchanged their first impressions.

Perkins was impressed both by the appearance of the young man and by his obvious attachment to his wife. "They'll do, Paul."

The Frenchman shrugged. "The voyage is still young."

"Love is an excellent cure for youthful indiscretions, Paul. The girl looks capable of keeping him interested."

"The girl," responded the partner with an open Gallic appreciation of women, "is capable of holding any man's attention. She has fire, that one, I think. We shall see if the Brownwell rogue has the sense to keep her interested."

Unaware that they were being so closely observed by the two men and completely ignorant of the fact that these men knew so much about them, Gilbert and Anne continued on their exploration of the decks that would be their home for two months or more. It was a beautiful ship; everywhere the wood shone under coats of varnish. The main salon rivaled all but the most expensive drawing rooms with its polished wood tables, padded chairs, and thick Persian rugs. At the moment a neatly dressed cook's helper was pouring wine for the several passengers assembled there. Paul Bouvier handled that end of the business, and he was cynically French in his philosophy that passengers should be well wined and dined and kept as inactive as possible.

Although the *Boston Queen* was primarily a cargo vessel, it had eight well-appointed guest cabins and an equal number for the ship's officers. The crew was housed at the forward end of the ship in the forecastle where their hammocks hung from a low ceiling like sheets bunched together on crowded clotheslines.

Anne and Gilbert had the only suite of rooms aboard, the space normally used by the captain and his family. Located between the official captain's quarters where charts and logs were stored and the smaller cabin of the first mate, the two rooms and small adjoining washroom were comfortably furnished with a large bed in one and a table and chairs in the other. Neatly lashed to the walls in both rooms were the Brownwells' trunks and other luggage. In one corner was a box of twelve bottles of brandy with a little note from Aunt Margaret: "For seasickness and whatever." With a glad cry Anne spotted the rows of empty ship's shelves framing the head of the bed, and she proceeded to drag books and writing materials out of her trunks and place them on the waiting shelves. As she looked in pleased reflection upon the familiar books that had surrounded her all her life, Anne felt at home. Remembering the one lacking touch, she dashed into the other room and returned with a vase full of a dozen beautiful handmade silk flowers which she had purchased on the last shopping tour in Le Havre.

Her husband stretched out on the bed and watched her in amusement. Looking down at him, Anne snatched one flower from the vase and, lying facedown beside him, tucked the golden rose behind his ear. Laughing at her, he removed it and wove the stem into Anne's own curly hair. "Not only do I have a playful wife," he teased her, "but a housekeeper as well. And now that you've filled all those shelves, what do you intend to do with those books and paper?"

"Oh, Tony, we have months ahead of us to read them together. I have some wonderful stories there."

Not having read any book for years, he contemplated his bluestocking wife seriously for a moment. "Anne, have you really read all these books?"

"These and many more. There are whole rooms full of books at Grayhaven." Anne did not yet realize that reading was not a universal pastime.

"How did you ever find time? From the way you ride I thought you spent most of your time on a horse."

Anne laughed in remembrance of the fights she and Paddy had had over his decree that she could ride no more than one hour a day. "Paddy never let me ride that much. He made me study, so did my Aunt Margaret."

"Then she really did teach you bookkeeping?" As he watched her vigorous nod, Gilbert felt a little intimidated by a not-quite-eighteen-year-old girl who knew so much. "What else have you done in that long life of yours?"

"Well, for years I helped keep my aunt's books. She has piles of them. And then, of course, there's the school."

"I thought your aunt's estate was a large farm."

"Most of it still is, but two years ago we changed Grayhaven and the grounds into a school."

"We?"

"Of course 'we,' it was mostly my idea; and after a while Paddy even let me teach."

"What did you teach, Anne? That stuff all women fuss over with thread and hoops and little tin things on their fingers?"

"Embroidery? I hated embroidery. I taught mathematics and Latin to older boys mostly."

Gilbert stared at his wife's glowing face for a moment before he moved restlessly to the edge of the bed. He was remembering the futile hours he'd wasted in classrooms, resenting the teachers who'd kept him prisoner and hating all the dull subjects he'd failed to master, mathematics most of all. Wanting to destroy Anne's enthusiastic confidence just as he'd wanted to strike out at his own teachers in blind frustration, he smiled sarcastically.

"At least your aunt didn't ruin all her land with a school."

"That's not fair, Tony," she gasped. "Grayhaven is a good school."

"You just try teaching your 'older' boys anything if they're hungry. Land's the important thing, Anne—land and the food it raises and the animals it supports. Farmers don't need mathematics and Latin to do their job, and without farmers everyone would be too busy grubbing for food to worry about school. You never worked around your aunt's farm, did you?"

"I kept books."

"But you never helped raise an animal. You don't even like them."

"I do, too; I like horses."

"You like to ride horses, Anne; you've never tried to make a friend of one. Come on, I'll show you what I mean."

Not waiting for her protest, Gilbert grabbed her hand and pulled her from the bed and along the companionway to the remote part of the ship denied to passengers. The sailor on duty in the hold let them pass after Gilbert's reassuring explanation, "It's all right, mate, we just want to check on our horses."

Anne heard the whinnies long before she could even see the stalls in the dim light. She felt her husband bend over a bin of some kind before he guided her down the narrow aisle between lashed-down stacks of cargo. Staring mutely at the two horses, she watched them strain to reach Gilbert's outstretched hands, each of which held a carrot. As she listened to him speaking softly to the magnificent animals and stroking their satiny necks, she admitted the truth of his accusations. She'd never even taken the time to pet them, much less to win their affection as Gilbert obviously had.

"Tony," she asked slowly, "did you know these horses before Harold gave them to us?"

"No, but years ago I helped the head groom when their sire was born, and I trained and saddle-broke that colt. Brun Roi was the finest animal I ever owned—ever worked with. He's Harold's favorite mount now."

"How old were you then, Tony?"

"About your age."

"Since you loved animals and farming so much, why didn't you just stay at Brownsville?"

"My father decided I was to become a navy officer."

"What about—afterwards?"

"After I was bounced out of Oxford first and then the navy? By that time Harold was in complete charge of Brownsville and Arthur owned Feldwood Park. I wasn't needed or wanted at either place."

"I'm sorry, Tony."

"Don't waste your sympathy, Anne, I had a better time in the city anyway. Come on, I want to show you one more thing before we explore the rest of the ship."

As he led her to another part of the hold past crates of cackling chickens, he paused beside one of the hutches full of silent rabbits. Swiftly Gilbert opened one of the lathed cages and gently withdrew a furry creature, cuddling it in one arm as he would a small child. After a convulsive kick the rabbit relaxed and submitted contentedly to Gilbert's fondling of its soft fur.

"Ever held one, Anne?" he asked quietly.

"I've never even seen one up close before," she whispered, staring in fascination, not so much at the animal as at her husband's hands and at the tender expression on his face.

"I made pets of so many of them at home," he admitted sheepishly, "I could never eat on the nights rabbit was served for dinner. Touch it, Anne, it won't bite you."

Reaching out a tentative hand, her fingers encountered the warm fur and she smiled in delight. "Tony, may we keep a pet in Boston?"

"We can do whatever we want in Boston, fondling; there won't be anyone there to tell us how to live our lives."

Gilbert had no illusions about attempting a job; even if he had the ability—which he knew he didn't—he had not the slightest interest in shipbuilding or money changing. During his two years in London he'd discovered that his only talents lay in the gentlemanly pursuits of gambling, drinking, and seduction. The seduction part he was now willing to forego, but the other two were his only real accomplishments. Once his luck at cards changed—only in the last year, he thought, had it really been bad—he could join the gentlemen clubs in Boston and augment his income. Moreover, despite his father's warning, he fully expected to be supplied with money beyond the dowry. Before his mother had left Le Havre, she'd given him five hundred pounds and promised to send more. He was also quite certain that her aunt had already given Anne a larger sum and would never refuse her beloved niece's request for additional amounts. Gilbert would have been badly shaken at the moment had he realized the reach of his wife's ambition or the extent of the stranglehold Margaret Gray had on his future.

Returning the rabbit to its hutch, he kissed his wife lightly and smiled. "Let's change our clothes and look over this old tub to see if it lives up to the grand name of *Boston Queen*."

He need not have wondered. In addition to the rabbits and chickens below there were live piglets and six milk-rich nanny goats and bins of varied foodstuffs. While the ship's crew might eat the traditional diet of salt pork and beans, the passengers and officers would gain weight from the rich cuisine of omelets, cheese, ragouts, buttery bread, raisin cake, and wine. Except for the time of serving, the meals were typically French; but Paul Bouvier had never been able to convince his senior partner that civilized dinners were served at nine o'clock in the evening. With Yankee logic, Perkins insisted that the largest meal of the day was most easily prepared during the daylight hours and that the night-time supper could be a cold spread.

So Gilbert and Anne's first introduction to their eleven fellow passengers was the pleasant one of dining on excellent food around two tables laid with linen and silver. At the one table were Captain Perkins, a Boston man and his wife, two American businessmen, Anne and her husband, and a middle-aged Englishman on his way to Bermuda. The people at the table presided over by Paul Bouvier were mostly French.

Before that first meal was half-over, Gilbert was bored by his dining companions, whose main topics of conversation were business and profits. He longed to be seated with the others where both the laughter and the wine consumed were more plentiful. Right after dinner he dragged Anne away from her conversation with the Boston woman to the other table where a faro layout was being set up. Without hesitation he accepted the invitation to join the game.

Because the two Frenchwomen were eager and talkative players, Anne sat mutely aside and watched with disbelief the enthrallment of the players even though they were not gambling for money. Looking up from the game and catching her expression, Gilbert pushed his chips toward the center of the table and stood up. "Come on, sweetheart, let's you and me go for a walk."

They found a secluded spot protected from the ocean spray and sat down on the deck with their backs against the aft structure. They didn't try to talk because the sound of the water and the sight of the long white plumes trailing the ship were entertainment enough, until his arms and hands relayed another message. Pulling his wife to her feet, he led her back toward their cabin, stopping only once at the ship's galley for a bottle of wine and a plate of cheese and fruit. That night they did not leave their cabin but recaptured instead the solitude of the inn. For the first time Anne's caresses were as bold as his, and his whispered encouragement made them both forget that other people existed.

Each afternoon for the next three days Gilbert would play the several games, and Anne would wait and watch until he rose to take her for a brisk walk around the deck. Once when the sky was overcast, they went directly to their cabin, where Anne rummaged through her books until she found the copy of *Robinson Crusoe* and settled down at one side of the table to read.

Into this third glass of wine Gilbert interrupted her concentration. "What're you reading?"

"One of my childhood favorites." She smiled. *"Robinson Crusoe."*

"That's the story of a ship's officer who was put ashore on an uninhabited island in the South Pacific," Gilbert volunteered. "Aboard my ship, the captain repeated it to everyone at regular intervals. I thought one time he was going to put me off the ship on an island near the coast of northern Australia."

"I think Daniel Defoe was writing about many other castaways besides Alexander Selkirk," Anne explained cautiously, curious about the first reference her husband had ever made to her about his naval career. "Does a captain really have a right to do something like that, Tony?"

"On a ship at sea a captain believes he has all the powers of God; but mine never carried out his threats—not until we returned to England. Why don't you read your story aloud to me?"

On the fourth page he interrupted again with an abrupt question. "Have you ever felt like an outcast, Anne?"

Afraid that Gilbert's strange mood signaled a return of the contempt he'd shown her during their first meeting, Anne responded warily, "Everyone feels that way some time."

Lost in his own thoughts, he ignored her hesitant answer. "I've been an outcast all of my life," he announced bluntly.

Keeping her eyes discreetly downcast, Anne listened with skeptical disbelief. How could a handsome, pampered aristocrat ever know what it felt like to be exiled on the fringes of society, to be treated like some unclean pariah? Gilbert's next words, however, taught her that there were different kinds of ostracism and varying degrees of exclusion.

"My father and brothers treated me like a useless ornament," he asserted flatly. "I was never included in any of their plans. The other relatives acted as if I didn't exist—I was twelve years old before I learned that those aunts and uncles and cousins belonged to my brothers but not to me. I didn't like school because I had no real friends at any of the ones I attended. As for the navy, I often wished I'd been put ashore—I'd probably have survived better than I did."

"What about London?"

"London was exciting because half the people there were exiles from something or other just as I was. What about you, Anne?"

"You met the three members of my family who admit to knowing me, Tony; and the only friends I ever had were the people my aunt paid to live with us."

"I knew we had something in common"—he smiled—"the day by that creek outside Le Havre. You were as defensive as a porcupine until I kissed you and I lost my temper because I thought—"

"I remember what you thought and how you treated me for the next week. Would you really have gone to Australia if you'd found a ship?"

"There were two ships I could have taken, fondling, but I didn't. I wanted to find out if you were just pretending or if you really were a passionate woman."

"Tony!"

"I'm happy to report you're just as much an outlaw as I am and a very satisfactory, shameless hussy. Put the book down, sweetheart, we've done enough talking for one day."

Anne was laughing when he kissed her, but she was very careful during the following hour to keep his opinion of her intact. Not every day could a neophyte schoolteacher win the accolade of "hussy," much less "shameless."

On the morning of their fifth day at sea, the faro game began after breakfast; and because the weather threatened, it continued all day. When Gilbert asked her if she resented his playing, she smiled and shook her head. On her way back to their cabin, she passed the open door of the captain's headquarters just as he looked up from the pile of work before him. As she hesitated, he called out to her.

"Don't come in, young lady, unless you expect to be put to work. If you are half as good with figures as your aunt claimed you were, I won't expect to have to look at another ledger for the rest of the voyage."

Anne smiled back at this kindly man with the shrewd eyes, walked over to the table, and sat down. "Just show me," she said. Until that moment she had not realized how much she had missed the challenge of work. She grinned still more when she checked some of his additions; he grinned back and admitted that his wife usually retotaled his figures. For hours she worked steadily, unmindful of the passing time. Finally the captain called a halt and escorted her back to the dining room for supper. The card game was still in progress, played now around the plates of cheese and bottles of wine. Gilbert looked up at her and reached out to pull her down to the empty chair next to his. The game went on, but as Anne rose to leave, he looked at her with a raised eyebrow. She smiled and nodded her permission and returned to work again on cargo ledgers. When the captain finally announced, "Time to stop," Anne departed with an armload of books and papers, leaving an astonished Tom Perkins behind.

Not one pang of guilt had she suffered about her absence until she saw her husband's scowling face as she entered their cabin. "Where in hell have you been?" he asked. When she told him, he exploded, "For God's sake, Anne, you're not some bloody tradesman's wife, and I won't have you acting like one. If you want to be a lady, damn it, you'd better start acting like one."

As she looked at him stretched out on the bed with both pillows stuffed behind his head, she snapped, "I will as soon as you start acting like a gentleman. In my experience a gentleman assists a lady when she's carrying heavy bundles."

Before she could reach the door of the other room, he was on his feet opening the door, laughing. "Touché, fondling. I'm going to have to watch that tongue of yours. It stings." Later while they were in bed, he tried a more diplomatic persuasion. "I'm sorry about my outburst, sweetheart; it didn't occur to me that you might not know how to play cards. Tomorrow I'll teach you piquet and whist."

Still concentrating on the world of business embodied in the books and papers stacked in the other room, Anne made a stupid, thoughtless answer. "Those are children's games, Tony; I played them when I was ten years old." Had he known a place to go at that moment, he would have stormed out of the cabin.

Not until early the next morning did either of them see the humor of the situation, and it was Gilbert who reached out to her first. Anne awoke to find his hand caressing her hair and his voice whispering in her ear: "I know a game that's not for children, sweetheart. Do you want to play it with me?" Her heart bursting with relief, she squirmed out of her nightgown. He laughed as he pulled her close. "Now that's one unladylike habit I do approve of," he said.

Whether Gilbert's invitation had been inspired simply by passion or by a vague realization that his girl bride was not as captive as he'd thought, his lovemaking that morning projected a possessive quality lacking in their earlier unions. He caressed her with a deliberate determination until her flustered breathing almost choked her, and he completed the act with an uncharacteristic regard for her emotional fulfillment. Afterward instead of the half-humorous comments he usually made, he studied her flushed face with a serious expression on his own.

"We belong together, Anne," he murmured, disconcerted a little when her only response was a giggle. Realizing belatedly that they had not yet separated, he tightened his arms around her and joined the laughter. "I'm glad you've acquired a sense of humor about the finer things of life, sweetheart, but I wasn't referring to that kind of togetherness. I was trying to tell you that you're easy to live with. You don't nag me and you don't break into tears when I yell at you."

Aware that this was the closest he'd ever come to a declaration of affection for her, Anne kissed him with a shy intensity. Even while he kissed her back, his mood remained pensively somber.

"Any regrets, Anne?"

Puzzled now, she stared at her husband in confusion. "About what, Tony?"

"About choosing me instead of my brother. With him you'd have had more than I'll ever be able to offer."

"More than we already have? Don't be silly. Even if Harold had asked—which he didn't—it wouldn't have made any difference. I didn't love him."

"Do you love me, Anne?"

In the soft glow of early morning her eyes were luminous. "So much, Tony, I can't imagine not loving you."

But even this unconditional declaration did not eliminate his strangely introspective mood. "Don't ever stop, sweetheart. I'll always need you," he mumbled as he held her closer.

For the rest of that day and the next two, they remained isolated from the other passengers except for the midday meal. Quixotically Gilbert insisted that their walks on deck be taken during the lonely hours in the late evening despite Anne's warning about the danger she'd encountered on the *Dover Princess*.

"I spent three years on ships that make this one seem like a millpond barge," he scoffed.

"Did you like the life, Tony?"

"No. Too much routine boredom and discipline. I prefer the freedom of land."

"Did your ship ever sail to Boston?"

"Once for provisions. It's like every other port city. When I said land, Anne Gray, I meant open land without people—like Australia."

"Gilbert Brownwell, what would we do in a wilderness without people? And how would we ever watch out for Aunt Margaret's investment from there? Just wait until you become a part of the business; it's more exciting than any farm ever could be."

Even without being able to see her face in the windswept darkness, Gilbert knew it would be glowing with an excitement he couldn't share. He shrugged lightly as he guided her across the slippery deck back to their cabin. The next day Anne was almost relieved when he was asked to rejoin the faro game. As he leaned toward her to ask permission, she grinned at him impudently and whispered, "I'm not a nag, remember?"

Their shipboard life quickly fell into a pleasant pattern of shared nights and a tolerated daily separation of card playing for Gilbert and ledger posting for Anne. Both felt secure in their chosen diversities, and neither partner noted the imperceptible erosion of the closeness they'd shared in Le Havre and during the few recent days aboard the *Boston Queen*. Stimulated by her first real taste of independence and by the challenge of learning about a business that would be a part of her life with Gilbert in America, Anne welcomed the boxes of neglected invoices and unrecorded bills of lading that Captain Perkins handed her each day. So engrossed did she become in the affairs of Perkins, Bouvier and Gray, she failed to notice Gilbert's increased moodiness and drinking. Not until the night he complained about his luck did she realize that the faro games were now being played for money.

"Why do you gamble, Tony?" she asked curiously.

"For the same reasons you get so lost in those ridiculous books that you don't even remember I exist; gambling fascinates me." He smiled at her.

Admitting to herself that she did tend to lose her awareness of outside activity when she was concentrating on something important, Anne remained in the salon the next day after dinner and studied the people playing with her husband. Although she spoke French fluently, this time she only listened and was a little startled by the easy familiarity of the players. From the ship's papers she had learned about the cargo and about this particular group of passengers; the four men were the owners of a large consignment of fine French wine stored below. They operated a major distributing business in Bermuda from where they wholesaled wine to merchants all over the French-English Caribbean. Three of the men were Frenchmen whose faces reflected the self-satisfaction of success. Surprisingly the fourth man was a German, whose French was impeccable but whose luck at cards was even more memorable.

The older of the two women was the wife of one of the Frenchmen; the younger one, her sister. It was their faces Anne watched the most carefully. Unmistakably upper class, the small dark-haired women wore their lovely gowns as gracefully as they played cards. Whenever they lost, they shrugged good-humoredly and reached for the next card. From the joking comments of the men, Anne learned that the younger Frenchwoman was a widow who could well afford to lose. She was on her way to Bermuda to marry a fifth partner in the wine firm, but her expression revealed little of love's eagerness. Instead she seemed content to hold court with the group around her now, treating them all equally to careless terms of endearment. Her *"Bonne chance, cher Jean,"* *"Félicitations, cher Rolf,"* and, when her wine was replenished, *"Merci, Gilbert cher"* were like lovely little notes of music. Anne envied the Frenchwoman's sophistication and the attention the men paid her, but she could not really be jealous since Madame Charbot called her *"chère Anne"* with equal warmth.

As Anne was watching the players, Paul Bouvier was watching her. During the five-week voyage he had seen and spoken to her many times, and always he found her unaware beauty a challenge .While Thomas Perkins admired her swift mind and her ability to master business problems, Paul admired the girl herself and even desired her. A complete realist, he accepted his attraction for her as a natural thing that did not distract from his deeper love of Lynette, but that existed because the girl was young and vulnerable.

Having watched the card game for weeks and mentally tabulated the losses and winnings, Paul knew that the young Englishman was a reckless, unskilled player. He had watched *"cher Gilbert"* escort Madame Charbot to her cabin and kiss her hand with easy charm. And Paul despised the idle aristocrat more than he had when he had first read the dossier about him.

The following afternoon two games were played in the salon. After exchanging a few pleasantries with Anne, Paul took her arm and smiled at the cardplayers. "If you will excuse us, Anne has promised to keep me company at the wheel. If she likes, she can become the loveliest helmsman on the Atlantic." Anne was delighted. The wheelhouse was out-of-bounds for passengers, and she was curious to know how a ship was operated. For an hour she stood with her eyes glued on the compass in its binnacle, and her hands gripped the wheel with a death hold. She did not know that Paul stood close behind her and watched her with a look of hunger. Nor did she notice her husband glaring at her from across the deck. All she knew was that Anne Gray was learning to guide a ship across the ocean, and she felt like a Viking conqueror.

At supper she was still glowing from the thought that she had held the *Boston Queen* on course for one whole hour. When her husband could finally regain her attention, he asked her coldly, "Did you have fun today, sweet?"

"Oh, yes, Tony, it was more exciting than anything I've

done since this trip started.'' She smiled a starry smile and hugged his arm. ''I'd like to learn to navigate and really run a ship.''

He hugged her back, but he still felt hurt that she could look so happy and excited without him. That night he drank too much wine and lost too much money. Anne was sound asleep when he stumbled into bed and didn't even stir as he kissed her. The next day after she had accepted Paul's second invitation to stand watch at the wheel, Gilbert lost even more money. By suppertime his anger was focused entirely on his wife. Damn it, how could he concentrate when she kept making a fool of herself over a man old enough to be her father?

It didn't improve his temper when he went to their cabin to escort her back to the salon to find her so engrossed in those damn ledgers that she did not respond with decent civility to his perfectly logical questions. ''What the hell do you think you're doing, Anne, fooling around with a man like that? Are you so stupid you don't know he's trying to get you into bed? Or is that what you really want?''

Strangely Anne didn't remember the earlier time he'd accused her of a similar intention with Harold; all she could think of was Suzanne Brownwell's final insult of ''miserable millstone,'' and she lost her temper. ''Your mind is as vicious as your mother's, Gilbert, and your conclusions just as stupid.''

When he slapped her face with the full power of his open hand, she stared at him in disbelief and walked stiffly out of the room. She didn't hear him start to apologize. By the time she reached the main salon, her head was high and her lips were softened by the same little smile she had learned as a girl. For three hours she carried on the liveliest conversation she'd ever had with her dinner companions. When Paul Bouvier joined the group and asked where her husband was, she smiled brilliantly and shrugged her shoulders. Slowly he reached out and touched the faint bruise mark on her face and frowned.

"I'll walk you to your cabin, Anne," he said quietly and helped her stand.

"It's not necessary," she protested; but Captain Bouvier was not an easy man to discourage. It was he who opened the cabin door and first viewed Gilbert sprawled on top of the bed in a drunken stupor.

"Is he often like this?" Paul asked sharply.

Fighting her tears, Anne shook her head.

"Is he violent when he sobers up?"

This time she shook her head more vigorously, but she really didn't know. She'd been out riding on both other occasions.

"Anne, did you know your husband has been gambling heavily and losing?"

That much she did know; on the day she'd taken the key from his pocket at the inn in Le Havre, he'd had five hundred pounds. When she'd looked yesterday morning as he slept off his excessive drinking of the night before, he'd had only a few pounds left.

"I know," she admitted, "but he hasn't much left to gamble with."

"Good. Are you afraid to stay alone with him?"

"No, I'm not afraid of him."

"Do you want me to help you get him into bed?"

"No, he's my responsibility."

"Good night, then, Anne. I'll look in on you tomorrow." Paul left them, more coldly angry than he'd been in years. A beautiful girl sacrificed to a *cochon* like this one who drank himself insensible after he'd struck her!

Sunk in her own misery, Anne peeled off her husband's outer garments and pulled the covers over him. Not until she went into the adjoining cabin did she remember her easy assurance that she was not afraid. Still lighted by a whale-oil lamp that had not yet guttered out, the room was a littered mess; and on the table was an empty brandy bottle, one from the box that had been Aunt Margaret's parting gift. The ledgers and what had been neat stacks of paper were strewn over the deck, and all of her trunks had been rifled. She cried out in dismay when she found one of her blue silk petticoats slashed to shreds. Willing herself to sit down and to study the shambles, Anne felt the cold fear of certainty grip her. Gilbert may have been angry enough to throw her bookkeeping material all over the cabin and drink himself into a comatose state, but he wasn't insane. Yet no sane man would slash a woman's petticoat unless—her breathing became tortured—unless he was looking for something of value. But what? The only pieces of real jewelry she owned were the two rings his mother had supplied for the wedding, and he was welcome to those any time for the asking. She jerked convulsively when the lantern flickered and went out, leaving her terrified in a pitch-dark cabin. Shaking in fear, she removed her dress and petticoats, returned to the adjoining room, and crept into bed beside the man who now seemed more a frightening stranger than the exciting lover she'd known for two months. She awakened late the following morning to find herself mercifully alone.

Ignoring a queasy stomach, Anne arose and dressed herself in the same clothes she'd worn the day before. Resolutely she began to clean the cluttered debris from the next cabin. She'd finished restacking the books and papers into neat piles and started on the contents of her trunks when she found the second ruined petticoat stuffed behind one of the open lids. The tears streamed down her face; she'd never even worn this beautiful garment and now she never could. Suddenly a memory of her wedding night stood out sharply in her mind. This was one of the three petticoats she'd searched for that night and never found. Frantically she tore through the contents of her trunks until she located the third one neatly folded inside the dress it matched. Her agile fingers located the coins within seconds, and she closed her eyes in sick dismay. Dear generous Aunt Margaret, who'd known all about Gilbert's gambling, was still trying to protect her!

With an almost detached sense of disbelief, Anne snipped the coins from the hem of the garment, counting them as she did so. Three hundred and forty-seven coins, three hundred and forty-seven pounds, seventeen hundred and thirty-five dollars! Logically she estimated the amount that had been stolen and giggled senselessly. Her third of the money was larger than the other two! Quickly she folded the one good petticoat and placed it back inside the dress. Then, using a piece of the torn fabric, she bundled up the coins; but before she tied the ragged ends together, she dug down into a trinket box, retrieved her wedding rings, and added them to her hoard.

Although she had never lacked for the material necessities in her life, money was rapidly assuming a grim importance to her. This money she held now might be all she could count on for her own support. Gilbert had already lost five hundred pounds in less than four weeks and now was threatening to lose the more than six hundred pounds he'd stolen from her. That sum was more than half of the two thousand pounds he would receive each year from her father. Yet it had paid for nothing except gambling debts. She remembered her father's promise to send her money any time she needed it, but Anne was rapidly becoming a realist. Her husband would probably have as much claim to funds her father or Aunt Margaret sent as she would. And they weren't the only ones whose fortunes could be jeopardized! She had just remembered her grandfather's letter of credit. Thousands of pounds at the disposal of a man who was sick with a disease more virulent than the plague. Her heart was pounding as she ran into the other cabin and grabbed her copy of *Tom Jones* from the bookshelf; and only when she found the letter of credit inside the cover could she gasp in relief.

The tears streamed down her face as she reached for the tinderbox and held it to the document until all that was left were blackened ashes. The three strong people who had always protected her now needed her protection; she would not allow their fortunes to be squandered by her husband, who had almost ruined his own father financially.

Resolutely she picked up the pile of ledgers and the sack of coins and walked calmly to the cabin two doors down. Captain Perkins admitted her with a smile which faded quickly when he noted the faint bruise marks on her cheek, which had now faded to a pallid blue.

Handing him the makeshift sack of coins, she announced without explanation, "I want you to lock this in your strongbox, please."

"How much money is it, Anne?"

"Three hundred and forty-seven pounds. Captain Perkins, what will happen if my husband asks for it?"

"He'll not get one coin of it. We'll keep it safe for you until you're provided for in Boston."

"Is it all right if I do the book work in here from now on?"

"Aye, you can use this half of the table. Is there anything you need?"

She shook her head. "Nothing but a chance to work."

"Then I'll let you get right to it." His face held a grim expression as he closed the door and went to locate his partner.

Left to herself, Anne arranged the ledgers in proper order and opened the top one at the appropriate page; but she couldn't focus her eyes on the columns of figures written there. Heartbreak even for a young woman of eighteen is an overwhelming emotion. What had gone wrong? How could two months of wonderful ecstasy be finished without her knowing why? And how could he have forgotten that he'd clung to her throughout nights of joyful love? Or that he'd asked her never to stop loving him?

"Are you all right?" Paul's voice cut through her tears with the efficiency of a knife.

"Just tired," she mumbled.

"I don't doubt it. You didn't report for breakfast this morning, so I've ordered our dinners served topside on the bridge. I need you to watch the instruments and stand lookout. There's a storm someplace ahead. You won't need a cape, I already have foul-weather gear waiting for you."

Gratefully Anne accompanied him, glad to be relieved of

the torture of recriminations. Before the long afternoon was over, the resilient fiber of her character had strengthened still more; and she was able to face her husband at supper without flinching. But the next five days seemed unreal to her. Although she succeeded in making all the ledgers current and gaining more knowledge about ship's instruments than she knew existed, she felt disoriented, cast adrift on an alien sea. She saw Gilbert at irregular intervals and was as icily polite to him as he was to her. By eating many of her meals in the cabin where she worked, she was able to remain out of the salon almost entirely during those five days.

The nights, though, were torment. On the first two Gilbert returned to their cabin only mildly intoxicated; he made no move to touch her, and she pretended sleep. The following two he didn't return at all. Toward dawn during the first of these lonely nights, Anne was awakened by a nagging memory of a description she'd overheard at her wedding breakfast, the description of her husband's former mistress—"beautiful, brunette, and short." Anne remembered Madame Charbot and knew where Gilbert was. "*Bonne chance*, madame," she whispered and wept bitterly into her pillow until she fell asleep.

Aroused from an uneasy sleep on the fifth night of Gilbert's on again—off again absence by the violent pitching of the usually stable *Boston Queen*, Anne realized with a terrified start that the storm Paul was worried about had overtaken them. Gripping the wooden sideboards that kept her from being thrown from the bed as the ship crashed helplessly into the giant troughs of the turbulent waves, Anne fought against her rising panic. Images of the stories she'd read of shipwrecks floated across her inward vision as she stared into the unrelieved darkness and whispered her husband's name over and over. Strangely, it was a peaceful memory that gradually eased her terror, the remembered sight of Gilbert swimming far offshore in Le Havre Harbor. He hadn't been afraid of the sea because his powerful strokes had kept him on the surface. Her last thought before drowsiness reclaimed her sensibilities was that the storm couldn't frighten him and that he would keep her safe.

Anne didn't awaken when Gilbert stumbled into the cabin sometime later, nor did she hear the profanities he uttered when he slammed into one of the trunks. Only as he flung himself fully clothed on the bed did she stir at all, reaching out to him blindly for the reassurance of the protection her imagination had created earlier. Even the violence of his reaction did not arouse her to total awareness. With a guttural curse he shoved her away, his hands and booted foot knocking her over the rail board. Dimly she heard the slurred words "cheating bitch" before her head struck the protruding timbers of the bulkhead and she slipped unconscious onto the dampening deck.

Minutes later, after she'd regained a small measure of mental control, she crawled groggily back into the warmth of the bed; and neither the throbbing pain nor shivering cold kept her from falling into a deep stuporous sleep. Awakening late the next morning, Anne's tortured memory returned in full; and she vomited helplessly, unaware and uncaring that her husband had already gone.

Despite the enormity of controlling a ship during a storm, Captain Perkins was fully cognizant of Gilbert Brownwell's total absorption in gambling and his neglect of a young wife. Worried about the girl he and Paul had sworn to protect, Perkins stopped by her cabin on the way to his own and found her lying on a disordered bed staring expressionlessly at the gray light filtering in from the one small battened-down window.

"How'd you get those bruises on your face, young lady?" he demanded sharply.

Her voice was as emotionless as her eyes. "I fell out of bed."

As his expert gaze checked the guardrail, he shook his head skeptically. "Was your husband drunk again last night?"

"I don't remember," she replied listlessly.

"Do you want me to move him to another cabin?"

A faint smile touched her lips. "That won't be necessary, Captain, my husband has already taken care of that detail himself."

With a troubled conscience, he ordered a steward to bring her food and clean the cabin before he returned to his own quarters for a badly needed rest. It was easy for a woman a thousand miles or more away to have demanded that he keep her niece safe from all harm, Perkins reflected uneasily; but short of using force, how was he to dictate to a self-possessed young woman who refused to listen to reason? Despite the violence of the storm, he was morally certain that the husband had caused those injuries.

As if rampaging natural forces joined the human ones to plague the beleaguered *Boston Queen*, a series of storms battered the ship for another seven days. Since hot food could not be prepared safely, the main salon was closed and the passengers ordered to remain in their cabins. Once a day rations of water and cold food—cheese, sea biscuits, raisin cake, and dried fruit—were distributed. Sensibly frightened, the passengers cooperated; even the gamblers obeyed the edict. They moved the game to Madame Charbot's cabin and continued their play during the gray daylight hours and their drinking when they could no longer see the cards or dice.

Alone in her cabin Anne's misery increased. Her bruised body ached, her head throbbed, and the nausea continued on a daily basis. Each subsequent morning of the storm she awakened with a queasy stomach and tried desperately and unsuccessfully not to throw up. Only by afternoon did she feel well enough to eat some food and contemplete the wreckage of her marriage realistically. That Gilbert was finished with pretending to tolerate her she had no doubt. The ugly name he'd called her and the violence of his rejection when she'd tried to touch him had destroyed what illusions she'd maintained with difficulty after the theft of her money and his first blatant infidelity. Stoically she shunned the sympathy the two captains offered during their frequent hurried trips to her cabin, requesting only that they bring her some work to do. Predictably Captain Perkins returned with the ledgers, but Paul Bouvier was far more inventive. He brought her a length of heavy manila rope and the large, crudely illustrated chart used to teach neophyte seamen the art of tying nautical knots.

"I've never met a woman yet who could tie anything but pretty bow knots," he warned her with a shrewd twinkle, "but if you're really serious about learning how to operate a ship, you'll have to master these kinds."

Pleased by his own stratagem when the guarded look in her eyes was momentarily replaced by the sparkle of challenge, Paul remained longer than usual, instructing her in the simpler knots. "How're you coping with your *mal de mer*, Anne?" he asked her casually, adding still another barb with his next words. "That's another thing a good sailor has to conquer."

"If you'd stop trying to put this ship on the bottom of the Atlantic Ocean," she flared, "I wouldn't have any trouble. The way you've hit every wave during this storm, even a fish would be seasick."

Paul was grinning when he let himself out of the cabin. He'd been right; this one had fire. She was too much of a fighter to succumb to motion sickness or the storm; and she'd survive the ordeal of an unfaithful and brutal husband once she was separated from him. Even more than Captain Perkins, Paul was convinced that her husband had beaten her or worse.

Anne's composure was even more intact than Paul surmised. During his visit she'd regained enough angry pride to contemplate her future without tears. When Gilbert shoved his way into the cabin a few moments after the Frenchman had left it, she glanced up only briefly and then with an expression of disdain.

Glaring defensively at his wife's averted face, Gilbert blurted angrily, "What the hell happened to you?"

"I've been seasick." She shrugged.

"So have the other inexperienced passengers," he insisted

callously. "I meant your face. How'd you smash it up like that?"

Startled out of her postured indifference, Anne half rose from her chair before she settled back with a defiant control. "You should know," she snapped, "you kicked me out of bed with your boots."

"You're out of your mind," he sputtered, "I haven't—"

Interrupting his protest with an icy contempt, Anne continued her accusation. "Before I struck my head, you called me a 'cheating bitch.'"

Gilbert's denial was explosive. "I haven't touched you since you started playing games with your damned Frenchman."

"I know you haven't," she returned with equal fury. "You've been too busy with your own games. Except," she added with biting vindictiveness, "on the first night of the storm when you returned here in your customary state of inebriation."

The faint doubt that clouded Gilbert's eyes was quickly erased. "There was nothing wrong with you when I left the next morning; you were in bed and asleep. But deny if you can that you've spent this morning with your lover. I watched him as he left here, and, lady, he looked more than self-satisfied.

"My aunt's partners," Anne stressed the words with deliberate malice, "have been kind enough to see to my welfare since my husband deserted me. What did you come for this time, Gilbert?" she asked with a faint trace of her old defensive smile. "I didn't think you'd spare the time for any useless conversation with me."

There was nothing faint about the enraged flush that mottled his face. Striding past her as sure-footedly as Paul had done on the pitching deck, Gilbert rummaged in the box containing Aunt Margaret's brandy and removed three bottles. He paused briefly at the door to regard his wife's rigid back grimly. "You're as much a cheating bitch as all the others," he muttered indistinctly.

Two days later he returned in a drunken mood more vicious than any he'd exhibited before. Seated at the table where she'd been unsuccessfully attempting to fathom the mystery of a bowline knot, Anne looked up sharply, her face reflecting a sudden fear as he began to paw through the contents of her trunks. Watching his vandalism with stony silence, she held her breath at his grunt of satisfaction. But that sound quickly changed to one of fury as he stood up and approached the table, holding the blue petticoat in front of him, its neatly raveled hemline plainly visible. His face, she thought with a sad regret, looked like that of an evil angel; his eyes glittered menacingly and his mouth was a cruel slash across his face.

"Where is it?" he raged at her.

"Where is what?"

"The rest of the gold coins your suspicious aunt sewed into your three petticoats to keep you safe from a wicked husband."

"What gold coins?"

"The last third of one thousand pounds, my lying wife."

"How do you know it was a thousand pounds?"

"Your stuffy family members are predictably consistent. They deal in nice round sums. Not six hundred and fifty-three pounds, but a thousand pounds. Where have you hidden the rest?"

Anne's hand gripped the end of the rope. "It's my money!"

"You don't own any money. You don't own any of these things, not these clothes or these books or these trunks." As he raged, he threw still more of her things about the room. "You're a smart enough girl to know the law, and the Boston law is the same as English law. A wife does not own a thing; everything belongs to her husband, including her body. Now where did you hide the money?"

"You'll just have to look for it, won't you?"

"There are other ways; a husband has the right to beat his wife."

"How like you, Gilbert, to take the coward's way of beating a wife to keep her terrified of a coxcomb who thinks he's a man."

Their voices had risen to furious shouts that matched in volume the violence of the storm outside.

"You," he raged, "you razor-tongued bastard. You don't have the sense to be afraid."

"Never of you, you drunken fool! You unfaithful mucky lecher!"

"Where's the money, bitch?"

"Where you will never get your hands on it, bastard."

As he came toward her with his hand upraised, she leapt up from the table, and her hand gripped the rope until her knuckles turned white. She raised it and with all the strength of her fury, she struck him across his cheek and shoulder. She heard him scream as she watched the deep welts turn red with oozing blood. When she felt him tear the rope from her hand, she turned to run. The first blow caught the back of her legs, and she fell forward to her knees. Instinctively she lowered her head toward the clammy deck and dug her arms into her thick hair.

Four times she felt the rope slash deeply into her back and waited without movement for the fifth because she could not move. Standing above her, Gilbert watched in a stupor as the bright red blood began to soak the shredded dress. Then, as the strength and anger left him, he began to shake in the terrible realization of his savagery. "Oh, my God, Anne. Oh, my God!" And Anne knew the storm was over as he sank to his knees beside her. She also knew that she had only minutes to get out of this cabin.

In a voice as soothing as one she would use for an injured child, Anne said, "I know, Gilbert, I know you didn't mean to hurt me. But now, you have to help me stand." After he had drawn her to her feet as gently as his shaking hands could manage, she murmured again, "Please wrap my cloak around me. I'm cold."

Frantically he grabbed her heavy wool cape and laid it across her shoulders, but not before he saw the blood again. His face went white and he groped for the chair, fainting as he sat down. Anne looked down on the blond head resting on the table. Slowly and painfully she raised her hand and caressed it. "Good-bye, Tony," she murmured.

Turning she walked stiffly out into the passageway and down the endless space, willing her numb feet to shuffle forward one at a time until they reached the tall man standing motionless at the entrance to the deck. "Hide me, Paul," she said and fainted.

He lifted her slim body and walked swiftly into his own cabin carrying the unconscious girl. As he removed her cape and laid her facedown on the bed, his face was that of a killer. With the cold deliberation of a strong man, he started for the door, only to be pulled back to the bed as he heard her clear voice say in what sounded impossibly like a chuckle, "He told me I'd wind up in your bed, Paul, and here I am," before she fainted again.

Chapter 8

MINUTES after Anne had fainted for the second time, Paul arrived with a badly worried Tom Perkins. As the younger man unlocked the cabin door, he motioned the older one to silence and led him over to the bed. When Perkins tried to speak, Paul silenced him again and shook his head. They must do what had to be done in silence.

With an expressionless face, the dark Frenchman opened his medical kit and removed the items they would need. His hands were steady as he forced the first dose of laudanum down Anne's throat. The half-conscious girl threw it up only to have the second dose held in her mouth by roughened, tender hands. For an hour the men worked, cutting off the back of her dress, cleaning the wounds, and smearing on a heavy oily paste. When they had finished, they covered the lacerated back with a piece of clean sheeting and tied her hands and feet loosely to the bed so that she could not thrash around. As an afterthought Paul moved her head to the edge of the bed and placed a bucket beneath it.

A short while later they sat at the captain's table and talked in whispers. "They should have been separated a week ago. I should have done it, stubborn girl or not," Perkins said in the sharp whisper of self-accusation.

Paul shrugged. "What is done is over, *mon ami;* now we must settle the little problem once and for all."

"How? Aboard ship, I grant you it's possible. We can lock them in separate cabins. But how will you keep a husband from his lawful wife when we reach Boston? Every court there will take his side."

"Very simply, *mon ami;* the husband will not reach Boston."

"You cannot murder him, Paul."

"An hour ago I might have done just that; but now, no, I will not kill him."

"Then what are you planning to do?"

Paul smiled sardonically at his partner. "I think, *mon ami,* that I will not tell you. What your Yankee conscience does not know will never distress you. I will handle the problem so that our young Anne will not be hurt again. Now I will need a bottle of your excellent cognac and a glass. Rest assured, Tom, my plan is the best one under the circumstances." The older partner watched Paul leave, and his shrewd eyes held a speculative look.

Paul rapped sharply on the next door down and entered without waiting for a response. He found the young occupant still slumped in the chair staring vacantly across the darkened cabin. "I didn't mean to hurt her," Gilbert whispered without looking up. "I didn't really mean to hurt her."

"That may well be, *mon ami,* but what is done cannot be changed." He poured a glass of cognac and shoved it in front of the young husband. "Now we must get down to practicalities. Which of these pieces of luggage are yours?"

Gilbert looked around at Anne's littered trunks and cringed

in memory. "None of these. These are all my wife's." The tenderness of the last word was unmistakable. "Mine are in the other room."

"*Bon*. This room will be kept locked for a Boston board of inquiry, and any evidence must remain untouched. Let us take the two chairs and go into the other cabin." Paul had heard the longing in the other man's voice, but he steeled his heart to do what was necessary.

Seated once again in the next cabin, Paul placed the glass on the trunk and refilled it.

"I think, *mon ami*, you should drink that before you hear what I must tell you," he said gently.

Eyes filled with self-loathing looked up. "That I'm to be charged with beating my wife? Oh, God, it sounds so—"

"No, *mon ami*, not that. Two hours ago your wife fell overboard and was lost." Paul watched the other man's face go white and heard the glass drop from his nerveless fingers.

The words when they finally came were without hope. "You searched for her in the water?"

"No one except God can stop a ship in a storm."

Anne's final words to him seared Gilbert like a brand in his sick heart: "Good-bye, Tony." She had called him Tony just as she had during their moments of love, but her voice had sounded so sad and final. Driven by a desperate fear, Gilbert asked another hopeless question. "Did you look everywhere aboard for her?"

"It was not necessary. She was seen going over the side."

Tortured eyes searched Paul's face. "Did my wife jump overboard, Captain?"

"The seaman who saw the tragedy did not think so."

Deeply shaken himself at the sight of Brownwell's grief, Paul watched as sobs shook his companion. Compassionately he touched the other's shoulder. "We all make mistakes, *mon ami*. And yours is no worse than many other men have made. I will leave you now to compose yourself. Do not, I beg you, do anything foolish. Remember that nothing would have made your wife prouder than your courage at this time."

Just as a drowning man sees his life pass before his eyes, so did Gilbert relive his during the next half hour. He hated every minute of those memories, except for Anne. He saw again the contempt in his father's face and wished that once, he could have seen approval on it. He heard his oldest brother's voice imploring him to stop his insanity. He shuddered with a sick revulsion when he remembered his mother's doting face and the everlasting lies she defended him with. In a long procession, he saw again the blurred and nameless faces of the women he had corrupted and been corrupted by, and the cynical men he'd lost his money to. He wept brokenly and tried to stop the inexorable, torturing recall of his wife's strong, slim body next to his and of her low voice vibrating in his ear when they had been together. But for her, his life had been a worthless existence, until her love. And he had destroyed her.

Calm now and dry-eyed when Paul returned, Gilbert did not care what his future held; he was prepared to follow, without thought, what the older man proposed.

The Frenchman noted the composure and nodded. "Within a few days we will arrive in Bermuda, and there we'll find some British ship headed for Australia. You served as navigator in the navy, yes? Navigators are always in demand for such voyages. It would be better for you, I think, *mon ami*, that you should work your way and have less time to think." The younger man shrugged, so Paul continued. "Just before I leave you on that ship, I will hand your new captain the envelope containing the two thousand pounds of your wife's dowry."

"I don't want it."

"Nevertheless, I will give it to the captain to hold for you until you reach your destination. What you do with it there is your concern. But remember, *mon ami*, you're young with a long life ahead of you. Do not, I beg you, waste any more years. One more thing; I will sell your two horses when I reach Boston, and send you the money."

"No. Give them away to whoever needs them." Gilbert

closed his eyes sharply against the pain of seeing Anne's long hair streaming behind her as they raced down the dusty French country roads.

Two days later the *Boston Queen* rode at anchor in beautiful St. George's harbor. In the dawn hours of the following day, a long boat holding four silent men and two trunks was lowered into the calm water. Two seamen rowed with rapid strokes across the half mile that separated the *Queen* and the British ship Paul had located the night before. On the way over Gilbert moved only once, to touch his pocket, which held a piece of torn blue cloth wrapped around one gold silk rose.

As they approached the side of the ship, a rope ladder was lowered, and a burred Scot voice hailed them. "I'm Robert MacKeith, master of the *Glasgow Lady*, and you be the navigator, lad?"

"I'm a navigator, yes, but I have no papers."

"Aye, my friend Bouvier had told me. But I'll not be holding up the ship over a technicality. If you prove yourself in the next five months, I can give you papers. Well, lad, from the look of you, I'd say you should live with the officers."

"If it's all the same with you, sir, I prefer to bunk with the crew."

"They're a scurvy lot, lad."

"So am I, sir." Gilbert's salute was mechanical as he turned to walk toward the forecastle with his shoulders stiff and straight.

Chapter 9

THE *Boston Queen* was the scene of bustling activity for two weeks following the departure of the *Glasgow Lady*.

Immediately after the *Queen* was towed to dock, all the passengers, save one, joyously disembarked, the gamblers permanently and the Americans for two weeks of vacation on the beautiful Caribbean island. Even the two storm-weakened horses were taken ashore and placed in lush pastures.

As the passengers were driven off in graceful open carriages, hundreds of dark-skinned loaders swarmed into the hold of the ship; their bodies glistened with the sweat of hard labor as they carried out the boxes and barrels of French wine on their powerful shoulders. With a rhythmic cadence their bodies moved to the wordless music they chanted. They carried out the bolts of French silk, Irish linen, and Belgium lace and the boxes of expensive kid gloves.

At last, when the ship was emptied, a group of specially trained dock experts entered the hold with boxes and containers. Three hours they worked with their poisons and their cats, emerging with sacks full of dead rats. Thus the ship was ready to be loaded with her third cargo in six months, eight hundred barrels of uncut Jamaican rum, the richest cargo of the West Atlantic trade. While the barrels were being lashed to the bulkheads, the ship's water supply was replenished and the food restocked. The four Americans and eight new passengers boarded, and the *Boston Queen* sailed for home.

During these weeks Anne remained facedown on her bed, knowing nothing of these changes. In her lucid moments she had only one wish, to die quickly rather than suffer this drawn-out torture. While her back burned with fire, her lower abdomen throbbed with a dull ache. And every day for three hours she suffered the terrible nausea which left her weak and empty. The two men who tended her with unfailing devotion worried about each pain and left the ship only when necessary, and then only one at a time. They sent out for cool tropical fruits to tempt her appetite. They wiped her face and washed her body, and kept her presence a secret from the other passengers, old and new, and from the crew. When anyone asked about the young couple, both captains replied in unison, "They've taken passage for Australia." A half-truth, they believed, was better than either the whole truth or no truth at all.

Four weeks after the ordeal began, it was suddenly two-thirds over. Her back healed completely, though she would bear the scars for life; and the abdominal pains stopped. Only the nausea continued; and for the thousandth time Anne cursed the rolling, surging motion of the ship.

As her health returned, so did her driving need to keep her mind occupied with thoughts outside herself. She was not ready yet to face either the past or the future, but she could find no real escape from disturbed dreams and tortured thoughts. Even her reliable old props of books failed her. Sad poetry aroused mindless self-pity, and romantic stories left her wanting the happiness she had lost. She paced the cabin feeling more and more a prisoner, and she cried easily and often.

Both captains were concerned about her growing unrest. Perkins wanted to tell her that her aunt had already planned the future, but Paul shook his head. "She must plan her own this time, and in America, I think. This girl is not one who can be easily content, like my Lynette. This one will want much more, and she will need her courage back."

That afternoon when he visited her, he found a weeping, unhappy Anne; and for the first time since the night she had come to him for help he did not pamper her. "*Chérie*, you are becoming a tedious woman. You weep because a husband left you. You weep because you were not happy with him. You weep because you're bored. You weep because you're not a little girl anymore, safe at home with an indulgent aunt. It is time for you to grow up. You will have to face many problems when you reach Boston. You are a woman alone, and that is never easy. And I think, *chérie*, you have another problem as well. Is that not so?"

Anne had been glaring at him with the anger of a child who had been scolded when she expected to be praised. But now she stared at him.

Patiently he continued, "*Chérie*, you have to face this

thing. There is nothing anyone can do for you this time. You will have to do it alone.'' As she continued to look at him without any comprehension, it was Paul's turn to stare at her. She had no idea what he was talking about. ''Each morning you are sick, each afternoon you are not, yes? You don't know what that means?'' She shook her head. *''Mon dieu,* what kind of crazy people are the English? They teach a girl mathematics and science and bookkeeping, but they don't teach her the simplest things about life. You are going to have a child, Anne.''

She started to laugh; Paddy's books again. They told her how children were conceived, but not one word about what happened to the mother. No one had ever thought to explain what the monthly flow of blood had meant, except that it was a natural thing. Since hers had always been light and painless, she had accepted it as she had everything else about growing up. It just was. And she had paid so little attention to it, she couldn't even remember the last time. She thought about Paddy and Aunt Margaret and about their avoidance of all such subjects, and she wondered if they even knew themselves.

She laughed until the tears ran down her cheeks. Smart, educated Anne, who didn't even know as much as the dumbest village girl of ten. She felt as light as a feather. All the time she had lain in bed believing that she was going to have that horrible nausea for the rest of her life. And all the time she was growing a child. A child all her own that she could love and teach. A little son who'd look like Gilbert. An angel babe she'd name Tony.

''I didn't know, Paul.'' She laughed again. ''I don't even know how old it is. Oh, Paul, I have so many things to do. Now I have to earn twice as much money—no, ten times.'' And she frowned in concentration about the ways and means. Even in this moment of shocked enlightenment, her practicality surfaced. A simple return to Grayhaven was now impossible. She would be doubly branded as a bastard with a bastard if she tried to teach village children, and the alternative home in England was far worse. Anne could not conceive of a more disagreeable fate than to raise her child under the spiteful domination of Suzanne Brownwell. She wished she knew more about Boston. Would she have enough money to support herself and her child until she could earn more? She couldn't ask her father or grandfather for help, not after the fortune they'd already spent buying her a husband. Nor could she burden Aunt Margaret with the problem of another unwanted child. "No," Anne corrected herself fiercely, "this child is wanted."

Paul shook his head as he watched her mental gymnastics and her changing facial expressions. This was a very unusual woman. She cried tears over nothing, but she only laughed when he had told her news that would have made most women in her circumstances faint with terror. She said not one word about infant clothes, only some nonsense about making money. He started to tell her about the ten thousand pounds, but Anne was paying no attention. She was too busy taking inventory of her assets.

"If I can get a job as a teacher during the day," she mused, "I can work as your bookkeeper at night. And I do have three hundred and forty-seven pounds. If I can invest a part of that money in a business, then it can start to earn an income, too." A sudden thought struck her. "Paul, how long does a woman have to wait after she has had a child before she can go back to work?"

His answer was positive and stern. "A woman with a *bébé* does not work. No one in Boston would hire her. For that matter, women are not encouraged to work outside the home at all. Especially in jobs like the ones you're thinking about. Such ones are for men." When he saw the building anger on her face, he softened his tone. "Do not worry so, *chérie*, we will take care of you."

"I won't be taken care of like some breeding sow," she stormed. "If no man will hire me, I'll work for myself. I don't need any pity or protection. I'm going to succeed on my own, Paul Bouvier, without anyone's help."

Paul left, not sure that he had done the right thing by

telling her about the child. But he was grateful that he did not have to live with an ambitious woman. Paul, after all, approved of his world and did not want the nice, comfortable arrangement changed. He had as yet no conception of how much this girl would change it.

When Captain Perkins brought her supper in, he was met with the blunt, unpleasant question, "Will you hire me as your bookkeeper?"

He squirmed as he hedged. "I will bring some work home each night, and you can go on as you've been doing."

"That's not what I mean. Would you hire me to work at your shipyards?"

"Well now, Annie, shipyards are mighty rough places, and the men aren't what you'd call gentlemen. It's no place for a lady." He did not mention her condition, so Anne concluded that he did not know about the child. And she vowed he would not learn about it for months yet, if she could convince Paul not to tell him or anyone else. But Captain Perkins had told her what she wanted to know. Boston men were just as stubborn and benighted as Englishmen.

She paced the floor, remembering the things Paddy had taught her about survival in a strange world. She remembered his answer when she had asked why he'd changed Ian's name to John. "It's best to use the enemy's own weapons whenever you can." She stopped her pacing and looked down at her long, lean body where not a trace of motherhood showed. She felt her brown hair, which was a nice nondescript color. And she made her decision. Since women were not welcome in the man's world, she would invade it as a man. She shuddered at the thought. Many of the crude taunts she'd faced in her girlhood had accused her of being manlike; and she had often prayed to be transformed into a small, defenseless woman toward whom men would feel protective. More so than most girls, Anne had worked to make herself look feminine with pretty dresses and polished manners. But ladylike ways would not help her now. As a woman she could not earn as much money as she needed, if Bostonians allowed her to earn any at all. As an educated young man, though, she was certain that she could find a good job. Thus it was that a little more than seven months before she gave birth to Gilbert Brownwell's offspring, Anne Gray gave birth to her own—a seventeen-year-old brother named Andrew.

During the last three weeks of her imprisonment she was too busy to be sad or sick. When her stomach threatened to rebel, she said, "Look, little child, if I have to put up with you, you have to put up with me. Now, I have too much work to do to be sick, so you just stop whatever you're doing to me." And someone listened. Anne worked all day and every day. She made four of her dresses larger. She cut up petticoats and made shirts, big loose men's shirts. From three dark-colored wool cloaks, she made three pairs of loose men's breeches. She polished her four pairs of riding boots. And she wrote long lists of things to buy and things to do.

At midnight, six hours after the *Boston Queen* had docked in its name city and the passengers and most of the crew were ashore, two gold-braided captains escorted a well-cloaked young lady to a waiting carriage. They smiled at each other in relief. What they did not know was that eighteen-year-old Anne Gray Brownwell, deserted wife, had become Anne Grey—spelled with an e—widow, and Andrew Grey, younger brother.

Chapter 10

THE Perkinses' lands were unique even for land-rich Americans. They occupied two miles of deepwater Boston Bay frontage and extended two and a half miles back from shore. Along the waterfront were the Perkins, Bouvier and Gray loading docks and the sprawling Perkins, Bouvier and Gray ship-yards. On the extreme inland part of the property, set far back from a wide public street, was the large weathered gray-wood Perkins home. Unlike the tall, narrow houses crowded together on Boston streets, this structure was isolated far south of the city proper and sat by itself on a large tract of open land.

Two hundred years earlier Seth Perkins had settled in this place because none of the other Puritans had wanted it. They'd pre-ferred the more attractive areas to the north, where they'd developed lovely little communities from Salem to Concord to Chelsea.

Seth Perkins had been a shipwright who wanted neither lovely communities nor interfering people around him, so he'd chosen the swampy land to the south, which extended almost to the area that would become Quincy a few years later. He was a practical and farsighted man. He built his shipyards on the same parcel of land as his home, leaving more than a mile between the two because he wanted no neighbors to block any future expansion of his business. In 1841, because old Seth's descendants had been taught to value isolation, the home still sat far apart from its neighbors, although waterfront businesses and commercial buildings were now crowding the northern boundary of the property.

The central part of the present home had been built a century ago after the original Perkins home burned down. It was a square two-story structure with few claims to architec-tural beauty. Stretching out at angles toward the road were two long one-story wings, built at separate times by different Perkinses. Had the two builders chosen the same angles, the home might have had some distinction. Since they had not, the house had acquired an added-on look and was merely a large comfortable home in an unfashionable part of South Boston. The only neighboring buildings were a huge barn to the north and a smaller structure that housed the carriages and horses. Both were built of the same gray weathered wood as the house.

When Anne had finally climbed into bed the night before,

she'd known nothing about the house or its occupants. Captain Perkins had led her down a dark hallway lighted only by the candles they'd carried, opened the door to a bedroom, and bid her good night. Inside she had found all of her luggage and trunks and the most comfortable bed she had ever slept in. Ten hours later she awakened in a brilliant sun-lit room with the calmest stomach she'd had in six weeks. As she was burrowing still deeper under a down comforter, a knock on the door brought the blood pounding to her heart. She had been locked in a ship's cabin so long with only two older men for visitors that she had become terrified of meeting anyone else. Her voice quavered as she said, "Come in," and the smile on her lips trembled; but the woman who entered was the least pretentious and threatening person Anne had seen in months. Gray-haired and sturdily built, the newcomer was an attractive sixty-year-old with no pretentions of vanity or social superiority.

"I'm Maude Perkins, the captain's wife," she announced cheerfully. "He tells me you probably won't want to be called Mrs. Brownwell at the moment."

In spite of the familiarity of the comment, Anne smiled in response; it was difficult not to respond in kind to the open good humor of her hostess, whose friendly hazel-brown eyes surveyed the young guest without censure.

"I'd prefer Anne, Mrs. Perkins."

"Which trunk's your robe in, Anne? I 'spect you want some breakfast before you take a bath. Imagine it'll take hours to get the nasty grime of months at sea washed off. If you're like me, your skin is probably wore to a frazzle with those saltwater wipe-downs aboard ship. Afterwards we'll get you unpacked and settled down."

Anne had been listening more to the sound of Maude Perkins' flat New England dialect than to the words themselves. But when the older woman moved toward her trunks, the girl remembered the confusion of the contents of those trunks with a thrown-together mixture of men's and women's clothing.

"I'll unpack later, Mrs. Perkins," she exclaimed in agitation.

Maude looked at her shrewdly and nodded. "All right, Anne. The kitchen's down the hall. You can come whenever you're ready, but don't bother to dress. Lynette and I are the only ones here."

Anne was out of bed before the door closed on the departing woman, her heart beating with another kind of fear. How was she going to explain her need to find a home of her own? Mrs. Perkins obviously expected her to remain here. Hastily Anne washed her face in the small necessaries room and donned one of her least wrinkled day dresses. Rigid training would not allow her to leave a bedroom in a strange house in anything as casual as a bed robe.

Locating her hostess again was a simple matter of following the aroma of cooking food that made her feel hungrier than she had in weeks. She walked down the hallway between a series of bed and storage rooms, opened a heavy oak door, and entered the kitchen, a huge room more like Alette's inn in France than the utility room of a home. Dominated by a stone fireplace with baking ovens on one side, the room contained a wall-long sink counter with its own water pump, a great black monster of a cooking stove, magnificent pine china cabinets, and a dining table and chairs similar to those aboard the *Boston Queen*.

Maude was seated at the table while a younger woman was attending to the food preparation at the stove. Both turned to greet the latecomer with smiles.

"This is Lynette, Anne," Maude introduced the pretty, dark-haired woman.

Having heard Paul refer to Lynette often, the English girl nodded and murmured, "Madame Bouvier."

There was a hushed silence before the Frenchwoman's laughter sounded. "I am not Madame Bouvier, Anne; she lives somewhere still in France. I am Paul's mistress. Please call me Lynette."

Gulping imperceptibly, Anne nodded again and repeated the name. "Lynette."

"It is shocking, no?" the dark-eyed woman asked.

"No," Anne answered promptly, having just remembered her own unconventional plans to pose as a man, "not at all."

Smiling now with gamine impudence, Lynette explained, "When I first arrive here, I pretend to be a wife. But me? I am not so good with telling that kind of lie. So I tell the truth to my friends, and they are still my friends. I am not so proper as Boston ladies, who are, I think, so proper they have lost all sense of humor. But I am happy because I do not try to hide. I hope you are hungry. Paul said you do not eat so well on the ship."

Hungrier by the minute, Anne nodded and sat down; the meal that followed was one of her most memorable. The food was heaped on platters and placed on the table—fried ham, a scrambled egg mixture, a bowl of tiny strawberries, and a plate of thickly sliced bread so full of raisins it looked more like holiday cake than the simple staff of life. Throughout the meal she listened to the others talk with limited attention; her main interest was centered on the necessity of locating a home for herself.

"Where in Boston are there houses to let?" she inquired during a lull in the conversation.

Maude looked at her sharply. "And just why would you be asking a foolish question like that, Anne?"

Startled once more by the blunt curiosity of her hostess, Anne answered more cautiously, "I'll need a home while I'm here in Boston."

"You have one, right here with Tom and me."

"That won't be possible," the girl gasped, panicked by the thought that her carefully laid plans were being threatened.

"'Spect it'll have to be, young lady, leastways until your aunt or father arrive to pack you home. They'd skin me alive if I let you loose on your own."

Anne was speechless for the moment as an angry flush of annoyance reddened her cheeks. "I beg your pardon?" she muttered finally.

"Best you read their letters before you start making plans," the New England woman stated flatly. "Tom's told me all about that scamp husband of yours and about your aunt's insistence that we take care of you. Of course, your folks don't know anything about what happened yet, but I don't believe it'll come as much of a surprise. The letters arrived a month ago, so I imagine they're all worried about you."

Only two of the five letters were addressed to Mr. and Mrs. Gilbert Brownwell; the other three were for Anne alone. She sighed in resignation as she noted the names of the senders— her father, her Aunt Margaret, her grandfather, her father-in-law, and lastly, her oldest brother-in-law Harold.

"I'll read them later and answer them today." Already she had decided on the opening sentence of all the letters except her aunt's: "Gilbert and I arrived safely in Boston last night." She was not going to surrender meekly to more long years of dependence; her life was her own to live for the first time. She had enough money and a plan for her own and her child's survival that she was determined to put into effect.

"Then if you're through breakfast," Maude reminded her, "let's get your bath over with, so's the stove can cool off before suppertime. It gets right hot in Boston by midday."

"What time will Captain Perkins return?"

"Don't expect him or Paul before dark. Their first day back at the yards is apt to be a long 'un," Maude called over her shoulder as she hefted a large cast-iron pot full of boiling water. Anne watched in dismay as both the women carried the water to the necessaries room in her wing of the house. Belatedly she lifted the third pot and followed them, empty-ing her contribution into the brass tub there. She watched as cold water was drawn by the pump on the basin counter.

"Tom's father was a handy man with pipes," Maude explained. "He insisted that everyone could pump their own when he installed these contraptions all over the house. When you finish you pull that plug in the tub and let the water out." Lifting a section of the floorboards, she showed her guest a foot-wide grating where the water would flow out. "Goes to a sump outside and then flows into long ditches filled with rock. Not much else to New England soil except rock," she added cheerfully, "so's folks around here has got plenty of good drainage. Saves a heap of toting water back and forth. This way, except for hot water, you're pretty much on your own in this wing of the house. The rest of us stick to our quarters, so we won't be bothering you."

Anne's bath was lengthy, but not enjoyable or leisurely. As she scrubbed her hair with vicious efficiency, her mind boiled with frustrated questions, the answers to which she didn't know. How was she to escape from this comfortable trap? How was she to get her gold coins back from Captain Perkins if he should decide to keep them from her? "Until you're settled in Boston," he'd said aboard ship; but how could she "settle" without them? And how was she to become Andrew Grey with this house full of curious new friends? There was no question in her mind about the sincerity of their offer of friendship; both of the captains had been too devoted to her welfare for her to doubt their good intentions. But she still lacked the freedom she would need. In a frenzy to get started, she emptied the water, hung the towels to dry, and cleaned the room. Only then did she begin with the most imperatively necessary first step—making certain that every one of the letter writers remained firmly entrenched in England.

Digging a packet of paper, quills, and ink from her school supply trunk, she wrote two sets of similar letters to the four men. Only in the one to Aunt Margaret would she tell a part of the truth; Anne knew her aunt too well to expect gullibility for a network of partial lies. The men, she reasoned accurately, would be relieved enough not to question her blatant disregard for accuracy. The first four letters all began with the reassurance that her marriage was intact and continuing in Boston and included a brief description of the happier days aboard ship. The three to her father, father-in-law, and grandfather she ended with a brief announcement of eventual motherhood sometime in the vague area of early spring. "I haven't told Gilbert yet," she wrote truthfully, "because he's worried about getting settled in Boston." Caustically she hoped he was worried about a hundred other problems as well. "And I don't intend to tell him for months; so I'd appreciate your not mentioning the event in your letters to us." In the missive to Lord Brownwell she added an additional request that he not tell his wife about the child. "I'm afraid she might feel it her duty to come to Boston," she wrote mendaciously. The only duty Suzanne Brownwell would feel, Anne knew with spiteful certainty, would be to rescue her own son from the catastrophe of fatherhood.

In the letter to Harold she substituted the mention of the child with a copious expression of gratitude for the three thoroughbred horses—carefully she had erased the word *two* and replaced it with the original number. Again the acrid memory of her husband's selfishness momentarily blotted out reasonable thought. He must have gambled the money he'd received for selling her mare as well as the other eleven hundred and fifty-three pounds.

Omitting Harold from the second set of letters, she fabricated even more untruths, reminding these three relatives first that she didn't want Gilbert to know about the child—not yet, at any rate. "He doesn't like Boston and he's restless. I think he'd have preferred Australia." After a brief description of the Perkinses' home and the families who lived in it, she dated the letters a month in advance and stored them in her school trunk. In two months, she promised herself, she'd write another set of letters to these three men, announcing that Gilbert, still unaware of the existence of his child, had gone to Australia to locate a permanent home for both of them while she remained in Boston. Perhaps she might tell her father and grandfather in that letter that the separation was permanent, but not Lord Brownwell. Even in her present resentful mood, Anne didn't really want Gilbert disinherited as his father had threatened. "Someday he might grow up," she whispered soundlessly, a sudden sweet memory pushing out all other thought.

Restlessly she walked over to the window and pushed aside the bleached muslin curtains. "I have no time for memories," she reminded herself sharply. "There's no knight in shining armor in my life. There's only me, if I want to avoid another eighteen years of being pitied. Me and Andrew Grey," she added. Her letter to Aunt Margaret was four pages long and began with the admission, "Gilbert left me in Bermuda" —just the simple fact, no details about the theft of the gold coins or the beating she'd received. "I intend to remain in Boston," she continued, "and take care of your investment. Because I'm expecting a child in spring, I couldn't face another ocean voyage for years."

Recklessly gambling on her aunt's own cynicism about male domination, Anne described her plans in detail—the refusal of Perkins and Bouvier to hire her, the creation of Anne and Andrew Grey, and her intention of becoming financially independent. Only at the last sentence did she remember to warn her aunt of the lies she'd told her other relatives. "They wouldn't understand, Aunt M, and this is something I must do alone."

It was midafternoon before she emerged from the bedroom with the five letters she wished to send. "Does America have letter post?" she asked Maude.

"Land sakes, yes, but you don't have to use it. The *Belle* leaves for England next week."

"I'd like them to go on a faster ship, if possible."

Lynette smiled. "I don't blame you. It is what Papa might do that worries you, *n'est-ce pas?*"

"Yes, I don't want him here."

"Then we send on a clipper ship. They go so much more like the wind. I'll drive you there."

"That won't be necessary. I can use one of my horses, if they've been taken off the ship already."

"Those poor critters can't be ridden for a week," Maude told her, "so you'll have to let Lynette drive you."

Sighing in resignation, Anne asked one last question. "I'll need some of my money for the expense. Did Captain Perkins leave a blue sack anywhere around?"

"No, Anne, he didn't. He put your gold coins in the bank this morning where they'll be safe. And don't frown at me.

You can get your money out just as soon as I introduce you to Wally Stanton. He isn't exactly a trusting man. Lynette will pay the shipping cost this time. Now go along and stop worrying."

With nothing else to do, the visitor accepted the well-meant advice and in the next three hours became an optimistic American without seeing one bit of the beauty of Boston. Lynette drove only along the bustling, dirty, crowded waterfront that stretched for miles along south bay, Boston Harbor, and the wide-mouthed Charles River. An expert driver, the Frenchwoman was not flustered by the raucous traffic of hand-drawn carts, heavy dray wagons, fancy carriage rigs, and impatient men on horseback. Calmly she urged her plodding horse along without interrupting the flow of talk. As a guide Lynette seemed to sense that her passenger's interest was more than casual, especially when she parked in front of the McKay docks where a sailing vessel was being loaded.

Not in Dover or Le Havre harbors had Anne seen a ship like this one. It was long and narrow and rode low in the water. On the almost flush decks there was only a half-buried wheelhouse, and the ship's bowsprit was not angled sharply upward as on the *Boston Queen* but seemed almost parallel to the water. Towering in the air were three square-rigged masts with so many rigging lines and reefed sails that Anne couldn't imagine anyone walking on the deck.

"It's a clipper ship, Anne," Lynette informed her, "the fastest ship in the world. But don't tell Paul or Tom that I bring you here. They hate them."

"Why, if they're faster?"

"It is perhaps because Mr. McKay builds them, but I don't think so. My Paul says they're the devil on men. His brother is captain of one in France, so Paul has sailed on them. But who knows? We go aboard, yes?" At Anne's eager nod, Lynette called to the man watching them from the deck.

"Jean, you leave tomorrow for Liverpool? You will carry letters for us?"

"Delighted to, Lynette. Paul know you're here doing business with the enemy?"

"Non, Jean Reeves, Paul does not."

The man laughed as he eyed Anne appreciatively. "Who's your friend, Lynette?"

"Anne Brow—"

"Mrs. Grey, sir," Anne interrupted quickly.

Minutes later aboard the ship, while Lynette went below with the letters, the captain asked politely, "Are you in America with your husband, Mrs. Grey?"

"No, Captain Reeves, my husband is dead." She took a deep breath and added, "I'm going to live in Boston with my younger brother Andrew, and he'll be looking for a job in shipping."

"Is he a seaman, ma'am?"

"No, he's a bookkeeper, but he does know something about shipping. Our grandfather is a shipbuilder in England, and Andy has helped keep the books for years."

"And you'll be wanting me to recommend him for a job with Donald McKay?"

"Yes. You won't regret it, Captain. My brother is a hard worker."

Long after Anne and Lynette had started the return drive, the Frenchwoman maintained a stiff silence. Finally she pulled to a stop along the turn-in road to the Perkins house and asked sharply, "This brother of yours, he is perhaps invisible?"

"Andrew will be along in a few days," Anne answered, her heart pounding, "or he will be if you'll help me find a house of my own."

"Paul, he will not permit it, Anne. Last night he say you need much consolation. That I do not believe. But he say not one word about this brother."

"He doesn't know about Andrew, nor does Captain Perkins."

However, Maude Perkins, at least, had gained an inkling of Andrew's existence. Disturbed about what she considered was an obsessive suspicion on the part of her young guest, she'd frankly gone to Anne's room to find out what "cock-burr was scratching the girl's thin hide." From one trunk she'd removed the wrinkled dresses, cloaks, and feminine accessories; in the second one she'd found a confusing jumble of boots, scraps of fabric, and a motley assortment of hand-sewn men's garments.

"Anne," she asked bluntly as the younger women entered the kitchen upon her return home, "did you bring some of your husband's things with you? I found some men's clothes in one of your trunks." The shrewd New Englander knew that such was not the case; she was too expert a seamstress not to recognize an unprofessional job of tailoring.

"Those things belong to my brother," Anne gasped and then became coldly polite. "I wish you hadn't touched my things, Mrs. Perkins. Tomorrow after you've introduced me to your banker, I'll locate a house in Boston and not trouble you again."

"You'll do nothing of the kind. And you have no brother. Anne, I've received two letters from your aunt. She wanted to be sure that some woman was looking out for you even if your husband had turned out to be a decent man."

Realizing that any more lies would be a waste of time, Anne became the aggressor. "Did my aunt tell you that I was a good bookkeeper, Mrs. Perkins?"

"She sure did and Tom said you did a dang smart job on our books."

"Did your husband mention the fact that he refused to give me a job at the shipyards?"

"Nope, he didn't tell me that, but he did say he wanted you to do them here at home."

"I'd rather be laughed at in public than shunted away and be hidden in private like some two-headed freak, Mrs. Perkins."

"Best call me Maude, since we're down to 'druthers,' Anne."

"How tall are you, Maude?"

"Taller than most, I reckon."

"But you're still shorter than your husband, who is five

inches shorter than I am. On the waterfront today I counted fewer than a dozen men who were as tall as I. So would you give me one good reason why I can't work at the shipyards?''

Lynette's sardonic chuckle interrupted the conversation. "Me, I can give you two. Paul and Tom. They're men, *chérie*. For them, women have only one proper place. Ten years ago when I first come to this country, I, too, have the idea to work. In France I sell gloves to fat mesdames for little money. In America I think I will earn more. But on the ship I fall in love with Paul and he say, 'No work, Lynette, my wife will not work.' What he means for me is that his woman will not work. I object, but it does no good so I stay home and do servant work. He is as *obstiné* as—as Poor Sam was.''

"Poor Sam was an old mule we used to have, Anne"—Maude smiled—"but Lynette's right about Paul and Tom and I 'spect about the lot of men in Boston. She's right about what they order their womenfolk to do, and it's mighty hard sometimes to be downright happy about those orders. Before Lynette came to live with us, I used to go half-crazy without someone to talk to way out here. Once I took a job working as scrubwoman in a hotel just to be with other people. That's the only time Tom ever lost his temper with me. Men just don't like women competing with them, I reckon.''

"No, they don't, and they pretend that they're thinking of our welfare just like Captain Perkins did when I asked him for a job. But I don't have a husband, so I can do what I want to do,'' Anne declared.

"I think you'd better tell us what you're planning to do, Anne, if you want Lynette and me to help you. That passel of men's clothes you got hid away won't do the job, if it's what I think it is,'' Maude scoffed.

Aghast at the accurate discernment of the older woman, Anne evaded a direct answer. "I'm not sure yet.''

"Why in thunder then are you so dead set on working? You could live here without doing a lick.''

Anne laughed hopelessly. "I could live with my aunt and do nothing but teach in a protected little school, or with my father, or grandfather, and probably with my father-in-law, too. And I'd be exactly what I always was—a woman who was too tall and who had an even worse disadvantage. Since my aunt has written to you, Maude, you probably know that I was illegitimate, and everyone knew that I was. Over here I don't think anyone will care; that is, if I can become a respected worker. So one way or another I'm going to work.''

Maude nodded. "Go get those britches on, Anne. Let's see if you've got any chance of fooling people.''

The young girl was shaking by the time she reached her room to take the first realistic step toward reaching her goal. During the twenty minutes it took her to change, the other two women exchanged some pithy comments.

"Durn fool men. Tom said her father and grandfather paid a passel of money for a no-good husband and then sent that young-'un off without any protection. Only the aunt's got a lick of sense. And you have to admit, the aunt's investment will most likely save the company. Anne's got good sense, too. Imagine recovering from the beating she took and the desertion of that scamp both, and still having the grit to fight. Will you be willing to help her, Lynette?''

"*Oui*, but I think we have one big job to do. The clothes will be no *problème*. She is tall like a man already and she have the small hips and long legs. But *oh là là*, she is so much the lovely lady! Jean Reeves almost fall on his face with the flattery today. Her husband was one big fool.''

"It'll mean lying to our men.''

Lynette chuckled. "So? Paul, he has lied to me. He always say, 'With a man, it is different.' I think, Maude, we spit in their eye this time, yes?''

"I don't want your children to hear us lie, though. When do they get home from school next?''

"We have the time, *chérie*.''

Time was what it took for the transformation. As Lynette had predicted, the externals were simple to arrange. One shopping trip into Boston stores and Anne possessed two well-cut men's jackets, three pairs of breeches, shirts, ties, and a heavy work coat. The hair took only hours to cut, and braiding the long shorn lengths into a coronet a few more. But learning to walk, sit, and think like a man took a grim two weeks. Lynette was a merciless monitor; her sharp eye noticed every feminine mince, every ladylike gesture, and every womanly flinch. If Anne giggled rather than laughed when she heard a crude story, the Frenchwoman scolded her. If she mounted a horse the wrong way, Lynette slapped her derrière or slapped her hand, if it gestured too daintily.

"Andrew Grey is a *poli jeune homme,* not a *joli homme* with a *problème.* You must think like a man or other men will ridicule you for being the wrong kind of man."

While Lynette worried about attitudes, Maude undertook more basic changes. "Your voice is good, but don't make it so pretty. Never heard a young English pup who didn't squeak a little. And don't have such good manners when you eat. Use your napkin to wipe, not to dab your face. And for goodness sake, take bigger bites. Better stick your nose up a little higher. Americans expect limeys to act conceited."

Each evening a tired trio of women served dinner for Paul and Tom; and for two hours afterward, Anne and Maude did the bookkeeping. The older woman had to restrain herself from making a sharp rejoinder every time her husband repeated his nightly speech. "Now, Annie, isn't this better than working with a lot of rough men?"

In the flickering lamplight the girl strained her eyes and concentrated on the columns of figures. Not once did she mention that she thought the men were lax about the way they handled money or the fact that they were too slow in locating buyers.

On the day Lynette pronounced Andrew Grey full-fledged, Anne waited until the men departed, kissed the two women who had helped her, and mounted her horse. With a definite plan in mind, she stopped first at the Donald McKay Shipping Company and applied for a job as bookkeeper. The manager nodded his approval of the smartly dressed young Englishman.

"Captain Reeves recommended that I apply here," Anne said in a pleasantly low voice.

"You're the one who's kept books for an English company?"

"Yes, sir. I've worked on the books with one of the partners for several years." Aunt Margaret would be vastly amused, Anne thought, if she could hear this conversation.

"You sound educated. How many years did you attend school?"

"Ten years." Lies were a matter of interpretation, after all.

"Well, we're expanding here, so I imagine we can put you to work. If you're any good with mathematics, we can try you at figuring out product costs. Ever been through a shipyard before?"

"No, sir, but I'd like to see this one. And I'd appreciate all the printed material on McKay clipper ships you have available."

"All right, young fellow, I'll gather it up while you tour the place with one of the plant men. If you're interested in the job, come back in a week and we'll start you off."

Two hours later the same young "Englishman" tied his horse in front of Perkins, Bouvier and Gray Shipyards and walked past twenty men working around drafting tables in the office without attracting any special attention. At the foreman's desk Anne halted and again asked for a bookkeeping job.

"Captain Perkins's wife usually does them, but I know she wants to be shut of the job. Besides, it'd be better if they were done right here on the premises. Know anything about shipping, lad?"

"Yes, sir," she answered, "happens I do know a little. But I know a lot more about bookkeeping."

"Let's give you a try. Used to be the bookkeeper here myself, so I'll know if you get the books out of whack. Let's find you a quiet place to work." Anne had already spotted a table behind a partition that was hidden from the view of anyone in the upstairs captains' offices. Leading the foreman there, she stood politely aside as he spread the books out in front of her. Two hours later she walked over to his desk and announced that they were all posted.

A cautious Yankee, his eyebrow raised skeptically. "Mighty speedy work, son, to finish that fast with a strange set of books. Let's check on what you've done." Anne was amused to watch him audit her figures, carefully licking the tip of his pencil after each column. Puzzled at finding no error in her work, he asked her to re-do the columns after he erased her earlier computations. As he watched her add with a speed that dwarfed his own, she was officially offered the job she'd been doing for weeks. When she asked for a tour of the yards, the foreman himself acted as guide. While she was impressed by the general friendliness of the men she met, she realized that the McKay organization was more efficient. Before she left that first night, she made a long list of the comparisons she'd observed.

Arriving at the Perkins home half an hour before Tom and Paul, she rushed to her room, where Lynette helped her revert back to a woman. With the braids neatly pinned around her cropped hair, she was on time to greet an apologetic Captain Perkins.

"I'm sorry, Annie, but the office foreman hired a bookkeeper today. I know I should have informed him that you were already doing the job, but I didn't. And now there's no way I can fire the new man without cause."

Anne nodded and turned away, keeping her face averted when Paul added a jovial comment. "Anne will soon find things to do; she's going to be very busy in a few months from now after she returns home." Her conscience at the moment was free from even the slightest twinge of guilt.

Within two weeks she had become an accepted member of the office workers and an invaluable assistant to the foreman. Because the books themselves required only a part of the day, she was free to run his errands; and in doing so, she learned a good deal about the business. She discovered that the company had almost been destroyed financially when the sale of the four ships just now being completed had been canceled. The owner of the Portland, Maine, company who had ordered them had been lost at sea in a North Atlantic storm. Now those ships were being offered for sale on the open market. It was the head draftsman who alerted her to the fact that the "open market" was rapidly being closed to everything but the faster clipper ships.

"McKay has a virtual monopoly in these parts," he asserted sadly.

"Why?"

"Speed. The clipper outruns our ships in less than half the time. Our hull speed is seven knots, the McKay clipper is seventeen. At top speed it takes us twenty days to reach England. The clipper can do it in fewer than eight. We've lost the mail contracts and most of the perishable cargo business."

"Then shouldn't we build a faster ship?"

"First we'd have to rebuild half our equipment. It's the hull design, Andy. The clipper's almost a double-ender with a small transom aft and a narrow beam even at midship. Our modified frigate has a wide curved transom high out of the water and a wide beam. McKay's and our ships are both about a hundred and sixty feet long, but our beam is forty-two feet, his is only twenty-seven."

"Can we carry more cargo?"

"Four times more, and our accommodations for passengers are more comfortable. Because we're slower, we handle better in harbors and our cargo arrives in better shape. We've other advantages, too. We only need half the number of crew because we don't carry all that canvas the clipper does. There's no doubt the clipper is superior on the long hauls through Magellan Strait and across the Pacific, but we're probably more efficient on the Atlantic."

"According to all that, we could charge less for cargo."

"Never thought of it before, but I reckon you're right."

Anne returned to her table and spread out all the material she had on McKay clipper ships. The first problem, she decided, was to compile an advertisement for Perkins, Bouvier and Gray frigates that would compete with the one McKay used for his clippers. The second job would be to send it to every Atlantic Ocean shipping firm on America's East Coast.

With the enthusiastic help of the head draftsman, who drew the diagrams and checked her statistics, the compilation was complete in four days and in the hands of the office foreman. Anne was amused to hear both men refer to her as "the cracker-smart young limey."

Her amusement ended two days later when she was summoned to the office of captains Perkins and Bouvier. They were studying the papers she'd prepared, and only Paul looked up as she stood quietly by their worktable. His face turned livid with fury when he recognized her.

"You'd better have a damn good explanation of this idiocy," he sputtered and walked around the table to plunk her down on a chair facing his partner.

Tom Perkins's expression had undergone several rapid changes from startled disbelief, to frowning irritation, and finally to amusement. "So you're the 'cracker-smart young limey bookkeeper.'" He smiled wryly. "I should have guessed."

If anything, Paul's anger had increased. "There's not a damn thing to laugh about. This fool girl is Margaret Gray's niece. Our new partner would not approve of this ridiculous charade."

"I've already written every detail to my aunt, and I think the only thing she's going to be angry about is that you refused to employ me as a woman."

Paul glared at her. "We still refuse, so now you can get home and take those breeches off and put back on the clothes of a woman."

Defiantly Anne shook her head. "I won't do it. I'll get me a job somewhere else."

Noting her increased determination, Tom asked quietly, "Have you already been offered a job with another company?"

"Yes, I have."

"Annie, I wish you'd spoken to Paul and me before you went to all this trouble. There's no need for you to work at all. Your aunt sent ten thousand pounds over to America just for your support. It's safely banked for you here in Boston."

As pleasant as this piece of news was, her reaction to it

was not one of relief or resignation. "My father and grandfather wasted almost four times that amount to buy me a husband, and I intend to earn ten times more than they spent. The ten thousand is only a start."

Perkins's patience was not inexhaustible. "That's up to you. But Paul's right about you working here. The men wouldn't stand for it."

"The men," she responded acidly, "have been standing for it during the past two weeks without a shred of suspicion. I've gone on errands to every corner of these yards and not once did anyone treat me as anything but a young man."

"Nevertheless—" Tom began, only to be interrupted by a slashing attack.

"Nevertheless nothing. In those two weeks I found out why Donald McKay sells his ships and you don't. The only part of this company that has been profitable in the last three years is your Atlantic cargo fleet. Yet those five ships use only half of the men you employ. So far you don't have one customer for the four new ships you're building, and you won't unless you tell customers about the advantages your frigates have over clippers. Did you read those papers I helped prepare?"

Tom nodded reluctantly. "Where did you get the idea for them?"

"I went through the McKay shipyards, and I was given a copy of their advertisement. So I wrote one like it for our product."

Smiling at her use of "our," Tom asked, "Do you like 'our product' better than McKay's?"

Embarrassed by his tone of mild ridicule, she admitted her ignorance. "I don't know enough to compare them, really. It just seems to me that they have different purposes. But I do know," she added more firmly, "that I want to work here, and I want to invest that ten thousand pounds in this company for ten percent of the ownership. I'd work without wages until we start to show a profit."

The older captain stared at her before he made some rapid

calculations on paper. "Ten's too high, but I might consider eight percent and a salary. Tell me, what would you recommend we do with the extra capital?"

"Send that advertisement to every shipping company on the list and then start two more ships on the unused launching rails."

Tom turned to his partner. "What do you think, Paul?"

"I say no. Having a woman working here is, for me, not good."

"Think back, Paul. She's right about our profits and I believe this plan of hers will work."

"I don't give a damn."

"Yes, you do. Besides, I'm thinking about what Anne will do if we turn her offer down. She'd make the same one to McKay, and I'd sure rather have her with us than on his side. Paul, why don't you talk to her while I check some of these statistics downstairs."

As the only conciliatory person left in the room, Anne faced the glowering Frenchman with uncertainty. "Paul, why do you—"

"Why do I object? Because I'm the only one who knows about the special reason that makes this plan of yours insane. What will this Andrew Grey say when his belly becomes swollen with a child?"

Flushing at the crude reminder, she mumbled unsteadily, "I promise to leave before that time." The only response she received was a shrug; but when Tom Perkins returned, the younger partner withdrew his objection.

"Good, but before we sign any contract with our new partner, Paul, she has to promise to continue living with Maude and me for her own protection. Agreed, Anne?"

"Agreed, Captain Perkins"—she grinned triumphantly—"but you'd better call me Andrew here at the yards."

Anne was laughing by the time she finally left the office, the proud owner of eight percent of Perkins, Bouvier and Gray; Paul, however, was still resentful of the intrusion of a woman into his securely male world.

Moreover, he was furious with Lynette for her part in the deception. For once, though, the good-natured mother of his beloved children had her say. "Monsieur Bouvier, you are not my husband, so you cannot order me to do, poof, what you want." When she felt Paul stiffen beside her, Lynette chuckled and snuggled closer. "*Chéri*, this girl has no chance unless she does this thing. She has not a good man like you; she has only sad memories at night."

Although his antagonism remained intact for another two months, he was forced to admit grudgingly that "Andrew Grey" was an excellent worker; but not until a near catastrophe occurred did he finally concede that she was also an essential member of the firm. He was supervising the launching of a completed hull when one of the forward launch rails buckled. As Paul screamed for the men manning the great log brakes to hold, a crew raced out from the sidelines with a replacement rail. In five minutes the system was operable again, and the straining men released the brakes slowly so the hull could complete its slide into the water. Never before had there been a standby rail crew on the site. When Paul checked the equipment list, he found the main list signed by the foreman; but beneath that signature was an additional list with the rail and the crew on it. That one was initialed A. G. At supper that night he asked her why she had added the extras.

Anne answered enthusiastically, "One day I timed the men sent to get replacement parts after a job was started. They wasted thirty minutes running to the supply barn and back. We can't afford the delay." Anne was not aware of the look the captains exchanged, nor of Paul's raised eyebrow and faint smile of approval. Human lives may have been saved this day because one observant young worker had taken the precautions that more experienced men, including himself, had overlooked. She was not, he concluded, an ordinary woman.

As the months passed, he almost forgot that she was a woman at all; and he began to doubt his own diagnosis of her condition. Her belly did not swell, as he'd predicted it would and as he vigilantly expected it to do. She continued to work twelve hours a day with an energy that defied his experience with breeding females. Watching her ever-increasing rapport with other workers, Paul shook his head in consternation; in this respect, too, she was unusual. He'd never known a woman to listen with such intent interest to the complaints of carpenters or the suggestions of draftsmen without showing restless boredom. But he quickly learned not to ignore the ideas for improvement she submitted to him or Tom. More of a seaman than a businessman, Paul was impressed by her inventive practicality, never more so than on those days when the first of the potential customers began to arrive at the shipyards in answer to the advertisement sent them. "Andrew Grey" had cataloged every man according to particular shipping interests. The material she handed the senior partners was carefully tailored for the precise nature of the cargo that was usually transported by the shipper making the inquiries. When the polite bookkeeper was asked a direct question during these conferences, the statistics Andy gave were accurate—so was the subtle persuasion buried within those statistics. Paul grinned appreciatively at her technique—it reminded him of the high-pressure tactics he occasionally used to sell cargo space.

For the most part, Anne was so engrossed in the pursuit of success for the company and herself that she lost all sense of her own identity while she worked. Meeting each challenge as it came and looking unceasingly for new ones became such an all-consuming drive that she had no time for remembering the past or worrying about the future. She ate breakfast and supper in her workclothes and slept ten hours in dreamless exhaustion. Frequently she even forgot her advancing condition while at home. The height she'd always hated became her greatest ally, and she remained largely unaware of bodily changes. At five or six months—she wasn't certain which—a slight bulge necessitated her changing into the looser breeches; but since the cold Massachusetts weather made the use of a large winter coat mandatory, she appeared no different even to

Paul's critical eye. No longer wearing any of the fitted dresses in her wardrobe, Anne herself was largely unaware of the extent of her altered waistline. Having never observed any childbearing women enough to know what the usual expectations were, she was convinced she was following a completely normal pattern.

In early January a blizzard blanketed Boston with impenetrable drifts of snow, and the shipyards, like most other businesses, shut down for a week. It was during that idle week at the Perkinses' home that Anne made her announcement—not voluntarily, but in reply to an innocent comment of Maude's.

"I declare, Anne, I don't see how with all the hard work you do, but you're actually plumping up."

For Anne the shock of discovery was only momentary; her sense of humor resurfaced with a buoyancy that aroused her laughter. "I don't doubt it, Maude, I'm going to have a child sometime in March." The silence that greeted the news amused her almost as much as Maude's remark. Because he had not been the one to notice, Paul was defensive. Lynette, who had been vaguely suspicious for weeks, was relieved, while Maude was delighted—once she stopped saying, "I don't believe it; I declare, it isn't possible."

Only Tom Perkins appreciated the humor of the situation. "You're a young devil, Andrew Grey." He laughed. "And just how were you planning on proclaiming this miracle to the men?"

"Andy's going back to England to see his family, while his sister remains in America." She grinned. "But Andy will be back, Tom Perkins, so don't you dare hire another bookkeeper. I can do all of my work right here at the house."

The first two weeks of Anne's enforced retirement were almost pleasant and certainly as busy for her as working at the shipyards. On one of the shopping excursions to Boston, Lynette took her to see the midwife who'd delivered her own children six and eight years earlier. Experienced by twenty years in the demanding profession of birthing live infants, the woman poked and prodded Anne for twenty minutes before she asked, "Are you sure about a March delivery?"

Her patient nodded. "My husband died in July."

"To be on the safe side, then, I think you'd better plan on hiring a wet nurse in advance, even though you'll probably want to feed the child yourself."

Reality crashed abruptly into Anne's consciousness; for once her "planning" mechanism had gone awry. Not once had she thought about her child as an ordinary human being with the human needs for food, clothing, and constant care.

"Can you recommend a good nurse?"

"Is your home large enough to give the woman and her own child house space?"

"It will be," Anne promised as she left the small infirmary with the name of three young Irishwomen who had been pronounced healthy and nonalcoholic by the midwife. During the crush of the next two shopping tours, Anne and Lynette managed to find two of the young mothers, whose own infants were still so tiny Anne was afraid to touch either child.

"You are, I think, a most unusual mama, Anne." Lynette laughed. "You are not so much afraid of anything as you are of one small *bébé. Don't worry, chérie,* you will learn."

But Anne knew that she would have to learn far more than most mothers. She was the one who must earn the living; and while she was working, one of the pretty Irishwomen she'd just met would share the task of motherhood. The day after the final shopping tour, which had deposited mounds of infant clothing and equipment in the large room next to hers, she went for a lonely walk. Worriedly Maude offered to accompany her, but Anne needed time alone to think.

"I just want to check on my horses and go look at that old barn. It seems so lonely standing there by itself."

"If you want to go inside, you'll need keys. Tom's grandfather was a suspicious old coot. Don't try walking up the stairs in that old eyesore, Anne; leastways not until someone's along with you."

It wasn't that she didn't enjoy the company of Lynette and Maude; it was the overwhelming sense of responsibility she'd felt since her talk with the midwife. Her child needed the security of a home, not just the borrowed rooms that had sheltered the mother. There was no Aunt Margaret here or father or grandfather to contribute the love that would be necessary; there was only one lonely woman without a home at all. Just when she'd first considered the barn as a possibility, she wasn't sure; but the sight of it had intrigued her for the months she'd been in America.

For a fraction of a moment, Anne experienced a stab of nostalgia as she looked up at the weather-beaten building; she could almost see the ancient oak tree that had sheltered her girlhood home in England. "Grayhaven," she murmured aloud as she mounted the stairs and unlocked the two oak doors that were more the doors of a home than those of a barn. Inside, her first impression was one of warmth; and not until she'd taken a dozen steps did she realize that no barn floor she'd ever seen before was decked with ship's timbers. It isn't even a barn, she thought, it's . . . what? She knew as soon as she saw the two smoothed-out wood tables with sawhorse legs. "It's a drafting room," she murmured aloud again and sat down on one of the stools to look around her. Supported by rows of heavy posts at either end of the structure were two wide lofts, not open barn lofts for hay storage, but neatly walled lofts with railinged stairs leading to each side.

But it was the two-story-high open room she was sitting in that reminded Anne of England. Even the great black wood-burning heating stove with the round pipe that extended upward through the roof made it feel like home to her. It was the windows, she decided, the narrowed lead-paned windows that were most like Grayhaven—and so many of them, the light poured into every corner. Within these walls a child could develop a sense of belonging. Anne jerked when Maude's voice interrupted her reverie.

"I always get to dreaming whenever I come here, too, Anne," the older woman said quietly.

"It's a beautiful place."

"An expensive one, at any rate. Even when it was first built to house sheep, it was no ordinary barn."

"Who turned it into a drafting room?"

"Tom's grandfather. He'd built more than a hundred ships at the yards. Proud ships that outfought the British, but old Tom always dreamed of designing a new kind of ship. When his son took over the yards, the father rebuilt this place. Wasted ship's timbers by the wagonful, and kept ship's carpenters busy for over a year putting in those costly windows and stuffing the walls with oakum before he covered them with wood. That was before my time, but folks in Boston still call this place 'old Tom's folly.'"

"What's upstairs, Maude?"

"Bedrooms and such. When the old man died, my Tom's father tried to get some return on the money wasted by renting rooms to bachelor yard workers. Didn't work, though, too far from girls and pubs for the young bucks. So it's stood empty now for twenty years." The older woman paused and looked keenly at her companion. "Anne, if you're worried that your child won't be welcome at our home, I want you to know, you're dead wrong. Paul broke my heart last year when he took his two away and plunked them in some durned school in Connecticut."

"I wondered why they were home so seldom."

"He didn't want people knowing they weren't altogether legal. As if that's near as important as giving them love. I never had any of my own; but Lynette, bless her, let me share the two tykes she birthed. And now if it's all right with you, I'll have still another to fuss over and love. Let's go home, Anne, we've got to get that nursery ready. One more thing, young lady, Tom's almost as excited as I am about your child."

The tears streamed down Anne's face in gratitude to this generous woman next to her and to another generous, childless

woman three thousand miles away. Together they had given
her a family to belong to, to share with, and to love. Her
child would have more people to love than just one unusual
mother who would leave him each day and go to work
dressed as a man.

Four weeks later Maude's promise of a family became a
warm reality. Early in the evening Anne felt her first sharp labor
pain, and every member of the household rushed to aid her.
Home from school, the Bouvier children retired round-eyed to
their bedrooms, their father raced to fetch the midwife, and
Lynette took over in the birthing room. Captain Perkins and his
excited wife quietly paced the floor. Three hours later, only half
an hour after the midwife arrived, Anne produced a long, skinny
manchild, and a breathless few minutes later an equally long,
skinny little girl. Aroused from the stupor of exhaustion, the
young mother whispered, "My God!" before she fell asleep.

In the morning she awakened to a chaotic world of two
nurseries containing four infants and the two Irish mothers
contacted weeks before. Anne lay in her immaculate bed,
afraid to open her eyes until Lynette's chuckle forced her to
accept the reality of her nightmare.

"*Deux bébé, chérie;* for you one is not enough. My Paul
say, '*Mon dieu,* even in motherhood this Anne Grey is not
content to be an ordinary woman.' "

Chapter 11

HER first year of motherhood began with another
Anne Grey gesture of defiance against the established role of
a woman—she didn't produce a drop of milk. As she lay in

bed recuperating during the first few days, she watched in dismay the enormous amount of care two small bodies needed and the work she'd delegated to other women. For the first week Maude remained stationed at the cooking stove boiling hot water for washing and cooking mush as a supplementary food for the older infants of Katie and Mary. Determined not to be a burden herself, Anne ignored the midwife's stern command to remain in bed for ten days and was up in three, submitting to the discomfort of the tightly wrapped binding clothes without complaint. Strongly muscled by months of hard work at the shipyards, her body quickly regained its resiliency, and she was able to relieve the others in the endless chore of "toting" items to and from the nursery.

But not until she solved the problem of Maude's overworking could Anne relax enough to enjoy motherhood. With Lynette's help she turned one of the unused rooms in her wing into a washroom. There, on top of the wood heating stove, hot water bubbled most of the day, and nappies were washed at regular intervals and hung to dry. Just as she had at the shipyards, Anne organized a work schedule for the two young nurses that reduced the chaos in the main house to an almost normal level—so much so that a worried Maude came to investigate.

"Land sakes, Anne," she remonstrated, "I didn't mind the work. It made me feel useful."

Grinning at the older woman, the young mother led her to a rocking chair in the large nursery room and placed an infant in her arms. "As resident grandmother," she announced, "you'll be very useful." Maude quickly became adept at soothing whichever child was crying, and the noise was reduced enough for Anne herself to become a practicing mother.

On the day the twins finally opened their eyes with the serious intent of seeing the world they had been unceremoniously shoved into, she discovered their beauty and their differences. Although both had inherited the pale blond hair of their father, Margaret Maude's eyes were a soft light brown while

Anthony Geoffrey's were as sharply blue as his mother's. Their personalities were also as markedly different. Tony, for such had been the name Anne whispered when first she held him, was the more serious of the two and the less demanding. Almost from the first, he seemed aware of the need to listen, and within months he had begun to articulate sounds that almost seemed like words to a thrilled mother.

For Margaret, an adoring mother was unnecessary. From the first week Tom Perkins had formed a special attachment for this tiny brown-eyed siren that assured her instant attention whenever he was near. Dutifully her first words when she finally articulated them at nine months were "Mama" and "Mary," but her next four were "Tom," "man," "boat," and "up." With a pleased grin Tom would pick her up and hold her, gently at first, and then, in response to her demand for motion, more playfully. It was he who first dubbed the little towhead "Maggie." This odd friendship between a disciplined man of sixty winters and an active infant girl was one of the cohesive forces in the home life of this household of unrelated people.

Just how much a part that relationship played in making this home a permanent one for her, Anne was never able to assess accurately, since the kindly man became fond of all the children in the nursery, not just the little girl who had captured some small strand of his heartstrings. Increasingly aware of the enormity of the disruption her twins had caused, Anne's thoughts returned often to that huge empty barn. It could become a home with a few alterations, and the Perkinses and Bouviers would remain friends and not disgruntled housemates. It was Tom himself who gave her the first opportunity to broach the subject. He'd just tucked the six-week-old Maggie into her cradle and turned to the young mother.

"Annie, how soon do you think you'll be taking your children to see their family in England?"

She shook her head. "Not for a long, long time."

"You'll have to, Anne."

"Why? I can support them and make my home here in Boston."

He peered at her intently. "I'd like nothing better, and Maude is as happy as a biddy hen to have a brood to mother. But we're borrowing someone else's grandchildren."

"That's just it, Tom. They have too many grandfathers in England, and I wouldn't be allowed to live my own life there. But I don't intend to ruin your home much longer. I plan to make my own home soon and I can tell you exactly where. I want to buy that old barn from you."

"No, Annie, I won't sell it to you. You're too young for that kind of responsibility. We'd all be worried about you, and it'd be too far away for us to be sure the little tykes were safe."

"Then I'll have to rent a home in Boston."

"That would be worse. There're some ugly types living there who could be dangerous. So if you're planning to stay in Boston, I want you right here."

"Are you certain you want all this clutter around?"

"Dead sure."

Brushing the tears from her eyes, she smiled impishly at the man who'd just solved her problem. "In that case, I'll be back on the job tomorrow."

"I'm not saying that you won't be welcome there," he equivocated. "The books have a way of getting behind without you; but you'll be working only part-time in the future. Four hours a day, at most."

"I need the wages for ten hours."

"No, you won't. Your investment should begin to pay dividends."

"That's really Aunt Margaret's investment. Nine hours?"

"Six."

Eventually they compromised on eight, and even then Anne found that many of the jobs she'd assumed earlier had been assigned to other workers, leaving her a much reduced work load. Within two weeks she had brought the books up to current and discovered in the process that the firm of Perkins,

Bouvier and Gray was at capacity production level with a
backlog of six additional orders for new ships and ten for
repairs. All six launching ramps held keels in varying degrees
of completion, and the crew organization she'd initiated
earlier was working at maximum efficiency. It was this
productivity that inspired Paul to question the need for the
continued employment of Andrew Grey at the shipyards.

"You can do the books at home now, Anne," he announced complacently, "so you can stay here with your
children and be the woman again instead of pretending to be
the man."

Tom shook his head stubbornly. "No, she can't, Paul. She
was the one who earned us most of the sales, and she'll be the
one the customers will want to talk to when they come to
check up on us. She knows more about the answers than we
do. Besides, you and I are too busy to take time out."

Thoughtfully that night, Anne contemplated a future without Andrew Grey just in case Paul's decision prevailed over
that of his older partner. She realized that her disguise had
become more vulnerable since the birth of the twins. The
presence of two blond-haired infants in the Perkins home was
difficult to explain, since their "widowed" mother was rarely
in evidence during the day. Keeping the identities of Anne
and Andy separate, she realized, was harder than she'd
anticipated, especially since Paul Bouvier's prejudice had
increased since the birth of the twins. The need, therefore,
she reasoned, was to acquire an alternate source of income.
Once again her thoughts centered on the gray barn, and once
again her inventive mind seized upon a solution. The old
structure would make a splendid private school, which could
be made to support herself and other teachers just as the
original Grayhaven in England had been doing for three
years.

Surreptitiously, to avoid both Tom's and Maude's sharp
eyes, she began to ride over to the barn during her working
hours. Carefully she measured the available space and drew
diagrams as she had for her aunt's manor house. To her

delight the alterations needed proved to be the simpler one of building partitions rather than removing them. After the fifth such visit, she reviewed her own financial situation. Her hoard of gold coins still amounted to more than fourteen hundred dollars, even allowing for another year of wages for the two nurses. With economic planning, she decided, it would be enough for a start; however, she would not be able to purchase the barn now. Somehow she would have to persuade Tom to rent it to her. Her next problem was to determine whether or not Bostonians would send their children to a school run by a young English widow of unknown background. Disguised as Andrew, she cautiously questioned dozens of her contacts along the waterfront—shippers, hardware clerks, store owners, and ship chandlers; every man gave her a like response. Boston schools were in a deplorable state because they were too few in number to accommodate the rapidly increasing hordes of children.

"It's the birth rate, son," one old-time Yankee insisted vindictively. "Furrin people just ain't got the sense to stop having children. Durn fools double theirselves every two years, they do." Anne flinched when she realized that in her eight months in Boston, she had tripled herself.

But the man who convinced her that her plan was feasible was a Scot shipowner. "It's the idea of public schools, lad. People wi' money dinna want t' send their bairns to school wi' street urchins." Anne had the answer she wanted; a private school could be profitable, and she could eventually emerge from hiding and become a respected teacher.

That night she approached Tom with a confident smile. "Tom, I've been thinking about the barn."

"The answer is still the same, Annie. I'm not selling it to you for a home. You've agreed to live here as long as you're in Boston."

"I don't want it for a home, Tom, and I don't want to buy it." She took a deep breath and plunged. "I want to use it on a profit-sharing basis."

He regarded her suspiciously. "Whenever you use that tone

of voice, Annie, it either means more work or more money outlay. Which is it this time?"

"It's neither, at least not for you. I want to rent the barn from you and open a private school there."

Condescendingly now: "What do you know about schools, Annie?"

"I helped start the original Grayhaven in England. All you need is a building, teachers, books, and pupils."

Paul's sarcastic voice chimed in, "And maybe a pencil or two. You have invented a thirty-hour day for all your little jobs: bookkeeping, teaching, and maybe a little something else—like two *enfants?* You are, I think, Anne, becoming a fool about work."

"Oh, no, Paul, I don't intend to teach full-time. Only on two mornings a week. Boys can't really take much more Latin and mathematics than that."

"Anne," warned Tom, "Boston has some strict new laws about schools. You can't even afford the building materials, much less teachers' salaries."

"I think I can," she insisted. "Remember that pile of long lengths of warped lumber you told your yard boss to throw out? Well, I put a hold on it, and I'll pay the drayage on it to the barn. By cutting it into short lengths, there'll be enough to build the partitions. I figured that I could pay two ship's carpenters to work on Sundays. I've also estimated the costs of cutting three more doorways."

"That old barn will need a lot of fixing before it'll be safe enough for children."

"Not as much as Aunt Margaret's home needed in England. The foundation is heavy stone and the floors and roof are sound. Even the steps are sturdy."

Hanging up the dishtowels behind the kitchen stove, Maude joined the argument. "It's a strong enough building to last for another hundred years, Tom, and you know it. And Anne will be a lot better off teaching school than she is gallivanting all over Boston dressed as a man. Even part-time. Besides, she'd have a future there."

Tom's voice was no longer so negative. "Was that what you had in mind, Annie? A permanent future here in Boston?"

Recalled to the imponderable realities of her situation, Anne shook her head slowly. "I'm not sure about my permanent future, Tom. I may want to return to England someday. I just think that a school here will be a good investment for me—for both of us."

"Just how much money do you have to invest?"

"I have over a thousand dollars."

"And where can you get teachers for that kind of money?"

"I think I know where I can find some who'll gamble with me. Will you think about my proposition, Tom?"

With a thoughtful nod, Tom Perkins returned to stirring his coffee; and Anne remained quietly at the table and played with the twins until she heard him clear his throat. She returned the infants to their cradles and waited. Again Tom cleared his throat. "That old building has been unused long enough. Go ahead, Annie. And if—mind you, I said if—you make any money, you can pay me a small amount of rent."

Greyhaven Academy, Boston, took four months to remodel; but when the work was finished, a practical school building was ready for children, and a staff of four full-time teachers were living on the top floor.

Acquiring this staff had been a victory for Anne in all ways, a victory of the spirit as well as the pocketbook. While she was still recuperating from childbirth, she had listened to the two Irish nurses talk about the "turrible" mills. Curiously, because she had never heard of their existence, Anne questioned the two young women. The hated institutions were the New England cotton mills, whose owners sent advertisements to Ireland during each recurrent famine, promising good jobs for anyone who would come to America. Each year thousands of young Irish immigrants fled from hunger and hopeless poverty in their homeland to work for starvation wages in the mills. As a reward for a twelve-to-sixteen-hour workday, they could afford to live only in shanties, where many died of malnutrition by the age of thirty-five.

Anne remembered Paddy and the fine Irish scholars who had come to England to teach and to be treated with contempt by many Englishmen. Because of the perpetual state of national poverty, Irish students were more seriously dedicated than wealthier English ones. They realized early in life that only with an education could they hope to break out of the misery of a ruined economy and find good jobs abroad. Among the thousands of Irish here in Boston, Anne reasoned, there must be some teachers. So, months before the school was ready, she went to see Mrs. Megan Shea, whose daughter Mary was the prettiest of the two nurses hired to tend the twins.

Just how Mrs. Shea broadcast the message throughout shantytown Anne never knew; but the following Sunday twenty applicants showed up in Mrs. Shea's tiny parlor. Anne was sickened by the look of many of them, already ill with consumption from their long hours in unheated mills. When she had finished with the sad job of refusing those and several others she found unsuitable, Anne was left with six potentials. To those six she submitted her proposal; their salaries would begin only after the tuition had been collected. In the meantime they could live at the school, and she would supply their food. Reluctantly two older men refused; their families could not exist even that long without the wages from the mill. But the other four were willing to gamble—one middle-aged woman, one man, and a young couple.

The oldest member of the group, the shrewd, sharp-tongued spinster, had served as governess to a wealthy Boston family for ten years before she was dismissed for her outspoken support of the Irish. "Bostonians treat the Irish with the same regard their forebears held for the Indians," she stated bitterly. Having been well educated in England, Maureen Breena spoke without a trace of brogue; but she was skeptical about Anne's whole idea. "Irish teachers here will never be accepted in Boston. Once parents find out we're Irish, they'll remove their children and ruin the school," she declared emphatically.

Thank God for Paddy, Anne exulted, and proceeded to describe his methods at Grayhaven, England, when faced with even greater prejudice. "We," Anne announced, "are going to become the finest English school in Boston with a staff of English teachers straight from the original Grayhaven."

Maureen Breena looked at this young Englishwoman with an admiration she usually reserved for Irish patriots only and promptly renamed herself Marian Brent. For good measure she added the title Dame before her new name, although she admitted that she needed two additional years of recognized service before the title could become official.

The young couple, whose teaching experience was limited to three years in Belfast before the school there had been closed, agreed to change their names from Shawn and Kathleen O'Brien to John and Catherine Bruce.

The fourth teacher present was the best trained and most bitter of the group. A brilliant Oxford scholar who had been teaching at that university, he'd been fired immediately from his post when his two brothers were arrested and convicted in Ireland for political activity against the crown. Matthew Conway, whose name was ruled to be Anglican enough already, had been in America only two months and had been met with repeated refusals in his applications for teaching jobs. He was eager for this opportunity of demonstrating to Bostonians the difference between a provincial education and a classical one.

Once launched on this shoestring road of deception, Anne found her co-teachers as imaginative and resourceful as she herself. After she had located a shipment of gray wool fabric that had become waterstained in transit, the two other women teachers contacted an Irish tailor, who made them uniforms as stern-looking as early Puritan garb. Inside each jacket, however, he stitched a tiny green shamrock.

In these new uniforms the five "English" teachers began their assault on the entrenched establishments of Boston. Stopping first at the education department in the State House on Beacon Hill, they were greeted by a harried secretary who issued them all the necessary permits with breathtaking speed. The Massachusetts school system had been at crisis level since 1837, when Horace Mann had forced the state legislature to pass a bill guaranteeing free education to all children.

"So far," the secretary affirmed, "we have only enough schools to take care of ten percent of the children; and at the rate the Irish, Poles, and Russians are invading this city, we never will catch up with the demand. The public schools we have are overcrowded, and the private schools are overwhelmed with applicants. Yours will be a welcome addition."

With all of the permits clutched tightly in her hands, Dame Marian nodded her head. "I can understand why private schools are in demand. Imagine how horrified true Bostonians must feel at the idea of their children attending school with uncouth Irish savages." The secretary smiled in agreement; he never heard the subtle sarcasm in her voice.

During the next busy eight hours, John Bruce drove the Perkins's carryall all over Boston making ten necessary stops. The first two were at the free Roxbury Latin School and the private Groton Academy, where the "English visitors" studied the curricula offered and listed the books being used. Next they canvassed the bookstores, seeking an owner who would extend them credit. Only in the fifth shop, Desmond's Book Emporium, did they locate such a man. In return for Greyhaven Academy's insistence that the proposed one hundred students purchase all their books from him, Mr. Desmond would give free copies and reference books to the five teachers.

Having saved the most critically important mission of the day for the last, the five determined educators invaded the newspapers. Without advertisements they could never hope to attract a hundred students by opening day in September. The *Liberator* refused to give them any published space at all, either paid for or not, since its owners had sponsored the campaign for free education. At the *Boston Gazette* the teachers received a cool reception from a bored reporter who accepted their prepared advertisement and Anne's money with little interest. But at the offices of the *Columbian Sentinel*, an angered Dame Marian changed both their approach and their luck. Demanding to speak to the editor, she boldly requested his advice about acquiring pupils with enough academic ability to benefit from a classical English education. Impressed by the haughty demeanor of Marian Brent and by the educational backgrounds of the other four, the editor wrote an enthusiastic news story about the proposed Greyhaven Academy and promptly enrolled his own three children.

It was his story that aroused the interest of more than a hundred eager parents; it was also his story that almost brought disaster to the entire enterprise. One of the readers was the Boston matron who had fired Maureen Breena from the position of governess. Having been unable to replace the excellent and inexpensive Irish governess and having failed to place her four oldest children in any of the famous private schools, Mrs. Wallace Stanton promptly wrote for admission to Greyhaven. When her request was ignored, the aggressive mother arrived in person at the school an hour before official registration was scheduled to begin. She took one look at Dame Marian Brent and exploded into outraged speech.

"This woman is not who she claims to be. She is only an Irish governess whom I fired for incompetence. Furthermore, I denounce this entire school as a fraud."

Until she heard the final word, Anne's heart had pounded sickly with the certain dread of defeat; but the word *fraud* galvanized her to a fighting fury. In a voice as icy and as British as her Aunt Margaret's, Anne addressed Mrs. Stanton. "Just because you feel socially superior to a governess you once employed does not in any way detract from her excellence as a teacher. Dame Marian Brent is precisely what our advertisement said, a woman educated in English colleges who possesses finer credentials than most of the teachers already employed in this provincial city. As for the school, I represent my aunt, Lady Margaret Gray, in its establishment. She is the owner and headmistress of the original Grayhaven in England. If you are challenging my right to do so, Mrs. Stanton, I suggest you write to Lady Gray or to my grandfathers,

Lord Stanley Ashton and Lord Gerald Gray. If those references fail to satisfy you, feel free to contact my lawyer, Mr. John Peabody, in London. In any event I will notify him about you." Only for lack of breath did Anne cease her tirade. For the first time in more than a year, the memory of her own identity had been unleashed; and the old familiar names had rolled off her tongue like an inherited litany. Plain Anne Grey she might be in America, but every word she had uttered during this emotional purge had been the truth; and it was the power of this truth that silenced and cowed Mrs. Stanton into a state of awe.

"Are you also a Lady Grey?" she stammered.

Anne's contempt for the woman was reflected in her smile. "In America? Hardly, since everyone is supposed to be equal here." Turning to the other teachers, Anne asked abruptly, "Dame Brent, are the Stanton children educated enough to qualify them for Greyhaven standards?"

Concealing her triumph, Marian answered gravely, "Since I educated the oldest four, yes. The tuition, Mrs. Stanton, will be three hundred dollars a year for each child."

Anne held her breath; this sum was double what the teachers had decided on the week before. To her amazement, the mother uttered no protest about the amount. Nor did any of the sixty subsequent families whose children were accepted. But one more crisis had to be resolved before Greyhaven could become a reality. The minute the victorious Mrs. Stanton had been driven off in her expensive brougham, Marian broke into laughter.

"Anne Grey, you are more of a blarney artist than any Irishman I know; but for Mrs. Stanton and others like her, you couldn't have thought of a more impressive lie. They all pretend that their ancestors came to America on the *Mayflower*. By tomorrow we'll have our one hundred pupils."

Before Anne could comment, Matthew Conway accused her angrily. "She wasn't lying. She is a bloody English aristocrat, and those names and titles she rattled off are her bloody damned relatives. I'd rather work in the rotten mills than associate with someone like her.''

"Then you'd be a fool, Mr. Conway," Anne bristled. "Those people are my relatives, but the only two who'd admit knowing me are my aunt and one grandfather. You aren't alone in having a problem family. But if it helps us attract more students, why should you care if Mrs. Stanton boasts that I'm related to the royal family?''

"Matthew," Marian reminded him sharply, "none of us here are what we say we are. So let's forget the past and work to make our school successful.''

But Matthew Conway's distrust of Anne continued for another six months until he received a letter from Padric Neill, headmaster of Grayhaven in England. By that time Greyhaven, Boston, had become a financial and academic success.

On opening day in early September, the selected students had walked with alert trepidation along the hard dirt path bordered by white-painted rocks to the double-doored entry of the school. They wore the specified neat gray uniforms made by the recommended Irish tailor, and they carried the required books purchased from Desmond's Book Emporium. They also brought their own lunches. Remembering the largess of hot lunches and horseback riding extended by Aunt Margaret in her Grayhaven, Anne was apprehensive about Dame Marian Brent's parsimonious thrift. But that proud Irishwoman had ten years of resentment to assuage, and she had no intention of giving away one penny in extra service. She was more than Anne's match in her determination to attain financial success.

From the first day of school in September to the last one in June, Greyhaven pupils worked at their plain desks under the supervision of teachers who were unrelenting in their drive to achieve academic recognition for the school. If a pupil proved frivolous or too slow to keep up, he was quietly replaced by another from an increasingly long waiting list. But so excellent was the teaching that none of the surviving students complained about the hard demands placed on them. Anne herself had to work to raise her own teaching standards to the level of her fellow teachers.

Early in its history, Greyhaven became firmly stamped with Dame Brent's severity, lacking completely the informality of its predecessor in England. The only exercise the children had during the eight-hour school day consisted of two running stints on hard dirt paths around the school. If the weather was too cold or the snow too deep, John Bruce led the students through a regimen of calisthenics in the large common room. No other concession was made to childhood's need for fun.

To Anne's consternation, the pupils not only adjusted, they soon became as ambitious as their teachers for success. She found that she had underestimated the intelligence of Americans. They were not the undemanding students of rural England; they wanted a six-year education in four, and their parents drove them to accomplish this miracle.

Financially successful beyond her expectations and expertly supported by teachers who relieved her of all but nominal duties, Anne was soon able to rededicate most of her own energies to the job of making Andrew Grey an indispensable employee at the shipyards. She worried occasionally about the few hours she was able to devote to her children, but they seemed to thrive under the care of their nurses and the indulgence of Maude and Lynette.

As they neared their seventh month, however, a crisis occurred. Within a week of one another the twins stopped nursing, seeking instead the more interesting diet of mush and applesauce. Anne almost panicked the day Katie decided to return to shantytown life and her pub-addicted husband. She worried that Mary might also return to her home, leaving Anne to face the terrors of the nursery alone or to hire an unknown stranger. The timetable of her goal to earn money drove her almost as hard as did her desire to be a good mother.

Anxiously she would arrive home from work each night expecting Mary to be gone. But as the weeks passed and the Irishwoman continued to tend her own small Danny and the twins as placidly as ever, Anne took steps to make the arrangement permanent. She called Mary into her room one night for a "little talk about the future."

To her amazement, Mary broke into tears, and Anne had her first lesson in humility. In eight months of close association with the rosy-cheeked Irish girl, she had never asked about Mary's own life or even what her married name was.

"Mum," the girl sobbed now in Anne's room, "if you could just be seein' yer way of kapin' me on, I'd work for half me wages."

When Anne assured her that a permanent job was just what she had in mind, the nurse sobbed even harder. Intrigued now by the girl's reaction, she began to ask the questions she should have asked months earlier to ease the anxieties of a lonely girl. As the answers came tumbling out, she learned that Mary had never been married and that her little Danny was the product of a brief romance with a light-of-heart Irishman who had promised marriage, but who had blithely skipped away from his promises. Thus a seventeen-year-old girl had become an object of scorn in the Irish Catholic community.

Remembering her own hatred of the terrible word *illegitimate*, Anne became very thoughtful. Since she had based her own new life on lies, she felt no compunction about adding to them. Seeking an ally for her plan, she ruled out Tom and Maude; they would be incapable of such a deception. She contemplated Paul, whom she knew had as little regard for unnecessary truth as she did; but he was away on a voyage. In some trepidation she approached Lynette, all too aware that Lynette's own children lacked legal status. She need not have hesitated; Lynette had already learned all about Mary and approved Anne's plan enthusiastically. She knew all the steps that must be taken. When Anne looked at her in confusion, Lynette laughed.

"With me, it's different. I have Paul. Long ago I decided that such little formalities are unimportant. Mary is not so lucky. She's a good Catholic girl who would die of shame if a priest tells her she is a sinner. Me, I'd spit in his eye. But we will save our little Mary from that priest.''

Three weeks later Lynette handed Mary a white leather folder containing three documents. The first was a marriage certificate dated two years earlier, the second was a birth certificate for Daniel Patrick Harrington, and the third was a newspaper article cut from a New York newspaper. It told of the death of Patrick Harrington in a dockside accident; the part that stated that he had left a young widow had been underlined. When Anne questioned Lynette privately, the Frenchwoman shrugged. ''Paul has many useful friends,'' was all that she would say.

Mary was jubilant. She practiced calling herself Mrs. Harrington with a fine rolling of her *r*'s and hugged her year-old son until he squealed in protest. ''Now,'' she exclaimed, ''I can take me Danny to the church.''

Anne and Lynette looked at one another; here was a complication they had not foreseen. Lynette was certain that Mary would have to undergo confession before Danny could be christened, and neither of the plotters was certain that Mary could be trusted to keep the secret. As tactfully as they could, they coached the young ''widow'' in her ''confession.'' She was, they told her, to admit that she had sinned by not having her son baptized at birth. In that way, they assured her, she would be spared from telling a lie.

On the first sunny Saturday in March, ten passengers crowded into the Perkinses' roomy old carryall. Lynette's nine-year-old son Louis rode between Tom and Maude on the front bench, seven-year-old Lisa rode with Mary and Danny on the middle one, and Anne and Lynette held the twins on the rear bench. They made two stops that day. The first was at a small Catholic church in a new Irish shantytown in North Boston. There, in a solemn ceremony, Daniel Patrick Harrington became a legal Catholic.

The second stop was at the Protestant Episcopal Church of Boston. Here the family procession once more trooped into a church vestry to witness Anthony Geoffrey Brownwell and

Margaret Maude Brownwell being duly baptized and christened. Lisa and Louis watched the priest and later the minister don their impressive robes and chant their holy words over the heads of three thoroughly indifferent infants. For Anne the most touching part of both ceremonies was the serious participation of Tom and Maude Perkins as they promised to serve as godparents for all three children.

That night at supper Tom and Maude insisted that Mary was now an official part of the family. From that time on all three babies—Danny, Anthony, and Margaret—received equal attention from the family members. The only sad note at that otherwise happy meal was Paul's hooded look of pain when Louis asked if he and his sister had also been christened.

Lynette put her arms around her son and daughter and hugged them. "Not yet, *mes enfants,* but when that day comes, oh, how we'll celebrate," she promised.

Glancing up, Anne met Paul's brooding eyes and realized with a shock that the laws that made his and Lynette's life incomplete also shackled her own. That night Paul remained awake for hours huddled at his desk writing letters. In his neat angular French script he sent out messages to all the agencies and lawyers he had commissioned to locate his missing wife, asking them to redouble their efforts to gain him a legal release.

Much later in her room, in desperation Anne, too, wrote letters, because for the first time in eighteen months she dreamed and had awakened in tears. She had at last come full circle, and she remembered the breathless happiness that she had found with her husband for those few short weeks so long ago. She fought the intrusion on her peace of mind with all her strength of will. But whenever she closed her eyes, she could see his face and hear his voice and feel his arms around her. "We belong together, Anne," he'd told her aboard the *Boston Queen.*

Shivering from the cold and from her troubled thoughts, she arose from bed and, groping about in the dark, located all the candles she could find to help dispel her gloom. Sitting at her worktable wrapped in a down comforter, she began to write to the four people who had always helped her overcome self-pity. As she wrote about all the separate parts of her busy life and about the people in America who were her friends, Anne regained her sense of adventure. There were still worlds that she must conquer before she could go home. Sixteen pages of writing and hours later, she sealed the letters to Paddy, Aunt Margaret, her father, and her grandfather before she returned to dreamless sleep.

The best thing about a treadmill existence, she was reminded the next day as she washed her hair and dried the dishes and played with three children on the floor of the nursery, was that it didn't leave much time for sentimental journeys. Her life was full and rich just as it was. She thoroughly enjoyed her style of motherhood, since she rarely had to change a soiled nappy or stuff pudding down an unwilling mouth. Her friendship with Lynette and Mary made up for the years when she had had no young friends at all; and Maude and Tom had become so much a part of her new family consciousness that she could not really imagine a complete life without them. Only with Paul did Anne retain any aloofness. On the nights he remained in the family dining room, she and Mary quietly took the children to their own wing of the house.

Greyhaven Academy helped fill a void by giving her back the opportunity to be a woman in both manners and dress. She even tolerated the growing domination of Dame Marian Brent because it reminded her of Paddy and his drive to make her reach for perfection.

Yet it was through Andrew Grey that she developed a sense of daring. As Andrew, she became a familiar figure along the waterfront as well as in the shipyards. Astride one or the other of her horses, she could locate needed hardware or deliver completed plans to customers. Gradually she came to know both proper and improper Bostonians she could never have met as Anne Grey. It was also as Andrew that she built a modest fortune.

Shortly after the first birthday of her twins, Anne received two letters. One contained a gift from Aunt Margaret of three thousand pounds, a thousand each for Anthony, little Margaret, and herself. Her father's letter contained two thousand pounds for the children. With her now elastic conscience, Anne quickly decided that this providential windfall should be invested as quickly as possible for the benefit of her children's future. To her surprise, both Tom and Paul refused to let her invest another penny in the shipyards. Refused was really too mild a word to describe their reaction to her request. They both roared "No!" in unison.

Tom explained that Anne's past success in expansion had already pushed production beyond his ability to manage, while Paul bluntly told her he now looked forward to his annual captain's stint abroad as a vacation. Both men advised her to look elsewhere for investment possibilities and pushed her firmly out of their office. With the five thousand pounds, which exchanged into twenty five thousand dollars American, Anne began her quest at Desmond's Book Emporium, where she purchased all the books and newspapers she could find on the growing world of stock exchanges. As she read the piles of accumulated material, she began to understand why rich men rarely had to work unless they chose to. She decided to join this elite circle. At night she worked endlessly on charts that mapped the trends of the ever-expanding industrialization of America. By June she had acquired enough knowledge to venture forth.

Elegantly clad in the about-town suit she and Maude had purchased when Andrew Grey was still under construction, Anne invaded the most sacrosanct of all male citadels, the Boston Stock Exchange. At first the somber brokers ignored the tall velvet-coated dandy who stood watching them with a polite but interested expression. However, one middle-aged man noticed that the eyes of the watching youth were not as young as his smooth cheeks, nor as gullible as a lad's should be. Anne walked immediately to that man's desk and carefully noted the name printed on the wall behind him, Charles R. Matthews.

"Mr. Matthews," she announced, "I am Andrew Grey of Grayhaven, England. I want you to assist me in making some American investments."

Such a blunt approach was so unusual in the hush-hush world of finance that Matthews sat up a little straighter and looked a little closer at this client. But, like all cautious men, he hedged. "That all depends on the type of investments you are thinking about, and"—he cleared his throat in the vaguely threatening manner of a judge about to pass sentence—"of course, on the amount of money." Obviously he expected only a few hundred dollars from an investor so young.

At that moment Anne would have liked to wipe the complacency from his face with a deck brush dipped in tar. Instead she maintained the look of a serious young man interested in the advice of his elders and betters.

"For a beginning," she declared modestly, "I would like to invest fifteen thousand dollars in railroads, five thousand in steel, and five thousand in steamships." She noted with satisfaction that his open mouth had effectively wiped all expression from his face, and Andrew Grey was immediately asked to sit down in the leather chair beside the broker's. For half an hour he studied Anne's lists and charts. Once again he looked closely at his client, but this time with respect. At the close of their transaction, he offered his strange young visitor a small glass of sherry in celebration.

In the following months she noted with an ever-growing excitement that her rail stocks boomed and her steel stocks forged steadily ahead. She wasn't particularly disturbed that her steamship stocks did little or nothing. People, she thought, were still too fond of sailing ships to accept any alternative.

She became busier than ever as she watched over her small but expanding financial enterprises. When Greyhaven closed for the summer holidays, she found the net profit impressive. Even with her teachers' salaries almost on par with those of other schools, there was enough to repay herself the thousand dollars she had invested, an additional five hundred dollars profit, and an equal amount to pay Tom Perkins for the rent.

Since the teachers had elected to live at the school during the summer, she had no maintenance expenses.

From the quiet dignity of Greyhaven Academy and the pretentious refinement of the Boston Stock Exchange, Anne's next adventure almost hurled her literally into the gutters of the waterfront. One hot summer afternoon as she was riding down a dingy side street, her horse was stopped by two drunken men who dragged her from the saddle and shoved her against a wall. She cringed in terror as she heard their taunts and watched their hands double into fists. "Spyin' limey divil," and "Bloody English mucker," they called her. Looking prayerfully for help from any direction, she could see only the swinging doors of a waterfront pub ten feet down the street. She didn't hesitate. Twisting her arm away from one man, she managed to kick the other and gain enough time to dart toward those doors. Her heart was pounding as she ran full tilt into the saloon and straight up against the barrel chest of the owner. With two mighty hands he lifted her bodily aside. Then, pushing the doors outward, he went into action, the like of which Anne had never seen before. Without seeming to move, he unleashed two blows, one to each of her attackers; and they became peaceful bodies on the dirty street.

Without a backward glance, Casey Ryan wiped his hands on his stained leather apron and stepped behind the bar. "And what'll it be ye're havin', lad?" he asked with a smile.

For the life of her, Anne could not remember the name of a single Irish drink. In desperation she said, "Rum."

He laughed his big booming laugh and slapped a mug of ugly black liquid in front of her. She swallowed one mouthful and turned a strangled shade of red. He continued to laugh. "I'm thinkin' ye're not yit man enough for this one, laddy. Maybe it's a bit of port that'll be more to your likin'." With a rapid flick of his hands, he removed the offending rum and slapped another mug in front of her. This time the sour red wine was at least a familiar drink to her, and she sipped it in grateful silence. Casey watched his young customer with curiosity, even more so when she asked him how he had knocked down two rough-looking men so quickly.

"Ye mean layin' out thim two divils? 'Tis asy once ye're shure of the trick. Thire's only one way to be winnin' a street fight. Ye've got to be hittin' the other cock first and hard. Niver let him see yer fist comin'. Thin ye drive from yer shoulder straight into his jaw or brisket."

Anne gulped hard. "Could you teach me to hit like that? Not to fight, really, but just to be able to hit someone like those two, hard enough to get away safely. I'll gladly pay you for lessons."

"So ye're wantin' to learn the Casey Ryan punch, are ye?"

Her gulp was much smaller this time. "Yes, I am." Of all her Irish friends, Casey Ryan was to prove the most gallant and unusual. Every working day for two months Anne reported early to the unopened pub for her lesson in the manly art of self-defense. Casey would spread a filthy mat on the floor, push back the scarred tables, remove his apron, and take a stance with his fists held up before him.

At the first lesson he solemnly accepted the one hundred dollars she had agreed to pay, and then proceeded to force her at an exercise pace that left her body drenched in perspiration and her muscles knotted in pain. The next day he taught her to drive her arm forward using her shoulder muscles. On his command "Punch," she would shove her arm toward the critical instructor. Relentlessly he forced her to repeat the move until he was finally satisfied. He taught her to curl her knuckles using her thumb as a lock, and to do it automatically as she shuffled her feet into a fighting stance.

Every day during that first week Anne dragged her tortured body back to work, then home to bed. In explanation to a worried family, she claimed to have fallen off her horse and sprained her shoulders. Merciful hands applied liniment with gentle strokes.

Only the memory of the terror she had felt when the two hooligans had attacked her kept Anne at her lessons. Doggedly each morning she punched the air, shuffled her feet, curled her knuckles, and felt ridiculous. Even when Casey let her hit the seaman's bag filled with sawdust, she still felt hopelessly inept. But she had failed to take into account the fanaticism of Casey Ryan when it came to pugilism. He wouldn't let her stop, and by the end of summer he had welded a very adequate puncher out of a very unskilled woman. On graduation day, Casey seated her ceremoniously at the bar, poured her a mug of wine and himself one of ale. Then he leaned over the bar toward her.

"Lass," he said and Anne stiffened, "I'll not be perfessin' to know yer business, or why a lady like yerself is paradin' around pretendin' to be a young lad. I know a divil must be drivin' yer, so I'll not ask quistions. But I will be givin' yer some advice. Ye've got a fair punch now, but ye're no match fer a man lookin' fer a fight. He'd kill ye, lass. Now I want yer to git yerself a leather jerkin like the loaders use to pertict yer chist. Good-bye, lass, I've enjoyed yer company, but me pub's no place fer a lady."

Anne never entered Casey's pub again, but she recommended it to every worker at the shipyard; and sometimes when she rode past and saw him standing in front, she would wave and smile.

Chapter 12

In the late summer months of 1844 at the start of her fourth year in America, Anne's heavy investment in work and time began to pay. When Perkins, Bouvier and Gray divided the profits for the first time in three years, Anne's eight percent paid over two times her initial entry money.

Almost simultaneous with the windfall was the unexpected sale of Greyhaven Academy. Led by the driving force of Marian Brent, the four teachers had searched among their students' parents and found two backers. At the end of the transaction, Tom Perkins and Anne Grey, who shared equally in the sale profits of the school, were each richer by twelve thousand dollars; and Tom had acquired an additional five thousand for ten acres of land.

Once again the velvet-coated Andrew Grey entered the Boston Stock Exchange, and this time invested one hundred and twelve thousand dollars in stocks. Charles R. Matthews poured his client an even larger glass of sherry. With most of her hopes now resting on the outcome of her investments here, Anne began to spend each Wednesday at the Exchange, buying and selling. She found an endless fascination in studying the fluctuations of the market, and she developed an instinct for timing that multiplied her profits. The looks of supercilious contempt had long since fled the faces of the brokers assembled there, and young Andrew Grey became a popular figure. Anne found herself becoming more and more caustic about a financial institution that respected an eighteen-year-old youth but would not even allow a twenty-two-year-old woman on the premises.

Her growing resentment at being a second-class member of society was to be reinforced half a dozen times in the next year. While teaching her classes at Greyhaven, an assignment for which she was now paid a salary, Anne was delivering one of Julius Caesar's speeches in Latin. With her undiminished talent for dramatic speaking, she had retained her pupils' undivided attention. Neither she nor any member of her class had noticed the three men sitting quietly at the far end of the common room. In some irritation she asked them their business and learned to her embarrassment that they were the committee from Harvard University requested by Dame Marian Brent to upgrade the rating of the school. As the sober men left the room, Anne hoped that she had not influenced their decision downward with her histrionics.

After the school was emptied of the children, the faculty members and the professors met in the common room for a discussion of the results. None of these lofty arbiters of Boston academia could fault the school. One even recommended that it be enlarged as quickly as possible. As they were leaving, the tallest of the three approached Anne and introduced himself as Winchell Rawlings, head of Latin at Harvard.

"The teaching of Latin, Mistress Grey," he intoned sonorously, "is an art of the highest magnitude. It is one understood almost exclusively by men scholars." Anne drew herself up until she was a good two inches taller than he and, school evaluation or not, was about to explode when his imperturbable voice continued, "But you, Mistress Grey, seem to be the exception." Then the forty-year-old balding scholar asked the open-mouthed Anne to attend a faculty dinner at Harvard with him.

Managing to close her mouth, she was about to tender a gracious refusal when she remembered that she had never been allowed at a university like Harvard before. She accepted the invitation with the mental reservation that at least there might be people there more interesting than Winchell Rawlings.

That Friday night, pandemonium reigned at the Perkinses' house, this was the first time in more than three years that Anne had attended a social event of any kind, even one with members of the family. During those years she had bought not one item of feminine attire, and Maude was frankly worried that her Anne might be at a disadvantage with the elite of Boston. Undisturbed, Anne shook her blue velvet traveling suit vigorously and held it up for inspection. As she looked at it she remembered the last time she'd worn it, on the day she'd met her husband. A little shaken by the memory, she shrugged away her bittersweet nostalgia and donned the suit. Philosophically she reminded herself that at least now her life was her own to live.

Old suit or not, in style or not, Anne was a dramatic figure at that dinner; but she found the other guests just as dull and rank-conscious as the upper-class people of England were. At the end of the tedious evening, replete with endless speeches of mutual praise, Winchell Rawlings asked her to accompany him on a tour of historic Boston the following Sunday. Anne had visited few of the notable sights in this famous city; so with the firm conviction that the word *tour* implied many people in attendance, she accepted.

How wrong she was! From the moment he handed her into his buggy in front of the Perkinses' house to the moment six hours later when he brought her back, he lectured without pause in the unctuous voice of a professional guide. On the crest of Breed's Hill he described the battle of Bunker Hill in gory detail, and he was particularly smug about the heavy losses of the British during that historic confrontation in 1775. At the two State Houses, one old and one new, Rawlings spoke without interruption on the details of construction, on the cost and maintenance, on the skill of the builders, and on every other bit of trivia he could dredge up from his well-cataloged memory. Nonstop, as they drove from spot to spot, he lectured. Even at the formal coffee shop where they lunched, he continued the improvement of her mind, this time in the hushed tones of an undertaker. Never, she vowed a hundred times that day, would she ever see this incredible bore again.

But on the following Friday when she returned tired and dirty from the shipyards, she discovered that he had called at the Perkinses' home during her absence, and that Maude had accepted for her an engagement to accompany him to a reception at Harvard on Sunday. In fury Anne stomped to her room, not in anger at Maude, but at the man himself and his arrogant assumption that she would be delighted to accompany him anywhere. At that reception she became the haughty English aristocrat again who mentioned her grandfathers, Lord Gerald Gray and Lord Stanley Ashton, as often as possible. She was the social lioness of the afternoon.

She was to see Winchell Rawlings one more time. The Sunday after the reception, he arrived unannounced and asked to take her driving. She had fled from the parlor before he'd entered and had begged every member of the family to tell him that she had just departed for India or darkest Africa. Not a single person would help her out. In muttering irritation she flung on a more attractive dress and arranged her hair. Then she sat on her bed for twenty minutes. "Let him wait," she muttered, smiling grimly. When she finally emerged, Rawlings was still lecturing, with Maude as the victim this time. The cowardly Tom, Paul, and Lynette had already made their successful escapes.

Ceremoniously he handed Anne into his buggy, and they took off at a trotting pace along the tree-bordered lanes toward the southwest. About a mile from the house, he pulled to a stop under a leafing maple tree. "Anne," he said (no more Mistress Grey, but Anne), "during these last weeks I have had the opportunity of studying you carefully, and I find you a very satisfactory person. Satisfactory indeed, with just the right amount of dignity and grace needed for Ha'va'd." He smiled graciously and pressed her hand. "I am therefore asking you to become my wife. However, I must warn you that you will have to resign from your tasks at Greyhaven, since there can be no question of your working as the wife of a Ha'va'd faculty member."

He hadn't even waited for her answer, she stormed silently; he probably assumed that she would not dare refuse the honor. Not once during any of their earlier excursions together had this stone-faced egotist ever held her hand or, heaven forbid, tried to nuzzle her cheek. Not once had he ever asked for her opinion or even inquired about her marital status. Not once had he shut up long enough to notice that she had been bored to the point of wanting to push him off the bridge into the Charles River during the "guided tour." Gently she withdrew her hand and turned to him with her sweetest smile. "I have been studying you, too, sir," she simpered, "and I find that neither my guardians in England nor I could possibly consider the teacher of a small provincial college as a suitable or proper husband."

Gathering her skirts gracefully in her hand, she stepped down from the buggy, catching only a glimpse of his suffused red face. With head held high, she turned toward home, performing for anyone who cared to look a spirited step from the Highland fling. One more blow struck against the citadel.

A second autocratic invitation to place herself under the protection of another domineering man arrived a month after she'd refused Winchell Rawlings's unexpected offer. It was contained in a letter from her father, a black-banded letter whose first page was the bleak, desolating announcement that her beloved grandfather had died.

"It wasn't unexpected, Anne; he'd been ill for months ever since your grandmother's death almost a year ago. As I promised you, I never told him that your husband had gone to Australia without you. That was a kind gesture on your part because in spite of his reassurances, he was as worried as the rest of us at the time of your wedding—perhaps more so, since he felt responsible. More than anything else the advent of your children released him from that sense of guilt. He was so proud of them and you. He enjoyed the cameo portraits of your twins, as did your father-in-law. On their last visit together they spoke fondly of you and boasted of their mutual 'immortalities'—young Anthony and little Margaret. I know you loved your grandfather, Anne, as I loved my father, but he didn't want either of us to grieve for him. He'd accomplished what he planned to in life, and was not unhappy at the end.''

Not until the final word did Anne accept the reality of his death. Unable to read further through the blinding rush of tears, she was numbed by a sense of loss as unlike the brief sadness she'd experienced at her grandmother's death as sunlight was to moonlight. This grief was an overwhelming sorrow, the other merely a passing regret. He'd been her most uncritical friend, the one with the greatest faith in her and the one who'd understood her best. "You're an Ashton, gel," he'd told her whenever she'd wanted to surrender to self-pity, "and we Ashtons are stubborn fighters." Stubborn he had been! Until she'd finally surrendered to his demands for a portrait of the twins and commissioned an impoverished friend of Marian Brent's to paint them, he'd threatened to come to Boston himself to see them personally. Worried about the multiplicity of the defensive lies she'd told him concerning her marriage, she'd sent the delicately done portraits to prevent his coming. But how she wished she hadn't now! If she could only see him one more time to tell him what his friendship had meant to a lonely girl, perhaps his death would not leave her feeling so incomplete.

Burdened by memories she could not share with her new friends, she postponed reading the rest of her father's letter for several days. But when she finally did, her stubborn Ashton spirit revived. "Anne," her father had continued, "I was puzzled by something Lord Brownwell said to me the other day. He implied that your husband was in Australia only temporarily and would be rejoining you in Boston soon. He also said that he'd not told his wife about the children as you'd requested. I imagine you had your reasons for the deception, but your actions will be difficult to explain when you return to England. I have decided, Anne, that you now must take your proper position in society." That unbelievable father of hers, she thought. "I have decided, Anne." Not "if you'd care to" or "if you could see your way clear." No! "I have decided." That single-minded father of hers, with his eternally protective attitude toward his women, could never conceive of a daughter who would prefer to take care of herself. He still thinks of me as an eighteen-year-old bride, she fumed, all alone and helpless. He doesn't have the vaguest idea that I'm a twenty-two-year-old woman who's been surviving without his help for four years.

Her father's final paragraph set her laughing. "To insure your protection on your homeward voyage, I am sending Roger Cavendish—you remember, Elizabeth's cousin—over on the next ship to escort you home." Her laughter flowed out at the thought of that short pipsqueak protecting anyone, including himself, and also at the thought that anyone could make her do anything she had not planned herself.

When her almost relative arrived in Boston, Anne met him at the dock in the chaise with one of her horses pulling and the other tied on behind. She recognized him instantly as he walked down the gangplank. Although he was four years her senior, he still looked much as he had at her ill-fated sixteenth birthday party seven years earlier, an immature milksop.

Roger Cavendish's thoughts about her were as derogatory; she was still too tall, and she still had the same look of conceited superiority. Within minutes he had found more reasons to admonish her. "Really, Anne, a lady does not drive alone." And minutes later: "Really, Anne, a lady does not try to handle a man's luggage." But she helped him anyway, because he couldn't lift his trunk by himself. "Barbarous country, this," he said when no willing dockhand rushed to lift it for him. He had, she thought, a very limited vocabulary and a very limited mind.

With forward-thinking malice, she'd booked Roger into a North Boston inn, as far away from the Perkinses' home as possible, believing that his basic laziness would prevent too much crosstown travel. She had no idea of the extreme severity of her father's instructions to him. He located her the first time teaching a class in mathematics, and he smiled complacently throughout the lesson. He could not even compete against her fourteen-year-olds, Anne thought scornfully.

The next day when he tried to locate his quarry and found her already gone, Roger asked the children at the Perkinses' home instead of the women. "Mama work." "Mama makes big boats." "With Uncle Paul and Uncle Tom," the three-year-old voices chimed before the women could silence them.

In fury at her daring to do anything so completely outside the realm of decency, Roger raced his horse—Anne's horse, really—until the poor thing lathered. But then she always was outside the circle of decent people, he thought with a complacent satisfaction. At the moment he was sorry that he'd promised Lord Ashton to bring her back. Damn, if she wasn't proving an evasive twit.

Anne looked up from her desk to see him wandering around obviously looking for her. Three times she watched his eyes slide over her; but on the fourth time, when they swiveled sharply back, she jumped to her feet, grabbed his arm, and dragged him outside. "Don't you dare, Roger Cavendish," she hissed into his ear, "don't you dare say my name. One more sputter out of you and I'll deck you on the spot." He stared at her in unbelieving horror, still rubbing his arm where she had gripped him.

In a quiet corner of the yard, Anne finally told Roger that he was wasting his time. She had no intention of returning to England, not until she'd met her goals and decided what her life would be. "Go back and tell my father that I'm living my own life," she said.

"I can't do that, Anne," he blustered. "I'm not to leave without you. I'm to stay right here and take care of you."

"Suit yourself, Roger, but I'm not leaving."

"Then," he lamented, "I have to stay in this godforsaken wilderness, too, until you change your mind."

"Boston's an expensive city to do nothing in."

"Well, if necessary, I'll have to work."

"Doing what, Roger? Just what are you trained to do?"

"I finished college."

"I should hope so, after eight years," she exclaimed impatiently. "But what specifically did you train to do in college?"

"Really, Anne, gentlemen do not train in college; they matriculate."

"Gentlemen can starve to death as well as anyone else in a cold New England winter." She noticed that he looked almost humble enough to be human.

"I say, Anne, you wouldn't know of some post or other I could fill for the time being?"

"I might."

"I wouldn't mind a bank position or something like that."

"Here at the yards, Roger."

"You mean working with my hands?"

"Occasionally we do use our minds here."

"Well . . ." He sighed and made the sacrifice. "At least I could keep an eye on you here and protect you if necessary."

That morning Anne began to train him as her assistant. Unfortunately his additions did not agree with hers. The next day she walked him to the carpenters' shed, but by noon the foreman walked him back. In the hardware department about four that afternoon, Anne heard the unmistakable sounds of a human explosion fomenting. Sprinting across the yard, she raced for the long, low building that housed the huge inventory of metal parts. There she found an angry Roger confronted by an even angrier group of workers.

Roger was shouting, "What difference does it make if I did mix the iron with the bronze? Iron is stronger, anyway. If you scum knew anything about chemical elements—"

Anne drew him forcibly away, but not soon enough to escape the taunt thrown at him. "Not every limey is like our Andy here; some are jest natchal-born bastards." Roger's face flamed.

Stopping at her desk, Anne picked up four or five manuals on shipbuilding. "Read them, Roger, before you come back." She stuffed them into a saddlebag, slapped the horse's rump, and prayed Roger would never return. But two weeks later he did, a much subdued man, and he found his life's vocation.

After three months at the drafting tables where ships' designs were measured to scale, even the foreman said that Roger was a natural-born ship designer. "He sees things in his head," the foreman said, "while the rest of us can only see them on paper." By that time Roger was calling her Andy like the rest of the workers.

With Roger, she had felt no real sense of conquest; he'd been too unarmed an opponent. Moreover, she'd begun to like him. But her next confrontation with an overbearing male almost finished her.

Paul was two months overdue on a quadrangular trip from

Boston to England, from England to France, from France to Bermuda, from Bermuda to the home port. Until a clipper ship had reported that the *Boston Queen* was still laid over in Calais, everyone had been sick with worry. And it was with glad relief that the dock oarsmen finally pulled the *Queen* ashore and tied her down. Anne was at the Exchange that day, so she missed the excitement. She learned later that Paul had not even supervised the unloading but had gone straight home.

He and Lynette were to be married. The news was shouted at Anne as she walked through the door, also the announcement that she had been unanimously elected to make all the arrangements. When she looked at Lynette's incandescent face, she would have arranged the wedding on the moon, had Lynette wanted it there. By suppertime her lists were complete. "The first thing, Lynette," she said, "is your wedding dress."

"Anne," the bride-to-be avowed, "I'll wear anything except white. That I won't wear."

"Then come with me, I have an idea," Anne insisted as she dragged Lynette and Maude to her room. Hanging in the back of her wardrobe was a heather-blue silk dress with one blue silk petticoat. Anne had never worn it and never planned to; some memories were best forgotten. Lynette exclaimed at the soft iridescence of the fabric and fingered it lovingly.

"I've never worn anything so beautiful, Anne," she revealed. "I would love it." Until late that night, Maude and Anne sat stitching by lamplight, shortening the waist and the hem. By morning it was finished, shimmering on its holder in Anne's wardrobe. Beneath it were matching blue slippers which Maude had lovingly created by covering a pair of Lynette's with blue silk scraps.

Early the following day Lynette, Paul, and Anne drove into the South Boston shantytown and ordered the priest to post the banns. Anne tried to make the ruddy-faced Irish cleric understand her instructions, but his brogue was as thick as the boatmen of the Killarney lakes of the "auld sod." Since she could not communicate with him in speech, she decided to write the instructions down for him, one o'clock at Greyhaven Academy the following Saturday, and hoped that he could read. At least, she thought humorously, he sounded so wonderful that no one would mind not being able to understand the words.

As Paul and Lynette returned to their less than holy communion, Anne approached Dame Marian Brent with a proposition. In lieu of rent for the common room and front lawns for Saturday afternoon, she proposed that she buy Greyhaven a piano—a modest one, she stressed, not a grand or even an expensive one. Marian smiled with the light of battle in her eye; and four hours later at the second music store they went to, the two women settled on a respectable spinet which Marian promised to play at the wedding.

Next Anne tackled the food and groaned. In that area she was an idiot. Not once in her life had she ever made a cup of tea or boiled an egg. She could scrub pots and dry dishes, but the secret of cooking was to elude her most of her life. She was determined to make all the arrangements herself, but late that morning she confessed her ignorance to Maude, who laughed. "I wondered when you'd get around to asking me, Anne. I watched you once when you tried to cook your infants' mush; I had to throw that pan away, you burned it so badly. Don't worry about the food, girl; I've got twelve friends among the foremen's wives who'll help out." Maude's shrewd eyes had caught Anne's hesitation and she added gently, "You know, Anne, that you have to invite everyone at the yard. I know it's a mite of people, but it's the only way to avoid hard feelings."

Two hundred people, Anne groaned, but only enough room for one hundred in the common room. All that afternoon she fretted until she remembered the outdoor fairs in England. If the food and refreshment tables were set up on the lawns, most of the people would remain outside. Early the next morning she sent a yard hand and a company wagon to Casey

Ryan's pub with a note signed, "Your grateful student, Andrew Grey; your friend, Anne."

In a New England fall, the only flowers still blooming were asters. Anne was again discouraged. How do you decorate for a wedding in early October? She looked at the gray walls of the common room and shuddered; but as she looked, she thought of the beautiful blue velvet drapes of Ashton Manor. She reached the biggest draper's shop in Boston just before closing and purchased two bolts of blue velvet. At least, she reasoned, there'd be enough to make the children winter clothes after the wedding. She also purchased all the flowers she could find, three pathetic bouquets of lavender asters.

At Greyhaven, after she stopped the chaise and dismounted, she carried her bundles in and began the work of decorating. An hour later she was still trying to hang the first width of drape. As she wearily climbed the ladder to try once more, she heard the sardonic chuckle of Marian Brent behind her. Looking over her shoulder, Anne saw the four teachers all smiling and shaking their heads.

"Anne Grey," Marian Brent scolded, "when are you going to learn your limitations? You're a good teacher and a great businessman and probably a genius at bamboozling. But as a housewife you're a disaster. Go home and get some rest. Let those who can, do."

An hour before the wedding Anne arrived on the scene in her purple velvet attendant's dress and stood in awe at what the teachers had accomplished. When nailed on sawhorses, the pile of boards had become tables that looked like carved artpieces with the row of autumn leaves tacked around the edges. Inside, the velvet drapes dropped in soft folds behind a blue velvet altar. Everywhere were great displays of autumn leaves.

As the bowls and baskets of food arrived, she looked at the women who brought them and thought that great talent had nothing to do with education. But it was with the arrival of Casey Ryan in a green-draped wagon and four green-aproned helpers that she felt her humblest. Unnoticed, unknown people, she thought, really contribute the most to life.

As she stood in position and listened to the music of the priest's voice and the happy sounds from outside, she remembered her own wedding and its bleak emptiness. When Paul placed the ring on Lynette's finger, Anne glanced down at her own two rings; this was the first time she had worn them in America, and she knew they were at best only cold comfort. Suddenly she remembered another lonely woman at the wedding, pink-cheeked Mary Harrington, who had no ring at all to comfort her. She removed one of her rings; and after the ceremony was over, she slipped it on the startled girl's finger. Mary protested that she couldn't accept such an expensive gift; " 'T'wouldn't be right, mum."

"The rightest thing in the world, Mary. You're as much a mother to my children as I am, and we love you very much." Later as she watched the young "widow" dance with unattached yard hands, she could see the sparkle of the ring; and she was glad that at least one memento of her own wedding had made someone happy.

Tired and lonely, Anne herself sought the darkest corner of the room and watched the others. Slowly she became aware of someone blocking her view and she looked up. It was the tall dark man who'd stood by Paul throughout the ceremony.

In soft, sensuous French he introduced himself. "I am Claude Bouvier, Paul's brother." She studied his face with interest; no wonder he had looked familiar—the same dark eyes, the same slow smile, the same charm—only ten years younger. "And you are the notorious Anne Grey," he murmured as he drew her to her feet. "It's time for you to stop hiding."

"But I'm not hidi—"

"Then American men are blind. You sit alone in a corner and look so sad. Yet you are the most beautiful woman in the room."

"But I'm not beauti—"

His voice flowed on in a soft whisper near her ear as if she had not spoken. "If you could see yourself as I see you, you would know that in this dress of blue violets, you are a siren no man can resist."

With the practical, no-nonsense part of her mind, Anne knew that the words were perfect because this Frenchman had used them so often; but no woman is really practical in the aftermath of a wedding. For an hour the two of them danced to music that was part spinet, part fiddle, and part accordion. Neither of them heard the music or saw the other dancers. Vaguely she was aware that he held her too close to him, but she really did not struggle to free herself until she caught Paul's sardonic look from across the room and the warning shake of his head. That look was like a shower of ice water tossed in her face; and she freed herself from the spell that the man and the music had woven. It was the sensible Anne Grey who excused herself from Claude Bouvier, saying that she had duties to attend to. But as she walked away from him, she heard his murmur, *"Au revoir, chérie;* when you become a woman again, I'll be back." He knew that she was running from him.

Out on the lawn she saw the real party in full swing. Mothers and children sat happily on the grass, eating from plates piled high with food, and the men crowded even more happily around the bar.

A dozen times Anne was stopped and asked where her young brother Andy was. "In New York," she answered, "on company business."

"He's a fine boy, mum," said a foreman whom Anne knew all too well. "You must be proud of him."

She replied quite honestly, "Andrew can be a nuisance to me at times."

"Aye, all boys can be annoying to their sisters. But your brother's a cut above the rest. He's going places, that one."

Momentarily she was startled; she had never really thought about "Andy's" future, and she wondered if Anne's life would become unbearably dull once "her brother" was packed away in a trunk. She couldn't imagine life without the freedom Andrew Grey had given her, but how long could he remain eighteen?

She was shaken out of her reverie by one of the young bartenders, who was offering her a mug with port wine in it. "Me boss sinds ye his best regards, mum, and asks that ye toasts the auld days with him one more time."

Anne recognized the mug as she raised it high; and over the heads of the men crowded around the bar, she toasted Casey Ryan and laughed as he pantomimed the famous Casey Ryan punch. At least that part of Andrew, she hoped, would never die.

At four o'clock the Paul Bouvier family and Tom and Maude Perkins left to board the packet for New York, and the party gradually broke up. By dusk, willing hands, spurred on by an extra mug or two from Ryan, had cleared away the debris and returned the tables to neat stacks of lumber. Anne's bolts of velvet were refolded, and Greyhaven Academy was itself again.

As she began her short walk home, she wasn't too surprised to find Claude Bouvier waiting as he had promised. At first he held her arm lightly as he pulled her close; but as the sky darkened he slipped his arm around her waist and pulled her tightly against his side. "You are, I think, *chérie*, a most remarkable woman. I grow weary of listening to praise about Anne Grey, teacher, and Anne Grey, mother. I wonder if Anne Grey can also be a woman?" His words almost vibrated inside her ear.

At the moment Anne had no doubt. For the first time in four years, she was being held by an attractive man and her heart was pounding. As she tried to pull away from the smothering closeness, she felt his arm tighten and his steps slow. "Are you so afraid of me, *chérie?*" he asked.

Not of him, her mind screamed, but of myself. A Claude Bouvier had no place in her life, and she was a fool to let him think so. Or to let herself hope, she added.

Just before they reached the front porch, they stopped; and she turned to say a half-relieved good night. But her words were stopped by his other arm completing the encirclement and his lips closing over hers. Only that one kiss, but it was one too many for Anne's peace of mind. Her dreams that night were disturbing ones that took her back in time to other kisses and another love.

Claude proved to be a quietly delightful guest who remained in his brother's quarters until late the next morning. When he did emerge, he charmed both Mary and her mother, Mrs. Shea, by taking over the cooking duties for the day. Seating the women at the table and tucking the three little children securely into their chairs, he admonished them all to watch an artist prepare an omelet. Round-eyed, the children obeyed as he beat the eggs and rolled the mixture into a frying pan. Anne entered the room at his greatest moment of achievement, the successful flip and return into the pan of the fluffy concoction. Her own cry of approval was drowned out by the excited shrieks of the spellbound children. Not until she sat down to join the audience did she realize that Claude was speaking an English as fluent as his French. What a fraud, she thought as she remembered his romantic language of the night before; but when he served her portion of the dish and forced her to look at him, she realized he didn't need any language to communicate his message.

All that day the usually active children seemed content to sit and watch as Claude prepared the dinner for both the family and the four teachers Anne had invited. Never had the kitchen smelled so good; and because he fed the children little bites and tastes of apple tarts and pumpkin rolls from the oven, they became his ardent supporters. Even Marian Brent succumbed to the interesting travelogue that accompanied the preparation of dinner. Except for Anne, perhaps, these people had seen little of the world; and his easy description of Paris and of the South Sea Islands opened windows in their imagination. Even the sensitive Matthew Conway emerged long enough from his cloistered environment of study to enter into the spirit of this expanded world of travel.

When the meal was finished and the children were tucked

in bed, Claude served the adults a special brandy he had brought from France; and Anne watched the four teachers, who ran Greyhaven with puritanical sternness, being transformed back into four very relaxed Irish people who sang and danced their way home. Even Mary and her mother giggled as they left the room to go to bed. But when Anne tried to follow their example, she found her path adroitly blocked by a smiling Claude, who led her back into the parlor and closed the door.

"Oh, no, *chérie*," he chided her, "we have some unfinished business to discuss." Once again he spoke in French.

Shaken by his nearness, she moved abruptly away and protested, "We hardly know each other, Claude. Before yesterday we'd never even met."

"For you, perhaps, *chérie*, but I've spent several months listening to my brother talk about the courageous Anne who isn't afraid of life. I am intrigued long before we met, and now I am so much more than intrigued."

"You cannot talk to me this way. If Paul told you so much, you know I am not free. You have no right to say these things, and I have no right to listen."

"So young to be so strong and so sure. But I think you're as lonely as I am, *chérie*."

"No!" Her denial was sharper than she had intended. "My life is full and I want nothing more." He laughed and once more drew her to her feet as he had yesterday before they'd danced; and he kissed her slowly and thoroughly until she trembled in response.

"You're lying, *chérie*, you do want more," and watching her eyes, he caressed her breast with one soft stroke. Only when he saw her stricken face did he relent and release the now struggling woman. "Good night, Anne." He smiled and murmured, "Sweet dreams, *chérie*." She remembered that smile as she fled from the room.

Tired and irritated the next morning, she pulled her britches and boots on with angry jerks punctuated with angry thoughts. "You're so sure of yourself, Claude Bouvier, so sure that I cannot resist you. I haven't fought this hard just to have another man desert me. You'd walk out with a smile, and I'd be back to illegitimate again." Only the night watchman was on duty at the shipyard when she started work, and all day long she fumed.

At supper that night, Claude mentioned mildly, "I looked for you at school today, but Dame Marian said you'd gone into Boston." Anne surrounded herself with the three children and went to bed at the same time they did. The next day at school when he walked through the room where she was teaching, he smiled and waved and sat down to wait. At the end of class, Anne left with her pupils and exited through the rear door. As if pursued by devils, she ran across the half mile to the Perkinses' home and spent the afternoon reading in her room. On Wednesday she arrived at the Boston Stock Exchange two hours before it opened, but on Thursday Claude stopped the game.

She had just added the same column of figures for the third time when her restless eyes saw the shiny boots standing by her desk at the shipyards. With a sick dread she looked slowly up past the slim body dressed for riding to stare into an unsmiling face and angry black eyes. "It seems, *chérie*, that my brother did not tell me quite everything about you."

In panic she hissed, "Get out of here, Claude. I don't want to see you anymore, so just get out of here."

He smiled at her, but it wasn't a pleasant smile, and his voice became louder. "I won't leave, *chérie*, until you move your ridiculous derrière off that stool and come with me."

Furious, she looked around frantically, but there was no way she could call for help from the workmen. "Shut up, Claude, and go home. You've no right to interfere in my life."

"If you want to keep that life, you'd better come peacefully; otherwise I will drag you out." He stepped toward her, and Anne stood up, her jaw clenched. With a burning resentment, she strode toward the door and out into the open air. Waiting for them was his horse, and tethered next to it was hers. He had dared to move hers from its usual place, she fumed, the big, strong, all-conquering male. Gathering the reins, she lifted herself astride with one fluid movement and, wheeling the horse sharply away from him, took off for home. Halfway there his horse blocked hers, and she was forced to stop.

"Oh, no, *chérie*, not this time will I let you use your children as a shield. This time will be on my terms." He reached for her reins, but she tightened her hold and pulled back; his hand gripped hers and slowly he increased the pressure until tears of pain glistened in her eyes. But she didn't utter a sound. Unrelenting he watched her face. "Your hand, *chérie*, will withstand only a little more until a finger breaks." Damn men, she cursed, damn their brutal strength; but she released the reins.

Without a word or a backward glance, he rode toward a distant area dense with trees. Twice she removed one foot from the stirrup and contemplated jumping from the moving horse, but his voice stopped her. "You'll only hurt yourself and tear those pretty men's pantaloons. You could never outrun me, anyway." He led her horse on as she dodged low branches and hated him. Finally, when he was satisfied with the surrounding privacy, he dismounted and tied the horses up; but before he could lift her down, she'd jumped off.

For the first time his smile was pleasant as he looked at her standing defensively still. "I thought you'd try to run."

Grimly she remembered Casey Ryan's advice: "Niver try to run, lass, unless ye're sure ye can get away. Stand and face the bastard and watch for yer chance." Anne stood, but her fist was clenched, her shoulders thrust forward.

When Claude noticed her stance, he threw back his head and laughed at her. "And did your teacher, whoever he was, tell you what to do against a man who also knows how to fight?"

Helpless though his words made her feel, her face retained its grimness and her eyes blazed. "If it's force that you plan to use, I've been there before; and I'll fight to kill you if you try."

Something in her unrelenting determination gentled him, and he spoke quietly. "No, Anne, I don't plan to hurt you. Or to force you. But between you and me there is a fire. We both felt it when we danced and kissed. It intrigues us both, I believe, until we think of little else." He stepped toward her, but stopped as she moved back. "All right, we'll talk about it. Sit down, *chérie*, I won't touch you." He sat down first with his back against the trunk of a tree, and Anne noticed the tension in his shoulders and the tautness of his face. Slowly she sat down as if all the strength had suddenly left her legs and stared at her hands. Oh, God, she thought, it isn't fair. I should have known that Paul's brother would not be cruel. He wants me just as I want him. But this thing cannot be.

"Anne"—Claude's voice sounded oddly light—"I told you that I was interested in you before I met you. That isn't quite true. I wanted you; and when I saw you standing by Lynette at the wedding looking so alone, I fell in love with you. Paul warned me that you were not free, and that you were too strong a person to be tempted. But he does not know about the fire in you. I thought if I could rush you into love before you had time to think, I could win you anyway. Anne, in France we could live like man and wife. Will you forget your other dreams and come with me?"

She closed her eyes against the sting of tears and answered slowly, "To live like man and wife, Claude, is not enough. We both know that. Paul and Lynette were lucky because his wife died. We would not be lucky, and all of our lives together the shame would burn us. My children would be castoffs, and any children we might have together would be worse."

"I would love your children, Anne."

"I know you would, and they would love you. But I won't let them face what I did." She paused and looked at him. "Paul didn't tell you that, did he, Claude? That I was illegitimate? Someone discarded by a mother who couldn't be bothered. I was luckier than most. I have an aunt who loves me more than a mother would, and a father who tried to make up for my not belonging. But I felt every snub and heard every sneer. I listened to an angry husband call me bastard and to his mother call me worse. Now for the first time in my life I don't have to listen anymore. As Anne Grey I receive respect and acceptance, and I won't give up my new security. Only if I could be freed from legal ties would I feel free to love you as I want to love you, Claude.''

He, too, was looking at his hands. "I would keep you free from hurt, Anne. There are places where no one would ever know."

"You and I could hide, Claude. But what about my children? How do we hide them? And if we were discovered, their father, who doesn't even know they exist, would be able to take them from me. Our love, Claude, even if it became strong, could never survive that."

"There's no chance for a divorce?"

"No more than in France."

"Not even after what he did?"

"A lawyer I went to in Boston told me that a husband has every right to beat a disobedient wife."

They looked at each other, and Anne knew she had won, if returning to a lonely life could be called a victory. He extended his hand and they rose together, facing each other with unsmiling, saddened eyes. He pulled her to him. "If I had known you were such an eloquent speaker, *chérie*, I would have seduced you first before we talked. But a moment of love would never be enough, would it, Anne?" She shook her head in sad regret. His kiss was tender and sweet, but it was a kiss of surrender and good-bye.

All the way back to her desk and the endless columns of numbers, the tears streamed down her cheeks and dropped onto her leather jerkin and made permanent spots of brown.

Chapter 13

DURING the week that followed Claude Bouvier's precipitous departure, Anne struggled with an increasing awareness of the probability of a permanent, personal loneliness. His farewell note had left her with something far less than peace of mind or even hope.

"Chérie," he'd written in a handwriting so like Paul's that she had smiled shakily, "time does not make it any easier to live alone with regret. You are a woman meant for love. Do not, I beg you, deny that fire within you and become bitter with age. Such would be a sad tragedy. If not with me, *chérie*, find your happiness with someone else. Claude."

For the first time in America she contemplated a realistic future, one that must forever ignore the siren persuasion of a man like Claude. She was committed to being Anne Grey, widow, with two children to raise. Over twenty-two years old and a woman now, she could not hide much longer behind the protection of her American friends. She must establish her own home soon. But the thought of returning to England made her shudder; there both she and her children would be disciplined into a conformity that seemed rigid in comparison to the less regulated society here.

Strangely, her tentative decision to choose permanent exile in America was strengthened by an urgent letter from Aunt Margaret which began and ended with a peremptory command to return home. The part in between was devoted to her aunt's reaction to a London *Times* article enclosed in the envelope. Dated several months earlier, it was the dramatic announcement of a tragedy on the English Channel in which the *Dover Princess* had gone down without survivors.

Anne's first reaction was one of disbelief; Captain Newland, she remembered, never sailed his proud ship into danger. But this time danger had overtaken him and all of the wealthy, important passengers aboard. From the fourth paragraph on, the article centered on five of those passengers—Lord Harold Anthony Brownwell, Sir Harold Brownwell, Sir Arthur Brownwell and his wife, Lady Vivian, and their two-year-old son, Felton. They had been returning from France when the storm struck. Anne reread the names with a sense of loss so keen that she felt stunned; these three men who had befriended her had been the Brownwell part of her children's heritage she'd wanted Anthony and Margaret to know. A grandfather who would have been their friend, an uncle who might have been their father had Anne not chosen the weaker brother, and another uncle who would have shared his own family with them.

The final paragraph told about the grief-stricken Lady Suzanne Brownwell who'd remained behind in Paris and the search for the surviving son, Gilbert Anthony Brownwell, in Australia. How unfair, Anne reflected with a painful emptiness, for three good men and a young mother and child to die while a vain, self-centered woman reaped the sympathy of a nation, wearing what her one-time daughter-in-law cynically knew would be the latest fashion in black couturier dresses. Deliberately Anne tried to block from her consciousness the name of Gilbert—Gilbert, who would inherit a fortune he had not earned and the respect he did not deserve.

Filing the letter and the newspaper article in the trunk where she kept all of her personal correspondence, Anne rearranged the carefully cataloged stacks, placing the letters from Lord Brownwell and Harold in the corner with her Grandfather Ashton's. She and her children now had only two relatives who would welcome them if she took her father's urgent advice to assume her "proper position in society." But without the protection of a kindly father-in-law, there was no position left for her in England except the miserable one of a deserted wife with fatherless children. At least in America she would be free of public censure and could retain her independence.

As her eyes rested on the letter from Claude Bouvier, she smiled with a sense of bitter defeat. His offer had been the only alternative to a bleak and empty future; she'd never received even one word of explanation from the man who owed her so much more than the debonair Frenchman did. Only once had she ever seen a sample of Gilbert Brownwell's handwriting, and that had been on an arrogant note announcing the sale of her mare two days after the wedding.

Reminded of her last tangible ties with the Brownwell family, Anne quietly left the house and walked over to the building that held the carriages and horses. Inside, she automatically picked out two lumps of coarse sugar Maude stored in an oilskin bag as treats for the half dozen animals. It was the soft whinnies of the geldings as she approached their stall that triggered still another painful memory for Anne—the visual memory of Gilbert's face aboard the *Boston Queen* when he'd revealed his love of animals. He'd looked so much younger that day, so much more vulnerable as he'd talked about his boyhood pets on his family's estate. If only he'd been able to transfer some of that gentle tenderness to her, Anne reflected sadly, perhaps he would not have changed so completely into the cruel stranger who'd deserted her. Half-blinded by tears that coursed down her cheeks, she stroked the arched necks of the faithful horses that had become her friends. In that one small respect, at least, her brief marriage to Gilbert had enriched her life.

"Best let sleeping dogs lie" was one of Maude's most often repeated homilies, and that night Anne wished fervently that she'd heeded the advice. The revival of old memories only intensified the loneliness she faced. Her fitful sleep was haunted by dreams exposing the sensuality in her nature that she'd successfully repressed until the intrusion of Claude

Bouvier into her life. But the dreams that desolated her were not imagined ones of Claude; they were vividly real ones of Gilbert. Oh, God, she didn't want to waste the rest of her life in a state of hopeless longing for what might have been!

As the days dragged on, her depression increased. During the absence of Paul and Tom, the work at the shipyards had been reduced to half; and Anne had additional empty hours to fill. Restlessly she turned her attention toward the children, but the approach of New England winter limited their activity to the indoors; and Anne was often frustrated in her efforts to increase the pace of their education. More often than not Maggie and Danny refused to pay attention to stories that lacked the happy nonsense of nursery rhymes and fairy tales. Only Tony sensed his mother's agitation and struggled to respond.

When the Bouviers and Perkinses finally returned from New York, the three small children shrieked their exuberant greeting to Louis and Lisa after the young French-Americans had raced all the way from the dock just to show Anne their proudest new possessions, two white leather folders containing parchment certificates of baptism into the Roman Catholic Church. Minutes later Lynette arrived in a state of even greater excitement to explain to Anne about the miracle. Paul, his proud wife announced, had adopted his own children so that now they were as legal as Anne's own. When Anne raised her eyebrow in skepticism, Lynette admitted that some slight evasion of the truth had proved necessary. She had presented papers to the court naming her a widow, a legal one, with two children whom her new husband wished to adopt. Briefly Anne wondered what had happened to Lynette's old "spit in the eye" philosophy; but when she saw the pride on Louis's and Lisa's faces, she knew that what had been done was morally right, if not completely honest.

As she waited for the others to come home from the docks, she felt part of her depression dissipate. At least her family was back and life would return to normal. That night at supper as she watched Tom and Paul at their accustomed places at the table and Maude bustling around serving the meal she had insisted on cooking, Anne smiled for the first time in days. Loneliness, she decided, was just a matter of degree.

However, life did not settle down to a calm routine. Within days of arriving home, Paul announced that, approaching winter or not, he was sailing the *Boston Queen* to England with Lynette aboard as an honored guest. His two children, he declared with greater pride than ever, could now be enrolled at Greyhaven Academy instead of the school they'd attended as boarders in Connecticut. In that way they could live at home while he and their mother were abroad.

Even their departure a week later brought little calm to Anne's life, because the shipyards returned to full production overnight; and whether she liked it or not, her working day was stretched to twelve hours once again. To her chagrin, easygoing Tom Perkins became a slave driver, demanding a complete accounting of every aspect of the business. Wearily she trudged back and forth from shed to shed collecting lists of inventories. For the three weeks Tom had been away, work had slowed on every ship under construction; but now he increased the pace of construction to a speed that surprised even the older hands. Usually work eased off during the winter months, but this year full production was scheduled on every day except the stormiest. Like the other workers Anne wore the irritating red flannels of New England winters, and like the others she huddled around the fires kept blazing in the metal containers on every dock. That few men grumbled was largely due to the extra wages Tom was paying them.

When she complained to him about her added work load, he grinned at her and scoffed, "You're the one who wanted expansion, Anne." Toward the end of January, though, he relented and told her that the heavy work schedule would last only another month. Dejectedly she continued to write out endless job orders and equipment lists. By the end of the day she was too tired to do anything but sleep.

Maude and Mary worried about this new Anne, who cried

easily and who lacked the boundless energy of the girl who never used to have moods at all, except of joyous challenge. Even when Tom finally called a halt to the driving pace of work, she did not bounce back.

On the twins' fourth birthday, she stayed at home to help them open their presents and to worry about their future. Were they American or English? She didn't know what they wanted any better than she knew what she herself did. She worried that they might resent her if she denied them their English heritage. But she worried even more about not being able to protect them from a childish father if she decided to take them back to her own native land. Had she known what was taking place in England, she would have worried still more.

Within hours of the *Boston Queen*'s arrival in London, Paul and Lynette, accompanied by the lawyer, John Peabody, were speeding toward Grayhaven where an anxious Lady Margaret Gray waited.

In the five years since Anne's departure for America, Grayhaven had changed beyond recognition. No longer was it a simple country school enrolling only local children; it now housed more than five hundred pupils from all over England. The old manor house had become the first of three dormitories, while the classrooms were moved to two large buildings in the center of the sprawling campus. On the perimeter of the cluster of buildings stood twelve new faculty cottages and Margaret's own larger one. Even Mac's old barn had been replaced by a more efficient building situated near the paddocks, which now held forty horses. Everywhere the green lawns were punctuated by small stands of half-grown trees. Margaret had created this new campus by pouring all the profits of her farms into its construction. But the essential character of the school remained unchanged; its student body was still largely made up of the children of middle-class parents, although Margaret had relented enough to admit a few offspring of aristocrats and gentry.

As the mud-splattered carriage drove up in front of her own

cottage, Margaret herself ran out to greet the arrivals. Her first words when she saw only three passengers alight revealed her deep disappointment and anxiety. "Didn't Anne come? Didn't that stubborn girl of mine have the sense to come this time?" Seeing the blank faces of Lynette and Paul, Margaret paused. "She didn't tell you, did she?"

"Tell us what?" Paul asked.

"That her husband will return to England in the next month or two as the new Lord Brownwell." Lynette was thunderstruck; she knew nothing of the background of Anne's husband. But Paul's face became guarded and thoughtful.

"I think, Madame Gray, that we must complete the other transaction first before we involve ourselves with Anne and her not-so-small problem."

"You mean the sale of the shipyards? But I wrote permission for that six months ago."

"I am sorry, madame, but both the Philadelphia buyers and Monsieur Gerald Gray all demanded your signature on the sale contracts."

"That brother of mine has become very cautious in his old age. Well, let's get the signing over with," snapped Margaret. When Peabody tried to insist that she read the contracts first, she shushed him up. "Fiddle-faddle, John. I've already made more money from that business than I'd expected. Besides, Anne will protect my interests." Noticing Lynette's complete confusion about the entire subject, Margaret observed, "I think there's been more secrecy than necessary in this whole thing." Curiously now she studied the French-woman's face, not yet aware of the new gold wedding band.

Intercepting his hostess's look, Paul hastily performed a belated introduction. "My wife, madame. Lynette and I were married before we left America," he said defensively. He need not have worried about any censorship from Lady Margaret; like Anne, her attitude toward truth was always tempered with mercy.

"Then I think it's time, Captain Bouvier, that you inform your wife that this sale will make you a very wealthy man."

Somewhat reluctantly, it must be admitted, Paul explained the details to an astonished wife. He would receive not quite thirty percent from the sale of the yards themselves and another forty percent for the sale of the lands between the Perkinses' home and the new Greyhaven Academy. As part of his profits he had elected to keep the *Boston Queen* and the *Boston Belle*. Lynette grinned her gamine smile when she heard the amount.

"Oh la la chéri! Now we can afford to spit in the eye of the whole world.''

Impatient to complete the signing so that the discussion could return to the subject of Anne, Margaret began to sign the papers even before her disapproving solicitor could read them. ''How did my niece take the news of the sale?'' she asked.

''Your niece, madame, knows nothing about the sale. She is not so manageable a person as my Lynette. She has driven us hard, that one.'' He explained how ambitious Anne had become for the acquisition of money and how she had refused to leave America until she'd reached her goal.

''How much is this goal my foolish niece has set?''

''A half a million pounds.''

''My Lord, even I don't have that much,'' a flabbergasted Margaret groaned. ''How could she ever hope for such an amount?''

''She has, I think, already acquired one-third of it.'' Paul grinned. ''Your niece, madame, is a very shrewd gambler. She buys and sells American stocks and has, I think, shocked even her broker with her success.''

Lady Margaret laughed. ''Anne always claimed that mathematics was the key to success. Tell me, will her share of the sale complete her goal?'' Paul shook his head. ''Then give her all my profits from the sale,'' she proposed impatiently.

Again Paul shook his head. ''You do not know this new Anne. She does not take one penny she does not earn herself. As for trying to fool her, madame, she knows more about the profits than I do.''

"Then, Captain, you will have to bring her back to England—with force, if necessary. She has to be here when that man arrives or as soon as possible afterwards."

Jarred by the notion that anyone could make Anne do anything she didn't want to, Lynette protested, "Madame, your Anne is too stubborn for even Paul to manage. She will not come, I think. She does not want this husband. Not once in five years does he write to her. He is a fool and what woman wants a fool for a husband? He is no good for her."

"Lynette does not know the entire truth, madame. I think I must tell it now." Paul leaned forward toward Lady Margaret. "Do you remember, madame, what you told us to do if the husband became a problem to your niece?"

Margaret nodded. "Then it was necessary for you to act?"

"Yes, most necessary."

"What did happen?"

"He was what you said, that young man, only worse. He drank, he gambled, he beat your niece. He was not even faithful, that one." In remembered anger, Paul told the story of Gilbert Brownwell's actions aboard the ship on that unhappy voyage and of his own part in solving the problem. "No one else, madame, knew of my decision. I alone take the blame for the lie I invented. I put Monsieur Brownwell on that ship to Australia. He was, I think, a very broken man. But what I did I do not regret, even though I do not know at the time that Anne is *enceinte*."

No one spoke, so Paul continued, "I am sorry if I cause you pain."

Lady Margaret's eyes were burning with a suppressed fury. "Paul Bouvier, you've caused me no pain. I would have pushed that animal overboard."

Chuckling in sudden relief, Paul admitted, "I did consider it, madame."

In his dry lawyer's voice, John Peabody erased the remainder of the emotional tension. "Then Lord Brownwell does not yet know that his wife is living or that he is a father?"

"No," said Paul, "there is no way he could know."

"And Anne, the Lady Brownwell, does not know anything about the reason her husband left her?" Paul shook his head emphatically. "Then," continued the solicitor cheerfully, "we have no problem, since she is in no way responsible for the separation. Even if her husband has been so hasty as to remarry in Australia, the new marriage would be ruled illegal since Anne is still his valid wife. Unless . . ." He paused and delicately chose his next words. "Unless Anne herself has given cause for a divorce. Has she lived a completely, er . . . ah, moral life in Boston?"

Lynette jumped to her feet and glared at the solicitor. "Anne is only work, work, work. In all this time she has no time for men!" she shouted. "Five times, monsieur lawyer, five times"—she held her fingers up for his elucidation— "five times only did she see another man. And never once at night. Four times"—again the graphic finger count—"four times with a bald old man." Paul winced, since that "bald old man" was three years younger than he. "Two times he took her to some dull thing at Harvard and once to see the hills in Boston. The last time Anne told him—pooh—to stay away. And once, monsieur, once she dance with my Paul's brother at our wedding. If anyone says different, I'll spit in his eye." Having delivered her defense, Lynette sat down, still glaring at the startled man, leaving little doubt whose eye she meant.

Even lawyers are human; for a moment Peabody almost smiled. "A most eloquent testimonial, Madame Bouvier. Most eloquent. But I must know all of these things if we are to protect Lady Brownwell. And now, Captain Bouvier, only you can answer the next question. Do the children resemble their father?"

"The little girl completely, the boy not so much. But they both have his color hair."

"Then you think they are sufficiently like the father to convince a judge, should they be challenged as the Brownwell heirs?"

"These *enfants*," said Paul in contempt, "could not be denied."

"Good. Now, is there anything else that I should know? Anything that would prove Anne an unfit mother?"

Paul and Lynette looked at each other uneasily. "Perhaps not unfit," Paul hedged, "but most unusual. There's Andrew Grey."

"I beg your pardon. You did say Andrew?"

"Andrew Grey, John, is my niece's disguise at work." Margaret interrupted. "When my partners were too hidebound to hire her as a woman, she worked at the shipyards as a man."

"Anne wrote to tell you this?"

"Of course."

"Did you ever write your niece telling her not to?"

"Certainly not. I approved and wrote to tell her so."

"Did you save her letters telling of this, er . . . transformation?"

"Every one."

"Madame Bouvier, I don't imagine Anne ever discussed her aunt's letters with you, but would you know if she saved any of them?"

"*Oui*. She is like a squirrel. Every piece of paper filed away."

Peabody sighed in relief. "Then in actual fact, we can prove that she had one of her guardians' permission for this subterfuge. And if she supported her children with her wages, she cannot be condemned."

Throughout the dinner and far into the night, the solicitor quizzed the Bouviers. Then next day he made them read his notes for accuracy. Two days later he returned to London well satisfied with the case. But his final words held a note of warning. "Under these unusual circumstances, the children can be protected, but Anne will not be allowed a divorce. Now we must prevent her husband from divorcing her. Everyone who lived with Anne must return with her to England. Lady Gray has stated that she will pay all expenses.

Next, you must bring me written testimonials from all her friends there about her moral character, and you must tell her to transfer her funds to England, if I am to protect them from her husband. And lastly, under no circumstances is she or anyone else to know what you told her husband, Captain Bouvier. Anne must continue to believe that she is a deserted wife until I can prepare her for the truth."

After Peabody had gone, Margaret sighed wearily. "John is an excellent solicitor and a dear man, but there are times when he tries my soul with his haggling over legal details. What I want to know are the important things. Why wasn't my niece told about the sale of the shipyards?"

"Because, madame"—Paul shrugged—"we were not certain she would permit the sale if she knew."

"Nonsense. She didn't own enough of the company to have any say."

He looked at the older woman and smiled sardonically. "She has a persuasive tongue, your niece. She has outspoken Tom and me for five years."

"Was she that difficult to work with?"

"Anne is never difficult, madame, she is efficient. *Mon dieu*, is she efficient! She has doubled the business with her efficiency."

"Then why in the world did you ever consent to sell a company that was expanding so profitably?"

"I for one did not want so much expansion, but that is not the reason I decided to sell. I am a Frenchman and I have not been able to live in France for fifteen years until my former wife died. Now I can return there to claim my half of the Bouvier estate in Calais, where my brother and I will operate a very small shipping business."

"It seems to me that Anne would have understood."

"She would have wanted to buy my share of the company, madame!"

"The foolish girl! Didn't she realize that she'd have to return to England?"

"I think she will not want to return even now. She has

enjoyed pretending to be a man so much, she will not want to become a woman again."

At her husband's lofty analysis of another woman, Lynette broke her silence. "You are *stupide, mon cher,* if you think so. Anne only pretends because all Boston men are *stupid.*"

Grateful for the Frenchwoman's understanding, Margaret asked, "Has Anne been unhappy in America, Lynette?"

"Not unhappy, Madame Margaret, but she will not be happy in England, I think, either."

"Oh, dear, perhaps I agreed to the sale too hastily. Anne may not wish to live in England after she settles her claim here. She may have preferred to remain in America and work with Captain Perkins."

Paul shook his head. "It would not be possible. Our partner wants to sell as much as I do. He is tired of work."

"Then perhaps I should go to America with you and Lynette to make sure Anne does not do anything even more foolish."

During the following week while Paul supervised the loading of ship in London, Lynette remained at Grayhaven, forming a warm attachment for the older woman.

"I think I want *mes enfants* at your school, Margaret," she announced. "I want Lisa to be strong like Anne and my Louis to be not so *préjugé* about women as his papa. We will make the arrangement, yes? And then we will tell Paul."

Margaret laughed. "I seriously doubt that Anne is any stronger than you are, Lynette."

Her face lighted by her gamine smile, the Frenchwoman shrugged. "But that is something we do not tell Paul." She chuckled.

On the last day, as the two women were preparing to leave for London, a worried John Peabody returned to Grayhaven with news that would necessitate Margaret's remaining in England. Lady Suzanne Brownwell had turned her son's inherited estate over to the management of a man with a reputation for duplicity and fraud. Angrily Lady Margaret

Gray prepared for battle, and the *Boston Queen* returned to America without her.

Chapter 14

THE episode that broke Anne's winter-long gloom and restored her natural buoyancy was the visit of a still vigorous Lord Gerald Gray to the shipyards. When he arrived, she was working at her desk with such heavy concentration that she did not notice him until Captain Perkins brought the visitor to her desk and introduced her as Andrew Grey, head bookkeeper. "Andy," said Tom casually, "will show you around the plant, since he knows more about it than I do." As he watched the pair walk off, Tom wondered how they'd hit it off. Long ago he had guessed the relationship.

Amused by this one more irony in her life, Anne played Andy to the hilt and was delighted when the yard hands dispayed their obvious affection for their "limey." When the Englishman asked if she was related to the owner, Anne responded with the proper horror of any well-trained underling. "Oh, no, sir. My name is spelled with an e."

She soon discovered that her grandfather was an astute businessman and that shipping was his business. In return he found this bookkeeper knowledgeable about every aspect of the shipyards. She quoted costs and production schedules. She introduced key men and told how long they'd worked there; the only one she did not introduce was Roger Cavendish. Despite his growing excellence as a designer, Roger was still prone to blurt out indiscretions.

When she returned the visitor to Captain Perkins, Lord Gray

was complimentary to a fault. "Tom," he said, "if you ever want to get rid of this lad, I could use him in my London plant."

Tom's eyes twinkled. "Not for a minute. Andy's the indispensable man around here." Anne was hard pressed to maintain Andy's seriousness at that moment. Twenty-three years ago, she thought, Lord Gerald Gray would have nothing to do with an unwanted granddaughter and still would not today in her own identity. But a beardless youth who knew the business and would work hard for low wages, now that was a real find!

In another moment of whimsy, Tom asked Gerald Gray to be his guest the following day at lunch in downtown Boston. "Andrew here can come with us and show us the Stock Exchange," he suggested innocently.

Anne's velvet jacket and polished boots looked dapper-dandy as she led the two older men around the Exchange and received the nods and smiles of the brokers who had come to respect and envy this young financier. Her face retained the proper soberness of respectful youth throughout that memorable day, but inside she was bubbling with glee. Still one more blow against the fortress of male superiority.

That night she whooped and played with the three children until Maude called a halt. Whenever Anne met Tom's eye, she broke into helpless laughter while he grinned back. Maude and Mary were delighted to have the old Anne back, but the next morning they heaved sighs of relief when she left for work.

By the time the *Boston Queen* arrived back in mid-April, life was normal again at the yard, the school, and the home. Anne had stopped worrying; the future would have to take care of itself. As she watched the *Queen* being docked, she looked up to see Paul at the wheel; and she remembered Claude's face vividly. But the bitter regret was gone now, and she recalled only the sweetness of that never-could-be love.

Minutes after the *Queen*'s lines were secured and the sails reefed, Anne's world exploded once again—not just one small part, but the whole thing. She absorbed the shock of the sale of the yard without much difficulty; Tom's demands for comprehensive bookkeeping had already made her suspicious. And she wasn't too sorry about relegating Andrew Grey to the storage bin; after all, he'd existed for five years without any noticeable aging. Even the most obtuse yard hands must eventually become skeptical.

Although the breakup of the family seemed traumatic at first, the lives of the separate members would still be intermingled in many ways. Besides, she would be able to see Aunt Margaret and her father. Nor did the acquisition of money remain a completely unfinished dream, since with her share in the proceeds from the sale of the shipyards and the sale of her stocks—Anne knew to a penny what these sums amounted to—she would have reached four-fifths of her goal.

What destroyed her equanimity and aroused an angry animosity was the knowledge that her return to England was imperative if she were to protect her children's birthright against the stupidity of her mother-in-law. According to Paul, Lady Suzanne Brownwell had not waited until her son's return from Australia before turning the estate management over to an unscrupulous outsider who would undoubtedly advise his client to eliminate as many claimants as possible. Anne realized with a dread certainty that Suzanne was vicious enough to deny Anthony and Margaret their right to the Brownwell name if she could. That there'd be a court hearing of some kind, Anne had no doubt. Gilbert's mother was too possessive to share her son willingly and too vindictive against a despised daughter-in-law not to extract revenge for an earlier defeat.

Oddly, though, even in her growing perturbation and despite her resentment against Gilbert, which had bothered her more in the past months than during the previous four years, Anne was certain that he would never hurt helpless children any more than he would animals. She was relatively sure that he wouldn't deny them regardless of his feelings toward her. Even when his anger at her had driven him to violence, he'd never been deliberately cruel; and in the happier moments he'd been considerate and caring. Unlike his mother, Gilbert would be capable of loving his children, if Anne could reach him before his mind had been poisoned by Suzanne and the unknown stranger who now ruled the estate. In her imagination Anne pictured the meeting of the father with the two handsome children who resembled him, and some of her nervous apprehension eased. If only he'd grown up enough to accept the responsibility for Anthony and Margaret, there might yet be hope for all of them.

As the six frantic months of preparation ground by, Anne found herself closing chapter after chapter of her American odyssey. In June she finished teaching in Greyhaven Academy. In July she sold all her stocks, except for the steamship ones. When Charles Matthews questioned her about hanging on to what he called "worthless paper," she answered sharply, "In twenty years these worthless pieces of paper will be worth a quarter million dollars. The future of shipping is in steam." Her prophecy was to prove heartbreakingly accurate for Matthews, who failed to buy any of the stock for himself.

In August the yards were taken over by the Philadelphia shippers, the American partners of Lord Gerald Gray; and the three "workmen" of the family returned to their home to begin the tedious chores of preparing wardrobes that would have to last them far beyond the voyage to England. Maude and Mary, who had been sewing children's clothing for months, welcomed Anne's takeover of the job. With the children and Mary in tow, she swept into one Boston clothing store after another, seeking and getting the best bargains in shoes, hats, and heavy coats for the children and Mary. Not one garment did she buy for the twins that she did not duplicate for the smaller Danny, in spite of Mary's objections.

Checking her own depleted wardrobe, she found that six dresses had survived the five years because, except for the purple gown and the blue velvet suit, she'd had no occasion to wear the rest of them. Since her height made the new styles look as ridiculous on her as the old ones had, Anne tried her surviving dresses on and looked at herself critically in the mirror. Satisfied, she packed them carefully into her trunks.

But some articles of clothing even the thrifty Anne had to replenish. At the finest cobbler's she ordered five pairs of shoes and two pairs of boots. Early years of embarrassment at the hands of clerks had taught her that readymade shoes failed to meet the exacting proportions of the Ashton foot. Locating a dressmaker who would follow instruction rather than trend, she ordered three suits cut to the designs she'd sketched on paper. These were to be, she thought ruefully, her "trial" suits. Aware of the power of innocence, she chose a soft blue velvet for one of these outfits with no trim at all except a lacy white blouse. The navy serge was piped in white and looked exactly like what a well-dressed schoolmarm would wear, but the violet silk was as daring as Anne herself. Hats she hated; but since, for all she knew, hatless women were stoned in England, she had four made by a French milliner, whose impudence subsided when Anne swore sweetly at her in French. On two of them she attached heavy veils in case she had to hide in court.

For the final purchase, she donned her "Andy" clothes for the last time in America. In a furrier's shop she had spotted a long Maine mink pelisse. Knowing that tradesmen were much more apt to overcharge women than men, she let Andy do her bargaining. In the serious, earnest voice she'd used so long, she told the furrier that she wanted it for an old-maid sister. Since the tall woman who had ordered it was dead, Anne was able to buy it for half price.

Left to the last minute was the hardest decision she had to make, to sell or to ship the two horses that had been her companions for five years. In the end, realizing that a lady arriving at a London dock does not leap on a horse and ride off toward the sunset, she reluctantly sold them. Because their bloodlines were excellent, the money she received for their sale canceled the bills she had accumulated in replenishing her own and her children's wardrobes.

The day before the *Boston Belle* and *Queen* were to sail

from Boston, both loaded with beaver pelts and cotton, a messenger delivered a letter to Anne that had just arrived from England on one of the fast new clipper ships. It was from her Aunt Margaret.

"Anne, dear," the message read, "your husband has returned to England. He seems to have forgotten that he is a married man because he is seen all over London in the company of a very ambitious woman. You must come home now and fight for your own rights and those of your children. Godspeed, dear." Had Anne not already been primed for battle, she would have exploded into renewed fury. Silently she passed the note to Paul and Lynette, but she did not see the worried looks the two exchanged. The next day as she boarded the *Boston Belle* she signed the ship's log as Lady Anne Brownwell, Anthony and Margaret Brownwell.

Five weeks later both the *Queen* and the *Belle* docked in London at the same time, and one large family walked down two gangplanks to be met by another large family waiting on the dock. Anne's eyes swept the assembled crowd searching for the one person she'd hoped by some miracle would be there. Unbidden she remembered an earlier ship's docking in Le Havre when she'd first seen the tall, pale blond Gilbert and fallen in love. Shrugging off her faint disappointment as the romantic daydream of a foolish adolescent, she kissed Aunt Margaret wordlessly and smiled through moist eyes at her father. In the noisy confusion of the greeting, one interesting moment stood out during a sudden lull in the general hubbub, when Lady Margaret introduced her brother to his granddaughter. Standing tall and straight, Lady Anne Brownwell nodded with gracious condescension. "Ah, yes, Lord Gerald Gray, I believe we've met," she murmured before she walked regally away. Blood is not always thicker than water.

While the other travelers accompanied the Ashtons to their large London townhouse, Anne left the docks with Lady Margaret and John Peabody to begin the legal preparations. On the way to his offices, she asked the solicitor to stop at the best house agent he knew. When Peabody protested about the priority of the pending legal action, she assured him that her mission would be brief. It was. Within minutes of entering the agent's office, she had delivered the specifics of her order—a small townhouse in a smart neighborhood at the lowest price possible, a vacant house that needed no major repairs. "If you can find me such a home, I will pay for it in cash," she informed the flustered agent; and she signed the order Anne Grey, schoolmistress. John Peabody took a long look at this client of his. She was no longer the impulsive girl he'd known.

Waiting for them in the carriage, Margaret had also been pondering the changes in her niece, the beloved girl she often thought of as a daughter. Since the birth of the twins, Anne's frequent letters had expressed the gratitude she felt for the woman who had mothered her. This harmless delusion had consoled Margaret over the years of separation and made Anne seem closer. She was momentarily thinking about her brother's reaction to the priceless snub Anne had dealt him.

"I might have known, Margaret," he'd muttered caustically, "that any girl you raised would be a social boor."

"I understand that you offered Andrew Grey a job."

"He seemed a likely lad at the time."

"That likely lad, Gerald, was your granddaughter."

Margaret had noticed other changes in Anne: the crisp authority in her voice, the warm attitude toward her American friends, her breezy manner, and the sudden switch to cold business. Watching Anne and Peabody walk toward her, Margaret was curious about the expression on his guarded face and the careful way he handed her niece into the carriage.

Once inside the lawyer's private chambers, the relationship among the three become impersonally legal. Peabody's opening gambit, Margaret thought, was a curious non sequitur unrelated to the case. He wanted to know the degree of Anne's sensitivity toward her own illegitimacy. "In a case like this, Anne," he began, "the central parties are often subjected to ridicule and derision. There will be many crude and cruel people both in court and out who will be insulting and offensive. Do you think you can handle that kind of an affront without loss of dignity?''

"Mr. Peabody," she responded, "I have a warm, loving French friend whose favorite expression is 'Me, I'd spit in his eye.'" The solicitor's hand judiciously covered his mouth; he, too, had met that warm, loving French friend. "Although I would not perform the threat physically," she continued, "my attitude toward such people would reflect that sentiment."

"How would you feel if one of the newspapers which deal in scandal were to lampoon your illegitimacy?"

She thought a moment before she answered. "I think I would write the editor a polite note suggesting that he had misspelled the word." She giggled. "And do you know, I believe he'd look it up."

Peabody agreed; that type of journalist would probably have to. His next question was more direct. "Have you really outgrown the bitterness that you once held toward the circumstances of your birth?"

Vividly Anne remembered her impassioned words to Claude Bouvier. "A year ago I would have said no. But today I believe I have. Illegitimacy can only hurt defenseless young people. It cannot destroy successful adults."

The lawyer expelled his breath in relief and changed the subject. "Now, Anne, we attack another sensitive issue. You have become a very poised, outspoken person. Unfortunately, in a courtroom such qualities in a woman are not appreciated. In fact, they can be very damaging to the case. In England I'm afraid that men expect women to be modest and un-assuming."

Just the way, she thought, that Mr. Peabody expected them to be. She was tempted to quote one of the men at the Boston yards, whose favorite advice was, "Keep the missus's belly full; then she won't git highfalutin notions." She resisted the impulse and responded more politically.

"For five years I was an eighteen-year-old boy working among hundreds of older men. How long do you think I would have lasted if I had been impudent or outspoken? About as long as it would take for one of them to knock me down. I had to maintain a respectful, serious attitude all the time I was at the yard. I'll use the same disguise in court.''

"How will you defend your posing as a man at all?''

"When I created Andrew Grey I was without a family, I was headed for a strange country, and I was with child. I believed that I had only a few hundred pounds to my name. When I asked my aunt's partners if they would hire me as a woman, they refused and told me that decent women did not work at jobs in America. But I felt that I had to work to support my unborn child and myself. I believed then as I do now that Andrew Grey was essential to my children's future.''

After she had finished with this recital, she leaned forward in irritation and said, ''Mr. Peabody, I think I have discussed my attitudes long enough. May we now get down to the job of establishing my rightful claims?''

"I agree, Anne. I had to know how you would react to unforeseen complications.'' He paused. ''Three months ago your husband married Edwina Doncaster in a very public, very social ceremony in Birmingham.'' He sat back and waited for the explosion, but none came.

"The poor stupid fool.'' Her voice was surprisingly mild in view of the disclosure. ''I thought he was smarter than that.'' Alerted now to the lawyer's style of questioning, she slowed down before she continued, ''Unless there is something invalid about my own marriage.''

Peabody assured her that hers was legal in all aspects. "Then how,'' she asked, ''can there be any doubt about my children or myself? I don't understand why there has to be any legal action at all. Is my husband so vindictive against me that he'd fight to ruin me and his own children?''

That she was really disturbed for the first time during the interview, Peabody was all too aware; and as a kindly man, he hated to continue. But the case was far more complicated than she realized.

"Anne,'' he warned, ''there are many facets to this hearing

we face. It may not be called a formal trial, but you unfortunately are going to be on trial, anyway." He ignored her gasp and went on. "I am going to tell you everything you are up against. Eight months ago when I first undertook your defense, I learned many facts which made immediate action imperative. I tried to contact your husband as soon as he arrived in England. I failed because he did not travel as a passenger on the ship, but as a member of the crew, using the alias of Gil Brown."

Anne remembered her husband's attitude toward work of any kind and could not believe that he would actually become anything so lowly as a deckhand on a ship. The lawyer continued, "The reason that your husband did not travel as a passenger became evident when I discovered that in the sixteen months since his father's death, his mother had mismanaged the estate so badly that there was no money available for her son's passage. Her late husband had borrowed a considerable amount of money to invest in sheep production. At the time of his death he was on his way home from France after selling holdings there in order to clear the debts on his English properties. Being a foolish, headstrong woman, his widow ignored the advice of the family solicitor and allowed a very unscrupulous man to take over her affairs. Consequently when the new Lord Brownwell arrived he found that his estate was bankrupt. I believe he deliberately sought a rich wife to reclaim it." Beautiful Gilbert Brownwell, Anne mused bitterly, a man who had sold himself twice for money.

Peabody's voice droned on, "When I first heard of his engagement to Edwina Doncaster, I tried to contact both your husband and the bride-to-be's father. But they were in France checking into the remaining properties your late father-in-law owned there. Nor would the young woman respond to my letters. I went to Birmingham to prevent the wedding from taking place, but Mr. Doncaster had protected both the church and his home from uninvited guests. I tried to have the truth published in the newspaper there, but Mr. Doncaster's attorney convinced the editor that I was misinformed. So your husband and Edwina were married.''

Again Anne opened her mouth to protest, again she was silenced by the lawyer's dry tones. "It was two weeks after the wedding that I succeeded in advising your husband that this second marriage was not legal. He did not deny my charge at that time. Both he and his family lawyer assured me that there would be no contest against your claim. But they were wrong. Prior to the marriage, your husband had foolishly signed papers putting all legal matters into his father-in-law's hands. Your enemy, Anne, is not your husband; it is Edward Doncaster, the man Lady Suzanne Brownwell trusted so blindly. He is a very dangerous and powerful man. He started out working in a coal mine, but he now owns half the coal mines around Birmingham. He has been charged with the fraudulent acquisition of three of those coal mines, but he has never been convicted. He retains a staff of lawyers who are as unscrupulous as he is.''

As she listened, Anne had a premonition of jeopardy both for herself and her children. She didn't know how this man could hurt her, but she knew with fearful assurance that he would try. Dreading the answer, she asked Peabody, "Why would this Doncaster even want to fight this case? If my marriage is valid and my children are the legal heirs, what can he gain?''

"Edward Doncaster wants to gain an entry into the upper levels of society. He has tried for years and has been badly snubbed. But if his daughter could become the legal wife of Lord Brownwell, he would have automatic access to the upper-class families in that area. You asked me how he could gain that goal. There is one way in which he could succeed. His lawyers cannot challenge the legality of your marriage successfully, since our evidence is too strong. But they may try. Nor do I think that they will be any more successful in their attempt to prove that your children are not the legal heirs.''

Hesitating for a moment to look at the tense young woman

opposite him, Peabody cleared his throat before he continued. "That leaves you, Anne. You are the only real threat to Doncaster and his ambitions. If his lawyers can prove that you are an immoral woman or an unfit mother, then Doncaster can try to force your husband to divorce you and to gain custody of your children. Since Doncaster controls your husband's estate, he might very well succeed. If his daughter could become the legal Lady Brownwell, her father would have an even better access to society through your father and Lady Gray, because Edwina Doncaster would then be considered the legal mother of your children."

Minutes passed before her shock wore off. At first Anne wanted to snatch her children and hide them. Then she contemplated violence against the man who threatened them. Finally her common sense and fighting spirit revived. "In that case, Mr. Peabody, you will just have to prove that I am both a moral woman and a fit mother."

At this pronouncement, Mr. Peabody smiled; here was a client who would not break under pressure. "Now, am I forgiven for asking all those questions? You see, I have to know everything you did in Boston and everyone you knew there. I have to ask you some very personal questions. My source of information informs me that one of the character witnesses against you will be your husband's mother."

"My God," cried Lady Margaret, "not that vindictive fool!"

"I'm afraid so. I believe she plans to accuse Anne of being intimate with Harold Brownwell prior to the wedding. Is that true?"

Anne stared at the lawyer with shocked eyes before she answered. "No. I knew Sir Harold for several days. We rode together on two of the three horses he gave Gilbert and me as a wedding gift. My husband had refused to accompany us on two of those rides. I respected and admired Harold, but I did not love him."

"Her next accusation may well be that you and your husband were intimate prior to the wedding."

"We were not."

"Anne"—he was deeply embarrassed—"forgive the next question. Were you a virgin at that time?"

"Yes." Amazing, she thought, how easily she could answer such questions without a qualm; but to keep her children safe, she would have answered the prudish Queen Victoria herself.

"It's too bad we're not living in the Middle Ages. There were always witnesses then. The stained sheets were hung from windows so that the neighbors would know."

Anne began to laugh; she'd remembered the sheet she had scrawled the message on. "I think there might be proof, Mr. Peabody." By the time she had finished with the story of the first two nights of her marriage, the lawyer was fighting laughter, and Margaret's face was beet red. "I don't think the daughters of that innkeeper would have forgotten that sheet, even after six years." Anne chuckled.

With a lawyer's thoroughness, Peabody made the notation in his records. "Were you equally as moral during the five years in Boston?" Her response, except for the language, was the same as Lynette's had been, and the lawyer nodded in satisfaction as he handed her a sheaf of fifty or more papers.

"These are documents signed by the people you knew in Boston attesting to your moral character. A few months ago I asked Captain Bouvier and his wife to obtain them for me. Madame Bouvier was particularly energetic on your behalf." Anne smiled; bless Lynette! "I asked for them," the lawyer continued, "when I heard that Doncaster's solicitors had sent two men to investigate you. My guess would be that they returned with most of the same information you've given me. Did they get more, Anne? Is there anything you haven't told me that could hurt you in court?" He held up his hand. "I don't want the answer now. You're to take these papers to your hotel room and study them tonight."

Anne frowned. "I won't be at a hotel, I'm staying with my fath—"

"No, you're staying with your aunt at a hotel and will be

until the end of the hearing. You are to travel to and from that hotel in the carriage we used today. The driver is my own man. You cannot risk being seen on London streets.''

Until late that night she pored over one recorded segment of her life after another. Lynette had gathered statements from all the people Anne had loved in America. Even Mary's statement was there, neatly written by Maude and painstakingly signed by the Irish girl. Tears rolled down her cheeks as she read about her life as it had seemed to the family around her.

Many of the shorter testimonials were about Andrew. Charles Matthews described him as a financial wizard. Shipyard people agreed he was a good lad who was always helpful on the job, while the waterfront merchants claimed that Andy was shrewd but honest.

The one that amused her were the eight words of the recommendation from Winchell Rawlings: "Mistress Grey is a good teacher and a moral person." She was grateful that he hadn't added "and she has a sharp tongue"; however, the "person" part did seem just a trifle too neutral.

Only two brief episodes Anne did not want to be known. The first had been neatly hidden by Claude Bouvier's warm statement. "Anne Brownwell is the most moral woman I have ever known and the most devoted mother." His choice of words made her feel guilty, since her feeling for him had been neither moral nor motherly. There was nothing at all about her second adventure; Casey Ryan was still her secret. But oh, how she wished that Doncaster's spies would encounter the famous Casey punch as they snooped along the waterfront. With a sigh she realized that even Casey must be exposed to the legal scrutiny of her lawyer. Reluctantly she wrote about her venture into the world of self-defense and the Irish gentleman who had guarded her secret.

While Anne struggled with her memories of America, Margaret sat silently by, wishing she could comfort this girl she loved, this courageous girl who had been spitting in the eyes of the world that had threatened her since she'd been a child. Now she was facing complete exposure for daring to challenge the world of men. For more than six months now, since Anne's defense had changed from a simple legal confrontation with a husband to a complicated case involving a far more vindictive man, Margaret had been paying hundreds of pounds to expert investigators of her own. Their reports detailing Doncaster's rise to power included pages of testimony of the many victims who had charged him with theft and assault; but he had never once been convicted. How unfair for his actions to be condoned by a society that would now try to condemn Anne's innocent life. Margaret prayed that her beloved niece would be able to withstand the hypocritical outrage of Victorian Englishmen, a breed of pompous moralists created by a queen who tried to rule even the most private lives of her subjects.

When Anne had finished reviewing all the papers the lawyer had given her to study, she turned to her aunt and smiled impishly. "I feel like some Amazon straight out of a Greek myth, but I'm still not one bit sorry about Andrew. I was successful in Boston and I will be equally so here. I may become the most scandalous lady in English history, but I am going to wind up the only legal Lady Brownwell."

The next morning her flags were still flying high as she strode into the lawyer's office. "Except for this one report," she declared as she handed him the one on Casey, "you now have a complete and accurate chronicle of my life from the day my husband scarred my back to this moment. You can prove where I was and what I was doing every day I was in America. And nothing I have done can make me anything worse than a rebel, a very moral rebel. I am not going to let that irresponsible husband of mine or his stupid doting mother defeat me. As for Mr. Edward Doncaster, he can buy his daughter another husband; mine has already been bought and paid for. Mr. Peabody, let's go to court."

"You'll do, Lady Brownwell. You'll do very well. I think you're ready now to hear the rest of the story. Anne, your husband has believed you dead since the day he beat you."

She stared at him in disbelief as he went on with the ugly

story. "To protect you from what he believed would be even worse abuse and danger, Captain Bouvier told your husband that you had fallen overboard within minutes after you'd left the cabin. From that day until two weeks after his marriage to Edwina Doncaster, Lord Brownwell had thought you dead."

Listening to these terse words of explanation, Anne remembered the years of lonely nights when she had cursed her husband for not writing or remembering. She wasn't aware that Peabody had stopped talking and was watching her with concern. "Anne, you must not blame Captain Bouvier. He acted to save your life."

She raised her head in surprise that he had misinterpreted her silence. "I couldn't blame Paul for anything. I asked him to help me. And he did. He saved my children's lives, and they are the most important part of my life. But I'm glad you told me. It was being a deserted wife I hated the most." She paused and asked hesitantly, "What did my husband say when you told him?"

"He was shocked and, I think, relieved of guilt. Since then, he has been very cooperative. He told me about the case Doncaster is preparing against you, a case he does not approve of, incidentally. But you must not hope for too much help from him, Anne. The papers he signed were very comprehensive. Doncaster's solicitors had wisely taken into consideration the possibility of a prior marriage. So even if he wanted to, your husband could not stop this hearing. And if we do lose, your husband will have gained custody of the children and the right to divorce you."

"He will never get my children, not in a million years. Even if my husband loses every possession he has to Doncaster, I will never give up my children." Her eyes were burning with such a fierce determination that Peabody knew he could not tell her the whole truth after all. He could not tell her that the courts had already placed her children into the temporary custody of her father, and that she could not even see them until the outcome of the hearing was announced. Let her keep her fighting spirit intact until that time.

Although Anne did not realize it, this was to be her last visit to the lawyer's office. Late that same afternoon Peabody arrived at her hotel suite with six strapping men. She smiled in glad recognition of all of them, but she had the grace to grin at the three who stared at her with open mouths. They were shipyard workers who had known her as "the limey." Even though they had been warned about her changed status, they were still shocked at seeing a lad they had known for five years suddenly appear as a woman. The other three, two squat French sailors and one weather-beaten Yankee, were part of the regular crew of the *Boston Belle*. On the trip over they had volunteered for the hazardous extra duty of taking care of three almost-five-year-old children as they'd raced about the ship. Many times Anne had seen one or another of these men pack all three children under his muscular arms and deposit them safely in a cabin. She had marveled at their patience when she herself had been willing to lash the bubbling little demons into their bunks.

These six men were to be her and Margaret's bodyguards. One would be on guard outside their door at all times. After the hearing began, all six would escort the women to court. Anne was to bless these men for their protection. Peabody did not explain to her the reason these guards had become necessary. Two men, one of them a known ruffian, had been seen watching John Peabody's office, and only his alert carriage driver had kept them from following Anne that morning. The lawyer reflected bitterly that the ugly rumors about Doncaster's methods of winning were proving true.

The days ground on for Anne, who followed the dreary routine her lawyer dictated. She read the material he gave her each day and answered his questions about the contents. She tried on her dresses for his approval; the navy he said was "too sophisticated," the violet silk was "just what Doncaster would have ordered," but the soft blue velvet he liked. "It has the right appeal for a helpless woman," he exclaimed enthusiastically. She could have kicked him. Before the remaining seven days of this sequestered ordeal were over, she resisted that impulse more and more as the lawyer made her practice walking, speaking, and sitting demurely. She felt like a character actress trying out for the role of Juliet or a caged lioness pretending to be a kitten.

On the fifth day a very welcome incident broke the monotony; she bought a townhouse sight unseen. Peabody escorted the agent to her room and remained while the salesman described the premises and building. Whereas it was in the best part of town, the agent warned her, it was not a fashionable house because it lacked enough room for gracious entertaining; the parlor could accommodate no more than twenty people. Furthermore, two of the six bedrooms had been placed inelegantly on the downstairs floor, an arrangement usually found only in cottages. A third disadvantage was the tiny servants' quarters over the small carriage house which presently housed two retainers. However, he assured her, it was an excellent property for the money.

Since the price was far below what she had expected to pay, she signed the papers and ordered Mr. Peabody to release the funds. She also asked her solicitor to deliver the keys to Maude and Lynette along with her note asking them to check the contents. At this juncture of the transaction, the agent interrupted. "It's furnished, Miss Grey, but the quality of the furniture is commonplace. You will probably want to replace most of it." Anne grinned at him and shook her head. Life in Boston had taught her that silk drapes and brocade chairs do not make a home. Her final order to the agent was to retain the retainers; she would pay their future salaries. As he left with the lawyer, the salesman shook his head. Women, he thought with his prudent businessman's mind, were too impulsive to be trusted with money of their own.

As Anne and Margaret settled down to the more cheerful contemplation of the new home, Peabody finished preparing his case. The eleven witnesses he would call were thoroughly rehearsed, and the two Brownwell children had been coached for their one brief appearance on the first day. As he sat back and pondered his chances, this cold, efficient man of law closed his eyes and crossed his fingers.

Chapter 15

AT Peabody's insistence, Anne did not attend the opening session of the hearing. Since her testimony would not be required during the preliminaries, he told her that he didn't want her exposed to unnecessary tension. Actually, his reasons for her exclusion were more fundamental. This was the day the validity of her marriage and the legitimacy of her children were to be determined, and he didn't want a demoralized client on his hands in case either decision went against her. Moreover, he did not want her present when he questioned her husband and Paul Bouvier about the events aboard the *Boston Queen*. As poised as she seemed to be, he didn't dare risk an emotional outburst this early in the hearing. In a magistrate's court there would be no jury that might be swayed to sympathy by a pretty woman's tears, only a coldly judicial magistrate who most certainly would be irritated by any excessive emotion.

Thus it was Aunt Margaret who answered Anne's frantic questions about the day's proceedings.

"Were there many people there?"

"A flock of vultures were crowded into the balconies when the hearing began. But right after the magistrate read some of the papers from the stacks the solicitors handed him, he announced that the case was too delicate for spectators. I wish you could have seen their faces when he cleared the courtroom. I imagine they're the same sadists who attend public hangings, especially the women."

"Was my husband there, Aunt Margaret?"

"He was there, but he wasn't sitting with the Doncasters. He had his own solicitor."

"How did he look?"

"Very different. Older, of course, but very changed. I don't think he smiled once during the whole session."

"Did you get a chance to talk to him?"

"No, he left the minute it was over."

"What did she look like—you know—his new wife?" Anne tried but she failed to conceal the angry tremor in her voice.

"She's short and dark-haired."

"She would be."

"She's not bad-looking, I suppose, Anne, but she isn't in your class. She looks too much like her father to suit me. He's as hard-looking when he smiles as when he scowls. Even if I didn't know all about him, I'd still think he was a criminal. And two of his solicitors look almost as nasty as he does. Those two didn't seem to do a thing except pass notes to the third lawyer. He's the one you have to watch out for, Anne. His name is Prichart, and John says he is very good at intimidating witnesses. I can believe it. Those cold eyes of his seemed to look right through me."

"What kind of a man is the magistrate?"

"I can tell you this, he's not the kind you want to try any of your sarcastic tricks on, young lady. Funny-looking wig or not, he's been sitting on that bench a long time; and he's no one's fool. He sat up there and took his time reading all the papers about your marriage before he called the lawyers to the bench. Prichart was the only one who went up for the Doncasters. But your husband's solicitor went up and so did John. The only one to object to what the magistrate said to them was Prichart; but evidently no one paid any attention to him because the next thing I knew, the magistrate announced that your marriage to Lord Gilbert Brownwell was unquestionably valid.''

"What about the children, Aunt Margaret; didn't he rule them as legal, too?"

"Later he did, but not right then. First, he sent a bailiff out to bring your father and the twins into the court. Anne, I wish you could have seen your father carrying them in. He looked so proud. It was the first time I'd really seen your children except for those few minutes at the dock. They're beautiful, Anne. Your little boy has the same expression you had as a child, big serious blue eyes looking all around him as if he wants to memorize everything he sees. But your little girl, Anne, is she always so precocious? No sooner had your father seated her at our table than she looked up at the magistrate and asked, 'Is he God, Tony?' I take back what I said earlier about your husband, he did smile then; and that little monkey of yours turned around and smiled right back at him. She certainly does look like him.''

"She has since the day she was born. Did her father come over to talk to them?"

"No, I don't think the court would allow him to. But the magistrate came down from his bench and talked to them. He told them that he had just read some interesting papers about them, and your son said that he would like to read those papers, too. Can Tony really read, Anne?"

"He's been reading since he was four. The magistrate didn't let him, did he?"

"No, but he asked your son who had taught him to read. And when Tony said that you had, the man nodded and then asked your daughter if she could read, too. That little minx declared, 'Naturally, I can do anything my brother can.' Can she really, Anne?"

"Your namesake, Aunt Margaret, has a will of iron. She learned to read about two months after her brother did. What else did the magistrate ask them?"

"Mostly about the other things they had learned. Tony said that they knew their numbers and that they were learning to speak French. Little Margaret actually said some words in French. The only other thing the magistrate asked them was if they liked being made to study. Both of your children said it was fun.''

"Didn't he ask them anything about me?"

"No, he just patted them on the head and told your father to take them out. After they were gone, he walked over to your husband and spoke to him. I don't know what he said, but both your husband and his solicitor nodded. When the magistrate returned to the bench, he announced that Anthony and Margaret were the legal Brownwell heirs. I think Prichart was about to object, but he didn't get the chance to before court was dismissed for the day.''

"Did you get to see my children again?"

"Yes, dear, your father and I took them to lunch.''

"Did they ask about me at all?"

"You're all they talked about, Anne. Poor little tykes, they miss their mother.''

All personal conversation ended abruptly when John Peabody arrived to inform them about the next day's schedule. "I think it will be routine again, since the court has to admit the rest of the evidence before we can begin to call witnesses. So I don't want you in court tomorrow, either. I don't want you to be upset or nervous before you do have to appear. The case is going well, so there's no need to worry about anything.''

But all the next day Anne worried anyway, and the only moments of relief in her lonely vigil were the few times her three bodyguards came in to check on her. By late afternoon she knew with a sick dread that the day in court had not been routine at all; and when Margaret and the lawyer finally did arrive, she was tense with anxiety. Seeing her in this state, Peabody insisted on doing all the talking himself.

"I was wrong about the routine today, Anne. Doncaster's lawyers had already entered a challenge that you were an unfit wife at the time of your wedding. And as I expected, they called on your mother-in-law. When I objected that you had to be present to face any witness against you, the magistrate promised that if he accepted the challenge, the witness would be recalled when you were present to repeat her testimony.''

"What did she say about me?''

"Just what we thought she would say. She was a very bad witness without any respect for the truth. Even Prichart was embarrassed. Her testimony was stopped when Mr. Chadwick, your husband's solicitor, asked to put your husband on the stand to refute her accusations. Since Lord Brownwell's testimony was in your favor, the magistrate denied the challenge of immorality at this time.''

"That woman,'' Margaret interrupted, "was so angry at her son, she made a fool of herself and was told to leave the court for the duration of the hearing.''

"At that point, I requested and was granted permission to get all the testimony about the actual voyage over with before you appeared in court, on the ground that much of it would be too upsetting for you,'' Peabody continued. "Our case went very smoothly for the rest of the day. Both Captain Bouvier and Captain Perkins were excellent witnesses, as was Lady Margaret.

"She began by describing the conditions she had made to the captains concerning your safety while you were on their ship. Since the magistrate had already read a copy of the dossier I had collected on your husband prior to the marriage, he ruled that your aunt had merely performed her duty as guardian; and he ruled out cross-examination.

"Captain Perkins told about all of the events from the time the ship sailed until it reached Bermuda, detailing your husband's actions. Prichart's questioning was stopped abruptly when your husband's solicitor stated that his client admitted that all the charges were justified: the drinking, the gambling, the . . . er, relationship with Madame Charbot, the theft of your money, and the beating.''

"He admitted nothing else?'' Anne asked, remembering the other acts of her husband, his striking her face and his violence during the first night of the storm.

"No, he did not. But Captain Perkins described the heavy bruises you had a week before the beating. What caused those bruises, Anne, and why didn't you tell me about them?"

"I just remembered them a minute ago."

"How did you get them?"

"My husband and I had an argument and for several days we didn't speak. Then one night he kicked me out of bed." Anne could hear Margaret's sharp gasp, and she turned to her aunt to explain. "Most of the time Gilbert was a good husband; but when he was drinking, he often lost his temper."

Peabody was frowning as he continued his narration. "The only slight problem we had today was with Captain Bouvier's testimony. He was challenged almost at once by your husband's solicitor, who asked him if he had been attracted to you himself."

"Mr. Chadwick asked Paul that?"

"Yes, and Captain Bouvier answered it somewhat in the affirmative, that he'd found you a very pretty girl in need of his protection."

"Mr. Peabody, I swear that Paul has never been anything but a friend. I'm sure that's all he meant by what he said."

Again the lawyer frowned before he continued. "When Captain Bouvier admitted lying to your husband by telling him that you were dead, the magistrate was very critical. I thought that we might have trouble there, but eventually he ruled that a captain of a ship at sea had the right to protect a passenger's life."

Hesitantly Anne asked, "Mr. Peabody, were any charges made against my husband for beating me?"

"No, Anne, unfortunately, even though society in general frowns upon it, wife beating is not a chargeable offense. But you do not have to be concerned about facing your husband in court; the Doncaster lawyers demanded that he be barred from any further sessions. Now, Anne, I want you to go to bed and get a good night's sleep. So far the hearing is completely in our favor, so you just stop worrying about it."

After he had gone, Anne said plaintively, "I didn't want him charged with anything, I just wanted to see him."

Margaret's glance toward her niece was sharply speculative. "Just as well your husband won't be there. You can see him after it's all over."

Surprisingly, Anne slept better that night than she had since leaving the *Boston Belle*, and the next morning a serene Andrew Grey awakened. Even in her blue velvet suit and mink cape, Andy's steady eyes and serious face stared back at Anne from the mirror.

But on the way to court the next day, an incident occurred that shook her composure badly. As the carriage with Margaret, Anne, and the six bodyguards arrived in front of the Hall of Justice, a milling crowd tried to rush the new arrivals. Nimble as only seamen can be, the two Frenchmen leapt from the carriage to confront the crowd, and almost immediately the two burliest Americans joined them to form a line. The other two guards lifted Anne and Margaret to the paving; and using the Frenchmen as a shield they pushed the women toward the entrance. Suddenly violence erupted as a group of eight hoodlums rushed the bodyguards.

Paul Bouvier had chosen the two French Basques especially for this job. These squat, powerful brothers were his top cargo guards, expert fighters with fists, feet, and knives. Armed with knives, they sailed into the crowd, a swinging fist alternating with the flashing knife. While the Americans were good brawlers, it was the deadly teamwork of the cargo guards that accounted for six of the eight assailants. But in spite of their valiant defense, Anne was injured. Just before she gained the safety of the doorway, an expertly thrown rock struck her shoulders with a force that knocked her to her knees. Shoving Margaret through the entrance, one guard blocked the crowd while the other carried Anne into a waiting room and laid her carefully down on the floor.

Minutes later a worried John Peabody and magistrate entered the room to view the injured woman. Deeply worried, the solicitor knelt beside her to check her pulse. Anne shook her head slightly and whispered, "Give me a little time and I'll be all right." Then she closed her eyes and went to sleep; twenty minutes later she opened her eyes and arose. Andrew Grey was back and in full control of Anne's facial features and emotions. With a deep admiration for her courage, John Peabody escorted her into the courtroom with a gallantry he seldom displayed.

The magistrate gaveled once and began to speak. "This morning," he reported, "a disgraceful assault took place in front of this courthouse on the first day the central figure of this hearing arrived. Since for the previous two mornings there has been no disturbance, I can only assume this welcome was deliberately arranged by someone in this court. Tomorrow there will be bailiffs and policemen stationed outside. Furthermore, I would like to caution all participants in this hearing to keep the testimony given in court limited to this court until the hearing is completed." During the last part of the warning, the magistrate kept his eyes turned toward Edward Doncaster, and Anne had her first chance to observe the man's response. The heavy, jowled face remained impassive, but the eyes were blackly defiant. Anne knew that today's testimony would be avidly reported by the scandal sheets Peabody had warned her about. Restlessly her eyes scanned the group clustered around Doncaster, straining to locate the woman who would replace her as Lady Brownwell if she could. But Edwina Doncaster was no longer in the courtroom.

As she searched, Anne saw Doncaster nod to the tallest of the three lawyers huddled around him; and in response, the one Margaret identified as Prichart arose and began his attack: "Yesterday much was made of a beating which allegedly took place on a ship bound for Bermuda. We were led to believe that the beating was serious enough to leave scars. Since that claim is only hearsay to those of us not privy to the incident, I demand that we be shown proof."

The first objection to this request came not from Peabody, but from a man sitting alone in the center of the courtroom. Anne surmised that he must be her husband's counsel, Alan

Chadwick, and she wondered if his objection was in her husband's defense or in hers. When her own lawyer rose to second the objection, Anne stopped him and nodded her agreement to the inspection. In the company of Lady Margaret and a woman summoned by a bailiff, Anne retired to a waiting room and removed her upper garments. With her fur cape held securely over her breasts by the woman prison warden, Anne stood with her back to the door and heard the footsteps of the three men who entered the room. The first voice she recognized was that of the magistrate, who questioned her, "That bruise on your shoulder is the result of the rock incident this morning?" She nodded and started to speak, only to be interrupted by the sharp tones of Prichart.

"According to the testimony there were four or five lash scars. I can see only three." Again Anne attempted to speak, only to be interrupted by the testy voice of the magistrate.

"Even if there were only one such scar, such a blow is too severe for a woman's body regardless of the provocation. This indignity is now finished, Mr. Prichart." The magistrate, Anne thought wryly, does not disapprove of wife beating in general, only to the degree of it.

Returning to the courtroom, she was in time to hear Prichart formally present the charges against her. "With the help of considerable attested-to material which we have gathered against this defendant and with the direct testimony of witnesses, we will prove that the woman whom this court has ruled to be the legal wife of Lord Brownwell is both an unfit wife and an unfit mother." He paused long enough to impale Anne with cold, hooded eyes before he continued, "We hearby ask that she testify in her own behalf so that we may refute her claims."

"You don't have to, Anne," Peabody whispered to her. "Let him produce his witnesses first." But she shook her head and walked over to the witness railing, where she was sworn in. Her hand was steady as she placed it on the Bible; so were her eyes as she watched Prichart walk toward her. His voice was cold as he demanded that she remove her veil, so that, he asserted, the court could determine the truth of her answers. She nodded and took off the offending veil. He studied her face for a long moment; Andrew Grey's polite young face looked back.

"Will you tell the court how your illegitimacy affected your childhood?"

"I did not know what the word meant when I was a child, sir."

"But you learned quickly what it meant when your father married, did you not?"

"No, sir."

"Didn't you wonder why you were no longer asked to visit your grandparents' home?"

"No, sir," Anne responded, "because at that time I began to study full-time with my tutor."

"I have here the written testimony of your stepmother, Lady Elizabeth Ashton, who states: 'Anne seemed embarrassed by her misfortune.' Were you embarrassed?"

"No, sir; since I had not caused my illegitimacy, I was not embarrassed by it."

"Not even on the occasion of your sixteenth birthday party?"

"No, sir, I was not embarrassed at that party; I was angry about the way my stepmother and other people held my illegitimacy against me, instead of against my mother and father."

"You were angry a great deal during your childhood, were you not?"

"Most of the time I was too busy with my studies."

"Ah, yes. Let's get back to your tutor. He was an Irish itinerant, I believe."

"Padric Neill is an Irish scholar, who is now headmaster at Grayhaven." Even in her defense of her beloved Paddy, Andy's voice remained politely informative.

"According to your tutor's written statement, very early during your studies, you showed a marked preference for subjects traditionally reserved for men. Why?"

"Since I learned Latin and Greek easily, I did not know they were reserved for men." To save her life, she could not have added a "sir" at this point.

"But according to your tutor, you requested that he teach you higher mathematics; and when he refused, you learned it on your own. Again, why?"

"It is the basis of all business, sir, so I was interested in it."

"You were interested in acting in all ways like a man, weren't you? I have here the statements of four people whom you accosted in the village of Ramsey. Would you please explain these episodes."

Controlling the cold fear she felt, Anne responded quietly, "The first two were pupils at a local school. One yelled obscenities at me and the other threw mud. I smeared dirt on one and pushed the other into a creek. This third man made improper advances and I shoved him off the sidewalk. The fourth was a man whom I hit when he attempted to restrain me."

"The point is that you acted violently in every case as a man would act. According to one witness, you were the most aggressive girl in the parish. Do you recall Reverend Myles Thompson?"

Anne stiffened. "I recall him very well, but he was not a witness."

"Mr. Prichart," John Peabody's voice rang out, "I investigated two of those incidents, and I found Reverend Thompson both inaccurate and prejudiced."

Prichart's face remained impassive. "I stand corrected, Mr. Peabody." Abruptly he leaned toward Anne and his voice became almost confidential. "Lady Brownwell, do you approve of arranged marriages?"

"No, sir, I do not," she answered cautiously.

"Then you did not approve of the marriage your father arranged for you?"

"I did not, sir."

"Then you never loved your husband?"

"Yes, I did. I fell in love with him after we met."

"But that love didn't last long, did it, Lady Brownwell? You soon found occasion to seek out the company of Captain Bouvier."

"Captain Bouvier was only trying to teach me something about the running of a ship."

"Always the same compulsion to act like a man, to delve into matters that shouldn't concern a woman." Prichart's voice sharpened as he pounced on the next question. "How did you get the bruises Captain Perkins described in court yesterday?"

Fighting the mounting pressure that threatened her composure, Anne took several deep breaths until she could answer calmly. "My husband shoved me out of bed one night, and I struck my head."

"Odd that he didn't admit to such an innocent action, Lady Brownwell, when he'd owned up to so many more damaging ones."

"I don't think Ton—I don't think he remembered," she stammered, shocked by the realization that she'd almost called her estranged husband by the love name of Tony. Despite her unwillingness to remember, she recalled other fragments of a destroyed love—words from the only declaration Gilbert had ever made to her—"We belong together" and "Don't ever stop loving me." I never really have, she thought with an aching sadness that was abruptly terminated by the impatient sarcasm of Prichart's voice.

"I dislike having to repeat questions, Lady Brownwell. I asked you why your husband beat you on the occasion of your last meeting with him?"

"Because I refused to tell him where the rest of my money was," she answered dully.

"The gold coins your aunt so cautiously sewed into the hems of your undergarments? Lord Brownwell had a legal right to that money, just as any husband has a right to any of his wife's possessions unless those possessions are secured by special provisions. The gold coins were not, so once again you proved an uncooperative wife—not merely uncooperative but unfit as well, because you're the one who deserted your husband when you asked Captain Bouvier to hide you. You weren't deserted, Lady Brownwell; you're the guilty one who left her husband. He believed you to be dead, but you knew he was alive. In all those years in Boston, did you ever once try to write to him?"

"No, because I believed that he had deserted me and would not have wanted to hear from me. Besides, I did not know where in Australia he was."

"But as soon as you heard that he had become Lord Brownwell, you couldn't wait to get in touch with him. You hired a lawyer immediately to fight for what you thought were your rights, didn't you?"

Jumping to his feet, an angry and worried John Peabody shouted his objection and explained to the magistrate that Lady Margaret, not Anne, had begun the fight. Nodding in agreement, the magistrate called for the lunch recess; and an exhausted and defeated Anne huddled alone in a witness room drinking two cups of cold tea while trying to rebuild her shattered defenses.

Back behind the witness railing after the brief respite, Anne faced an even more relentless attack from Prichart, this time on the subject of Andrew Grey. His opening comments were directed toward the magistrate.

"We come now to the segment in this woman's life when she began to live her fantasy about being a man in earnest. Here we have a woman whose early life had been marked by her tendency toward masculine interests and violence; therefore, after she deserted her husband, she virtually became a man." He swung around toward Anne abruptly. "Tell us in your own words why you changed into this Andrew Grey."

"I was left alone and I had to support myself and my unborn child in a world where women were not allowed to hold good jobs."

"But the truth of the matter is that you did not need

money. Your aunt had already supplied you with ample funds. Furthermore, you could always go to your father for support."

"I refused to be a burden on anyone."

"So you persisted in your deception. Tell me, Lady Brownwell, how much money did you make with your questionable financial dealings in American stocks?"

"About four hundred thousand pounds, sir."

"And you made this money while posing as Andrew Grey, far more money than you actually needed. I suggest that it was love of money which became your central interest, not the support of your children." On and on he drove Anne with questions about her work at the shipyards and her activities in the Boston Stock Exchange. Without warning, he switched to her part in the establishment of Greyhaven Academy. She was forced to admit that she had encouraged the four Irish immigrants to assume English identities, and to admit that she had told no one outside the Perkins household the complete truth about her marital status.

"Did you ever tell this Winchell Rawlings that you were a married woman?"

"No, sir."

"Why not?"

"At first I thought he was only interested in me as a teacher."

Prichart's face was a mask of contemptuous disbelief in her claim. "But after he proposed, you certainly could not have doubted the source of his interest in you. Why did you not inform him then?"

"Because I was not interested in him as a man; I did not even like him."

"Had you 'liked' him, your answer would have been different, would it not?"

"No, sir, it would not."

"We will now examine another phase of this remarkable life you were leading. I have here the statement of an American cabby whose regular station was the section of the Boston waterfront directly opposite the pub of one Casey

Ryan.'' Although her face did not change expression, Anne could feel the rapid increase of her breathing and sick thudding of her heart. Prichart continued, ''According to his testimony, this American claims to have seen you enter this pub every morning during the summer of 1843. Were you not in fact becoming a public drunkard?''

In a voice as devoid of emotion as the lawyer's, Anne described her entire relationship with Casey Ryan, including her desire to learn the famous Casey punch. When she finished, Prichart looked at her with even greater contempt before he resumed his cross-examination.

''Not satisfied with the success of your earlier street battles with men, you decided to become an even more proficient street brawler. Tell the court if you ever used this newly acquired skill of yours?''

''No, sir, I have never had the occasion to.''

''Did you ever threaten to?''

Oh, God, she thought, not even Claude Bouvier can remain my secret. Aloud she answered without hesitation, ''Once.''

''Describe the circumstances to the court, please.''

''On one occasion I believed that a gentleman would not accept my word that I was not free to form an alliance with him.''

''Who was this gentleman? And just how did you get yourself into that predicament?'' It did not occur to Anne that by blackening the character of Claude Bouvier, she might have spared herself the anguish of the truth. Instead she described those six days in detail. When she had finished, Prichart demanded to know, ''Then you returned this man's physical passion?''

''I was attracted to him, yes. But I would not endanger the future of my children, even for my own happiness. So I refused him and he accepted my refusal like the gentleman he is.''

''A very noble sentiment, Lady Brownwell, but tomorrow I

will produce witnesses who will prove that you are more of a liar than you have already admitted to being."

Awakening in an exhausted state the next morning, Anne dreaded the even worse ordeal she must face that day. Nor did another violent incident that occurred once again on the sidewalk improve her spirits. Although the bailiffs and police had cleared a pathway, Anne and Margaret were forced to remain in the carriage by the command of one of the French brothers. He had spotted a flash of steel in the hand of a spectator. Pointing to the man, the Frenchman yelled, *"Le voilà!"* to his brother. Like great gorillas the two leapt toward the man. When they finally released him, all of the tendons in his fingers had been slashed with his own knife.

Strolling over to investigate after the incident was over, a laconic policeman looked at the fallen man and clucked sympathetically, "Well, well, Willy. I see you've cut yourself. Let's you and me wander over to the jail for a bit of plaster and a talk with my super."

More aware than ever now that Doncaster or someone he employed was her deadly enemy, Anne found Andrew's composure very elusive that day. She sat down warily next to Peabody, grateful for the heavy veil that covered her face. When Prichart arose to address the court, she shuddered; and although she was not called upon to testify once, she lived through torture for five long hours.

"Yesterday the defendant admitted to being a violent woman who wanted to act like a man. Time and time again she admitted that she was a liar. Today I will call upon two witnesses who will prove that she also lied about public drunkenness." The first man Prichart called was unknown to Anne, but she recognized the type as one of the many waterfront loiterers. In a bellicose voice the witness claimed that he had seen Andrew Grey enter many waterfront saloons and emerge in a drunken state of unsteadiness.

Immediately Peabody called upon Captain Perkins to refute the man's accusations. Impressive in his brass-laden uniform, Tom Perkins proved an unimpeachable witness. No matter how vicious Prichart's attempts were, the captain remained steadfast in his defense of Anne. "Because I had been entrusted with Lady Brownwell's safety by her guardian, I was careful about her errands into Boston. I timed the lengths of her visits there, and not once was she late in returning to the shipyard. And not once did she ever exhibit any signs of having had a drink of alcohol."

Anne recognized the next witness, a young shipyard worker. She watched as he swaggered toward the witness railing and spoke in a belligerent voice.

"When she was posing as the limey, Andy Grey, she thought she was the cock of the walk. She strutted all over the yard, drunk most of the time. Oh, the limey was careful not to git cotched by any of the bosses. But all of us young bucks knowed she drunk as much as we did behind the lumber stacks."

Peabody consulted the three shipyard workers at the table and then rose to confront the witness.

"Mr. Wilkins, when did you leave your job at the shipyards?"

"I quit two years ago. No use slavin' for dirty bosses who gave all the credit to a smart-aleck limey."

"Did you indeed quit, Mr. Wilkins, or were you dismissed?" Peabody asked and then called one of Anne's bodyguards to the stand, the foreman who had fired this ex-employee for theft of company hardware and for drunkenness on the job. In a slow, positive voice, the foreman defended "Andy Grey" as a reliable, sober worker and condemned Wilkins. In rapid succession Peabody called the other two shipyard workers, who supported the foreman's testimony. From her seat Anne noticed that the magistrate was looking through the dozen or more other shipyard testimonials that Lynette had collected, and she watched him jot notations down from several of them.

Prichart, however, was not completely silenced: "The witnesses I produced were impartial men who had nothing to gain by lying; whereas all of the defense witnesses are dependent upon the goodwill of Lady Gray, who is very biased about her niece. However, we will leave the subject of the defendant's drunkenness to a future time. Right now I am far more interested in her quality of motherhood. Because of her obsession to make money, this woman spent more than eleven hours each day but Sunday at one or the other of her jobs. Adding this number to the hours needed for sleeping and eating, I estimate that Lady Brownwell had no time left to do more than pat her children on the head once a day while other women performed the main function of motherhood for her.''

With varying degrees of anger both the Perkinses and the Bouviers defended Anne's actions as a mother. All claimed essentially the same thing, that she had spent hours every evening playing with all three children or teaching them, and at no time were they ever neglected. But the witness who proved most eloquent in her defense was Mary Harrington. As the red-cheeked Irish girl mounted the stand, Anne prayed that her children's nurse would not become excited and reveal the secret of her name "Harrington"; but she reckoned without Mary's intense loyalty.

Recognizing this witness to be an uneducated one, Prichart was particularly caustic, but he, too, underestimated the Irishwoman. She answered his questions with an angry assurance of right, and he could not shake her with his insults. Even when he stopped asking, Mary was not finished. "My mistress is a saint," she declared. "She's the best mither in the whole world, with me Danny as well as her own two. Nivver once did she fail to be there whin they needed her. What's washin' a nappy or sucklin' a babe compared to that? And I'll be thankin' yer, mister, to be kappin' a civil tongue in yer head whin yer talk about her." Dismissed or not, Mary stomped down from the stand and took her seat; and almost everyone in court smiled at her performance.

Momentarily, Anne noticed with pleasure, even the talking machine that was Prichart was silenced; but he was soon back with another witness, this time a Boston dandy in a beruffled shirt and tightly fitted suit. This was the first educated witness Prichart had produced, and he stood aside in anticipation.

"While she lived in Boston, Lady Brownwell admitted to having romantic relationships with two men. She claimed they were very innocent friendships, but I believe we can prove that she had far more not-so-innocent ones with other men," Prichart stated.

Consulting a small leather-bound book, the young man spoke with an accent that was straight from "Ha'va'd". He had first heard of Anne Grey, he claimed, from several upperclassmen who had told him that she was "available." She had first answered his summons to come to his room at an inn where he lived on April 19, 1842, at which time they had been intimate. She had come again on April 21, and then on six more occasions later in the same year. She had proved, he asserted, very available.

To refute this damning testimony, Peabody called upon Maude Perkins, who in her firm New England voice was as unemotional as a court bailiff. She insisted flatly that on the first two dates Anne had been recovering from the birth of the twins; and that on the other dates named, she had been at home just as she had been at home on all but one night of her five years in America.

"Are you quite certain that the defendant was at home?" Prichart asked.

"Absolutely."

"While she was under your roof, she occupied a separate wing equipped with its own outside door, did she not?"

"Yes, she did, but that old door has not been unlocked in years, and Anne never had a key to it."

"But there were windows in her room, windows which a tall athletic woman like the defendant could easily negotiate. I suggest, Mrs. Perkins, that not only on the one night was she unaccountably missing, but on any other night as well, she could have been away from home without your knowledge."

Before Maude could make any response, Mary Harrington had had enough. Leaping to her feet, she shouted from the floor, ignoring Prichart's attempt to shut her up and the magistrate's pounding gavel. "On that one night, she was at me mither's house, talkin' to the tachers she was hirin' for the school. As fer her lavin' her room through the window, I had to wake the mistress up many nights whin the children needed her. She was always there waitin' fer me. So, Yer Honor, yer can't believe what that dirty-minded lawyer is sayin'." Mary may not have been a dignified witness, but she was an effective one. The day's hearing was over a minute after her explosion.

That night Anne slept little, if at all; for the first time she admitted to herself the strong possibility that she might lose her children. In between her moments of despair, she thought long and hard about the man who would cause her to lose them, Mr. Edward Doncaster. Her mind was still concentrating on these two gloomy subjects as she and Margaret boarded the carriage the next morning. Vaguely she noted that there were only four of the guards aboard and that the driver, Peabody's own man, had four large pistols resting on the bench beside him.

The French brothers had gone ahead to await them. After yesterday's knife incident, they knew that today's attempt could be even more deadly; but for once they misgauged the place of attack. About two blocks from the Hall of Justice, the carriage was blocked by a crowd of shouting people. Grabbing his four-in-hand reins, the driver wrapped them around the post just tightly enough to keep the massive horses at a slow pace. Then he rose to a standing position with a pistol in each hand. Deliberately he fired them three feet over the heads of the crowd. "The next shots," he shouted as he picked up the other two pistols, "will be aimed four feet lower." Most of the hoodlums gave way instantly as the horses plodded slowly toward them, but a few of the thugs crowded close to the sides of the carriage. Anne and Margaret pressed themselves against the floor trying to protect their heads from the rocks being thrown at them while the four guards tried to beat the attackers off with their fists.

Both sides of the combatants paused as they heard pounding feet approaching. From around the corner the two French guards ran at top speed with knives drawn and their faces set in the savage glow of battle. For the assailants who could not escape, the injuries meted out that day were lethal or nearly so. But the passengers, too, had been hurt; Margaret was unconscious and Anne's temple was bleeding from a rock wound. Two of the carriage guards had also been hit.

Not daring to risk her aunt's life, Anne ordered the driver to get them to the nearest infirmary, where Margaret was put to bed and the wounds of the other three were bandaged. More than an hour late in arriving before the magistrate and feeling almost as vulnerable in court as she had on the street, Anne reported the attack, the third in as many days. She was too upset to notice that the magistrate had been angry before she spoke to him or that he held a small stack of newspapers in his hand, newspapers with smeared ink and slanderous reports about her real and imagined escapades in America. The lewd caricatures of herself as a huge busted Andrew Grey leering out at readers she never saw, either. Both Chadwick and Peabody rushed to escort her back to her customary seat, where she sat pale and shaken.

The magistrate waited for her to be seated before he began to speak. "Several days ago during this hearing, I issued orders that the testimony heard in this court was to remain secret. Someone here—certainly not the defendant, but someone—saw fit to give out not only what has been said here already, but what presumably was to be today's testimony. I promise you that I will investigate this matter thoroughly and punish the culprit.

"My second charge against the plaintiffs concerns the three attacks made upon the life of the defendant near my courtroom." Anne wondered if he would have cared had the attacks been in another part of town. "Again," the magistrate continued, "I promise to investigate this matter thoroughly.

"My third charge against the plaintiffs has to do with the caliber of the witnesses they have thus far produced. All three were proved to have lied during at least part of their testimony." The magistrate paused to look at Prichart. "I am going to deny your petition to allow your next six witnesses the right to speak. After reading these papers containing their probable testimony, I will waste no more of the court's time. I have already ordered my bailiffs to remand all nine of your witnesses into protective custody. If they were Englishmen, I would sentence them to jail for perjury; but since they are Americans, I am going to hold them until they can be placed upon the first ship bound for Boston. Both the court costs for their maintenance in England and for their passage home will be borne by Mr. Doncaster, because his hired agents failed to check their reliability before bringing them here.

"Therefore, without further delay, I am going to announce my decisions concerning this hearing." Fighting now to retain her semblance of innocence, Anne looked up at the magistrate, only to find his cold eyes waiting for hers. "Young woman," he began, "I cannot condone any of the life you lived in America. I disapprove of your lying, I disapprove of your masquerading as a man, and I disapprove of your greed for money. However, none of these qualities were listed in the charges against you. To the charge of drunkenness which the plaintiffs leveled but failed to prove, I can only declare you innocent. To the charges of immorality, I can only make the same declaration, since the witness they produced was proved to be lying in part, and since the two men you admitted knowing both supported your plea of innocence." The old devil, Anne thought, is actually sorry that he can't convict me on both counts. "I can therefore," the magistrate stressed, "find no evidence to support the plaintiffs' claim that Lord Brownwell has grounds for a divorce.

"On the third charge of unfit motherhood, I must likewise absolve the defendant. I have spoken with her children, and they seem content with her quality of motherhood. Furthermore, since many respectable English mothers also delegate some of their duties to nurses, I cannot condemn the defendant for a similar practice. I therefore am returning the custody of her children to her." Anne's head jerked at this announcement; she'd had no idea that for three weeks she had not been a legal mother. "With the proviso," the magistrate pounded on, "that she realize that in England the father always has the primary custody of all children. What her husband decides, she must accept. This hearing is now closed."

He rapped the gavel once and stood up, his eyes still on Anne as he made his way toward her. Furious at his prejudicial idea of justice, Anne continued to wear her little smile and to meet his eyes as he stopped by her table.

"Young woman," he asserted sternly, "I am going to give you two pieces of free advice. I warn you not to attempt posing as a man in England. We are much more careful here in monitoring the activities of our women. My second advice concerns your physical safety. Until I can ascertain the people responsible for the attacks, I recommend that you retain your bodyguards. Good day to you, madam." Without any forgiving warmth, he walked away in majestic serenity, well satisfied that justice had been served. Anne had been acquitted.

She watched him leave and turned to Mr. Chadwick, now sitting next to her. "I would like to see you in private, if at all possible," she whispered. He nodded and suggested that his office would be the best place. Thus, while her own lawyer and the other witnesses at her table went to rescue Lady Margaret and to report to the Ashton townhouse for a celebration, Anne walked the four blocks to Chadwick's office, flanked by her two French bodyguards. On the way there her fists were clenched in the pockets of her mink cape, and she almost hoped that some of Doncaster's paid ruffians would attack.

Once seated in the office, she dropped all pretense at youthful innocence and became the businesswoman she was as she asked the lawyer bluntly about the condition of her husband's estate.

Fascinated by the metamorphosis in the attitude of a young woman he had sympathized with in court, Chadwick was taken aback by a question that seemed decidedly mercenary. Perhaps Prichart had been correct in his claim that her only interest in Lord Brownwell was monetary. His answer was blunt. "Your husband has refused to fight Mr. Doncaster in court. He has agreed to forfeit his entire estate in payment for the monies loaned to forestall bankruptcy and for damage done to the reputation of Edwina Doncaster."

"You have no chance to save any of the estate?"

"Only if your husband chooses to fight. And he won't. Through both legal and illegal means, Doncaster has gained a stranglehold on the estate, and Lord Brownwell lacks the capital to mount a successful fight."

"Then, Mr. Chadwick," she instructed coolly, "I want you to do something for me. It may not be completely honest, but I am not dealing with an ethical man. I want you to purchase the Brownwell country estate. I know it is the least valuable of the three Brownwell estates in England, so I imagine that it will be the first one Doncaster places on the market."

"I'm afraid that he'll ask a large price, Lady Brownwell."

"Not," she countered, "if it should suddenly become less attractive."

"What exactly do you have in mind?"

"The estate is in the middle of sheep country. Supposing a mysterious disease kills those sheep, and some 'expert' expresses the opinion that the soil is poisoned?"

Chadwick was laughing outright now. "Lady Brownwell, what you are suggesting is chicanery."

Anne grinned back. "Oh, it's that, at least, Mr. Chadwick. Can you arrange such a natural catastrophe? Remove the sheep one night and display a huge filled-in area the next day. Then a bogus land agent can tell Mr. Doncaster that he will have to let the land go fallow for ten years to keep the disease from spreading."

"It might work."

"It would, especially if the news were spread around. And if there should suddenly be some vandalism to the manor house. Not extensive, just a few broken windows, a little mud smeared on the walls, and a few of the pictures slashed. Not the good ones, of course, just some of the daubs found in all old estates. And if the local gossips should spread the rumor that the house is haunted, or that it's bad luck to the owners, don't you think that Doncaster would be easy to convince that he was stuck with a bad investment?''

"Very. That gentleman hates to lose."

"All right, Mr. Chadwick, I want you to find two men who will be our substitutes in this deal. Your name and mine must not appear. One of the men could be the housing agent who tells Doncaster that he has a potential buyer who is too uninformed to realize the estate's drawbacks. However, the buyer only has seventy thousand pounds in cash."

"It's worth a hundred thousand."

"Not if our plan succeeds, it isn't. Do you think you can handle it, Mr. Chadwick?"

"I think it's just possible, Lady Brownwell."

"Very well. I will put the money where it will be immediately available. When you obtain the papers of ownership, I want you to register them in my husband's name; but do not inform him under any circumstances. Agreed?"

"Agreed, Lady Brownwell. Now, is there anything else you need my assistance for?" The irony in his voice just missed sarcasm.

"As a matter of fact, yes. I want your agents to investigate the Birmingham coal industry. I want to know the company which has the best chance of competing with Doncaster's, a company with a brainy enough management to look ahead."

"And if my agents should find such a company?"

"After the estate deal is finished, you and I will go to that company and I shall invest in it." She began to laugh. "Do you think I'm crazy, Mr. Chadwick? You've been staring at me as if I have snakes wriggling out of my head. I do have a reason."

"You're after Doncaster, aren't you? He's a dangerous man, Lady Brownwell."

"I know. I was almost another of his victims. However, I do not plan to let Doncaster know anything about my participation. Keeping my name out of both deals will be your job, Mr. Chadwick. Now here is my home address. If you have occasion to need me, I'll be there. If I should have to accompany you, please bring a carriage large enough to accommodate my two bodyguards; because until I get my husband out from under that man's domination, my life is in danger. Only when Mr. Doncaster has money troubles enough of his own will he give up on my husband. I intend that he begin having such troubles immediately."

"If your husband should ask, am I free to give him your address?"

"Yes. I should like him to meet his children for their fifth birthday on March twenty-second. Will you relay my message to him?"

"I shall be delighted to, Lady Brownwell."

"Please call me Anne. I'm really too simple a person for titles. Good-bye, Mr. Chadwick." After she had gone, he sat there contemplating the ramifications of the two plans she had proposed. Both of them bore the stamp of a very original mind, one remarkably unhampered by ethical considerations. With such tactics, she just might succeed in destroying the financial empire of Edward Doncaster, a goal Chadwick himself endorsed wholeheartedly.

Chapter 16

ALONE in her sitting room, Anne was staring moodily out the window watching the children playing in the private neighborhood park across the quiet street. As usual these days, they were playing with Jacques and Auguste, her two faithful bodyguards. For the past three months they had become more companions to her than guards, since she had received no further threats of any kind.

Immediately after the trial she had lived in a whirl of excitement; one party after another had united her two families. She'd learned to like her two pretty half sisters, now sixteen and seventeen, and had envied them their coming-out giggles. She had loved her half brother, Geoffrey, who at fifteen was taller than she, a boy who looked so much like Anne herself that twice Tom Perkins had called him "Andy."

She had had quiet talks with her father and listened to his praise of her character and fortitude; but she'd sensed in him a relief that he no longer had to worry about her. Her vindication in court and her establishment as Lady Brownwell had made him feel free from the responsibility for her former degradation.

"You're safe now, Anne, with a lovely home and family and a title which you've earned. I knew that someday you'd be accepted in society." Her father, she thought with amusement, was still a snob, a wonderful, naive snob.

During those happier days, watching Lynette and Maude bustle around the kitchen preparing the frequent meals for the eighteen hungry guests, Anne had felt as secure as she had in the old Perkins home in Boston. With Lady Margaret keeping the three children enthralled with stories of fairies and frogs, the young mother had basked in the warm security of continuing generations. But even Margaret, she sensed, had believed that Anne had reached her stride and could now manage alone. "If you get lonely, dear, bring everyone down to Grayhaven; Paddy and I will put you all to work." However, Anne knew that she had outgrown Grayhaven.

Gradually her families had drifted off to return to their own worlds, leaving Anne in what they thought to be her snug little nest. The Ashtons had gone home to prepare for the season when the East Midlanders all joined the "hunt," taking Tom and Maude with them. Surprisingly, Tom and her father had become warm friends, each sharing the other's different interests and finding the exchange rewarding. Practical, prosaic Maude was popular with everyone, especially with the two Ashton girls, who enjoyed her uncritical mothering. Paul and Lynette had deposited their children at Grayhaven and had sailed the *Boston Queen* to France. At last only Margaret was left, and finally the day had come when she, too, had declared that she was restless to go home. "Anne dear," she'd said at parting, "you have weathered all your storms and are now free to live your own life with your children. Remember, though, if you or your children should ever need me, I'll be here."

Of all those dear friends, Paddy alone had understood her dilemma. "Well, Anne, what are you going to do with your life?" he had asked her. And she had answered him with a vague unease, "I don't know." Only he knew the extent of her restless ability and her need for a purpose in life. But he, too, had returned to his beloved Grayhaven to begin a new term and to meet the challenge of new students. Anne was left as the lonely "head of house." How she hated that phrase!

Her household was a delightful one, with employees who were more friends than servants. Mary, of course, still bubbled with enthusiasm, finding London a paradise of interesting fairs and exhibitions. Many days she and the two French brothers packed the excited children off to see some display or other at the shining new Crystal Palace built to honor Queen Victoria's expanding England.

Somewhat removed from the central group were the retainers who had come with the house. A quietly dignified couple in their midfifties, Robert Glenn and his wife Laura lived in their neat little apartment over the carriage house enjoying their books and hobbies in placid seclusion. Four hours each day they earned just enough money to keep them content; Robert maintained the grounds and the outside of the house while Laura cleaned the inside. Nothing seemed to bother them, neither the oddity of the woman they now served nor the scrambling children who often played in the tiny backyard talking to Robert as he worked.

By far the most exuberant addition to the ménage was Marie, who doubled as cook and general morale booster for the entire household. Her advent had come about the day the amateur cooks, Maude and Lynette, had departed. Anne had never learned to cook, and she could stand Mary's Irish stew no more than once a year. After eating a breakfast prepared with a degree of adequacy by Jacques, Anne had mentioned her need for a good cook. The two brothers had winked at her and at each other, held their fingers to their lips in the gesture that only Frenchmen can use properly, and cried "Marie!" in unison.

Marie was their sister, who now resided in England, they'd explained, because of a slight altercation with the French authorities. When two local gendarmes had accused her of concealing smugglers in the family inn along the rugged Atlantic coast of southern France, Marie had taken offense. More properly, she had taken action by using Basque foot fighting to down the two officers who had come to arrest her. When Anne had asked the brothers if Marie had been guilty of smuggling, they'd shrugged good-naturedly; and Auguste had explained, "To a Basque, smuggling is an honorable profession. Who knows about Marie, she has always been an independent woman."

And what a woman she was! As short and squat as her brothers, her rugged face was wreathed in a smile, and her energy was limitless. But it was her cooking that made her the most popular person around. The children haunted her kitchen, sampling the flaky cookies and the apple balls, and watching wide-eyed as she flipped an omelet in the pan. Within a week of her arrival, everyone adored her; and Anne could not imagine ever having been without her and her cheerful, democratic love of people. Already Marie had become a legend in the food shops; bargaining was a game of skill she played, and the merchants enjoyed matching wits with her.

As Anne watched the children from her window, she thought of their ever-increasing rate of development. Three hours a day now they spent studying, and they competed against each other in speed of reading and simple additions. Their lesson time was the only part of the day that made Anne feel that she had any constructive purpose in life. She enjoyed watching their personalities deepen; Danny and Margaret had developed a classroom rivalry that often required Tony's gentle diplomacy to smooth over. Her children, she thought, and Danny was included, were her only touchstone in this lonely new life. She had lost the interest she had once held for making money. Two months earlier, when Alan Chadwick arrived at her home jubilant over the purchase of Brownsville at the price Anne had dictated, she experienced very little excitement. Only his success in locating a coal mining operation owned by a vigorous and shrewd pair of brothers aroused her sense of adventure, especially when the lawyer described the difficulties involved.

"You can't invest as Lady Brownwell; the Blakes would insist upon your husband's approval. Nor will they accept a woman as a partner. I'm afraid they're typically English in that respect."

"Typically male, you mean." Anne smiled cynically. "I wonder what the magistrate would say if I resurrected Andrew Grey?"

"Even old Percival Suffield might approve if you succeed in damaging Doncaster. He's been unable to find any evidence to connect that suspect with those damnable attempts on your life. But you can't pose as Andrew Grey this time. That young man has become as well-known to the British public as Tom Jones. I had in mind an older man as a disguise for you—gray-haired and dignified, maybe even a little crotchety. Someone connected with railroads to explain your interest in coal. With your acting ability, you should have no difficulty giving a convincing performance. And you'd be safer from

Doncaster's spies once we reach Birmingham. Since our appointment there is arranged for the fifth of March, just four days from now, I've hired a theatrical man to supply your costume and to accompany us as a bodyguard. Your own men would be too conspicuous."

Impressed by the thoroughness of the lawyer's preparation, Anne was thoughtful. "Why are you going to all this trouble, Mr. Chadwick?"

"I have two other clients who want Doncaster destroyed as much as you do. Moreover, I have my own score to even with him. Are you still interested in the venture, Anne?"

She nodded slowly; even if the revenge part failed, coal was still the best investment on the English Stock Exchange. And the "venture" gave her a glorious seven-day reprieve from boredom. Expertly disguised as an elderly man, Anne acted her way convincingly into the confidence of both of the Blakes, who accepted "Hanley Krebs" as a silent partner and the one hundred thousand pounds Anne wanted to invest. By allowing Chadwick to do most of the talking, she avoided risking the disguise with unnecessary speech. She listened quietly when the older Blake described his expansion plans. With her investment money the company would be able to acquire a mine that adjoined the existing Blake ones and to purchase more efficient equipment.

"In two years," he promised the new partner, "we should be in a position to compete with Doncaster on an equal basis. Meanwhile we are making inroads on the open market with lower prices."

After this final successful conference at the Blake offices, Anne met Chadwick's other two clients who formed the second half of the lawyer's conspiracy. The older of the two men was Weston Kenrick, an ex–mine owner who had been Doncaster's first victim. During the final year of his ownership, the Kenrick Mine had been plagued with constant labor unrest and a hundred or more costly and unexplained accidents. Forced into bankruptcy and a public auction, Kenrick discovered that the only "public" to offer a bid was Edward Doncaster, whose criminally low bid was readily accepted by the corrupt political authorities. For the past twenty years, Weston Kenrick had devoted his time and knowledge to the ruination of his enemy.

The second man was his son, Cedric Kenrick, who had inherited the Bank of Leeds through his mother's family and who had also become one of Doncaster's victims. At the insistence of Lady Suzanne Brownwell, he had been forced to relinquish all Brownwell accounts and mortgages to Edward Doncaster. His bank had suffered badly through this loss of income. At Alan Chadwick's request, he had acted as the agent who negotiated Anne's purchase of Brownsville. Like his father, Cedric was bent on revenge, a goal that he firmly believed could be achieved by Anne's current investment and a proposed future one with the Blake brothers.

The challenge of meeting these men and the excitement of those few days in Birmingham furnished the only relief Anne experienced from the numbing sense of stagnation that now dominated her life. During the weeks that followed the Birmingham adventure, her interest in this venture had gradually diminished; and she found herself repeating Paddy's question more and more frequently. "What are you going to do now?" What? She was a court-upheld aristocrat, but except for her family she had not one friend among her peers. She was a legally bound wife without a husband. At this thought the dull knife twisted once more around the region of her heart. He had not even come for his children's birthday or sent one word to her personally. Chadwick had tried to warn her. "Lord Brownwell," he had explained, "has been very cold and remote since he signed his estate over to Doncaster. He won't let anyone approach him. I think that he feels too defeated even to see his children. So if you want a reconciliation, Anne, you will have to take the initiative."

But how, Anne asked herself for the thousandth time, can a woman with no experience in the game of pursuit ever hope to claim a man? Even one she legally owns? She had listed all the ways she had read about: the "accidental" meeting, the arch invitation, and the feminine cry for help. For her these stratagems were ridiculous. The one unbidden item on the list was "go to him," a suggestion she had scratched off time after time. And now, in her desperation, she considered it again. Twice already she had driven her light carriage past the run-down flat in which he lived, only to flee in shy terror. But now time was running out. At her last meeting with Chadwick, the lawyer had told her that her husband was once more considering Australia. For a week she'd known and made no move, cursing herself for cowardice.

The one tiny incident that finally aroused her fury occurred when she looked up from the book she was reading to find her son standing near with his intent blue eyes watching her. "Mama," he asked, "why don't I have a father?"

A flash of anger exploded in her. You do have a father, Tony, but he's more of a child than you, she fumed silently, and it's time he grew up. Calling for Marie to take over, Anne fixed her hair and put on her violet silk suit—her fighting color, she mocked herself as she called Jacques to find her a hansom cab. Thirty minutes later she stood before a shabby door and knocked; no, she pounded with a force that matched her pounding heart. When the door finally opened, she faced her husband for the first time in almost six years. As she swept past him into the room, she didn't even know if he recognized her. His eyes held only that startled look of unexpected shock.

Steeling herself with the memory of her son's words, she turned to look at the man whose face had so intruded into her dreams. But the face she saw now was a greatly changed one. Gone was the boyish charm with the soft brown eyes and curved lips stretched into a practiced smile. This man stared back at her with an unsmiling face and a wary look. His body was lean and muscled instead of merely slim, and his hands were no longer the graceful ones that had shuffled cards; they were almost as labor-hardened as Jacques's.

"Why didn't you come?" she demanded.

He shrugged.

"Gilbert Brownwell, what kind of a man are you?"

"I'm known as Gil Brown around here," he answered noncommittally.

"Well, Gil Brown, you have two children who—"

"So I've been told." Something in that insulting shrug unstrung her; he wouldn't even admit his fatherhood, and not once had he said her name.

"What else have you been told?" She hated the quaver in her voice.

"That you're once again my wife"—he paused—"after an absence of six years. Courts do make such arbitrary decisions." My God, she thought, he really hates me for breaking up his new marriage; and no words would come to her defense. He continued to watch her as he asked, "Why have you come? There's nothing for you here." His gesture swept the dull brown room. "And nothing left of the once mighty Brownwell lands for your children."

"They don't need the mighty Brownwell lands, Gil, they need you. They're your children, too."

"I'd have thought your Aunt Margaret or your Lord Ashton would suffice." He remembers their names so easily, but he can't even say mine; the dull pain increased and she turned away. Something in her face, the look of hurt withdrawal, touched him. "Come on, you need a cup of tea." Not brandy or wine, but tea, and she watched him move about the small kitchen with easy familiarity. "Not really very elegant here, is it?" He shrugged. "But it's better than most of the places I've lived in lately."

"I'm sorry about your loss to that—that—"

"Crook and bastard? His kind always wins."

No, they don't, she wanted to cry out; but she didn't dare. "You'd feel differently if your new marriage hadn't been broken up," she challenged him, remembering Aunt Margaret's description of the attractive, hard-faced woman in court.

He laughed without much humor. "If it's any consolation to you, she was worse than her father. At least I escaped the fate of becoming the permanent target of the worst shrew in England.''

So great was Anne's relief that she returned his laugh. "Poor Gil, stuck twice with sharp-tongued women."

"Bought and paid for, you mean. Well, at least I've canceled my debts."

"Not to me you haven't. You still owe me."

For the first time he really looked at her. "There's nothing left to pay with. Do you know what I've become since that last blow-off of ours? What a hell of a cover-up that word is. Since I beat the skin off your back. Even now I can't stand to remember that."

"Why should you remember? I hit you first. Why didn't you tell about that in court?"

He fingered the scar that ran down his outer cheek. "I've grown fond of it. It got me into places I couldn't have gone without it."

Intrigued now, Anne asked, "What places, Gil? What have you done for the last six years?"

"I was a seaman for seven months with men I didn't know existed. They were dirty, foul-mouthed, and stupid; but they taught me what I am. I'm a laborer. I'm a good camp cook and I'm a top sheepshearer, and now I grade the same wool I sheared in Australia in a warehouse in London. How's that for a husband, Lady Brownwell?"

"My name is Anne!"

"I remember." Both of them were aware of the tension, but he eased off first. "Tell me what you've done."

"Gil Brown, don't you even know what went on during the rest of that hearing?"

"I read the results and saw some of the dirt published about Andrew Grey. Did you really do that? Dress like a lad and work like a man? That I'd like to have seen." He laughed.

Stung and angry, Anne's voice rose. "Andrew Grey kept me from wallowing in self-pity all those years."

His voice also sharpened. "And were the rest of the things I read about you just as true?"

Because she had never seen any of the papers that had caricatured her as a lewd adventuress, Anne was startled. "What things?"

He wasn't looking at her now. "Oh, the tales of your midnight meetings with half the men in old Boston town."

Her shock turned to fury. "That bloody rotten ex–father-in-law of yours! He couldn't kill me physically so he's tried to do it this way. If you'd heard one word at that trial, you'd know that—that creature paid liars to smear me, but every one of those lies was thrown out of court." She was standing now and glaring at him. "Not one night was I away from home, Gil Brownwell, not one night was I with a man. I had two infants and a twelve-hour-a-day job. Just like you, I've learned to work." She sat down hard.

"Was what you said earlier true, that Doncaster tried to kill you?"

"Three times he paid thugs to do it for him. If my lawyer hadn't hired six bodyguards for me, I'd be dead."

"The damn bastard. I wish I had killed him."

"How did you ever get mixed up with a man like that?"

"When I finally came back from Australia, he was entrenched at Brownsville with the very available Edwina, holding the mortgages on most of the Brownwell properties. My stupid mother had turned everything over to him. I just tried to save something, but as usual I failed."

"So now you're going to run away again." His eyes narrowed; she must be a shrewd guesser, since he had told no one his plans except his lawyer.

"Where would I go?"

"Australia." She wasn't a shrewd guesser, she had asked Chadwick.

"You've been busy, wife."

"Someone had to be, husband."

"It's no use. I haven't got a thing to offer."

"May I come again, Gil?"

In spite of his somber shrug, Anne read a hopeful permission in his eyes, or perhaps it was just a reflection of her own eagerness. He was no longer a shadowy figure she'd once fallen in love with; he was a flesh-and-blood man who was far more attractive than the immature weakling he'd been. Remembering the flattery he'd once used so glibly, she wondered if the emotion he'd displayed during their one happy month together had been real or pretended, or if he even remembered that month after believing her dead for six years. Forget the past, she scolded herself sternly, just build a future if you can.

Three days later she returned to the flat, and this time he greeted her with a smile and actually cooked a dinner in her honor. But she still could not break down the barricade of his stiff pride. He touched her only once when he removed her fur cape. "You're very elegant looking, Lady Brownwell," he said lightly.

A week later she arrived with the twins and watched for an hour while their father squirmed. She had not told them who he was; at least she had been fair enough to spare him that emotional shock. During that visit Margaret was her usual confident little self, talking to "the man" as if she had no doubt that he was a friend; but Tony appraised his father with a thoughtful expression. The only words he volunteered other than to answer the stilted questions Gilbert asked were, "You look like my sister." His father nodded and turned away, but not before Anne saw the glisten of tears in his eyes and the way he watched the five-year-olds with hungry eyes.

On the way home she was very pensive. "The time has come, the spider said, to spin another web," she murmured to no one in particular. It was time, she decided, for her husband to become her husband again, and after that the father of his children.

The next week was a busy one. Anne released a restless Jacques and Auguste from their jobs as her bodyguards and watched them leave in a rush to return to their beloved sea. She gave Robert and Laura a month off to visit his brother in

Scotland and told Marie to stock the pantry with some easy-to-cook food. "Just some tea and bread and eggs and things," she suggested casually. And finally she sent Marie, Mary, and the three children to stay with Aunt Margaret— "Until such time," her note read vaguely.

After seeing her family off on the public coach, Anne went once more to the dingy flat, this time in the morning. With her fingers crossed, she informed the landlady, "My husband is moving back home again."

" 'Bout time," that worthy woman grunted. "Single men make me nervous." Together they packed up all of his things, and the landlady summoned a dray to haul them while Anne wrote her husband a brief note.

Leading the driver of the dray into her home, she watched him mingle her husband's possessions with hers, and she hung Gilbert's clothes up in wardrobes, elegant suits she noted and most of them very new. A wave of jealousy swept over her as she remembered the reason for that wardrobe of clothing; seven months ago her husband had been a bridegroom trying to please a demanding new wife. I wish he'd tried as hard to please me, she complained silently.

Late that afternoon the quiet of the sedate neighborhood was rudely shattered by the sound of a door being angrily pounded. On shaky feet Anne went to answer the imperative summons. As Gilbert shoved the door open, she moved quickly out of his way and reclosed the door. He doesn't drink anymore and he's stopped gambling, she mused, but he's retained his temper; the thought did not displease her too much. At least he was still among the living.

"What the hell do you think you're doing, Anne?" he roared. The first time in six years he'd used her name, and he had to yell it at her. Smiling like a gracious hostess to hide her trembling lips, she ushered him into the parlor. Deliberately he sat on one of his own chairs.

"I was tired of coming to see you," she said. "I thought it was time you visited me."

"Well, now that I'm here, are you or are you not going to

offer me some tea? I've worked for ten straight hours and I'm hungry."

In dismay she fled to the kitchen and stared at the rows of pots and pans. Filling a large one with water, she fumbled with the wood stove until it lighted. That, at least, she congratulated herself, I can do right, and promptly broke the four eggs she planned to boil. Fifteen minutes later her husband pushed open the door and gazed at the mess. "One thing you didn't do in Boston was learn to cook," he said as he swept the ruined food into the garbage. "Now just stand back and watch an expert."

Actually, she thought as she enjoyed the meal, his cooking was excellent, but his sense of refinement left something to be desired. He had blown out the candles she had placed on the kitchen table and relighted the lantern. "I like to see what I'm eating," he declared emphatically. A very different husband, she reflected, from the smiling man who had tried to seduce her with candlelight long ago at a Le Havre inn. He had also become as elusive as an eel. With businesslike efficiency he washed the dishes, said good night, and went to bed in one of the small downstairs bedrooms.

Anne tossed and turned in a slowly growing anger that night in her room upstairs. He hadn't asked about the children, he hadn't tried to kiss her; after the first minute, he hadn't even had the common decency to be angry at her high-handed rearrangement of his life. "All right," she promised him, "if you want to play by unfair rules, this game is going to become very rough." In the morning he was gone before she awakened, but he had taken the house key she'd left on the kitchen table.

With all her hopes hanging on that slim thread, she plotted her campaign like a general. She washed her hair and fussed over a choice of dress. She rushed to a very special shop that specialized in hot dinners for home consumption; she even bought a bottle of wine the chef had recommended. Gilbert wouldn't have to cook tonight. She laid out a table in front of the fireplace and placed matches by the candles. For hours she waited, but he didn't come, not at six, nor at seven, nor at eight. By ten she had thrown out the spoiled dinner and gone to bed. Her invitation had been declined by a husband who preferred not to be one.

The crashing sound of a door being slammed awakened her to trembling terror. With shaking hands she lighted the candle by her bed and pulled on her robe, then listened without breathing to the slamming, banging, cursing sounds coming from the hallway down below. Oh, God, she wished that Jacques and Auguste were here. Frantically she looked around for a weapon but could find nothing better than the candlestick itself. Her heart was pounding as she crept down the stairs, expecting some unknown assailant to lash out at her.

Pausing at the foot of the stairs, she strained to locate the source of the sounds of furniture being pushed around and of continued curses. Slowly she inched toward the back hall and stopped. The noise was coming from the room Gilbert had slept in last night. Relief poured through her, and with it came the anger of a discarded wife. Inside the room, her husband was fumbling blindly with the rope ties of a seabag. He stumbled as he pushed himself off his knees to glare at her intrusion. He was drunk, not silly drunk, but angry drunk. Anne looked at him in disgust; six years had taught him not a thing, not a single redeeming thing.

"What are you doing?" She put her candle down on the dresser and surveyed the mess.

"What's it look like, lady? I'm packing. I'm getting out of here so you can get back to your own kind of life."

"And where do you think you're going this time of night?"

"Australia, lady, where I should have gone three months ago."

"The devil you are!" she screamed. "You're not going to run out on me again, Gilbert Brownwell, not again, not again. Do you hear me?"

"Who ran out on whom, lady? I was shoved out. I didn't run out. I was shoved out by your lying captain, your great big, protective, lying captain. Who thought of the trick, lady, the trick to dump your husband on another ship so you two could be alone? Oh, yes, and the trick to tell poor old husband you were dead?"

"You're drunk."

"But not too drunk to know what's going on. Your big French captain is back in town, lady."

What an ironic coincidence, Anne groaned faintly. The *Boston Queen* was back, carrying the only man Gilbert might believe was responsible for his bad luck.

"What's the matter, lady, didn't you expect him yet? Did you get lonely while he was gone and decide to look up an old husband to fill in? Well, it won't work. He can have you. Now get out of here so I can pack."

She gritted her teeth. "You're not going anyplace tonight. For once in your life, act like an adult. Just go to bed and sleep it off. And quit making so much noise; I don't want the neighbors disturbed." She took his arm and pulled him toward the bed. Halfway there he stiffened and, with a wide swipe of the arm, threw her hard against the wardrobe; then he stumbled toward her.

She watched him come closer and something snapped into place. She stepped aside and, with an automatic reflex, drove her fist into his jaw with all the power her shoulder could deliver. With supreme satisfaction she watched as his angry face became a peaceful one and as his body crumpled slowly into a restful position on the floor.

For the third time she undressed a drunken husband and dragged him to bed. She looked down on him and wondered why she bothered. Disgusted with herself as much as with him, she began to pick up his clothing strewn around. She jumped as a small dirty object fell out of the pocket of his leather work jacket. When she saw that it wasn't alive, she picked it up and untied the soiled string that bound it. The object inside looked like a dead flower; an odd souvenir for a man to carry, she reflected, and she held it closer to the candlelight. As she recognized the blue of the torn cloth and the silken petals of the flower, the tears came slowly to her eyes. All those years he had carried around something of hers. In the dim light she looked at her husband—her difficult, proud, foolish husband—and her tears fell unchecked.

Softly she blew out the candle, removed her robe, and slipped into bed beside him. As impossibly temperamental as he was, he was the only husband she wanted. She put her arms around him and went to sleep. Hours later when she felt his breathing pattern change and his muscles tense, she awoke only long enough to snuggle closer against his back. Gradually he relaxed and drifted back to sleep.

Heavy groans and the ugly sounds of illness awakened her the second time, and she scrambled up to hold his head over the basin and lead him back to bed. Compassionately she wiped the beads of perspiration that stood out on his face, now more gray than tan. She forced him to swallow the headache powder she dropped into a glass of water. When his discomfiture had subsided, she went to the kitchen; and with determination not to be beaten again by the mystery of a cooking stove, she brewed a pot of tea and made some toast. As she carried the tray to the bedroom, she fished out the tea leaves floating on top and held a cup of the dead brown liquid to his lips.

"It tastes like sheep dip," he complained; but he drank two cups and ate the burned toast. Later, while she was dressing in her own room, she heard the rattling of pots and hurried to the kitchen in time to see her husband finish brewing a second pot of tea and stacking a plate with golden toast. He held his head stiffly as if a sudden move might jar it off his shoulders, but his healthy tan was back, except for the livid bruise darkening his jaw.

"What in the devil did you hit me with last night?" he asked.

"My fist," she answered with a giggle; and between bites of toast, she told him about the Irish pub owner and his famous Casey Ryan punch.

"Was life really that hard in Boston, Anne?"

"Not really," she remembered. "Parts of it were exciting. But it wasn't what I wanted."

"What do you want?" His voice was casual but his eyes avoided hers.

"You," she answered simply and heard his breath ease out.

"And the children? What will they think about a strange man thrust into their lives without any warning?"

Her voice was soft and she longed to touch him. "Not so strange, Gil. Your son has already asked me if you were his father."

"You told him?" But before he could frown, she shook her head.

"You don't have to tell Tony anything. He always knows somehow."

"And Margaret?" How easily he said the name, as if he'd practiced.

Anne laughed. "Your daughter feels that anyone who looks like her cocksure little self must be perfect."

"Australia will be hard on them." Then he hadn't been so drunk after all last night, she mused.

"It doesn't matter. Wherever you want to go, we'll go with you." This time she did touch his hand when she leaned forward to look at him. "Tell me about your life in Australia."

As if the floodgates had burst open, he talked about the freedom he'd found there. "For the first time in my life I had to work to stay alive. I worked with criminals and other drifters like myself, but I survived." He talked about the endless fields of green grass which could turn to brown stubs overnight during a drought. He described the leathery gray eucalyptus trees and the strange creatures that clung to the drooping branches. He told about the magnificent quiet which bound men together in a land peopled mostly by black aborigines. But when he talked about sheep, his voice sharpened with enthusiasm.

"Sheep," he explained, "are the dumbest creatures God ever made, but they can survive on grass cattle won't eat, and their herds increase every year ten times as fast. For cattle you get paid only once, after the slaughter. But sheep are a never-ending supply of income because you kill only the excess of lambs each year." His eyes were shining as he continued, "Wool is the crop, Anne, wool means money. If only I had a piece of land left out of the estate."

"You do, Gil, you still own Brownsville," she said quietly and shivered as she felt his stiff pride return. Reckless now with fear, she plunged on, telling about Chadwick and his part in regaining the forfeited acres. Defensively she described her scheme to defraud Doncaster in order to force the price down to seventy thousand pounds.

"Where did you get that kind of money, Anne?" She tried to, but she couldn't avoid the demanding sternness in his eyes. So, months ahead of schedule, her cautious schedule for revealing only one asset at a time, Anne had to tell about the Boston Stock Exchange and her eight percent of the shipyard profits.

He whistled in awe as he appraised this formidable wife of his. "And what other, er . . . surprises are you planning to spring on me when you think I might be ready for them?" he asked; and once again she did not dare disobey his command. Taking a deep breath, she briefly outlined the action she had taken to invest—she gulped when she named the amount— with the competition of the Doncaster mines; but she stopped far short of revealing the name of the company or the details of her masquerade.

He threw back his head and laughed. "My Lord, Anne, no wonder the man tried to kill you."

Hurt by his laughter, she defended herself. "That conceited baboon doesn't have the least idea that the pathetic woman he tried to destroy in court has a brain in her head. But he is going to find out, and soon," she promised.

Still laughing, her husband reached over and ruffled her hair. "I hope I'm around to watch."

The rest of the day was aimless as their tension dissipated. Anne watched him prepare Australian stew with long strips of dried meat in boiling water, and he watched as she put candles on the table in front of the fireplace. This easy camaraderie lasted through dinner; but soon after, their banter stopped; and they were silent as they washed the dishes and banked the fire. It was Gilbert who reached out first and took her arm; and in a not-too-steady voice he asked, "Are you sure, Anne?" She could only nod her head as he led her down the hall. When he held out hesitant hands to help her undress, she shook her head in a sudden overwhelming shyness.

Silently they climbed into bed, only to lie there side by side without touching. Anne held her own silence as long as she could, then she propped herself up on one elbow and hissed in his ear, "Gil Brownwell, either you make love to me tonight or I'll blacken the other side of your jaw." The bed shook slightly with his suppressed laughter, and their paralyzing tension changed to the compelling desire that had been building throughout the day-long emotional tug-of-war They reached for each other and their lips met with the sweet abandon of a surrender that bridged the years of separation and blotted out the bitter memories.

Compelled by the need for complete possession, they clung together, responding to the magic elixir of unleashed desire. His hands caressed her taut breasts with a tender urgency until her answering passion overwhelmed them both. Without restraint they joined together in a fierce reunion of body and spirit. No conscious signal was needed by either lover to time the compulsive thrusts that drove them toward a simultaneous climax and the searing violence of ecstasy. As if the thought of a separation, however brief, aroused the specter of the loneliness they'd endured, they remained locked together in a passion that seemed insatiable. Even in the quiet moments they moved slowly against each other without volition, the mental discipline of the empty years forgotten; and their tongues continued the languorous exploration of repossession. When Anne's muscles cramped, Gilbert pulled her on top of him without a break in the rhythm of their lovemaking.

Finally, as their desire abated for the moment, they held each other gently in exhaustion as they slept. Toward morning, before they awoke completely, they came together again; this time their movements were a slow adagio, and their union as effortless and natural as breathing. When they climaxed, their sounds of ecstasy were muted and drawn out. Once again they slept in drowsy awareness of each other.

Arising late, they buttoned each other's robes and walked barefoot to the kitchen with their arms entwined. They drew water into large pots and placed them on the stove, then dragged a huge old bathtub to the center of the kitchen floor. As the water warmed, they sipped tea and reached their hands out in a mutual need to touch. Still silent, for they felt no need for talk, they bathed together and washed each other. As Anne felt his fingers slowly trace the ridges on her back, she leaned back against him and whispered, "The scars of battle, sweetheart, a battle long forgotten and forgiven." But he shook his head and climbed out of the tub.

Anne observed the way he stood with his back to her as he fixed a plate of toast and avoided her eyes. With a haste born of a wisdom she was just beginning to acquire, she dried herself and buttoned her robe, then waited for him to sit down at the kitchen table. She put her cup down and, with a sigh, went to him and sat on his lap. Deliberately she blew into his ear and sinuously wiggled her hips until she could feel his response. "If you go moody on me again, Gil Brown," she whispered into his ear, "I will glue myself to your lap, and you'll become an impotent old man before you're thirty-one." What could he do with a wife like Anne, but laugh and hold her close.

Chapter 17

ISOLATED in an exclusive neighborhood of insular people who associated only with selected friends, Anne and Gilbert spent another five idyllic days. Freed from prying eyes, they explored their own complex reactions to the rebirth of a love that had only begun to develop six years earlier. During those years of separation each partner had erected walls around a vulnerable heart to prevent future pain. Neither one dared take the conventional path of reconciliation by admitting the loneliness of empty nights. They could only reach out now in a blind, sensuous response to an emotion that frightened them by its intensity. As if they were afraid to risk their fragile relationship with separation, they remained within touching distance of one another. Even the few outdoor chores were performed together. When they watered the garden or cared for Anne's two carriage horses, their hands would meet and cling. When they remade their bed, more often than not they would interrupt the task with a compelling embrace and a return to the compulsive lovemaking that marked their reunion. Wary of each other's pride, they made no vows of eternal love; but each responded with unbanked passion whenever they touched.

Gilbert referred to the past only once. "I'm glad you named our son Tony."

"Why?"

"That's what you called me whenever you were happy."

One day when the weather turned cool, they dragged their

304

bedding to the floor in front of the fireplace; and there, behind closed drapes and locked doors, they learned to accept the joy of their reunion without the mental reservations of recrimination and lingering fear. Nothing seemed to intrude on their pervasive need to be together; one dinner burned as they made love, and one bath turned cold. Even as Gilbert prepared their simple meals at the stove, he wanted Anne near and so would stand with one arm around her. And Anne, in total surrender, basked in the knowledge that his tenuous need for her was growing. The closest either came during the first four days to anything like a pledge was the moment he reached out for her one night after she had rolled away from him in sleep. His heart was pounding as he pulled her close. "I thought I had lost you, Anne; never leave me again." And even half-asleep, she understood that hers had not been the only lonely life.

Gradually, the past, which had marked them both with the taint of distrust, faded into unimportant memory; and they began to have confidence in the future to which they were legally bound. When on the fifth morning he pulled her close and whispered, "Let's go home, sweetheart," Anne's heart soared. She had become a wife again, included in his life. All that day he packed boxes of food and ordered her to select a few practical clothes for both of them. "We're going to be working hard, so come prepared."

Faced with a dilemma, since all her practical clothing was in the wrong gender, Anne hesitated to follow his instructions, fearful of risking any more disclosures about her past life. Impatient with her absence, he came to her bedroom and stood watching her try on the pants and boots of Andrew Grey before the mirror, her face clouded with anxiety. When she glanced up to see her husband's reflection, she flushed red with embarrassment; but his laughter was not unkind. "You make a very tempting picture, but I don't know how much work I'll get done with your backside so neatly displayed at all times."

She smiled in relief, "Oh, I wear a loose jacket so it doesn't show."

"It doesn't matter what you wear, I know what's underneath." Then he became very serious. "But I don't want you to wear them in public," he warned. "I won't have other men enjoying what's mine." Nothing he would ever say again would match those words as a declaration of love and possession, and Anne pressed herself against him in exultation.

During their four-day trip from London to the north of England, she sat demurely beside him in pretty dresses and feminine shoes. Because the two horses needed long hours of rest at night, they were forced to reduce the number of miles they could cover. In the late afternoon of the first day out, they drove into the walled coach yard of an inn on the northern outskirts of Bedford. It was there they set the pattern for travel that they found most enjoyable. Registering as Gil and Anne Brown, they ordered their dinner served in their room; and each room became their own special island without the prying eyes of strangers. Two nights more, one in the bustling town of Nottingham and one in the village of Pontifract, they stayed at inns where they made love and slept and even talked about the future.

Brownsville lay only a few miles from Pontifract, so Anne's first glimpse of Gilbert's boyhood home was in the slanting sunlight of early morning. She smiled in delight at the beauty of the Aire River which flowed along the southern boundary of the huge estate. She gasped at the spread of the massive oak trees that dotted the green fields creating cool patches of shade. But as they entered through the wide-open gates, it was her husband's turn to gasp. Everywhere for two hundred feet on either side of the driveway that led to the distant manor house the scene was one of shambles. The large metal lettering of the name Brownsville dangled loosely, held only by a single chain. Broken branches and debris littered even the driveway itself, and large patches of dead, brown grass made the entrance look desolate.

"The place is ruined," he despaired as he stared at his

home. Chimney pots and shattered glass lay in untidy piles around the house; and pieces of broken furniture were strewn across the yards, haphazardly mixed with rusted plows and hoes. Large globs of mud strained parts of the tan brick walls, creating a look of decay. One of the massive entry doors was hanging from one hinge, and the draperies behind the broken windows fluttered outward. "It'll cost a fortune to repair," he asserted gloomily.

But while he looked at the obvious damage, Anne was studying the roof. Every visible one of the manor's own chimney pots was firmly in place, and most of its windows were intact. She began to laugh. "Someone brought all of this stuff in," she declared, "all of this worthless junk. Someone hauled it in. None of it even comes from Brownsville." As he checked the truth of her words, he joined her in laughter. The hired "vandals," whoever they were, had proved inventive and highly convincing. Cleverly they had limited the "destruction" to the grounds around the house and driveway, leaving the working fields and out-of-sight structures untouched.

All that day the couple rode the carriage horses around the estate, sitting astride on saddles they had dragged from the undisturbed tack room. Anne gazed in wonder at the magnificence her money had purchased so cheaply: the windmills which could pump the water from the river, the long shearing sheds, the empty water troughs, and the rows of sturdy open cotes.

Gilbert, too, was amazed at these structures. "My father must have really expanded into sheep production; none of this existed when I lived here." As they continued their ride, the eerie silence began to disturb them; not one animal was in evidence, not one cottage was filled with people. They were alone in a vast expanse that normally held scores of people and thousands of animals.

Reluctant to move into the large manor house, they settled for the servants' wing which housed the kitchens and storage rooms. As Anne carried in the last of their clothing and hung it in the wardrobe of the largest of four bedrooms, her husband unpacked the boxes of food and dusted off a few of the pots and pans. When she rejoined him in the huge kitchen, he was staring doubtfully at the smaller of the two stoves. "I'm sure it must work," he said. "I just wish I knew how." Without much hope he turned to Anne.

She shook her head in awe; she had never seen monsters like these before and had no idea how they operated. But having learned from shipyard experience to leave a man alone when he was concentrating on the wonders of a piece of metal gadgetry, Anne left the kitchen and entered the main house through the connecting hallway. She located the two dining rooms first; one was a huge formal expanse which opened onto a brick terrace, while the other was a cheerful family-sized room. She noted quickly that although the furniture and thick carpets were intact, all of the cabinets and china closets were empty. Wandering through two sitting rooms, a library, and an office den, she reached the large central hallway with its graceful flight of stairs rising to the upper floors. The softly lit walls were covered with the portraits of her husband's relatives. Anne stood for a moment before the likenesses of his father and brothers, remembering their kindness to her. Their sightless gray eyes stared back, and she moved away sadly, but not before she noticed with relief that there was no portrait of his mother. That relief was premature. In a huge space over the fireplace of the drawing room was the life-sized image of a thirty-year-old Lady Suzanne Brownwell smiling serenely over the entire room. Anne shuddered and vowed that someday that visage would burn in the fireplace it now dominated. She glanced back to find her husband also looking at his mother's portrait, and her heart sank until she heard his words.

"I always hated it there. We had to treat it like some kind of shrine. Come on, let's go back to where we can be comfortable. We've got a year of work to do before we can play lord and lady here."

He was right, Anne reflected as they sat on the sofa in front of the fireplace in the servants' sitting room. They were more comfortable here; and she wondered if either of them would ever be able to live up to the elegance of the big house next door. Intimidated by the sheer size of this new home, she clung to her husband that night and didn't even mind that he laughed at her fear.

"I don't believe it," he teased her. "You've never been afraid of anything in your whole life before. Now you know how some of us feel most of the time." He didn't seem displeased at all that his wife had at least one Achilles' heel, and his lovemaking that night was tender and protective.

Early the next morning, they set out in the carriage to locate a man called Grimes, the wizard who had transformed Brownsville. Unfortunately, all Chadwick had known about the address was that the man lived in some nearby village. By noon they had located his house, providing the ramshackle, spread-out structure before them could ever be called a home. What didn't sag with age was concealed behind the piles of assorted junk that almost obscured the building. Broken wagons and buggies of all descriptions lay about in helter-skelter confusion. Rusted farm equipment was surrounded by broken chamber pots, cracked mirrors, and seatless chairs; in every corner the debris of past glories was piled. The Brownwells had located the source of the debacle at their estate.

The man who bounded down the stairs to greet them and to protect his treasure trove from the inquisitive eyes of strangers was dressed in an assortment of clothes that Anne assumed must have come from the same junk store the rest of the debris had. His baggy leather trousers were cheerfully held aloft by one suspender, and the sheepskin vest covered nothing but browned skin and a hairy chest. Under a thatch of uncombed dark hair, shrewd eyes studied his uninvited guests.

As he approached, Anne stepped forward and smilingly nodded at him. "I'm the person who requested those 'alterations' at Brownsville."

The look of admiration on Grimes's face was obvious. "So yu're the missus with the narsty mind the lawyer fellow told about. Devilish clever, missus, rooked that barstard coal man good, our little touches did. Watched the day he sent that snoop of his'n 'round tu 'valuate the damage. Fool shyster couldn't get his own horse away fast enough, so skeered he 'uz of poisoned grass. Mu brothers and me laughed all the way tu home." Suddenly he jerked his thumb at Gilbert as if her husband were standing twenty feet away instead of four, and demanded, "Who be yu friend, missus?"

Before Anne could begin the introduction, Gilbert stepped forward and held out his hand. "I'm called Gilbert Brownwell, among other things, and I'm a sheep man from Australia."

"So yu're the new mister up tu the old place. Mu name be Grimes." As the two men shook hands, Anne silently appraised their host, thinking, That artful devil knew exactly who we were the minute we stepped on his property, but he's not about to call anyone by a title. He was just like most of the Americans she had met, proud men who hated any caste system. She decided that she liked this rugged individual in spite of his blunt manners and uncouth appearance. It was just as well she had a full reserve of her own thoughts, because the two men seemed intent on ignoring her.

"Yu run a few sheep in Austrilia, did yu?"

"I didn't run them, I worked them."

"Shear man? How many?"

"Fifty some odd."

"I'm a sixty-a-day man muself. Two of mu brothers be as good. Third one's slow, only fifty-two. Tuk five hundred head of sheep offen the place like yur missus ordered. Fine Southdown breed they be. Also tuk yur twenty head of beef. Only tuk ten horses off. The old missus sold t'other thurty the year before. Got stung real good, she did. Fool woman let some fancy talker have them cheap. Good horseflesh, too. Got the whole lot of yur animals hid good three mile from here. Had to sell yur lambs, though. 'Tworn't enough grazing fur them all."

"Then we owe you wages for the lambing and shearing in addition to the other expenses."

"No, yu don't, mister." Grimes became very defensive.

"Sold yur wool and lambs at standard price. Tuk out only what I thought 'twas due and put the rest in the bank. Wouldn't cheat anyone related to the old mister. Worked fur him six years afore him and his oldest two was tuk. Lived in them cottages, we did, until the old missus throwed us out when that furrin barstard came around tu help out. Help out; he stole the place, is what he did! Slaughtered two thousand head of sheep, he did, and then told the old missus they 'uz wurthless. Robbed that fool missus good."

Anne wondered how Lady Suzanne would react to Grimes's description of her; the "fool" part she might be able to stand, but the "old" part would be a crushing blow. Anne liked Grimes more and more.

By the end of this odd dialogue, the Grimes brothers had been rehired as permanent sheep men and ordered to clear away the debris they had scattered around the estate and to return the animals to their own pastures. Later, as Anne remonstrated with her husband about Grimes's lack of respect for his rank, Gilbert shushed her up.

"He could call me Dingo for all I care. He's a real sheep man and they're all as independent as hell. That's the only reason we got them. The other owners around here are a stiff-necked bunch who would hire a polite flunky every time over a real worker who doesn't bow and scrape." His years in Australia had made a democratic man out of her once arrogant aristrocrat husband, Anne concluded.

During the next few days, they watched a strange caravan of vehicles travel in and out, carting away the scattered junk, while the Grimes family members scrubbed the walls, rehinged gates and doors, and boarded up the broken windows. When they had finished, the manor house emerged in much of its old elegance, except for the dead grass surrounding.

"Only lime, missus." Grimes chuckled. "Burns the grass real good but don't last much past the first good rains."

Two weeks later four of the ten cottages were occupied by the Grimes brothers and their families. Anne learned that Grimes himself was an avowed bachelor who didn't believe in marriage for himself. "Too much interferin' with a man's thinkin'," was his explanation. Because he was the unchallenged spokesman for the entire family, Anne caught only glimpses of the other three brothers and their wives and children. From a distance the brothers looked like replicas of Grimes himself, and even their wives had the same broad-beamed silhouettes.

No sooner had the human contingent settled down than the animals arrived; and Anne had her first glimpse of five hundred brown-faced, white-coated creatures being driven by six of the most threatening dogs she had ever seen. The brutes would creep along on their bellies after twenty or more sheep, ready to spring in bared-tooth fury if one of their pleasant-looking charges dared to stray. These were Grimes's own dogs, and he spoke of them in the same tone of pride a doting mother might use.

"I don't work sheep without my beauties," he boasted. "Yon dogs got more sense than most of t'other people I know." Anne sincerely hoped that she and her husband were no longer considered "t'others" by this forthright man whose advice she was finding more and more accurate.

Her husband, too, was finding him an invaluable adviser. One afternoon when he returned from checking the windmills and water troughs, Grimes was waiting for him.

"Don't mean to be nosy, mister, but yon middlin' number of sheep ain't enough to eat the bloom off the clover. The old mister run more than two thousand afore he made a go o' it."

Having been contemplating the same problem, Gilbert admitted that more sheep were necessary. "But," he insisted, "I want to try the crossbreed which produces silk wool. Wouldn't know where I can get five hundred merino ewes, would you?"

"Heard tell of a Highland man who tried them more'n a year ago. Too cold up there for merinos, though. Might be willing to sell."

Anne wandered over in time to hear a complicated deal being put together in which the Southdown rams would be traded for merino ewes, if Grimes's Scot cousins would handle the transaction. She was to remember her simplification three months later when she met Grimes's Scot cousins. Their methods of dealing made Yankee traders look like timid shopkeepers.

Amused by her husband's enthusiasm as they walked home, Anne made a suggestion. "Sheep are sheep, Gil. Let's just buy some locally." Half an hour later she was still regretting her comment when her ears were overflowing with ewes and rams and qualities of wool. She almost wished the old Gilbert were back.

That night she made another mistake. Realizing her total ignorance about sheep, she went to the library next door and brought back an armful of books and pamphlets. During the next weeks her husband's constant request of "Look it up for me, Anne" almost made her rude enough to scream "Look it up yourself!" She was rapidly losing all love for those sweet creatures which looked so pastoral in the clover. They were cantankerous, temperamental, disease-prone, stupid animals. Furthermore, the idea of one ugly ram servicing—that word she hated, too—thirty-five ewes warmed her deep resentment toward male domination to the boiling point.

For days now she had been trying to get her husband to drive her to Grayhaven; already they were weeks overdue in retrieving their children. And frankly she was beginning to feel that he ranked those dumb sheep above anything else. Finally, after listening to another of his "Just wait until"'s, she exploded. "Either we start for Grayhaven tomorrow, or I'll castrate every one of your precious rams." Seeing his stricken face, she thought she'd gone too far; but she soon learned that his fear lay in another direction entirely. Gilbert Brownwell was the basest of all cowards; he was a terrified father.

All the way to Grayhaven he drove in moody silence; and that night at the inn he made her promise never to leave him alone with the twins. "I've never even held a child," he groaned, "much less been a father. What can I say to them?" Anne began to understand his fear and to worry along with him. She needn't have bothered.

As they approached the gates of Grayhaven, a lonely little
boy came shyly out to meet them. He approached his father's
side of the carriage and with his heart in his eyes reached up
his hand and said, "Hello, Father, I'm your son, Anthony
Geoffrey." Without a word Gilbert handed her the reins and
stepped down from the driver's seat. A second later a whirl-
wind rode up with blond pigtails flying. As she ground her
pony to a halt and jumped off, she shouted, "Papa Gilbert, I'm
your daughter, Margaret Maude."

Anne looked at her husband and relaxed. He had a child in
each arm, and on his handsome face was a smile of idiotic
bliss.

Chapter 18

LIFE, Anne concluded two days after their arrival at
Grayhaven, was one long series of twists and turns in which
her best plans became twisted and turned into something very
different. Mary Harrington, that greatest of all possible gifts
to mothers—an all-purpose nurse—was not coming to
Brownsville. For two long months Anne would have to be a
full-time mother; it was her turn to be terrified of children.

Lady Margaret explained Mary's perfidy: "Your little Irish
widow is a natural housemother. She's taken over the
younger boys' dormitory, and the children adore her." Very
quickly Anne discovered that the little boys were not the only
ones who adored the pink-cheeked nurse. One of Paddy's
new Irish teachers also thought she was a "foine" woman;
and Mary's shining eyes told Anne that his admiration was
returned in full.

The second heart-stopping crisis turned out to be a gentle hoax. Aunt Margaret insisted that she wanted to keep Marie as well. "Anne, she is a jewel, not only the best cook I've ever known, but an amusing, witty friend. I'll be lonely if you take her away."

Anne cried out in agony, "No, Aunt Margaret, you can't have Marie, too. I'll have my hands full just trying to keep up with the twins; and you know I can't even make a good cup of tea, much less fix a decent meal. Gil will just die if he has to do any more of the cooking."

Margaret grinned at this topsy-turvy niece of hers who could do most things a man could, but who had never mastered the basic jobs of womanhood. Well, Margaret amended, some of the basics. After watching her niece and Gilbert together, Margaret guessed that at least one womanly function Anne had mastered well.

"I was just playing an old lady's game, dear. Marie is not a servant to be bartered. She does exactly what she wants to do. And right now she wants to get as far away from the sound of five hundred boisterous children as your carriage can take her. But I will miss her; and remember, Anne, even though she is a superb cook, she is not really a servant. I know you would never treat her as such, but there is that mother-in-law of yours."

"That woman will never live with us, Aunt Margaret; she's too destructive." Margaret nodded and hoped that her niece could prevail in keeping the husband and his mother apart. Anne had not seen the vindictiveness of Lady Suzanne Brownwell in court; Margaret had, and she feared for Anne's happiness if Gilbert ever had to choose.

The farewells from her Grayhaven friends, both old and new, were not so painful this time because at Paddy's insistence the twins were enrolled for the spring term. "Your little boy," her old tutor said, "is a serious student just as you were eighteen years ago, and is just as sensitive as you were. He will benefit in increasing his self-confidence. As for your little girl, I'm sure you realize better than anyone else that she has a wild streak that needs the taming we can give her here.'' Anne looked fondly at her oldest and best friend and knew that she trusted him with her children above all other people, even her beloved aunt. In his gentle, stubborn way, he could force Tony and Margaret to develop their abilities to the fullest.

But still, as she kissed Danny and the Bouvier children good-bye and hugged Mary and Emily, her own childhood nurse and friend, Anne felt a part of her life slip away. Even when Mac Dougall teased her about being bossier now than she had been as a girl, she felt sad. As she kissed Margaret and Paddy, the two people who had molded her life, she fought her tears. Life never seemed to give her the time to thank all these friends properly.

On the two-day trip home, she found herself more in the company of Marie than her own family. The twins insisted on flanking their father on the driver's bench, and she could hear snatches of the conversation that seemed to exclude her. That night in bed, though, she rejoined the magic circle. Gilbert was more carefree than she had ever known him to be, more confident and relaxed. "For a lonely drifter from the wilds of Australia, I'm not doing so badly. I have two great children and a very satisfactory wife. Sweetheart, I'm a happy man." He didn't mention his sheep once.

With amazing swiftness Marie and the twins adjusted to life at Brownsville. Margaret and Tony found an endless fascination in watching the sheep; and Grimes's dogs, which terrorized Anne, were as playful as puppies with them. Having lived in a comfortable farmhouse most of their lives, the children felt at home in the modest servants' quarters, especially in their favorite part of it, Marie's kitchen.

That resourceful woman mastered both of the huge stoves on her first day of residency, and they seemed to respond to her understanding and stop their annoying tendency to burn one dinner and undercook the next. After the first dinner she prepared there, Gilbert saluted her as a superior fellow artist and promptly resigned his position as resident chef. But

Marie was expert in more areas than the kitchen; she was very perceptive about human relationships. Realizing that with Lord Brownwell she could be friend but not family, she made the acquaintance of the three Grimes wives; and soon these women, who were still strangers to Anne, had become the confidantes of Marie. Throughout the Christmas season, she delighted in taking them the special treats she loved to make. Frequently she would prepare the meals for Anne's family but eat her own with her new friends.

Anne was grateful to Marie because her frequent absence gave the children a better chance to know their father; it also gave their father a better chance to know himself. One night when Margaret handed a book to her papa and asked him to read her a story, he murmured something about reading being her mother's department. But Margaret shook her head and declared, "No, Papa, I'll read you a story." And Anne watched her daughter, as she had since the child was four, take a case out of her pocket and carefully put a pair of glasses over her pert little nose. Proudly she boasted to her father, "I have to wear glasses because I'm farsighted. Tony doesn't get to."

While Margaret was talking, Anne was casually watching her husband's face; and something about his expression triggered an understanding that made her angry at her own blindness. Gilbert needed glasses and he couldn't read without them. Her beautiful, vain husband needed glasses and had probably known about his need for twenty years.

In bed that night he asked her, "When did she start wearing them?"

"When she found out that her brother was learning to read faster than she was." Timidly she added, "She has your eyes, Gil." He grunted.

The next time Margaret brought her father a book to read, he lifted his daughter to his lap and unsmilingly imitated her. He removed a case from his pocket and carefully placed his new glasses on his nose and boasted, "I get to wear glasses, too." Anne never had to read another word about sheep.

She just had to learn to live with them, literally. The day before the children were to leave for school, a distant sound penetrated the stillness around them, the sound of a bagpipe being wailed discordantly into the air accompanied by the anguished bleating of sheep. As she and the children hugged the fence near the main gate, they watched a procession approach that would always be remembered as the twins' favorite Christmas present.

Four large, creaky wagons were drawn slowly into view, each one packed with forty merino ewes; but it was the appearance of the two men in each wagon that kept the audience spellbound. They were dressed alike in stained leather pants and huge sheepskin coats. Worn at rakish angles on their heads and surrounded by a ruff of wiry hair were Scottish bonnets, and each man's was the plaid of a different clan. Four of these men were Grimes's Scot cousins, the other four were relatives of the Scots. All the way to the special area fenced off for the merinos, the bagpipe continued its mournful caterwauling.

That evening the children received their final holiday treat when the Brownwells walked the half mile to the cottages farthest from their own home and watched a celebration. Six brawny Scots danced to the piercing wild tunes being played on two bagpipes. As they whirled and leapt in the flickering light of a campfire, Anne thought they looked like great hairy beasts from Greek mythology bounding about the furnaces of Vulcan. The children thought them beautiful. On the way home Gilbert grabbed Anne around the waist, and together they performed the leaping march of the Highland fling until Anne was breathless and the children exhausted from laughing at their undignified elders.

Twice more in the cold month of January these Scot sheep traders made an equal delivery to Brownsville, until the merino ewes grazing in Brownsville clover numbered almost five hundred. In between these deliveries, two incidents occurred at the estate that renewed Anne's almost forgotten terror of attack. One afternoon when she, her husband, and

Grimes were just finishing a long ride of inspection, they saw two mounted figures approaching them from the road. Anne stiffened as she recognized the hard features of Edward Doncaster and the cynical ones of his lawyer, Prichart.

"Lord Brownwell," the solicitor began without preamble, "we have reason to believe that you committed fraud in acquiring this property from my client. We intend to prosecute you to the full extent of the law."

Having had nothing to do with the methods Anne had used in her purchase of the property, Gilbert was taken aback by the accusation. However, Grimes was neither reticent nor afraid. With his bull-like voice, that unrepentant hypocrite declared in the righteous tones of a church deacon, "The lord and lady here had nought to do with what happened. Mu brothers and me 'uz patrollin' outside the grounds as we 'uz wont to do, when we seen a dozen men sneak acrost the fence. They 'uz yourn, Mister Doncaster, we seen 'em around the place plenty of times when yu 'uz here with the old missus. We watched 'em do turrible things that night, and mu brothers and me'll swear to what we seen in any court."

Looking into the glaring face of the visitors, Anne could not resist one final "Andyism." "Mr. Prichart, sir," she said in that earnest young voice, "our lawyer, Alan Chadwick, negotiated the sale. Should we inform him that you plan to sue him, too?"

Doncaster had not spoken a single word, but Anne saw his face darken in rage as he turned abruptly and rode off. She remembered that rage three nights later when the entire estate was alerted by the bleating of frightened sheep and the barking of excited dogs. As the two Grimes brothers on watch alerted the others, three of the lambing cotes burst into flame; and in the frantic confusion the vandals escaped. At dawn Gilbert found twenty sheep with their throats cut. He reported the crime and his suspicions about the criminals to the rural constable at Pontifract, whose advice was almost as disturbing as the raid. "Best double your guard. The party in question," he warned, "has a nasty reputation around here since he ordered your father's sheep slaughtered. He might not stop at just one strike against you.''

Even the usually imperturbable Grimes was nervous. "Dirty barstard," he muttered to whoever would listen. Nights passed in cold sleeplessness for all the estate people as they tried to patrol the fences they had just mended. But no one felt confident about resisting another raid until the eight Scots returned. With hearty laughter they took over, and in a few hours they had prepared what they called a Scottish reif trap. Reif, they explained, was the old Scot word for the robbery that had been a way of life among feuding clans for centuries.

After first tearing down the mended fences where the raiders had entered earlier, they placed twelve specially constructed hayricks in a wide circle around the break. These were hollow ricks to allow for swift firing and burning. That night and the next two, twelve men sat huddled by those ricks armed with pitchforks whose prongs had been honed to gleaming points. The thirteenth man patrolled in front of the broken fence. Each night the dogs were removed to a far pasture so they could not warn off intruders.

During these tense nights Anne had become increasingly afraid for her husband's safety. The logical target for any attackers hired by Doncaster, he towered over the other men; and his distinctive hair gleamed pale silver in the firelight. Since all the men had refused to let her join them and aid in the fight, Anne had told Marie her suspicions. That redoubtable Basque woman, whose fighting prowess has already been established against French gendarmes years before, recommended that she and Anne set up their own small defense ring near Gilbert each night of the vigil. While Anne armed herself with a heavy hoe, Marie chose a large, lethal-looking kitchen knife.

On the fourth night the Scottish reif trap closed, not with a snap, but with the terrifying sounds of Scot battle cries. When the first shout of warning was sounded by the thirteenth man on patrol, the hayricks burst into flame; and the twelve defenders, with their gleaming pitchforks in hand, advanced toward the dozen or more men caught in the light of the fires. The faces of these vandals were smeared with black, and they carried knives in well-trained hands. As she watched in horror, Anne saw four of the attackers rush toward her husband with their knives raised. Marie was in instant motion running across the twenty feet that separated Anne and her from Gilbert. After one paralyzing moment Anne, too, ran toward the converging men, with her hoe raised for attack. Gilbert met the first man with a powerful thrust of the pitchfork which downed the man, but which cost the victor his weapon. As the second assailant leapt over his fallen comrade, his eyes concentrated on his blond-haired target, he failed to see a short, squat figure intercept him. Marie's foot caught him squarely in the middle, breaking two ribs and rendering the man unconscious. Backing swiftly away, the Frenchwoman shoved her kitchen knife into her employer's hand in time for him to meet the third assassin, who had slowed down enough to exercise greater caution than his injured partners had.

Seconds earlier Anne had reached the combat area by circling behind the fourth man and had landed a crippling blow to his shoulder with a wild swing of her hoe. As the man whirled to face this new enemy, Marie again unleashed her foot in a thrust that landed with a dull thud in the small of the man's back. As he fell forward Anne's hoe landed again, this time on the hapless thug's head. It would be months before he regained enough of his wits to understand that the army that had attacked him had consisted of two women.

Freed once again to turn their attention back to Gilbert, both women noted with satisfaction that the years in Australia had indeed taught him to deal successfully with the scum of society. Wielding the knife as expertly as his opponent, he had inflicted three slashing cuts which had all but eliminated his enemy's will to fight. As the beleaguered man watched two of the Scot defenders approach him with their pitchforks aimed murderously, he threw his knife down and raised his arms in the universal gesture of surrender. The battle was over; and except for two slight cuts on Gilbert's arm where the thug's knife had penetrated the heavy sheepskin coat, none of the Brownsville people were hurt. But all fifteen of the marauders had been badly mauled with varying degrees of injury. Knives had been a sorry choice of weapon against pitchforks.

While Gilbert ordered the two Scots who had come to his aid to ride into Pontifract for the constable, Grimes took over the grisly task of dragging the groaning bodies into the circle of fire where they could be watched. The redoubtable foreman had also taken over the lighter chore of praising the defenders.

"Ye be a fair fighter, Mister Brownwell, and the missus be a sly one. But t'other be an expert with her feet. Never seen that kind of scrappin' afore. Takes a man a mite by surprise t'find a lady so resourceful." No one else had ever seen that kind of fighting, either, and a smiling Marie was soon surrounded by an admiring circle of Scots and Grimes men, leaving Lord Brownwell to face his disobedient wife.

"I thought I told you to stay at the house."

"Those men were hired to kill you."

"You could have been hurt."

"And you could have been killed."

"I'm grateful, Anne, but I don't ever want you involved in anything like this again. I don't suppose you remembered to bring any bandages with you. I think I could use one around my arm."

Men, she thought, were very illogical creatures; if she and Marie hadn't helped him, he'd need a lot more than bandages right now. Using the kitchen knife, she obligingly cut strips of cotton from her petticoat and wrapped them around his blood-smeared arm, noting that none of the cuts would require a doctor's stitching. When she finished, she looked up at her husband to find him grinning at her.

"At least, sweetheart, you had the sense not to try using your fists this time."

"If you don't say 'thank you' properly, I just might be tempted."

He kissed her, lightly at first and then not so lightly. "I think I'll have a talk with Edward Doncaster," he declared as he pushed her gently away. "Not only is he interfering with my sheep farm, he's kept me out of our bed for a week, and that's something I won't stand for."

But it wasn't Doncaster who kept him out of his bed for another three weeks. It was a Southdown ewe who dropped her lamb on the cold, wintry ground just minutes after the cheerful Pontifract constabulary staff had driven off with a gory load of fifteen bloody cutthroats. Cursing the stupidity of sheep in general, Gilbert ordered the weary defenders to prepare the cotes and breeding pens. Gray dawn was just breaking as Grimes's remarkable dogs began the job of separating nine hundred ewes from the rest of the flocks and driving the reluctant, bleating creatures into the fenced pens surrounding the fire-warmed cotes. Fourteen newly born lambs had to be rescued in the process.

Unlike most animal mothers, ewes walk casually away from their offspring without a backward glance. Unless human hands carry the shivering little bodies to the safety of the warm hay piled in the three-sided cotes, the lambs perish; and so does most of the profit of sheep farming. Hours later, propelled by some belated sense of responsibility, the ewes begin searching for their young, callously pushing aside any that are not their own. Some ewes, for one reason or another, never locate their lambs, and these orphans must be nurtured on cow's milk.

Anne was disgusted with this cruel, indifferent quality of motherhood, and she was thoroughly annoyed by the number of hot meals she and Marie were asked to lug down for the men. But she had no intention of becoming a sheep tender herself, not until she was offered an invitation that she couldn't refuse.

On the third night of the marathon vigil, she was waiting to speak to Gilbert after delivering the sixth serving of food for the day when callused hands grabbed her and pulled her backward inside one of the cotes. Terrified, she opened her mouth to scream, only to be silenced by the warm laughter of her husband as his hands reached for the buttons on her dress. Giving her no chance to protest, he began an urgent assault on her senses with kisses that were hot and demanding. Anne was to blush profusely whenever she remembered her response. Whatever it was—the flickering light of the open fire, the pervasive mood of tension, or the star-lit beauty of the chill night—her pulses were racing and her caresses as compulsive as his. Without removing their clothing they made a kind of love that was total and almost savage in its domination. Afterward he held her tightly and his soft exultant laughter tickled her ear.

"I used to dream about you when we were apart."

"Gil Brown, you thought I was dead then."

"That didn't stop me from dreaming, especially around a campfire. But you're better than any dream, Anne Gray. You're more alive than I ever thought you could be. Stay with me tonight. Better still, stay with me every night."

"I'd just interfere with your work."

Again his soft, lazy laughter sent chills of intense pleasure down her back. "I like your way of interfering. You may be the most intellectual bookworm in Yorkshire, but you're also a very sensuous, exciting woman. And you're mine."

What woman could resist that kind of blarney? Anne asked herself with amused skepticism; it wasn't like Gilbert to articulate his feelings. But in the weeks that followed when she became as adept as her husband at taking care of the harvest of lambs, his praise became even more specific and open; and he waited for her each night with welcoming arms. The compliment she loved the most, even though she blushed every time she remembered it, was the one Gilbert paid to her on the rainy night she wore her oldest Andy Grey outfit. Carrying her into "their" cote, now shared by a dozen orphan lambs, he had removed her boots and trousers with warm hands that caressed and stroked.

"You have beautiful legs, Anne. Did you know that the dumb books the schools give boys to read call them limbs?"

She giggled. "The book I read called them parts."

"Well, you have beautiful parts that I love to have wrapped around me like you did last night."

"Gil!" She flushed hotly at his reminder, but he was in the same exuberant mood he'd exhibited for a week.

"I shall expect the same treatment from now on. You are becoming a very necessary habit." What woman could resist that appeal!

During the middle of the first week, Anne had discovered that she wasn't the only one to succumb to the prevailing mood of the season. Marie was also spending her nights at the breeding pens and returning to the house each morning with a happy smile. Anne could only guess about the uninhibited Frenchwoman's choice of partner, and not once did she guess right. In the third week of lambing, Anne was decorously approached by Grimes, that confirmed and vociferous bachelor, who announced proudly that he and Marie were keeping company.

"Come t'end of shearin', we plan to marry up. Yu mightn't approve of what we're doing, missus, but she's too much woman to be let alone." His voice was as serious as a medieval knight making a pledge to help a damsel in distress. When Anne recovered from her amused shock, she realized that these two wonderful people had probably found a love as strong and exciting as her own.

After the season finally ended and the pens were emptied of all but sixty-odd ewes, Anne estimated that rams were as inefficient as female sheep. These arrogant idiot creatures had impregnated only seventy-five percent of the ewes assigned to them.

Manlike, her husband was defensively forgiving. "That's a great yield. Most farmers survive on sixty percent. What with the thirty orphans we saved, we'll end up with seventy-three percent. Meanwhile, sweetheart"—he grinned at her—"I want you to talk to these maiden ewes and give them some instructions on how to please a male. Perhaps next time they won't be so reluctant.''

Try as she might to express shock at this outrageous suggestion, Anne burst into laughter. She was becoming accustomed to this lusty and changed husband of hers and was finding him almost irresistible. That shared laughter would be the last they would enjoy for weeks. Like everything else important in Yorkshire County, spring justice was sandwiched in between lambing and shearing, since the county's economy was based on sheep. Thus the Brownsville residents were summoned to the Assize Court of Leeds to give testimony at the trial of their attackers.

On the day they packed for an indefinite stay in Leeds, Anne was dreading her reappearance before a judge; she was also alarmed by a second summons she'd received from Cedric Kenrick, warning her that the final step in the Blake brothers' conspiracy was imminent. In the busy excitement of the recent months she had almost forgotten the commitment she'd made with the Kenricks and Alan Chadwick prior to her reunion with her husband. This trip would give her a double dose of Edward Doncaster, a man she now feared and hated more than ever. Automatically she dressed in the blue velvet suit she'd worn at her last trial involving this man.

Gilbert regarded her critically. "You look like a sixteen-year-old girl in that thing and as innocent as one of our lambs. Wear something else."

Stung by his ungracious criticism, Anne returned his scrutiny and frowned. Her handsome husband was elegantly garbed in a cream-colored suit topped by a light brown coat that fit his muscular slimness with a graceful perfection. Bitterly she remembered that this suit had been part of his ''trousseau'' for a marriage to another woman.

"And you look like a bridegroom," she blurted, wanting to hurt him as the memory had hurt her.

He studied her averted face and put his arms gently around her. "I feel like a bridegroom, and I want my bride to wear the same outfit she wore to my old flat the first day she came husband hunting.'' Unerringly he went to her wardrobe and returned with the daring violet silk suit she'd had made in America; and long before he finished dressing her in it, she was blushing at his uninhibited comments and caresses.

"Now," he concluded smugly as he lowered the low neckline another quarter inch, "you look like the woman I wanted to seduce that day."

"You didn't even remember my name that day!"

"I remembered everything about you, including the fact that you had a sharp tongue and the education to make me feel like an ignorant fool."

"They why—"

"What chance did I have? You also had a well-educated right fist. Come on, Lady Brownwell, let's go to court. I want to show you off."

He knew his Yorkshire countrymen far better than Anne did. From the moment they stepped out of their carriage in Leeds, they were on display as heads of every description swiveled around to peer at the famous or otherwise celebrities. As he nodded to a woman in a carriage across the street who was studying them avidly through her lorgnette, Gilbert whispered in Anne's ear, "That's Lady Crandall. At one time she wanted to lead a lynch mob after me. I hope she's had a long cold wait for us this morning."

Inside the austere courtroom the same degree of curiosity about them prevailed; but at least in there Anne had someone to stare back at—the twelve men lounging casually around the jury box, three of whom strolled over to talk to Gilbert about sheep.

"Are they all sheep farmers?" she asked in horror after the three jurors returned to the box.

Her husband grinned at her. "You didn't expect Leeds to choose an impartial jury, did you? This is a wool town. Look, they're bringing our lads in now." Anne looked up at the sorry bunch of men being led or carried in. Three were propped up on litters, two unrecuperated from pitchfork injuries and one with his head swaddled in bandages, the victim of a hoe attack. In the daylight, the others looked like frightened, harmless little men; but Anne remembered the terror they had caused her a month ago.

All speculation stopped when the bailiff rapped for order and announced the imminent entrance of the judge, who turned out to be a smiling, affable man whose wig bounced merrily over his hairless head as he nodded to his friends among the jurors and even to Anne and Gil. She remembered Magistrate Percival Suffield, who had scowled at her with disapproval for three days, and wondered if she would have fared any better under this jolly man. An hour later she knew that she would have been lucky to have escaped jail with this judge. He was callously efficient in the speed with which he dispensed with the preliminaries, announcing that since the defendants had committed the crime in front of fifteen reliable witnesses and been apprehended at the scene, they had agreed to forego legal counsel. Anne wondered if anyone had even asked the defendants. The prosecutor, too, was unmercifully brief in his description of the crime; four men were being accused with attempted murder and eleven men with the intent to kill sheep and set fire to the premises of Brownsville.

As soon as the judge announced that the witnesses would now give testimony, Anne knew with a certainty that she'd be sworn in first. She was the one that the crowds of spectators had come to see. When her name was called, she walked to the witness railing with the haughty grandeur of a queen about to be condemned and executed, fiercely glad that her husband had forced her to wear her most sophisticated outfit. Dramatically she took the oath to tell the truth and waited for the ordeal to begin. Oddly enough, the judge was the one who questioned her.

"Were you present at the scene at the time the alleged crime was attempted?"

"Yes, Your Honor."

"Did you see the four men who attacked your husband with knives?"

"Yes, Your Honor."

"Thank you, Lady Brownwell, you may step down."

Anne could not believe her ears; she was being dismissed without being asked a single critical question. She had been paraded in front of the curious rabble of Leeds like some circus freak and then dismissed like an unimportant chambermaid. She was fuming as the bailiff led her out of the courthouse building and into the street. Mounting the carriage Gilbert had paid a street urchin to watch, Anne picked up the reins and drove to Cedric Kenrick's bank four blocks away with little regard for the sedate rules of traffic. After paying the bank doorman to watch her carriage, she strode regally into the bank, where no fewer than three smiling employees escorted her into the very private office of the owner. Cedric rose graciously to welcome her.

"I was hoping that your testimony would be brief, Lady Brownwell."

"I wasn't asked to testify, not even against the man I struck down."

Cedric smothered a smile. "I don't believe your action was officially recorded. I imagine your husband will be given the credit for striking that blow."

"How about Marie Pascale? She fought two men."

"I believe Mr. Grimes will be given that credit. I'm afraid we're a bit old-fashioned in Leeds."

"If there's no official record, how do you know what happened, Mr. Kenrick?"

"I investigate every incident I can concerning Mr. Doncaster. I talked with both the Pontifract constable and with twelve of the defendants."

"Did they admit that Doncaster hired them?"

"Doncaster didn't, at least not in person. Only two of the men even know him by sight. The others are waterfront scum from Liverpool. The two, however, have worked for Doncaster before. In return for a guarantee that they would not be hanged—"

"How could a banker be able to guarantee that, Mr. Kenrick?"

"Judge Ackley was with me at the time. He, too, has a long-standing grudge against Mr. Doncaster. He was forced by contrived evidence to turn over your husband's estate to Doncaster prior to Lord Brownwell's return to England. Ackley hates legal trickery and lies." That was the moment Anne decided that grumpy Percival Suffield had been a blessing for her.

"When the two men received the judge's guarantee that he would not ask the death penalty, they told everything they knew. At Doncaster's order they had hired the men who killed your sheep in an earlier raid, but they both swore that Doncaster had not hired them to murder your husband and you. I'm afraid they were telling the truth. Edward Doncaster would not risk being involved with murder so openly as to hire the assassins himself. Both men swear that they have no idea who was behind the hiring. They never even saw the man who paid them the money. He talked to them only in an unlighted room, and neither man could identify the voice. Now, we could have Doncaster charged with the destruction of your sheep, but he would avoid conviction simply by paying a large fine. So that leaves us precisely where we always have been. Are you still willing to invest another hundred thousand pounds to accomplish our purpose, Lady Brownwell?" he asked abruptly.

His question took her by surprise and she nodded doubtfully. "I suppose so, since I have already committed myself."

"Good. Alan Chadwick, my father, and I will match that sum."

Anne smiled in relief. "Then as new partners you can do all the negotiating with the Blakes, and I won't have to go to Birmingham."

"Yes, you will. We will be partners with you, not with the Blake brothers. They are well satisfied with the partner they have and have refused any others. So your Mr. Hanley Krebs will have to be our spokesman."

"Mr. Kenrick, there is no way I can learn to speak like an old man."

"Alan assures me that you are an accomplished actress. If you write out your speeches and memorize them, I'm certain you can convince the Blakes."

"I haven't the vaguest idea of what I'm supposed to talk about."

"I have all the material here. Both my father and Alan have gathered every fact we'll need. You will study their notes and put them into your own words."

"By when?"

"Six weeks at the most."

Anne blanched. She had expected the answer to be six months at the earliest, but the banker's next words destroyed that consoling fiction.

"The Blakes and some of their mine owner friends have succeeded in stealing almost every customer Doncaster has monopolized for years by undercutting his prices—the railroads, the steamship companies, and thousands of private customers. The Doncaster Mining Company is facing bankruptcy and is left with mountains of unsold coal. Doncaster has to sell at least two of his ten mines to break even this year."

"That's nonsense. He stole enough from my husband's estate alone to be a wealthy man."

"He would never risk his private fortune merely to satisfy his company's creditors. Your husband's estate and Doncaster's earlier fortune are now legally in his daughter's hands."

Anne sucked in her breath slowly. She had the husband but her rival had the husband's fortune. Hastily she changed the subject. "It is going to be very difficult to posture as Mr. Krebs in front of my husband. He will not understand the necessity—"

"Your husband cannot go to Birmingham."

"He'll insist on going, otherwise he'll not permit me to do so."

"He can't go. In the first place he would be in considerable danger there. One attempt has already been made on his life. In the second place, he is too well known there not to be recognized. During that . . . er . . . difficult period of . . . er . . .

transition, he was entertained everywhere; and with his distinctive appearance, he'd be impossible to disguise. In the third place I'm certain that you do not want him running into Edwina Doncaster.''

Anne stared at the banker and answered honestly, ''Not under any circumstances.''

''Your husband would not let you go alone?''

''No. Gil has even refused to let me come to Leeds alone.''

''Can you fabricate some family emergency?''

''I hate to lie to my husband.''

''Very commendable, Lady Brownwell. But without your presence in Birmingham, our plans to shut down the Doncaster mines will have to be forgotten.''

''Tell me, Mr. Kenrick, what good will it do to ruin his business as long as his personal fortune remains intact?''

''The mining company supports his lawyers and the army of thugs he employs. It also pays the corrupt public officials of Birmingham enough money to protect him from prosecution. If we succeed in closing down that mining company, Doncaster will not be able to pay these people. Remember that he no longer controls his personal fortune, his daughter does. Without his paid army and the support of the corrupt officials, he will be in a position to be sued by creditors and by the people he has bilked. In the case my father has prepared against him, Doncaster will be charged as a criminal. We are hoping he will be convicted and sent to prison.''

''Are you certain your plan will work? Can we really destroy his mining company so quickly?''

''Technically, yes. We've known how for years. But it took your rather unique idea of working through another coal company to make our plan feasible. And now we need your Mr. Krebs to ensure the cooperation of the Blake brothers. Will you help us?''

''Yes, and I have an aunt who will supply me with a family emergency.''

''Good. Then everything's arranged. You and I will drive

by private coach to Birmingham. My wife will accompany us, naturally.''

''The train would be faster.''

''At present, there is no train direct to Birmingham, except through Liverpool. And that would be too public an exposure for all of us. Secrecy is going to be the essential element. We will meet Alan Chadwick and my father at the Newhall Hotel and discuss any last-minute changes in plan. Mr. Philip Trent will also be there to aid you with your costume. Now about our timing. Just as soon as Doncaster puts some of his mines up for public sale, we'll have to be ready to move. I'm afraid I'll be able to give you no more than one day's warning. Can you manage?''

''I hope so, Mr. Kenrick.''

Anne was sitting in the carriage studying the voluminous notes the banker had given her about the Doncaster Mining Company—forty pages of facts to be digested into several short speeches. She looked up in time to see her husband and Mr. Duncan, the oldest of the Scot cousins, emerge from the courtroom.

''The trial's over,'' Gilbert announced.

''What trial?'' she asked and heard the hearty chuckle of the Scot as he climbed up to the driver's bench while Gil joined her inside. ''Did Marie get to testify, Gil?''

''She was asked the same two questions you were; but according to Grimes, she didn't want any publicity. Anne, did you know she left France because of trouble with the police?''

Anne nodded thoughtfully; she'd almost forgotten; but now at least she understood why neither she nor Marie were mentioned in the evidence. ''How did the trial come out?''

He shrugged. ''Since they were guilty, they were declared guilty and sentenced to hard labor. They'll probably wind up in Australia.''

''Where are we going now?'' Anne asked.

''To look at some sheep.''

''Oh, Gil, not again! What kind this time?''

''Duncan has made a deal for some pedigreed Leicester

and Rambouillet rams at the auction. They're expensive, but they produce the best wool when bred to merinos.''

"How much?"

"You'll just be angry if I tell you."

"How much?"

"Each ram costs the same amount as thirty ewes. But our credit is good, so we'll be able to borrow from the bank."

"No, we won't, Gil; if you're going to borrow money, you're going to borrow it from me. And I'll charge you the same interest the bank does."

At his sharp question, "Do you mean it, Anne?" she knew she'd walked into a trap—a fifty-thousand-pound one. Rams were not the only deal Duncan had made. That night at the Yorkshire Hotel, Lord and Lady Brownwell dined with the most progressive mill owner of Leeds. By the time the after-dinner brandy was served, the Brownwells were half owners in a new mill designed to produce only the expensive, silklike wool fabrics.

Gilbert boasted, "Next year, we'll be producing nothing but merino wool; our yield will supply the mill and our farm will be self-supporting." Anne sincerely hoped so. After her trip to Birmingham her own fortune would be reduced to sixty thousand pounds.

For the two weeks Gilbert stayed in Leeds completing the business details while Anne was secluded in their bedroom at Brownsville creating a "talking" Hanley Krebs. By perching a pair of spectacles on her nose, she achieved a disfiguring squint; and by leaning heavily on a wooden stick, she simulated a realistic stoop. Only the voice proved troublesome; but by the middle of the second week she'd perfected a dryness that suggested old age. Between sessions of acting practice, she learned forty pages of facts and memorized the speeches she wrote. Satisfied at last that her basic preparation was sufficient for a two-day performance, she emerged from the bedroom to find her husband waiting for her with a wolfish grin and impatient arms. His kiss was more than an invitation, it was a command.

"How long have you been back?" she gasped when she could catch her breath.

"Long enough to light a fire, and don't change the subject." His expert hands were almost through unbuttoning her dress.

"Gil, Marie will see—"

"No, she won't. Grimes is back, so she's gone for the night. Any more objections?"

"No."

"I should hope not. You even get to wear your Andy Grey getup tomorrow when we start the shearing."

Sharply reminded of her own project, Anne protested, "I don't know anything about shearing."

"You don't have to. I've got another job for you, and you'll need to wear trousers."

"I thought you didn't like me wearing them in public?"

"I was referring to your fancy captain when I told you that, not our farm workers. And I'm not sure I'd even mind the Frenchman anymore; that is, if you remember everything I taught you at lambing time." Anne flushed deeply at his words; they'd both revealed a primitive streak in their natures during those nights in the cote. That he'd already remembered their lack of inhibition was evident in the grin he flashed her as he pointed to the sheepskin object on the floor.

"It's a shepherd's sleep sack. I had ours made double. We'll use it whenever we're camping out again, but tonight we'll just pretend." However, there was nothing of pretense about the passionate lustiness of his lovemaking inside that furry sleep sack in a room lighted only by the fire. He was as insatiable as any sailor after a long voyage instead of a husband after only a two-week absence, and Anne exulted in his uncomplicated exuberance. She giggled when she thought about the fireplace in the manor house next door with Lady Suzanne's portrait above it, and she wondered what her elegant mother-in-law would think of Gilbert as he squatted before the fire and roasted their camp dinner.

"Someday I'm taking you and our children to Australia. I want them to know what's important in life. As for you, I'm taking you wherever I go from now on, including the shearing pens tomorrow morning. Come on, wife, let's climb in and get some sleep. I don't want Grimes to outshear me by too many.''

Tousle-haired and still flushed, Anne awoke the next morning to find her husband gone. Hurrying to the sheds, she located nine sweaty men behind mounds of wool gripping nine indignant sheep, while four other workers shoved the shorn creatures through a trough of evil-smelling liquid.

''You bale, weigh, and mark the wool,'' Gilbert yelled at her without a trace of lingering affection in his voice.

It sounded like an easy enough job until she tried to straighten her back at the end of the day. Those nine men had sheared five hundred sheep, and she had bailed a third of that number. Not since her days with Casey Ryan had her muscles been as sore; she felt as old as ''Hanley Krebs,'' and all she could smell was sheep dip.

Marie smelled it, too. When Gilbert and Anne dragged themselves home, their normally good-natured cook pointed to three large barrels of hot water standing ten feet from the rear of the servants' quarters. Obligingly the lord and lady of the manor stripped off their clothes, climbed into separate barrels, and scoured themselves with a bar of soap strong enough to remove all but the last essential layers of skin. While they were thus employed, Marie lifted their discarded garments with a stick and shoved them into the third barrel, where an even stronger concentration of soap reduced the offensive odor to a bearable mustiness. For three weeks the Brownwells spent twelve hours a day in workclothes and twelve in nightgowns, during which time they helped shear their own sheep and seven thousand belonging to neighboring farmers. Lord Brownwell and the Grimes brothers were what they'd boasted of being—top shear men.

Gilbert also had become a work addict. Jubilant over the financial success of the shearing enterprise, he dispatched Duncan and his Scots to buy every merino ewe they could find. Gambling on the probability that most English sheep men were ignorant of the successful Australian experiments in cross-breeding the versatile Spanish merino, he hoped to keep the new mill in Leeds completely supplied with fine, silky wool by the following year.

On the day Marie and Grimes left Brownsville for their wedding trip to London, where they would stay in Anne's home, Gilbert and the remaining Grimes brothers began the Herculean task of reorganizing six hundred acres of pasture to accommodate an expected two thousand more sheep in time for breeding. Hiring an additional ten laborers, he ordered the construction of thousands more feet of fencing, a dozen more cotes, and twenty more water troughs. On the day when the resulting activity was at its most chaotic, three of the Scots' wagons returned with full loads, and a messenger arrived from Leeds with the verbal command of "tomorrow morning" for Anne and a letter from Aunt Margaret for Anne and Gilbert.

Nervously Anne packed her clothes and waited for her husband to report home for the evening meal, which one of the Grimes women had prepared. Silently she handed him Margaret's letter, a letter Anne had written herself and asked her aunt to send a copy of to Cedric Kenrick.

His response was short and pithy. "Out of the question, Anne; I can't get away right now."

"I can," she reminded him.

"Not without me, you can't. I haven't forgotten that Doncaster is still as free as a bird and much more dangerous."

"I'd be perfectly safe on the public coach."

"You weren't even safe here on the farm."

"You went to Leeds alone."

"I outweigh you by four stone, and I wasn't taught to fight by a gentleman pub owner in Boston."

"Gil, I want to see the children."

"Your aunt said they were just homesick."

"I've never been away from them this long before. Besides, Aunt Margaret has been ill and I want to find out if she has recovered."

"And I'm being a dog in the manger by keeping you here, is that it?"

"No, but I don't understand your objections. I'll be safe enough and I'll ask my brother to escort me and the twins back here. 'I'll only be gone two or three weeks."

"In three weeks I'll take you there and we'll bring the children back ourselves."

Anne studied the stubborn expression on her husband's face and felt like a prisoner. Admittedly everything she'd just told him was a lie, but it was a reasonable lie. Mothers were supposed to console lonely children, and wives were expected to visit sick aunts. Moreover her husband hadn't worried about her safety when he'd left her alone on the farm while he'd remained in Leeds. Anne's irritation grew. During the past year she had made few demands on him and had allowed him to make almost all the decisions. But this trip was one decision she had made herself; and if it accomplished the purpose, it was a good decision regardless of the lie. She took a deep breath.

"Gil, I'm going to Grayhaven tomorrow morning. If you don't want to drive me to Pontifract, I'll ask Duncan to take me in his wagon."

"It doesn't matter that I don't want you to leave?"

"It matters very much, but you have work to do and I feel obliged to go alone."

His "Suit yourself, Anne" were the coldest words he'd spoken to her in a year; and she was tempted to tell him the truth so he'd have a real reason for his anger. Silently she left the room to complete her packing, feeling less guilty by the moment. Men, she reflected with a flash of her old resentment, liked their women to be obedient chattels who never questioned their lords and masters. By the time he joined her in bed, her mood was one of defiance as she turned to kiss him good night. He spoiled her defensive righteousness by responding warmly after a second's hesitation and by making expert and passionate love to her. Holding her close to him, he continued to caress her boldly.

"Don't become too civilized for me while you're with your family."

"You're the most important member of my family," she reassured him, feeling the burden of guilt again.

"I hope you feel the same way after your father and aunt finish reminding you of all my faults."

In a flash of understanding, Anne chuckled. "If you'd come with me, you'd find that most of the time they'd be too busy telling you about all of mine." But Anne vowed that she'd never again lie to her insecure husband or leave him for as much as one night.

Chapter 19

STUDYING the faces of the three men who were her partners in a complicated conspiracy, Anne was both puzzled and irritated that their tense concern was greater than her own. Since she was the one who faced the ordeal of a difficult masquerade and since hers was the larger investment of money, she thought their worried expressions reflected a singular lack of confidence in her acting ability. During the two days of travel with Cedric Kenrick and his wife, the banker had been almost jovial as he'd listened to Anne practice her prepared speeches. Not until they joined Alan Chadwick and Weston Kenrick in a private sitting room at the Newhall Hotel in Birmingham did Cedric's face assume a funereal expression. Alan Chadwick was also frowning with concentrated concern, a look that was uncharacteristic of this normally pleasant lawyer. Certainly during the earlier meeting with the Blake brothers he had been relaxed and confident.

Anne turned her attention to the third man, Weston Kenrick, whom she'd met only once before. Somewhere in his middle sixties, he projected the image of a successful, well-preserved businessman; and unlike his son and the lawyer, he did not appear unduly apprehensive as he studied Anne's notes. But she knew that the bad news must have come from him since he was the originator of most of the plans. He shook his head as he laid the papers on the table.

"The Blakes won't accept this proposition as things now stand," he announced matter-of-factly.

"Why not?" Anne demanded hotly. "I followed all your instructions."

"Your preparation is excellent, Lady Brownwell. It's your false identity which is no longer convincing," he explained.

"How can that be? They saw me only twice in that disguise, and both brothers seemed to accept me then."

"They did, Anne, at that time," Chadwick assured her, "but they have reason to be suspicious now. It's really my fault; I should have been much more thorough in preparing a background for Hanley Krebs. What has happened is that we underestimated Doncaster's intelligence system. He evidently knew far more about the Blakes' finances than we thought. When they expanded so suddenly a year ago, he assumed correctly that they had acquired a silent partner. In view of the phenomenal success the Blakes have had with the railroad and steamship companies, he also assumed correctly that the Blakes had access to inside information about his own operation. And he was right again. I have been supplying our friends with all the facts Weston has been able to obtain. I'm afraid Doncaster reacted typically; he paid a Blake employee to spy for him. A month ago Farley Blake caught one of his secretaries going through the locked files.

"Since that time, Doncaster's solicitors have been busy investigating our Mr. Krebs. Needless to say, they have discovered nothing except that Hanley Krebs is a client of mine. Unfortunately the incident aroused the Blakes' curiosity about this new partner. They will probably demand a complete disclosure from you tomorrow.''

"Why should they care what I am, Alan, as long as my money strengthens their company?''

"Because Doncaster or one of his lawyers cleverly circulated a rumor that Krebs was working for them. And the Blakes are afraid you might be trying to ruin them. Well, Anne, can your devious mind invent a miracle solution to our dilemma?''

The one advantage, she reflected, of being a woman in a man's world is that you don't expect fair play. Conventional men like the Blakes always do. The secret of dealing successfully with people like that is to know enough about the situation to make a lie believable.

She was smiling when she answered Alan's question. "I think I can. Before either brother can challenge me tomorrow, I'll tell them that Hanley Krebs is an assumed name and that I'm a far younger man disguised with theatrical makeup. They will accept that as the truth since it mainly is. Instead of railroads, I will tell them I am in shipping and shipbuilding, which is almost the truth. I worked in shipyards for six years, I own stock in the two largest American steamship companies, and I am a member of the British family that owns one of the largest companies in this country. Incidentally, that company is converting to steam and has already contracted to buy Blake coal.

"To explain the necessity for the disguise, I will also tell the truth up to a point. I am afraid of Edward Doncaster because he has tried to have me killed three times—perhaps four. The reason I will give them will be a lie, but a believable one. I will claim to have successfully persuaded all steamship companies to boycott Doncaster coal because he attempted to gain a monopoly with the intent to overcharge his customers. According to Mr. Kenrick's notes, the steamship companies voluntarily refused Doncaster, but the Blakes probably don't realize their refusal was voluntary, especially if I drop a few names of my relatives and the owners of other shipping firms. My final admission will be a signed pledge to reveal my own identity as soon as they have purchased the Doncaster mines in question.''

Of the three listeners, only Alan Chadwick greeted her solution with approval; but then he was the only one who had been exposed to her flexible philosophy of business ethics. Cedric Kenrick's face mirrored his professional disapproval of a woman capable of such glib duplicity, while his father looked as outraged as Paul Bouvier had the day he'd discovered Anne at the shipyards. Weston Kenrick had been willing to use her money and to accept the necessity of a male disguise for her. But the idea of any woman, except the queen, being in charge of any enterprise was untenable.

''I think not,'' he stated flatly.

Anne shrugged. ''All right, perhaps you'll approve of my second plan. It will take five years longer but it will accomplish the same end. You own the two-hundred-foot-wide strip of land adjacent to the Doncaster mines in the existing coalfields of south Staffordshire. According to your notes, you have obtained the mineral rights to additional acreage. We will open our own company with your land and my money.''

''No, Lady Brownwell, I will not be involved in any company in which a woman has an actual part in the management. I will most certainly not be your partner in a company of our own.''

''Then you have no choice but to accept my proposal to the Blake brothers. I will most assuredly not be a manager there. Besides the destruction of Mr. Doncaster, my only desire is to see my investment earn more money. I know nothing about coal, so I'll let you experts accomplish that goal for me. Moreover my husband will not permit me to take an active role in any business. He feels much as you do about women,'' she added with remembered resentment.

Pushed to the wall, the old man conceded grudgingly. ''Then I suppose I must agree to your earlier suggestions, and I apologize for any affront I may have caused you.'' His stiff formality softened a bit when he asked a more personal question. "Have you really had practical experience working in a shipyard, Lady Brownwell?"

"Six years of it," Anne affirmed, surprised and pleased to find one member of the British public who had not heard of Andrew Grey. She hoped that the Blake brothers would be as ignorant when they met an older Andy the next morning.

She couldn't be certain about their ignorance as she and Chadwick were ushered into their office, but she found both the Blakes vastly changed from the gracious men she'd invested with a year before. Just as the older brother, the one whose desk plate read Farley Blake, cleared his throat, Anne rose swiftly from her chair.

"Gentlemen," she began in a voice considerably younger than the one she'd practiced for Hanley Krebs, but far more autocratic than the polite one she'd used for Andrew Grey. Giving them little opportunity to interrupt, she made the introductory speech she'd outlined the night before, ending it with a challenge. "I am in a position to invest two hundred thousand pounds with your company, providing you are interested in my proposition. If not, I will investigate another firm."

Predictably, Farley Blake demanded, "For that size investment, do you also plan to become one of the company's managers? If so, we are not interested. My brother and I work alone."

Impatiently she assured them she did not. At her reassurance the brothers nodded in unison, and Anne was given permission to state the proposition. Her first move was to unfold a large map of the entire south Staffordshire coalfields, a map considerably more complete than any of the Blakes.

"This map was drawn by one of my associates, Mr. Weston Kenrick. You are undoubtedly familiar with his name and with his background as a mine owner and mining expert. You will notice that he has carefully detailed the production yield of each mine as well as all other critical facts. Of the twenty-two mines still operating in the south Staffordshire fields, eight are individually owned, four belong to you, and ten to Doncaster. His mines are all connected by a private railway which feeds directly into the large terminal of the publicly owned railroads. In that way Mr. Doncaster has cheap transportation for his coal, so much so that his mining operation is now entirely dependent upon his private railway.''

"We also have a private railroad, Mr. . . . er . . . Krebs," Leland Blake asserted.

"I know you do, but you also have access to a public road and can dray your coal out in wagons. Mr. Doncaster no longer has such an access—a condition I will explain later. Now about my proposition. Because you gentlemen have successfully undersold Mr. Doncaster for a year, you have accomplished our initial goal of forcing him into financial difficulties. Last week in the *Manchester Guardian,* he advertised his mines seven and eight for sale. They are only moderately productive, but I want you to buy them.''

Leland Blake shook his head vigorously. "No, the production figures are not good enough to risk sharing a railway with Doncaster. We'd be lucky to get a third of the coal past his mines nine and ten.''

"You're not going to share the railway with him. Over a period of years, Mr. Kenrick has purchased the two-hundred-foot-wide strip of land which runs adjacent to all of the Doncaster mines. Last month one of the landowners who sold him that strip of land also sold him the mineral rights to the fields opposite Doncaster's number seven. That landowner will allow you to install pumps, vents, and escape shafts; but he will not allow coal to be brought up to the surface of his farmlands. You will have to use Mr. Kenrick's strip of land for that purpose. You will also build a new railway on that strip of land after you have purchased mines seven and eight and tear up Mr. Doncaster's rails going through those two mines.''

Farley Blake sucked in his breath. "It's a daring plan, but Doncaster will probably retain ownership of his railway system.''

"Not according to these advertisements in the *Manchester*

Guardian. Mr. Doncaster has no idea that Kenrick owns the land adjacent to his mines. The sales have all been recorded in Coventry rather than in Birmingham. All he knows is that the original owner denied him access a few years ago, so he would naturally assume that you would also be denied access. He is most probably convinced that the only access for coal from mines seven and eight are through his own.

"You will get three mines for the price of two, one of them a virgin area beneath farmlands, an area Mr. Kenrick is certain contains deep strata of coal. By tearing up Doncaster's railway you will virtually bottle up his mines one through six. Are you interested, gentlemen?"

Both men nodded vigorously, but Farley Blake was the more cautious. "What is Mr. Kenrick's price for this land?"

"Forty thousand pounds and a permanent job as a consulting expert with your company. That money must come from you. The two hundred thousand pounds I am making available will be needed to purchase the existing mines and to build the railway. It may even be sufficient to start developing the third mine."

"What are your expectations, Mr. . . . ."

"Krebs will do for the time being. I will expect you to make a fortune for me at the same time you're making another for yourselves. So far I am very pleased about the returns on my earlier investment. Gentlemen, the contracts are all in this container. Study them at your leisure, but do not delay contacting Doncaster if you decide to accept our proposition. Naturally you will mention nothing of these plans to Doncaster. You can contact me through a Mr. Philip Trent at the Newhall Hotel."

Only Leland rose to escort Anne and Alan Chadwick to the door; Farley was already poring over the case containing the contracts. Having maintained a solemn face until he and Anne were safely in the carriage, Chadwick now burst into laughter. "I want to be present when they meet Lady Brownwell."

She grinned back at him. "They're not going to. I'm going

to pay you to deliver my signed statement to them; that is, if they decide to buy those mines."

"They decided to buy the minute you told them that they'd get three mines out of the deal. You're a very persuasive speaker. How in the world did a properly brought-up English girl like yourself develop such a remarkable talent in salesmanship?"

"By having to deal with properly brought-up men. It's a stupid social system, Alan."

"In your case, I think it is, Anne."

Dealing with three properly brought-up men and one extremely proper woman for the next two tense days of waiting proved almost beyond Anne's endurance. Imprisoned in their individual rooms or in the common sitting room for precautionary reasons, they quickly exhausted their topics of common interest. Mrs. Kenrick silently and placidly embroidered on the dress skirt she was covering with pink rosebuds while her husband and father-in-law read. Only after Chadwick invited the actor to join them did Anne lose the sensation of being entombed.

Philip Trent was an entertaining man whose endless anecdotes about theatrical people were amusing and perhaps even partially true. He had an equal fund of stories about the gentlemen cadets at Sandhurst, where he'd been employed as a fencing instructor in between acting engagements. Trent was also an avid cardplayer and an expert with dice. Anne lost four pounds to him before she changed the stakes from shillings to copper pennies. Twice during those two days Alan Chadwick was summoned by the Blakes to explain the contracts, and both times he returned to announce that Doncaster had not yet responded to the Blakes' offer.

Just before dinner on the third night the awaited news arrived. Doncaster had agreed to sell, providing the Blakes' "silent" partner was present at the meeting.

"It's a trap, Anne," Chadwick exclaimed.

"Doncaster couldn't possibly know that I'm Hanley Krebs," she protested.

"Prichart would know the minute he saw you. He had too much opportunity to study your face at the hearing, and he knows me well. Both he and Doncaster would guess your identity if we walked into that office together. I can't allow you to risk the possible danger."

With dramatic delicacy, Philip Trent cleared his throat. "Alan, you've been paying me to act as bodyguard for Anne, and I haven't as yet earned my salary. I'll go to that meeting with her and claim to be your clerk. Every solicitor has clerks. I'll announce that you're down with a cold as bad as the one I'll invent for Hanley Krebs. Anne's face will be such a shambles, no one will want to get close to her. Just give me two hours to visit the backstage of one of the local theaters to procure the necessary props."

When the lawyer hesitated, Trent reminded him sharply, "I am an excellent swordsman." To demonstrate, he twirled the beautiful ebony walking cane he carried and, with one swift movement, unsheathed a slender lethal rapier. "I'll borrow one of these for Anne and teach her how to hold it. Even if the intentions of those dastards are the worst, Anne and I will get safely away."

Before Cedric Kenrick or his father could express an opinion, Mrs. Kenrick murmured, "Oh, I don't think you have to worry about Lady Brownwell's safety. From what I've read, she's well able to defend herself."

It was the first time Anne had heard the woman say much more than "Yes, dear" to her husband, but this remarkable statement about Anne revealed the reason for the silence. Mrs. Kenrick was not pleased about having to associate with a picaresque adventuress like Anne Gray. Most certainly this smug lady was not the wife she had pretended to be. Both her husband and her father-in-law nodded readily in agreement as if they were well accustomed to agreeing with her suggestions. Anne, it was decided, would attend the meeting with Philip Trent.

Hours before the scheduled appointment, Philip was preparing her face, smearing rouge on the tip of her nose until she looked like a rheumy old man with a chronic cold. The skin under her eyes was darkened with a blue salve which dyed the skin and heightened the impression of impending pneumonia. Philip swaddled a long wool scarf around her neck and pulled mittens over her hands. Peering through spectacles and bent over a cane, Anne couldn't recognize her own image in the mirror. Stuffed into her pockets were two large handkerchiefs, each containing a different theatrical aide. One held a pungent substance that made her sneeze vigorously, and the other was impregnated with a chemical that irritated her eyes to instant tears. One small experimental tryout of both handkerchiefs was all Anne needed to convince herself that she was indeed the victim of a miserable cold. She envied Philip Trent, whose only disguise in addition to his own elegant clothing and sword cane was a lofty expression of superiority.

At his suggestion Anne entered the Blakes' office with a sneeze moist enough to cause the four men already seated there to react with prudential distaste. Trent and Farley Blake performed the required introductions hurriedly.

Trent's opening declaration was delivered in a voice of aggrieved protest. "Both Mr. Krebs and my associate, the solicitor who heretofore handled this transaction, have contracted vicious colds in your unhealthy city, gentlemen, and we consider this meeting an unnecessary imposition." Anne sneezed repeatedly. "Mr. Krebs could have signed the necessary papers from the safety of his bed."

Farley Blake cleared his throat nervously. "I apologize for the inconvenience, but Mr. Doncaster insisted that—"

Impatiently Prichart interrupted, "We insisted with good cause. After weeks of intensive investigation, we have been able to find no one who has ever heard of you, Mr. Krebs. Even before the Blakes made this offer for Mr. Doncaster's two mines, we were curious about you and we inquired. It is our company policy never to deal with unknown strangers, so until we are satisfied with your identity, this transaction will not be completed."

Anne applied both handkerchiefs liberally and began a

violent paroxysm of sneezing and coughing. Coldly Philip Trent answered the challenge. "Since my client's money is above reproach, I fail to see how his lack of local fame is pertinent. Nevertheless, he has instructed me to reveal certain facts. For fifteen years he has lived abroad where he earned his fortune speculating in foreign industries. He is currently involved in the development of the steamship industry of Germany, France, and America. None of these countries are producing enough coal for this expanding industry, therefore he is in England to secure a permanent supply."

Doncaster whispered something to Prichart who immediately returned to the attack. "Why were we given the false information about his interest in British railroads?"

Trent shrugged. "Not that it is any of your business, but my client has invested heavily in railroads to ensure the transportation of coal to the port cities of England."

"We could find no such record," Prichart snapped.

Again he received a theatrical shrug. "I should hope not. As a representative of foreign interests, my client preferred to remain anonymous. British prejudice, you understand."

"But why this sudden need for more coal?"

"The Blake Company at present is unable to supply my client's growing needs."

For the first time Anne heard Doncaster speak for himself. "Mr. Krebs, why did you select such a small company? My firm could have met all of your demands."

Delicately Trent phrased his answer while Anne sneezed noisily in agitation. "Not being an expert in coal production, Mr. Krebs invested with the company which was most accommodating about prices."

Doncaster was on his feet, declaring vehemently, "We are now willing to undercut any price, Mr. Krebs, and we can supply you all the coal you want without any unnecessary delay."

Trent smiled with icy contempt. "Such a move would be unethical, Mr. Doncaster, as well as poor business." Anne jerked Trent's arm and whispered in his ear. As he resumed talking, Anne sneezed repeatedly. "Mr. Krebs is ill and desires to return to his hotel. If you are unwilling to sell the two mines to the Blake Company, he informs me that he will make arrangements with the German coal companies in the Saar Basin. Good day, gentlemen."

As Anne and Trent arose from their chairs, Prichart jumped to his feet and, without consulting Doncaster, announced placatingly, "Let's not be hasty. My client is satisfied with your offer, Mr. Krebs. If you're willing to sign the bill of sale, we can terminate this conference now."

Nodding with a weariness that the constant sneezing had produced in reality, Anne moved to the desk and signed the several papers rapidly. Sneezing repeatedly, she extended her hand toward Doncaster who backed warily away. Leland Blake had the door open for her long before she reached it. Leaning heavily on her cane, she walked slowly to the waiting carriage, maintaining her character until she was safely inside where she sneezed one last time even without the aid of the handkerchief and relaxed in tired relief.

Trent was enthusiastically complimentary. "You're an excellent actress, Anne."

"So are you, Philip. Why is it that you're no longer on the stage?"

"Like you, I'm too tall for my contemporaries. The one time I played Romeo, my face was level with the top of the balcony and the audience laughed. Occasionally I still play character parts. But you would look marvelous on the stage."

Anne shuddered. "I'll never act like anyone but myself again. Once I wash this horrible stuff off my face, I'll never wear anything that remotely resembles a disguise."

Her resolve lasted throughout a two-hour bath and the modest celebration that followed Philip's account of the successful sale. However, during the dinner hour two disturbing messages were delivered to the assembled conspirators. One was from the Blakes informing them that the sale was complete and the deeds duly registered in both the Birmingham and the Coventry Hall of Records. The message also contained a discouraging request. Since the dismantling of the railway tracks in mines seven and eight would commence the next morning, the Blakes wanted Hanley Krebs available to answer any legal court summons a furious Doncaster might demand.

Anne protested in dismay, "I have to leave for Grayhaven."

Sympathetically Chadwick soothed her. "If such a summons is forthcoming, it will probably arrive during the next several days. You can have the same cold, and I'll do all the necessary talking in court. Then Philip and I will drive you to Grayhaven. Meanwhile I think it best, Cedric, that you leave for Birmingham immediately."

The second message arrived ten minutes later. It was a politely innocuous note from Charles Prichart thanking Hanley Krebs for his patience and wishing him a speedy recovery from his cold. Chadwick frowned heavily.

"This note means that Doncaster knows where we are. He must have had you followed. With that degree of distrust, he undoubtedly has his men watching this hotel. Anne, you will have to continue as Krebs and eventually leave the city as such. And here's another nasty complication. Weston, every one of Doncaster's hired cutthroats knows you by sight, and some of them may even know you, Cedric. Both of your departures will have to be delayed."

Unimpressed by the lawyer's apprehension, Mrs. Kenrick snapped contemptuously, "Nonsense. My husband is a respected banker who often visits this city. I have no intention of enduring this ridiculous situation another day."

Weston Kenrick, too, was undisturbed by Chadwick's concern. "I have been dodging Doncaster's spies for ten years. Tomorrow I intend to begin working at the Blake Company."

Only Cedric seemed worried as he turned to ask Anne, "Were you aware of Doncaster's suspicion during the conference at the Blake office?"

She shook her head uncertainly; her eyes had been too blurred by tears to see the facial expressions of the others clearly enough to interpret their emotions. Trent came quickly to her defense.

"Anne's performance was excellent. Neither Doncaster nor his lawyer revealed any suspicion or disbelief. And none of them could have recognized me since I haven't played the local boards in years. I think they had us followed simply as a prearranged contingency. However, Alan is right in suggesting extreme caution in our departures. We don't want to give the enemy any further chance for learning the truth about us. May I suggest a little judicial theatrical makeup for all of you."

Mrs. Kenrick reacted to the suggestion with scorn. "Certainly not! We'll leave at ten in the morning as we planned."

More cautiously, her husband compromised. "No, we won't. We'll leave the hotel before dawn by a rear exit." His father merely smiled in his haughty British fashion and bid the others an abrupt good night.

Only Alan and Philip remained with Anne, escorting her to her room after reaffirming their promise to remain with her in Birmingham. During the following three days they joined her in the sitting room to share the meals and to play endless games of cards and dice. Philip's cane remained within easy reach at all times. As the hours passed, Alan relaxed his tense watchfulness and had even regained a measure of his normal confidence until an agitated knocking sounded. Instantly Philip unsheathed his sword and stationed himself near the door while Anne fled to the adjoining necessaries room which held the commode and washbasin. When Alan opened the door, Anne heard the familiar voice of her Aunt Margaret and ran back into the room, her face a mask of apprehensive terror.

"What are you doing here? Are the children with you?" she shouted, only to have her frantic questions fade to a whisper. Standing behind her aunt was Gilbert, looking at her with the same remote iciness he'd displayed over a year ago in the shabby parlor of his flat.

Anne's heart plummeted as she listened to her aunt's exasperated scolding. "What in the world have you been up to, Anne? Gilbert and I have been worried witless. We're in Birmingham only because he fortunately remembered that you had invested money with some coal company here. This is the fourth hotel we've searched, and we wouldn't have found you here if it hadn't been for that man.''

"What man, Lady Gray?" Chadwick asked swiftly.

Gilbert answered for her, "One of Doncaster's lawyers, the worst one. A bootlicker sneak named Eldon—no, Eldritch Philbrick. He was standing by the reception desk while Margaret was talking to the clerk.''

Without much hope, the lawyer demanded, ''Did he recognize you?"

Gilbert shrugged angrily. "Of course he did. He was the one who suggested that my wife might be the woman registered with the Trent party.''

Anne heard only the coldness of the words *my wife;* she didn't think about the dangerous implication of his words, but Alan did.

"I'm afraid, Gilbert, that you've placed Anne in a great deal of jeopardy.''

Margaret's voice rose shrilly. "I knew it. As soon as Gilbert told me about that last vicious attempt on your lives, I knew you were in danger. Anne, whatever possessed you to come near that terrible man's city?''

"She had no choice, Lady Gray," Chadwick replied hastily.

"She had a choice," Gilbert contradicted the lawyer. "She could have consulted me, and I would have come in her place. Instead she chose to lie to me.''

Chadwick attempted a futile explanation of the planned conspiracy to destroy Doncaster, ending it with a terse defense of Anne's participation. "You couldn't have replaced her. She had to continue her pretense of Hanley Krebs. Lacking her remarkable acting talent, you would have been recognized instantly.''

Gilbert shrugged again, his face still impassive as he moved over to the table to accept the glass of brandy Philip Trent obligingly poured for him. "Might I inquire how my wife reached Birmingham during each of these extraordinary trips?"

"This last time she came with Cedric Kenrick and his wife."

"So my banker is also involved in this insanity. And the first time a year ago?" Gilbert persisted.

As Chadwick hesitated and looked over at Anne, she blurted angrily, "I traveled with Alan and Philip, and I was disguised as a man." Before he could voice any disapproval about her admission, she asked the question that had bothered her since his arrival: "Gil, why did you go to Grayhaven?"

For the first time he faced her squarely. "I had the odd notion that you might be glad to see me. Instead I found your aunt in perfect health and the children happy and well adjusted. Tomorrow I'll drive you and Margaret back there before I go home."

At this point the lawyer lost his temper. "Didn't you understand anything I told you, Lord Brownwell? You have already endangered your wife's safety with your ill-advised trip here. If you attempt to leave this city without protection, you'll complete the job."

"I am capable of protecting both Lady Margaret and her niece. Doncaster may be dangerous, but he's no fool. He wouldn't dare attack us on the open road. But if you're so concerned about safety, why don't you secure a room for Margaret and spare her the necessity of confronting Philbrick again?"

Anne sucked in her breath; her husband sounded as rude and petulant as he had when she'd first met him. Chadwick, too, was highly irritated with his client. Ignoring Gilbert, he turned toward Margaret. "Lady Gray, the room Mr. and Mrs. Kenrick stayed in is still available. If you haven't dined yet, Philip can order your dinner sent there."

Hastily Margaret demurred. "Gilbert and I had tea several hours ago, so a dinner will not be necessary; but I am tired. If one of your gentlemen will escort me to the room, I'll bid all of you good night."

Miserably, Anne watched her husband pour himself another brandy before she spoke. "Aunt Margaret, you can share my room. I imagine Gil will prefer one of the empty ones."

Smiling unpleasantly, Gilbert raised his drink in a silent toast to her. "I'll share your room, Anne; I have no intention of wasting another week looking for my runaway wife should she decide to leave me again. Good night Margaret; I'll have one of the hotel maids awaken you in the morning. If you don't mind, I'd like to get an early start." Anne's eyes were stormy as she kissed her aunt and watched as a sympathetic Philip escorted the older woman from the room.

The lawyer tried once more to reason with a stubborn client. "Gilbert, you're risking three lives tomorrow if you persist in this insanity. I urge you strongly not to take this precipitous action."

"I'm afraid your advice is too late, Chadwick, and misplaced. It was your idea, not mine, to place Lady Brownwell in this dangerous position."

"It was not Alan's idea, it was mine," Anne cried defiantly.

"Then the stories I read about Andrew Grey were not as exaggerated as you claimed. You travel around the country in the company of two men like some barmaid, you take part in an unethical business deal disguised as a man, and you treat me like one of your six-year-old children by telling a pack of lies. I believe I have a right to be angry." The children, she noted, had become exclusively hers again, and Gilbert was pouring his third glass of brandy.

"I'm sure no one else is interested in your opinion of me. Good night, Alan. Thanks for your support and I hope you and Philip get home safely."

Gilbert reached the door before she did, his brandy forgotten. Silently he allowed his wife to lead the way to her room and just as silently followed her inside. He was in bed long before she was, watching her pack her clothes into valises and brush her hair. Her rigidly maintained composure was beginning to crack as she joined him in bed only to lie there tensely expectant.

"You're a bigger gambler than I ever was," he told her in a cold and speculative voice, "and you don't really want anyone else in your life, do you? All that work you did on the farm was just to keep me from asking questions about your really important business deals."

"I started this investment a long time before you and I—"

"Before you decided you might need a husband. But what do you need one for if you refuse to consult me about gambling a huge sum of money on a wild scheme for revenge?"

Resentfully Anne remembered the huge sum of money he'd spent on a woollen mill without consulting her—and her money at that. Tired from the strain of eight tense days and as many lonely nights, she suppressed the urge to lash back at him with a reminder that he was the one who'd dragged a murderous Doncaster into their lives. But what would it do except increase his cold anger? Frustrated and hurt, she turned away and buried her face in the pillow, trying to blot out the sound of his voice.

"Don't tell me Anne Gray can't think up another lie? Something brilliant enough to convince me that your charming actor isn't a replacement for the French captain? He's just your kind, isn't he? Old enough to be your father, but very much the protector with his little pig sticker which he learned to use by dancing around onstage dressed as Mark Anthony or Hamlet. But then he's an actor, someone a great actress like you would find more interesting than a dull farmer."

Anne listened with hopeless resignation and wished she had the courage to put her arms around this unreasonable husband and tell him to stop being ridiculous.

"Just out of curiosity, Lady Brownwell, why did you find it necessary to pretend that great love for me if you'd already made other arrangements? Or were you planning to return home as if nothing had happened? If you were able to return at all. Did you dreamers really believe that Doncaster would let you ruin him financially without striking back? I'll be lucky if anything of value is left at Brownsville by the time I get back there.''

The guilty feelings she'd been repressing for days surfaced violently at these words. Her reckless decision had put everyone she loved in danger; he had a right to be angry with her. Sick at heart, she waited for his next accusation, only to realize in disbelief that he'd already finished with her and gone to sleep. That was the final crushing insult! Exhausted and despondent, she slowly lost her own hold on consciousness and drifted into uneasy slumber. Her last awareness before sleep chained her mind was a distorted image of her husband on the night he'd been attacked. The faces she saw were the violent ones of the hired assassins as they'd raised their knives to kill.

Tortured hours later Anne was awakened by a vigorous shaking accompanied by Gilbert's urgent voice. ''Wake up, Anne, wake up! You've been shouting and crying in your sleep. What's the matter with you? It's not like you to cry over anything, much less a dream.''

Still gripped by the formless terror of the nightmare, her convulsive weeping continued; and she welcomed the tentative arm he placed around her as a drowning man clutches at a lifeline. Awkwardly he patted her shoulder, offering nothing more than comfort for a distraught woman. Certainly he had no intention of responding to her trembling body. But the habit formed by a year of passionate relationship overruled their other emotions, her fear and his anger. Automatically they reached out with hands that caressed knowingly without reluctant hesitation. As his sensitive fingers measured the degree of her ready surrender, he muttered, ''Not even you are that good an actress,'' and released the last restraints on his own desire. There was nothing of their usual joyous sensuality about this physical union; it was a relentless drive to reestablish possession, and the ecstasy of their abrupt climax was sharp and intense.

Still holding her tightly to him, he growled softly, ''Now

let's get some sleep. We have a hell of a day ahead of us tomorrow." Anne smiled blissfully in the dark and closed her eyes.

They were awakened by a persistent knocking in the early hours of a gray dawn. Still lulled by the euphoria of their reunion, Anne's alarm system failed to respond; and it was a half-asleep husband who stumbled to the door and admitted an agitated Alan Chadwick into the room.

"We have an emergency," he announced tersely. "You two get dressed as quickly as possible and meet us in the sitting room. I hope to God you're willing to listen to reason this morning, Gilbert; we're all going to need clear heads." He was gone before either occupant could demand an explanation.

"He would ask for that," Gilbert groaned. "You'd think I'd have learned better than to drink brandy without eating dinner first. I don't suppose you have any headache powder with—" Anne was already searching through her valise. Silently she handed him the packet and poured a glass of water. Neither one spoke during the busy minutes of hurried washing and dressing; both were remembering the lawyer's tense warning.

Lady Margaret was presiding over the makeshift breakfast table when they entered the room where Farley Blake was pacing nervously and Chadwick was staring into space with grim-faced concentration. Margaret kissed Anne and Gilbert and poured them cups of the strong tea she'd been brewing.

"You're going to need all the food you can get down, too," the lawyer insisted. "This is going to be a difficult day. "I'll explain while you eat. Anne, I've already told Farley about our deception. Your explanation about the disguise had already prepared him for something of this nature, so he wasn't as surprised as he might have been. At any rate such a disclosure is completely irrelevant now. Yesterday afternoon when Leland Blake and Weston Kenrick were directing the removal of the railway tracks in mine seven, they were forcibly kidnapped by a large force of Doncaster's guards. Two hours ago this message was delivered to Farley Blake at his home."

The "message" was a reverse contract returning mines seven and eight to the Doncaster Mining Company. It had already been signed by Leland Blake.

"My brother would not have signed unless his circumstances were desperate," Farley Blake stated heavily. "Lady Brownwell, I want you to sign this paper using the name Hanley Krebs. Since there is no sum of money mentioned, I imagine the purchase price we paid will not be returned. I can only hope my brother and Weston will be spared."

Gilbert looked up from the contract he was reading and shook his head. "Doncaster wouldn't dare let them live, Mr. Blake. If he did, he'd face kidnapping charges. If you and Anne sign this paper, you'll be signing a death warrant. I lived with the Doncasters and know how ruthless they are. I also lived with them long enough to know something about the operation. He runs the entire business from his office building at mine number ten. That's probably where he's hiding your brother. If we can find enough honest policemen here in Birmingham, we could attempt a rescue effort. But don't be too hopeful. He controls the two constables at Staffordshire and half the police force of this town."

Chadwick nodded in agreement. "I found that out when I attempted to register an official complaint two years ago after Doncaster appropriated your estate from your mother. Not only the police, but half the city's officials are on Doncaster's payroll. Under these circumstances, if we returned this signed contract, Leland and Weston would simply disappear; and I doubt there'd be an official investigation. I don't imagine any of the Birmingham officials would even try to arrest Doncaster. We have no choice but to wait here until we hear from Philip Trent."

Missing the affable actor for the first time, Anne looked sharply at the lawyer, who continued speaking in his calm, deliberate voice. "He's gone to the local military garrison to enlist aid."

"The military won't interfere in civilian matters without an order from a government official," Gilbert declared emphatically.

"How about your guards, Mr. Blake? Will any of them fight with us?"

"Most of them were knocked around yesterday when Doncaster's cutthroats attacked. Some of them might be recovered enough to help, if the odds are not too hopeless. What about those soldiers, Chadwick? Can Mr. Trent get them to cooperate?"

"I believe so. As Anne already knows, Philip is slightly more than an actor. He is involved with activities at Sandhurst Academy."

At Gilbert's raised eyebrow, Anne hastened to explain. "He teaches fencing to the cadets."

"Don't be silly, Anne. Military academies don't employ amateurs," Gilbert exclaimed.

"You're right, Gilbert," Chadwick admitted, "Philip is not quite an amateur. But even with the help he can muster, we'll still need to find a civilian official with the power to arrest Doncaster."

"Will the head constable of Coventry do, Mr. Chadwick?" Margaret asked. "He was very cooperative when I investigated Doncaster before Anne returned to England."

"Beasley would be excellent," Farley asserted, "but we have no way of getting through to him. Some of Doncaster's men were outside the hotel when I arrived. I don't believe that they'd permit even a messenger to leave now."

"That won't be necessary," the headmistress of Grayhaven announced calmly. "Last night I sent a message to Mr. Beasley requesting his aid in escorting Anne, her husband, and myself safely to Coventry. I didn't mean to question your ability to protect us, Gilbert; I'm just a cautious old lady when it comes to the Doncasters of the world."

He smiled at her in grudging admiration. "No wonder Anne thinks she can whip the world. She takes after you. Did your constable promise to send help?"

"Mr. Beasley himself will arrive at nine o'clock."

"So that leaves only the five of us without means of

self-defense. Alan, didn't any of you think to bring weapons?" Gilbert demanded of the lawyer.

"As a lawyer I can only use them in self-defense, but Philip is well armed."

"So am I," Farley Blake acknowledged, removing two six-barreled pistols from the pockets of his greatcoat. "You're welcome to use one of these, Lord Brownwell."

During this exchange Anne had remembered the sword cane still in her room with the rest of the Hanley Krebs costume. She was on her feet and hurrying to the door when her husband's sharp command stopped her. "Where do you think you're going?"

"I have a weapon in my room. I was just going to get it."

"What kind?"

"A sword cane I used as a prop."

"It's a poor weapon for street fighting, but it's better than none at all. I'll go with you."

Back in their room, he inspected it carefully and finally grunted his approval. "At least it's not just a cheap stage sword. Can you use it, Anne?"

"Philip taught me how to hold it, and I'll use it if I have to."

"You may have to. I wish we had Grimes and our Scots here with us."

"Will it be that awful, Gil? Even with soldiers on our side?"

"I doubt if they've ever encountered thugs like the ones Doncaster employs. And that reminds me, we'd better wear some sensible clothes. While I put on my sheepskin jacket, you take off that pretty-boy blue velvet dress and get on your man's costume. You'll be less conspicuous; and if you have to, you'll be able to run. I'd insist that you and Margaret stay here at the hotel if I thought you'd be safer; but as things stand, you probably wouldn't be."

"Gil, this really isn't your fight."

"I've got more reason than anyone to hate Doncaster. Anne, I guess I owe you an apology for some of the things I said to you."

"No, you don't; you had a right to be angry with me. Besides," she added with a happy grin, "I liked the apology you made last night better."

"That was not an apology; that was a lesson in the law of ownership. And if you hadn't gotten us involved in this mess, there'd be time for another lesson. But right now we have to get back to the others."

By the time they reached the sitting room, the "others" assembled there had doubled in number; and only Margaret's warning kept the Brownwells from walking into a trap. Her shout of "We have company, children" gave Gilbert the time to shove Anne behind him and to pull the pistol out of his pocket before the door was yanked open by Charles Prichart. The cold welcoming smile on the lawyer's face faded quckly when he saw the gun, but his anger changed to caution as he obeyed the command to join the two uniformed men across the room.

"Anne, lock the door in case others of Doncaster's cutthroats are outside," Gilbert ordered sharply.

At this insult Prichart exploded into speech. "I beg your pardon, Lord Brownwell, I resent that implication. I am an officer of the law and these gentlemen are—"

"I know who those 'gentlemen' are, Prichart. Alan, these men are Doncaster's bought-and-paid-for constables of Staffordshire. And what were you 'gentlemen' ordered to do? Kidnap the five of us or merely hold us captive while your employer completes the other half of this dirty business?"

"Kidnap, Lord Brownwell? Hardly. These constables are here for the purpose of serving you and Lady Brownwell with papers demanding the return of Brownsville to its rightful owner, Mr. Edward Doncaster. They are also here to charge Mr. Alan Chadwick with complicity in defrauding my client of said property."

Alan's voice was deceptively nonchalant. "When were these papers prepared, Mr. Prichart?"

"Immediately aftcr my client and I served notice of this action to the Brownwells at the site of the disputed property."

"Why the delay in serving these papers, Mr. Prichart?"

"We were waiting for Lord Brownwell to arrive in Birmingham."

"In other words, the authorities of Yorkshire County denied their legality."

"I can assure you, Chadwick, they're completely legal in Birmingham."

"Just how did you intend holding my clients if they refused to sign these release papers?"

"If Lord Brownwell refuses to comply, these constables are empowered to arrest him."

"When did your client notify you that Lord Brownwell was in Birmingham?"

"My client didn't. Mr. Philbrick did after he spoke to him at this hotel. At that time we also uncovered the identity of Mr. Hanley Krebs. Allow me to congratulate you, Lady Brownwell; your disguise was most convincing. So was the performance of your clerk, Mr. Chadwick. Where is the estimable Mr. Trent this morning?"

"He's on an errand. But let's return to the business at hand which happens to be kidnapping. As a solicitor and as constables sworn to uphold the law, your complicity in such a crime could earn you a severe prison sentence, if not a worse penalty."

"What are you talking about, Chadwick?"

"Edward Doncaster's kidnapping of Leland Blake and Weston Kenrick from the premises of mine number seven. This document, which was delivered to Farley Blake this morning, constitutes irrefutable proof of the crime, as will the testimony of a dozen witnesses. Now, you three have a choice: you can either help us in our effort to rescue the victims or you can submit to arrest when Mr. Beasley arrives from Coventry."

"Who the hell notified Beasley?" Prichart shouted, momentarily forgetting his dignified courtroom demeanor.

"I did," Margaret confessed with sharp asperity, "and I hope he bears you the same degree of malice he did when I had your client investigated. I'm certain he will be delighted to arrest you on the charge of kidnapping or on any other charge related to your client.''

Whether it was the mention of Beasley's name or the sight of Leland Blake's signature on the contract paper, both the constables and Prichart rejoined the forces of law and order and promised their support. Since Gilbert kept his gun trained steadily on them, no further mention was made of Doncaster's claim to Brownsville.

Smoothly Chadwick continued his questioning, this time of the constables. ''Were either of you gentlemen present at mine number ten yesterday afternoon?''

The shorter and more frightened of the two men answered, ''We are never at Mr. Doncaster's mines unless we are ordered to arrest a troublemaker.''

''Then you don't know your way around the premises well enough to act as guides?''

''No, sir,'' the relieved man admitted.

''But you would be willing to arrest any of Mr. Doncaster's . . . er . . . guards who might attempt to impede Mr. Beasley?''

It was the other, more truculent constable who answered. ''You haven't got the manpower here even with Beasley's two lickspittles to get into the grounds of mine ten, much less reach Doncaster in that fort he calls an office. And his guards know my partner and me. If we were to try to arrest any of them, they'd tear us apart.''

''That is what I thought. You two will remain here in Birmingham in protective custody during our efforts to rescue the kidnap victims. But before you become too consoled by the prospect, you'll be held by the military. In that way the rest of us can be assured that you will not be free to warn Doncaster. So, Mr. Prichart, that leaves you as our friendly guide in our law and order efforts.''

Prichart's expression was sour and his voice demanding. ''Chadwick, what does the military have to do with this operation? It's a civilian matter and the military cannot act in a civilian case unless—''

"Unless an emergency is declared, Mr. Prichart. I'm sure Mr. Beasley will be delighted to declare such an emergency. If by chance he is reluctant, I have been empowered to do so. By way of consolation, Prichart, you must realize that this emergency could never have been declared as long as there was no direct evidence connecting your client to a crime. But now that there is positive proof, the procedure is legal."

"I'm sure this talk of legality is of interest to lawyers," Farley Blake reproached Chadwick impatiently, "but not to me. I want my brother rescued. Just when is this army due to arrive?"

Chadwick consulted his watch. "Within the half hour, Farley, we'll be under way." They were under way in twenty minutes, almost immediately after Anne admitted Philip Trent into the room, a Philip Trent dressed in a splendid uniform of subdued blue with just enough gold medal decoration to be impressive.

His opening remark to Anne was the last lighthearted comment of the day. "An old actor can never resist the temptation of wearing a costume, Anne. And I see you decided to be practical and wear yours, too." But Philip's uniform was no costume; he wore it with military authority as he took over the leadership.

"Mr. Beasley has agreed to be the arresting officer, Alan. His men have already rounded up six of Doncaster's guards who were watching the hotel, but I'm afraid we may have lost the element of surprise. Two others were mounted and rode off before we could intercept them. Undoubtedly Doncaster will be warned in time to organize more thoroughly. However, we have a sixteen-man troop from the garrison, eight of them riflemen and eight of them subaltern officers. What is the situation here?"

Briefly Chadwick introduced the apprehensive constables and reported on the extent of weaponry. Philip nodded. "Good. Lord Brownwell, you will ride guard for Alan's driver, and Mr. Blake will take charge in the cab. You gentlemen from Staffordshire will accompany the prisoners to the garrison, and the rest of us will ride to the coalfields. Anne, I wish we could leave you and Lady Gray here at the hotel, but Birmingham is not yet entirely safe.''

With these brief instructions, the nine people left the room and walked to the front of the hotel, where what amounted to a procession was already waiting. In the lead was the police wagon of Coventry with Chief Constable Beasley and one assistant on the driving bench and a second man guarding the rear door of the prisoner cage. Unceremoniously the Staffordshire men joined the six already in the locked enclosure, and the police wagon moved off. The carriage Anne was in was the same one used during her first trip to Birmingham; it was the post chaise type built for speed, but not for the comfort of passengers. Facing Alan and Prichart and sandwiched tightly between Aunt Margaret and Farley Blake, Anne envied her husband, who was seated on the roomy driver's bench. Following closely behind the carriage were sixteen mounted men of the Royal Lancers, 17th Regiment, led jointly by the commander of the Birmingham garrison, Lieutenant-Colonel Graham-Bentley, and by Philip Trent.

The first stop in what was to be a swift journey was a momentary pause before the steel gates of the garrison, where the six prisoners and two constables were placed in charge of the soldiers waiting for them. From that moment on, Anne's only awareness was the discomfort of the swaying carriage and the acrimonious exchange of words between the two lawyers.

''What is a colonel of the Royal Grenadiers doing here?'' Prichart demanded.

''Philip? He was assigned by Parliament to head the investigation into the corruption of Birmingham. I met him two years ago when I first registered my complaint against your client, and again last year after Lady Brownwell presented me with her delightful plan to entrap Mr. Doncaster. Philip decided to use that plan and to enlist the aid of Weston Kenrick. The rest you already know,'' Chadwick explained.

"Not quite. Just how is it that a grenadier's colonel is permitted to act as a spy?"

"Philip is also an actor and well-known in theatrical circles. He could not very well be a successful investigator of a city controlled by corrupt officials in a full-dress uniform. And most certainly not in a city like Birmingham, where many officials are involved in smuggling, theft, extortion of the railroads, and a hundred other crimes. Your city is crisscrossed by canals and connected directly to both coasts of England by navigable rivers. It is the railroad and industrial center of the nation. Parliament wanted it cleaned up; and now it will be. Once your client is convicted, the other criminals can be exposed."

"You are precipitous in your self-congratulations, Chadwick. My client has not as yet been apprehended, much less convicted. You will find that Edward Doncaster is very difficult to find if he does not wish to be found."

Prichart's gloomy words proved discouragingly true once the searchers reached the number ten mine and were met by a dense human wall of jobless miners standing defensively in front of the locked gates. No amount of threats on Constable Beasley's part could budge the miners; but after an uncomfortable delay of critical minutes, one shout by Farley Blake turned some forty of the unhappy miners into vengeful allies.

"All colliers who want jobs with the Blake brothers will be given jobs in return for your cooperation in identifying those guards and miners who attacked mine number seven yesterday afternoon." Even before he finished speaking, some of the miners had their picks and fists in motion. What no outsider could have accomplished in a day of investigation, these men accomplished in fifteen minutes. Ten of their fellows were dragged out and dumped unceremoniously at the constables' feet even while the gates were battered down by other miners. Inside the yard where the guards had been lined up in defense, the violent assault continued; and only a dozen of the thirty guards escaped injury. Seven had been spared by the miners themselves, and five had been admitted into the safety of the fortresslike building.

The capture of the accused guards and miners was the last action Anne and Margaret would see for three worry-filled hours. Their carriage was driven to a safe distance away from the mine, and both Gilbert and Philip insisted the women remain inside. Mr. Prichart, too, was ordered to remain on the bench beside the driver. On Anne's first attempt to leave the carriage, "to stretch her legs," she discovered that two of the young lancer's officers had remained behind to guard her and her aunt. Anne was furious at her husband, who had kissed her briefly and left without a word of his intentions. As the minutes stretched into hours, her anger changed to anxiety and then to desperate concern when Alan Chadwick finally returned to the carriage and reported the news.

The office building had been successfully entered only after Farley Blake had paid six miners to hack a way through the brick walls, and one of the miners was shot in the process. Once inside, the searchers found only three frightened clerks and four defiant guards, two of whom were killed when they resisted arrest. Mystified by the whereabouts of Doncaster and the other guards, as well as Leland Blake and Weston Kenrick, Beasley was about to order a search of the mine when one of the captured clerks asked to speak privately to Farley Blake. In return for the promise of leniency, the clerk showed the searchers the cleverly concealed opening of a special tunnel which led from the office through a passage in the mine to a distant escape shaft. The clerk admitted that Doncaster frequently exited through that tunnel whenever he was threatened by unhappy miners. It was also the place where the special "guards" hid whenever they were being hunted.

Farley Blake had once again paid the miners, this time with the princely sum of ten pounds per man, the help him search that tunnel for his brother and Kenrick. To protect the miners from a possible attack from the fugitive cutthroats, a small group of armed guards had accompanied them, led by Farley

Blake himself. Not until Alan was escorting the two women to a private luncheon room in the main railroad yards did Anne learn that her husband was one of the men down in the mine.

"I shouldn't worry if I were you, Anne. Gilbert is well able to handle himself in a fight, and one of the Coventry constables and six of the lancers are with him. Moreover, I believe that some thirty miners volunteered for the job. So there's very little danger."

Three hours later, though, even Alan had lost his optimism, and Anne was frantic. She and Margaret watched in gloomy silence as the soldiers drove off with two wagonloads of prisoners to secrete them in the garrison in Birmingham. They also witnessed the arrival of a doctor, who was hurried inside the office, presumably to treat the injured miner and perhaps the injured prisoners. Sometime during the midafternoon Prichart was summoned and taken into the office, but he was returned in a half hour by an angry-looking Beasley.

The first awareness that the searchers had returned was the sight of twenty miners pouring out of the office building to be greeted by the small knot of men waiting in the yard. Not caring if one of her day-long lancers guards offered to use his saber on her, Anne stumbled from the imprisoning carriage and ran toward the office, her heart pounding with the bottled-up fear of waiting. It almost stopped beating when she looked through the open door into the crowded office. The floor seemed littered with bodies, and her eyes moved frantically from one crude litter to the next, searching for the still form with pale blond hair. She fought the arms that were dragging her outside; and not until her name was urgently repeated for the third time did she look up at the speaker. Nothing about him looked familiar. The elegant tan trousers and the sheepskin coat were coal-blackened beyond recognition, and the face and hair were hidden behind a streaked film of soot. But it was Gilbert, unhurt and beautiful. Others of the rescue party had not been as fortunate. Three times they had been attacked by fugitive thugs who struck without warning in the stygian darkness of the coal pits; four lancers and six miners had been injured. But in the end the kidnap victims had been found, unconscious but alive; and nine attackers had been dragged out in varying stages of impairment. In the giddiness of her own relief, Anne was unprepared for the gratitude of Farley Blake.

"Your husband," he exclaimed in the half-dead voice of exhausted relief, "kept the rest of us going. Thank God he was there; and thank God he knows where the black-hearted devil who caused this is hiding."

All the beautiful euphoria of Anne's relief fled; this ordeal was not over yet. "No, Gil," she whispered sharply, "you can't go down there again. I won't let you."

"The bastard isn't in the mine, Anne. He left his men there while he saved his own skin. The escape tunnel goes halfway to the Pinnacles, and that's where he's hiding now, in that damned fortress he calls a country estate. If we don't go after him tonight, he'll escape again."

She shook her head stubbornly. "Let the others go alone."

However, at the moment the "others" were busy establishing order to the chaotically crowded office and directing the loading of the three wagons that had arrived only moments before carrying six Blake Company guards. Accompanied by the doctor and the three miners who had been helping him, the kidnap victims and the men injured while rescuing them were placed gently in the largest wagon and dispatched to the garrison hospital. Following quickly was the second dray, into which Constable Beasley had ordered Doncaster's men dumped unceremoniously. At the last minute he added the outraged lawyer Prichart to the unsavory load. But it was the third conveyance that carried the most damning evidence—Edward Doncaster's office records, including the ones found inside the escape tunnel. Carefully listed on the pages of those neatly kept ledgers were the names of Birmingham officials and the amounts of money paid them over the years. So valuable did he consider this cargo that Philip Trent ordered Lieutenant-Colonel Graham-Bentley and four lancers soldiers to ride guard under the civil authority of Alan Chadwick during the transportation to the safety of military strongboxes.

Not until this third wagon had departed did preparation begin for the final assault on the estate called the Pinnacles. Anne shivered with fear when all but six of the miners adamantly refused Farley Blake's offer to pay twenty pounds to any man who would accompany him.

"They claim the moors thereabouts have an evil reputation," the mine owner admitted. "What the devil kind of a place is it, Lord Brownwell?"

"The ugliest monstrosity in England," Gilbert answered brusquely. "It's an imitation of a castle which some coal baron built a century ago on the remains of a small thirteenth-century keep. It gets its name from the dozens of turrets the builder designed to make it look like the original. But inside all that ugly stone, it's just an inconvenient house with four stories of drafty rooms."

"It's slightly more than that now, Lord Brownwell," Philip Trent declared. "Since your brief stay there, Doncaster has added an eight-foot stone perimeter wall and topped it with steel spikes. He also built a stone gatehouse that is stronger than the original castle. Three nights ago on my last unannounced visit there, I managed to dispense with the watchdogs and locate a way into that guardhouse. So I can get us into the grounds. I'm hoping that you know an equally painless way into the house."

"Three of them, Colonel," Gilbert responded with a sour smile. "The coal dump, which would be possible but damned uncomfortable; the kitchen entry, which would be simple to break into; and a door the grounds keepers use. It's those men we'll have to watch out for. Not even the other servants trust them."

"Then we'll stand a better chance to take them by surprise in the dark."

Looking around at the small number of men left in the office, Anne was appalled by the calm assurance of her husband and a suddenly overbearing Colonel Trent. "Philip, there are only five soldiers left," she cried in exasperation.

"Five lancers officers, Anne, and all of them my personal students. With Lord Brownwell and myself, we have a force of skilled fighters that could take Buckingham Palace, if need be. Now let's join the others in a camp dinner and prepare to depart."

"He's enjoying himself," Anne raged privately to her aunt, "and so is Gil."

"I imagine the colonel knows what he's doing, and your husband has proved more than adequate today. Stop your complaining and remember that it was your idea to precipitate this emergency," Lady Margaret admonished her niece and then added cheerfully, "I haven't had camp food since I was a girl, so stop pouting and eat dinner."

Unhappily admitting the truth of at least a part of her aunt's accusations, Anne vowed that she would not remain lumpishly seated in a carriage during the coming attack. With her sword cane she was better armed than either the miners or the guards, and she had a great deal more to fight for than twenty pounds—her reckless husband's life, for one thing! But as in her earlier clashes with masculine authority, she was powerless to resist being ignominiously placed in the carriage with her aunt and driven across a desolate stretch of road ten minutes after Gilbert had departed on horseback with the lancers and five minutes after Constable Beasley left in the police wagon loaded with Farley Blake and twelve miners and guards.

By the time the carriage reached the Pinnacles, the gates were open and four bound and gagged men lay limply in the padlocked prison wagon. Without a word Philip signaled the group toward the dark, forbidding house. Two hundred feet away from it, the men dismounted and formed into two groups, leaving the Blake mine guards to watch the imprisoned occupants of both vehicles. Anne's one furtive attempt to leave the carriage ended when a vigilant husband clamped his hand over her mouth and whispered sternly, "So help me, if you make one more move or sound, I'll lock you in that cage with the others.''

Rebelliously she remained seated and agonized beside her calm aunt until the first lights began to show through the windows on the main floor. She watched with tense expectancy as the other floors were lighted one by one. And still she waited with the chill fear of frustration, jerking violently when the large brass-studded front doors were thrown open and a grim-faced Gilbert strode toward the carriage.

''You'll be safer inside,'' he warned them as he helped Lady Margaret down from the carriage. ''That is, if you keep out of the way.'' Unceremoniously he pushed them through the door, past the chamber which seemed thronged with people, and up the wide, thickly carpeted stairs. In an ornate alcove off the large metal-railed landing overlooking the crowded room below, he deposited them on a velvet-covered bench.

''Don't move from this spot before I call you,'' he ordered as he pulled the draperies halfway across the enclosure. ''You can see everything that's happening from here.''

''I don't see Doncaster, Gil. Didn't you find him?'' Anne demanded.

''According to the servants, he's in the cellars with three bodyguards. We're going down for him now. Quit frowning, Anne, we outnumber them two to one. Beasley is in charge of the prisoners we've already taken, but don't bother him with questions.'' Without a backward glance he plunged down the stairs and disappeared somewhere in the rear of the house. Only then did Anne and Margaret look down on the scene below. What they saw did not add to their peace of mind. Two wounded lancers officers were being tended by housemaids, and three bandaged miners were seated limply in chairs. Holding a heavy truncheon in his hands and looking as if he would like some more heads to use it on, Constable Beasley watched as two Blake guards tied the hands and feet of the assorted humans stretched out on the floor. Using lengths of the heavy gold cord pulled from the elegant red velvet draperies, the guards secured the men and the women the constable indicated with a vindictive wave of his hand. From her vantage point, Anne approved the action. After a long day of violence, she no longer had a shred of sympathy for anyone who had ever served the Doncasters. Her degree of suspicion was such that she wondered why even a group of frightened servants had been spared.

Relentlessly, as the minutes ticked by, Anne tried to focus her attention anywhere but on the oppressive and apprehensive silence in the room below. She studied the blind marble faces of the four pseudo-Greek statues that occupied the alcove with her and her Aunt Margaret and the pretentious replicas of medieval flags suspended from the towering ceiling of the main hall. It was during her perusal of the red cross of St. George that she heard the first sounds from the rear of the house. Restrained by Margaret's firm hand on her arm from running down those red carpeted stairs, Anne gasped as Edward Doncaster stumbled across her line of vision prodded none too gently by Philip Trent's expertly held saber. Almost on their heels was a pair of smiling lancers officers relentlessly propelling a loudly protesting lawyer Philbrick. Entering the room more slowly were two miners carrying a limp body between them, and a third lancer carrying three picks and as many sabers. Looking upward, Philip Trent projected his dramatic voice.

"We found the scurvy lot hiding in a trench between the original castle hold and the foundation of this anachronism of an eighteenth-century home. Had it not been for them sneezing from coal dust inhalation, we night never have found them. These three surrendered, the other two did not. No one in our party was hurt."

Anne heard the words and knew with the objective part of her brain that Philip had spoken loudly so that she could hear him; but she had spent so many of the last twelve hours being afraid that only the sight of Gilbert safe and sound could assure her completely. Dimly she realized that Farley Blake and another miner were also missing, but so were the two bodyguards whom Trent had said refused to surrender. With a vicious satisfaction she watched Beasley attach professional manacles and leg irons to Doncaster and then shove the dethroned coal king to an ignominious position on the floor.

In a sudden passionate intensity to see this man punished beyond the simple embarrassment of arrest, Anne almost missed the quiet arrival of her husband and the two mining men. Even when he flashed a smile in her direction, her face was too rigidly set for an easy response. Stiffly she and Margaret rose to leave the confining alcove, when her aunt's hand tightened once again. Impatiently Anne started to jerk free when she, too, heard the faint noise of a door being pushed stealthily open about twenty feet from where she stood concealed behind the draperies. The first glimpse she had of the intruder was of a feminine hand holding a large pistol with businesslike efficiency. The second was of the satin-clad woman herself walking swiftly toward the metal railing only eight feet away from the two horrified watchers. The high-pitched shout of "Lord Brownwell!" silenced all sound in the room below; and with a sinking heart Anne saw her husband's blond head snap back to stare at the short, dark-haired woman who had been his wife for two weeks.

Long before the others did, Edward Doncaster realized his daughter's intention. "No, Edwina, not this way. Surrender the gun. There's nothing they can charge you with."

Ignoring her father's warning, Edwina's eyes and the gun remained riveted on her blond target. Without moving, she issued a sharp command. "Philbrick, take the keys from that animal Beasley and remove those damned things from my father." As the lawyer shook his head in defeat, Edwina's sharp voice sounded again. "Father, if you can, walk to the door and hide outside. I'll bring help later."

At her father's helpless words of resignation—"I can't move, Edwina"—his daughter's resolve hardened; and her voice held a tinge of arrogant gloating as she turned her attention back toward her intended victim.

"You have been a difficult man to kill, you and that bastard bitch of a wife. But before you die today, I want you to know that I was the one who paid to have her killed in London, and I was the one who hired those men to murder you and her at your farm. Not my father, never my father! He believes in only beating his enemies. Like today, I sent those men into the tunnel to finish the job. Don't move, Mr. Farley Blake; your brother may have survived today, but you will not. You will die for ruining my father, and Lord Brownwell will die because he chose her over me.''

Anne never heard these final words. She was listening to the lilting Irish words of Casey Ryan: ''Niver take yer eyes from the cock ye're plannin' to hit.'' Nor the hen, either, she thought as she strode silently across the eight feet separating from from the murderous Edwina and brought the heavy handle of her cane smashing across the woman's hand. She didn't hear the gun or her cane strike the stone floor far beneath her; she was concentrating her energies on driving her fist into the open-mouthed face in front of her. Her second blow was also flawlessly executed, landing squarely into the region Casey had called ''the brisket.''

Kneeling beside the unconscious woman, Anne remained oblivious to the staring faces below and to the pounding feet of the men running up the stairs. She was remembering another edict of her old instructor: ''Niver turn yer back until ye're shure the cock can't bash ye from the rear.'' Methodically she tore the wide velvet ribbons from Edwina's dress and bound the fallen woman's hands and feet, completing the job with efficient nautical knots. Only then did she look up into the stormy eyes of her angry husband and the amused shock on the face of Philip Trent. White-faced with gratitude, only Farley Blake forgave her for being a woman and mumbled a devout ''Thank you'' as he helped her rise.

Below in the room looking up in fascination were forty people who'd never seen the famous Casey punch nor a woman who could deliver it with the mastery of a trained pugilist. Long before this night was over, a hundred other miners would have heard the story in varying degrees of embroidered inaccuracy at the pub in Staffordshire. But the next day in the Birmingham barracks of the Royal Lancers 17th Regiment, thirty smiling officers silently toasted the English lioness.

Chapter 20

THREE eventful years later Anne could recall that night with laughter; but for the weeks following she found no humor in the memory, only a deep hurt from her husband's furious reaction. His anger was quickly turned to admiration by Constable Beasley's thoughtful verdict that she'd saved two lives at least and by Philip Trent's unstinting praise of her courage and skill. But it was Farley Blake's reiterated and sincere gratitude that shamed Gilbert.

"You saved my life, Anne; I honestly didn't think Edwina would kill me," he apologized.

Anne shrugged coldly. "The female of the species! Your Edwina was more dangerous than her vicious father."

His fervent words "God, I hated her!" did much to quell Anne's own resentment toward her husband; but the feeling of having been condemned by prejudice persisted throughout the trial. Even from prison Edwina's money reached out to extract revenge, and the scrabbly journalists of London once again lampooned Anne with libelous caricatures picturing her as an Amazon in men's clothing. Gilbert also was ridiculed as a timid husband who cowered before his towering wife. He bore up stoically under the attack until the day their children were included in the degradation. Dressed in an elegant green velvet jacket over a ruffled shirt and accompanied by Alan

Chadwick, Lord Brownwell invaded the dirty print shops of the two most scurrilous editors. Both men made the mistake of believing the lies they had printed about his cowardice and attacked. For weeks following their ill-considered action, they were unable to leave their beds long enough to print a word, much less the complete retraction they'd promised.

Due largely to the political upheaval in Birmingham, the Doncaster trials were held in London; and the Brownwells were constrained to testify repeatedly. Strangely enough, the central investigator, Philip Trent, had disappeared the day after the violent capture; and neither his name nor his contributions were ever mentioned in the papers or at the trial. Because of her passive role as spectator, Lady Margaret, too, was not asked to testify, neither at the brief summary trial for the daughter nor at the protracted, complicated one for the father.

Despite Charles Prichart's eloquent pleas of "justifiable jealousy" for Edwina, she'd convicted herself before witnesses to the extent of eliminating all doubt about her guilt. Her trial lasted two days and she was sentenced to fifteen years in the penal system of Sydney and exiled for life to Australia, her fortune confiscated. Even briefer was the trail of Eldritch Philbrick. Whereas Prichart and Carlisle, the other two Doncaster lawyers, were allowed to defend their clients, Philbrick was considered to be criminally involved, since he had been the one who had located and paid the various criminals and cutthroats the mine owner and his daughter had employed. His sentence was five years at Verne Prison on the Isle of Portland working on the harbor being built by the Royal Navy.

Involved with more than a simple kidnapping charge, Edward Doncaster was also tried on a dozen counts of acquiring property through criminal means. Convicted the first day of the kidnapping of Leland Blake and Weston Kenrick, he endured a grueling three weeks of sitting in court while one after another of his properties were returned to its rightful owners. Alan Chadwick's determined fight to regain the Brownwell estate for the present lord met with only partial success. Since Doncaster's acquisition was ruled to be not entirely fraudulent in this instance, only the large country estate of Feldwood Park in Essex, inherited through Gilbert's brother, Sir Arthur Brownwell, was recovered.

At the trial's end, three of Doncaster's properties were ruled to have been legally acquired—mines nine and ten and the Pinnacles. These and his money were promptly confiscated, and he was sentenced to life imprisonment in the infamous prison pens on Van Diemen's Land off the southern tip of Australia, a verdantly wild place known as Tasmania in honor of the aborigines the early British settlers had hunted to extinction. Immediately upon the conclusion of the trial, the three confiscated properties were placed on the public auction block. Competing against a score of bidders, the Blake brothers paid dearly for the two mines, but their offer for the estate was the only one tendered; and the Pinnacles became the most valuable asset of their entire company.

Ironically, Doncaster had unknowingly and honestly owned the largest deposit of coal in England, a deposit so close to the surface it could be strip-mined without the expense of tunnels or shafts and without danger to the miners. In this enterprise the Brownwells were full partners, a decision reached in the hurried conference in the cellar between Farley Blake and Gilbert. Even the miner whose pick had uncovered the coal was paid an ample finder's fee.

Just why an experienced coal miner like Doncaster had never suspected the existence of this rich deposit until the night he'd hid in the ancient cellar was explained by his basic ignorance of English history. When the original castle had been built in 1301, the reigning monarch, Edward I, had decreed death to any subject using the noxious black stones as fuel. Thus the land owners of that era had deliberately ignored the forbidden mineral and covered the ugly outcroppings with their stone buildings. For Doncaster and Edwina, the Pinnacles had proved an unhappy place, but for the Blakes and Brownwells it became a source of easy wealth. Even the building itself earned money. The Church of England purchased the stones to use in the construction of a hospital for miners. By donating a worthless piece of land to the charitable cause, the Blakes were spared the cost of dismantling the pseudocastle; and at the same time they gained a greater medical security for their workers.

As dramatic as these events were, Anne much preferred the memory of the nonviolent changes that had occurred in her private life after she and Gilbert had returned to Brownsville. Of the two thousand additional merino ewes Duncan had located, six hundred had come from the chilly Isle of Tiree in the Inner Hebrides off the windy coast of northern Scotland. Because of a late winter there, these animals had not been shorn. As happy as a schoolboy on vacation, Gilbert tackled the job with only Grimes and Anne as coworkers. In that way the other estate people could continue their assigned jobs of constructing the many improvements he had ordered. Even Anne found the hard work a welcome relief from the tension of London until the day the pleasant harmony of Brownsville was almost destroyed. Her mother-in-law returned.

In the early afternoon of the final day of shearing, a strange carriage drove up and parked in front of the boarded-up manor house. Smelling of sheep dip and sweat, Anne and her husband walked from the pens to greet their visitor.

They arrived in time to see Lady Suzanne Brownwell descend from the carriage and stare at them in icy fury.

"What have you done to my home?" she demanded.

Stung by the imperious tone of voice and unpleasantly reminded of the years of her domination, her son shouted back, "It's not your home and hasn't been since you let that vulture steal it. It's Anne's and my home now."

"Where did you get the money to buy it?"

"I didn't. Anne bought it with her own money."

"You mean that Margaret woman bought it."

"No. Anne earned the money herself in America. Don't you ever read the papers? My wife is a very famous woman."

"Notorious, you mean. I haven't forgotten the things they

said about her at the trial. You were a fool to take her back. You had a chance then to make something of your life."

"What as? The husband of that bitch you picked out?"

"At least Edwina was a lady who always looked like one and not like some peasant farmhand."

Anne looked from one handsome face to the other, alike even in anger, and decided that she'd heard enough. Walking back to the carriage, she helped the maid dismount and led the tired woman to the door behind which she knew an avidly curious Marie would be standing.

"Marie, this is Lady Suzanne's maid. Would you see that she is comfortable and then prepare some tea for our guest? I'll find Grimes and tell him to take care of the horses so that poor driver can relax."

Grimes was waiting for her around the corner of the house. "The old missus come back, did she?"

"Not to stay, Grimes," Anne reassured him. "I want you to turn the carriage around and water the horses. That 'old missus' will be leaving in two hours." His shoulders were shaking with laughter as he turned to do her bidding. She didn't look back as she continued to the rear of the house, stripped off her clothing, and climbed into her barrel of tepid water. Had the water been ice cold, Anne would not have noticed. Automatically she scrubbed her hair, her mind a welter of cold, angry thoughts. She didn't look at her husband when she heard him approach.

"I'm sorry, Anne, I didn't invite my mother here," he apologized.

"Are you planning to ask her to live with us?"

"Good Lord, no! But how will we get rid of her? She says she has no place to live and no money."

"Your mother has enough money. She receives a hundred pounds every month from a fund Doncaster set up for her. He didn't want her interfering with you and Edwina." Anne's voice seemed devoid of emotion.

"How do you know?"

"From the trial. It was listed on those financial sheets that Alan showed us."

"Then she's a liar as well as a bitch. What can I say, Anne? And what can I do about her? I thought she was settled in France with her cousin. Do you know that she has six more trunks of clothing stored at the dock in Hull? She was all set to move in with us."

"Do you want her to?"

"God, no! I couldn't stand her, and I imagine you'd like to throw her in the trough of sheep dip."

"And hold her under," Anne muttered. "Gil, will you trust me to solve this problem?" Suddenly the humor of the situation struck her. He looked ridiculous and miserable hunched down in his barrel. "I promise you she won't go to debtor's prison."

There was no answering laughter on his face. "If she stays here, we'll be the ones in debt," he growled.

"Oh, she won't stay here," Anne assured him airily as she climbed out of the barrel and toweled her hair vigorously. "Just give me half an hour alone with her."

Twenty minutes later a well-scrubbed, neatly dressed daughter-in-law entered the comfortable sitting room to face a hard-eyed opponent.

"Where is my son?" Suzanne demanded.

"He won't be here until you've either listened to what I have to say or left my home permanently."

"This is my home and my son's home."

Anne ignored the challenge. "Which will it be, Lady Suzanne? If you don't listen to me politely, I promise you that you'll be on that rented carriage and headed off this property within ten minutes." Anne paused and waited for a response; when none came, she continued. "Gil and I own a small townhouse in London."

"I have my own townhouse in London," the woman snapped.

"Except for what's in your seven trunks, you don't own a thing. But you may live in our townhouse under certain circumstances. You will not redecorate it in any way except to add the contents of those seven trunks. You will never treat the people who maintain that home except as what they are—my friends, not my servants, but my friends. If you wish to hire a cook, you will pay her salary out of your own income. The house is within walking distance of shops, so you won't need a carriage.''

Suzanne's eyes were narrowed with speculation as she studied her faintly smiling daughter-in-law. ''And what if I refuse?''

''You won't,'' Anne stated flatly. ''You haven't anywhere else to go. One more condition, Lady Suzanne: You'll visit Brownsville only when you're invited. Now about today. After you have visited pleasantly with your son for the next hour, you will leave to spend the night at the inn in Pontifract. Gil and I will pay your hired driver to take you to London tomorrow, and we'll have your other trunks shipped there next week.'' Anne looked up to smile at her glum husband standing in the doorway. ''Come on in, Gil. Your mother and I have reached an understanding.''

The words almost choked her, but Lady Suzanne did reply. ''Anne has offered me your London home.''

He stared at his wife. ''I didn't know you owned that house. I thought you only leased it.''

''We own it, Gil. And your mother can live there quite comfortably.''

But Mother was a long way from being subdued. ''I can, providing I can take my own belongings from the house next door.''

Gilbert glared at her in disbelief. ''You don't own another damn thing here. You already sold the china and the silver which were not yours to sell, and you took every artpiece of value.'' Anne smiled contentedly; he had taken a more thorough inventory than she had. ''Furthermore, Mother, Anne and I will not be responsible for any debts you incur in London.''

"I paid all your debts for a good number of years, Gilbert."

"I know you did and you ruined my father financially in the process. Mother, Anne and I are living like a couple of grubs to build something for our children. We're not trying to be unkind to you, we just can't afford to live the way you and Father did."

Anne looked at the bleak face of her guest and relented; more specifically, she responded to a flash of inspiration. "There is one very fine artpiece you may have, Lady Suzanne. Your portrait! It would look magnificent above the fireplace at the townhouse."

Not daring to look at her husband, Anne studied the expressions on Suzanne's face as it changed from disbelief to joy. "I was wearing my white satin ball gown when I posed for that artist. I would love to have the picture, and I will enjoy living in London in my own home again." The ugly tension had disappeared, and Anne fled to the kitchen with the empty teapot. When she returned a half hour later with hot tea and a tray loaded with Marie's delicacies, Gilbert was patiently listening to his mother's unceasing flow of talk. When Lady Suzanne was driven away two hours later, the carefully wrapped portrait was secured on top of the carriage; and long before she left, one of the Grimes brothers had already ridden into Pontifract to make sure she would receive excellent service at the inn.

Laughing with relief, Gilbert grabbed Anne and whirled her around the lawn until she forced him to stop. "If you don't put me down gently, you big oaf, I'm going to drop your lamb right here on the grass."

She would always remember the stunned-idiot expression he wore as he carried her into the house and laid her down on the couch.

"You're going to have another child?" he asked. She nodded.

"When?"

"In three months."

Quickly he ran his hand over the length of her abdomen, gently tracing the slight bulge there. "Why the devil don't you show like other woman? I thought you were just putting on a little weight. Are you sure of the time?"

She laughed. "Absolutely, and if you weren't so dense, you'd have guessed long ago. You've been kicked often enough."

He grinned sheepishly and blushed. "I wondered what those were."

Just as he'd taken to fatherhood with a total commitment, so he became a doting father-to-be. Anne was not allowed out of the house without his loving attendance; he urged food on her and rest as if she were as delicate as a flower. Remembering the hard work she had done only weeks before, Anne was both touched and irritated by his constant concern for trivialities. But she knew better than to depend on him for essentials. It was to Grimes and Marie she went for midwife and wet nurse information. That practical, resourceful man solved both problems instantly. The oldest of his brothers' wives "birthed" all Grimes infants, he said, and a niece of hers whose husband was at sea had just had a child. He was even prepared for twins since another of the Grimes women was still nursing her youngest offspring.

Gilbert was like a small lad at Christmas when he and Marie went to Leeds to buy infant clothes; he bought so many useless toys and garments that Marie was forced to return the next day to exchange most of them for the needed items of blankets and nappies. He was equally enthusiastic about his attic searches for the old furniture stored there. In rapid succession he unearthed a cradle, a crib, a high chair, a rocking horse, a small bathtub, and even a tiny hand-painted chamber pot. Soon the nursery was as crowded as a junk store. One day he emerged from his treasure hunt with his now familiar idiot smile. Lovingly draped over his arms was a six-foot-long christening dress complete with ribbons, lace, and a matching bonnet.

In the predawn hours when Anne felt the first pain, she

roused him sharply and cried, "Hurry." Wearing only a robe over his nightclothes, he ran barefoot across the grounds to awaken Marie; but even with this speed, the necessary people arrived only just in time. Anne's second son was already uncurling his long legs and getting ready to emerge one hour after the first pain. He measured twenty-five inches. Three days later when he opened his eyes, Anne knew his name; the large eyes were a beautiful soft gray. "Harold Gilbert Brownwell," she announced to the father as he sat admiring his son. He nodded and kissed his wife gratefully.

Anne had hoped that she would be able to nurse this baby, but again she did not produce a drop of milk. With tears of frustration, she complained about her lack to her husband. He was anything but sympathetic as he blew into her ear and whispered, "I don't think that yours were intended for that purpose," and looking into her eyes, he caressed her thoroughly. Anne cursed the time they had to wait but silently thanked the rams and ewes for making her husband into a very lusty man.

As it turned out, it was just as well there were two wet nurses available. Harold Gilbert drained them both. In three months this hollow baby was consuming bowls of warm mush and mashed-up fruit. "He's going to be a giant," groaned Anne, who had forgotten that the same words had often been used about her.

"I like them tall," her husband responded smugly. "The view is much better from up here." He was, thought Anne, a thoroughly ridiculous father. Twice a day he would return to the house to pick his child up and talk to him seriously. She firmly believed that Harold would grow up to smell like a sheep, so often did his father visit him during working hours.

Arriving home when the baby was a month old, the seven-year-old twins were introduced to their new brother by a very careful father. As he led his tall children over to the crib, he asked them casually, "This is the newest addition to our family. Do you think we should keep him?" Two startled faces swiveled around and up to stare at their smiling father. Only when they were sure that he was joking did they smile back at him. As Tony studied the tiny face that seemed to study him in return, he was thoughtful. "He looks like the two men in the pictures in the big house."

"Those are pictures of my father and my oldest brother," Gilbert admitted, wondering how Tony even knew about them. He would have been very astonished to learn that Margaret Maude and her brother knew his boyhood home almost as well as he did, having spent many hours tiptoeing through the rooms whenever Marie's and Anne's backs were turned.

Margaret's appraisal of her brother was more practical. "He's too skinny." She soon made it her business to watch him as he nursed, explaining to the nurses that this baby was a special child who couldn't help it because he was so long and needed so much food. When her young Uncle Geoffrey, who now commuted regularly with the twins between Brownsville and Grayhaven, saw the baby, he made the mistake of calling Harold another "Ashton pole bean." Margaret was incensed; "My brother," she informed Geoffrey coldly, "is a beautiful baby." Anne and her husband exchanged looks over this byplay; who would believe that their wild tomboy had such a maternal streak?

That night at dinner in the now crowded servants' quarters, Gilbert announced, "I think it's time to move into the big house while everyone's home to help with the work. Tomorrow while your mother and Marie go to town to hire some people, the rest of us are going to search for buried treasure." After the episode of the baby furniture, Anne knew that her husband's memory for boyhood household goods was as accurate as a shopkeeper's; she groaned silently about the amount of useless items her family would unearth.

Early the next day, even before she and Marie left the house, Anne could hear the sounds of boxes being rustled in the storerooms and attics. In the villages where they stopped first, the two women hired painters, glaziers, and chimney cleaners. In Leeds, however, where the serious shopping for draperies had to take place, Anne relaxed and let Marie take over. Whereas she was economical, Marie was a price expert. Her merest shrug was an eloquent "Too much," her raised eyebrow meant "Ridiculous," and a slight head shake meant "We'll look elsewhere." But if a bargain was finally struck, her enthusiastic *"Bon"* had made the tradesman her friend.

When the two women arrived home, they were greeted by four happy hunters standing proudly by their trophies. Tony had found a slightly rusted suit of armor, which he was manfully polishing. Seeing the look on her son's face, Anne knew it would be on display somewhere in the house forever. Her husband and half brother were admiring their find, which they had spent hours cleaning. It was a gigantic picture which Geoffrey assured her had been painted by the outstanding landscape artist of a century before.

"It must be the picture my mother's portrait replaced," Gilbert exclaimed. "I think it's beautiful." He would, Anne thought as she counted the white creatures with brown faces that grazed beneath the painted blue skies; but even sheep were preferable to the former occupant of that hallowed spot over the fireplace mantel, so she smiled her approval.

Margaret Maude had found the only real treasure of the day, a huge box of silver flatware used fifty years earlier, badly tarnished but still beautiful. Anne blessed her daughter and mentally counted the money saved.

For the next three weeks while the professional workers painted and repaired, the amateur treasure hunt continued until the lawns were littered with vases and pictures being cleaned, metal objects polished, and broken toys repaired. Anne found herself becoming as eager as the others to discover what lay beneath the accumulated layers of dust. She found two ancient tapestries which when gently cleaned with soap and water revealed much of their original color and medieval charm. One of the interesting results of these attic raids was the discovery that her brother had an unerring eye for value. While Gilbert was too sentimental and Anne too practical, Geoffrey knew the names of artists and the commercial worth of the antiques. When he approved a find, Anne made a mental note to place that object on more obvious display.

As both the professionals and amateurs finished their restorations, Grimes and Marie brought cleaners and gardeners in from the surrounding villages; and these two majordomos watched to see which ones polished the most vigorously and dusted the most thoroughly. At the end of their weeks of supervision, Brownsville Manor had three permanent maids and two gardeners. One gardener and two maids, Anne noted, looked suspiciously Grimes-like.

When the house was ready, its stripped-down look disappeared as the attic yield was distributed around. But it would be months before the family stopped feeling lost in their huge new quarters; they missed the coziness of smaller places. Just as she and her husband clung together for companionship that night in their large bedroom, they discovered the next morning that both twins had dragged their bedding into Geoffrey's room to sleep. During the weeks of transition, even after the children had returned to school, their parents often asked Marie if they could dine with her and Grimes in the kitchen.

Gradually, however, Lord and Lady Brownwell emerged from the two grubby sheep hands who still labored most days with those demanding animals on whose woolly backs rode the future of Brownsville. The first social appearance of these novice aristocrats occurred the night of the housewarming ball. Besides their twenty-odd family members and immediate friends, forty of the local elite and gentry were invited. A month before the momentous occasion, Gilbert asked Anne casually whether or not she had planned her dress. She shook her head; she hadn't "planned" a dress since America.

"I remember one dress you wore before we were married, the night you wouldn't even look at me. It was a purple velvet one and it made you look very seductive. As I recall, I was very jealous of my brother that time." Anne remembered that particular dress very well—blue violets, Claude Bouvier had called it—and it still hung limply in her closet. Immediately she ordered a duplicate made with just the merest nod to fashion changes; the idea of a jealous husband was too much of a temptation to resist.

On the day the dress was finished, Anne and Marie drove into Leeds with a long shopping list which kept them busy until the shops closed. They ordered stacks of gleaming white china to be delivered, cases of champagne and wine, and boxes of special foodstuffs Anne had never heard of. When they arrived back at the estate in exhaustion, they found Lord Brownwell busily roasting a spitted lamb while an interested Grimes looked on in awe. He had never seen a man take over in a kitchen before; but if the mister did it, it must not be too lowly a job. Gilbert ordered the two women to sit down while he served dinner. Touched by his consideration, Marie gratefully rested her tired feet. After dinner the host poured four glasses of brandy, although Anne noted in relief that he did not touch his when he rose to make a short speech.

"My wife," he announced, holding up an object Anne guiltily recognized as her surviving wedding ring, "does not wear this ring." He was right; except for the night of Lynette's wedding in America and for the three days of the hearing in England, she had not had the ring on her finger. Even though it held a row of small perfect diamonds, she had hated it since her wedding day because it had belonged to Lady Suzanne. "Beautiful rings were meant to be worn by beautiful women," her husband continued, "so it would give Anne and me pleasure, Marie, if you would accept it as a token of our gratitude. You've made our home very special." Anne's smile seconded her husband's; and they watched as Marie—the practical, no-nonsense woman—pushed it on the little finger of her right hand. She didn't even wipe away the tears that ran down her plain, beautiful face.

That night in their own room, Gilbert asked his wife, "Would you wear a wedding ring if I bought you one?" Mutely she nodded and fought her tears as he picked up her hand and slipped a plain gold band on her finger. Moments later he opened a large jewelry case and fastened a beautiful necklace of amethysts and sapphires around her neck. "They are your colors, sweetheart, so I had it made for you. This time they're from me with all my respect and gratitude." As he wiped the tears from her cheeks he grinned and slapped her bottom. "I'll deliver my love personally as soon as you get properly undressed for bed." She didn't need a second invitation.

Looking back over the ball which had quickly followed their own special housewarming, Anne dusted off her memories one by one. First to arrive two days before the celebration were the nine from Grayhaven: Paddy and Lady Gray; Mary and her new husband, Dwayne Brodie; and the five children whose lives had been so closely bound up. Anne watched her beloved family move admiringly through the rooms, and she noted the changes in each person. Louis at fifteen was rapidly developing Paul Bouvier's wolfish look and charm, while the petite Lisa was pretty and French to her fingertips. Pink-cheeked Danny was a happy little lad whose athletic abilities had made him a school hero. Although still the wild hoyden, Margaret Maude already exhibited the beauty and impish smile her father's heritage promised her. But Anne's special concern was for Tony, whose handsome, sensitive face mirrored his love for everyone. How, she asked herself for the hundredth time, did two people who had stumbled around for years in the pitfalls of human relationships ever give birth to this perfect diplomat?

She watched as her son escorted two people across the room, the only two from Grayhaven who might feel awkward as guests—Mary "Harrington" and Dwayne Brodie, who had already taught his glowing wife what he taught his students, to speak the English language musically with only a trace of Irish lilt. Anne remembered the years of undemanding love and loyalty this warmhearted woman had given her and her children, a girl from shantytown, Boston, who in the past year had reached out to acquire a quiet dignity to match the pretty face. Tony squeezed his mother's hand before he guided his "special" guests toward his father.

"Does he frighten you with that gentle intuition of his,

Anne?'' She swung around to see Padric Neill standing behind her.

"Paddy," she gulped, fighting the tears that flooded her eyes. He looked the same to her as he had twenty-one years ago, with his twinkling eyes probing into her thoughts.

"Anthony is like you in many ways, Anne; but in that respect, he's unique. Whereas you had such a ferocious drive you tired me out, he always takes into consideration the way other people are feeling."

She frowned slightly. "Paddy, I don't want him to be afraid of anyone."

"No danger of that. He can outfight his sister, if he thinks someone is being unfairly treated. Hello, Lady Margaret, I was just telling our young mother that her son is one of our finest."

"Tony?" Aunt Margaret smiled fondly and then said an amazing thing for her: "He's sensitive, like his father. Come along, Anne, Gilbert's waiting for you to open your house-warming gift from Grayhaven. He wouldn't even touch the ribbon until you were there."

The gift was twenty volumes of classical literature, each book identically bound in brown leather with the name Brownwell etched in gold beneath the title. "These are wonderful." Gilbert smiled. "Now Maggie won't have to tell me the stories anymore; I can read them for myself." Perched on his shoulders, his blond daughter grinned down at him.

The next day the Ashtons and Perkinses arrived, Maude and Tom riding with the lord and lady while the younger members rode in a following carriage. How wonderful they looked together, Anne thought. Maude and Tom had bought a home near Grayhaven to be with their five godchildren. Without sacrificing any of their American bluntness, they had become an accepted part of rural England; and Maude's kitchen was a favorite meeting place for the friends of all the children here today.

At fifty-one Lord Geoffrey looked forty, tall and still slim enough to appear almost boyish when he smiled, as he did often in his complacent satisfaction with life. His pride in his family was evident as he walked forward with his son to greet his oldest daughter. Had a portrait artist been there to reproduce these three faces on canvas, he would have found only the slight differences of age and gender. All three looked like the tall Vikings from whom they had most probably descended.

Elizabeth and her daughters were another of nature's triangles, the mother just slightly plumper, but otherwise alike. Young Elizabeth, already an ambitious woman, had her husband in tow, a vain man who obviously believed that respect came with rank alone. The self-absorption of these newlyweds was both pathetic and embarrassing; within minutes Anne became weary of listening to the long list of titled notables connected to his family. Caroline, the younger girl, still had a spark of fun that was being fanned neatly at the moment by a merry-faced young man, who though he held rank, held it very lightly. The most interesting of these three women was the mother herself. Elizabeth's face reflected the discontent of a woman whose demands of life had never quite been met. Her husband and son had eluded her domination, and not even her rise up the ladder of aristocracy had earned her the respect she craved. Although she now accepted Anne as an equal, she still retained traces of her earlier resentment.

In the afternoon hours before the ball, the big house stood waiting in a kind of limbo, with activity limited to the kitchen. It had become a well-organized factory with dozens of varieties of food divided into hundreds of servings, all carefully labeled for easy service. For days Marie had trained her now regular sisters-in-law and four village helpers. Not once had she been questioned by Anne, and not once had she asked for advice. She and Lady Brownwell had developed a firm partnership in the management of the manor. Anne had frowned with worry when she'd announced that there would be sixty people at the party; Marie had smiled and exclaimed enthusiastically, *Bon. Pas de problème.* Don't worry, *chérie.''*

Out on the sweeping front lawns another group enterprise was under way. The children and young men, Lord Brownwell included, had divided into teams and were madly kicking a ball back and forth, with shouts of "Foul!" and "Goal!" so intermingled that the terrace watchers could not determine the winners from the losers. They did notice, however, that Danny outran the other players and, to Anne's slight embarrassment, that her daughter was his fastest competition. When the game ended, their host led the grass-stained, sweating men and boys behind the kitchen wing, where eight barrels of warm water awaited them. Here the spirit of the game continued without stop, this time with bars of soap and handfuls of water thrown from barrel to barrel. Little Margaret was incensed when her mother led her upstairs to the refinement of an indoor tub, where a patient Lisa tried to explain the facts of life to this determined rebel.

By eight o'clock the youngest children had been fed and relegated to their vantage point at the head of the stairs, forbidden to come down any lower. Even nine-month-old Harold was allowed to sit by his sister to watch the party below unfold. Because their parents were coming, Lisa and Louis were dressed to attend their first ball. At eight-thirty Anne and her husband descended the stairs and walked hand in hand from one room to another, where everything looked beautiful to their uncritical eyes. They kissed Marie and wished her luck and waved to the Grimes brothers outside awaiting the traffic of expected carriages. In the music alcove were four musicians, who were eating the dinner Marie had already served them. They were village men whose evening apparel may have been old-fashioned, but whose music, according to Grimes, was "toe-tappin' lively." As the reception line queued up, even Anne was impressed by the display. Three ladies, two lords, and several embryo aristocrats should be enough to impress even the most haughty of the locals who were already arriving by twos and fours. Gilbert and Anne took turns introducing them to the assembled families and friends.

Just before the reception line disbanded, Paul and Lynette arrived and everyone present stared in awe. Paul, with a silver glint now in his dark hair, was impeccably garbed in an evening suit so new in cut and dashing it could only have come from Paris tailors. He still looked, Anne reflected, like a good-natured wolf; and she remembered the times they had clashed back in the shipyards. She also remembered his protection and her friendship with the gamine Frenchwoman who had cheerfully admitted to being his mistress in straitlaced Boston. Tonight Lynette was the undisputed queen of the ball. From tiara to ivory satin shoes, she looked like an elegant French sophisticate; but underneath the glitter was the old Lynette. Fifteen minutes after she arrived, Anne heard the words "Me, I'd spit in his eye" being addressed to Lord Ashton, who had never lost his admiration of pretty, petite, dark-haired women.

Fast on the heels of the Bouviers came Lord Gerald Gray, alone now since he had become a widower two years earlier. From across the room Anne could feel his eyes on her, and she walked over to greet him. "Still looking for a bookkeeper, Grandfather?" she asked and kissed the top of his balding head.

"Still think you're a promising young worker," he answered, pleased in the way of old men at a pretty woman's flattery.

The last arrival, one invitation Anne had not expected to be accepted, was the still impressively regal Lady Suzanne Brownwell, who had, her daughter-in-law suspected, deliberately waited in order to make a more dramatic entrance. When neither Anne nor Gilbert rushed forward—she was still held fast by her grandfather and her husband was serving the drinks to the men, Lady Elizabeth Ashton did. Perhaps she, too, felt a little of the isolation of incomplete acceptance. With the remarkable memory natural hostesses seem to acquire, she introduced Suzanne with unerring accuracy to forty or more guests. As Elizabeth finished her sponsorship, a forgiving son escorted his mother to the supper table, where she studied Marie's production with a critical eye.

All the beauty of that scene, Anne recalled—the lamp-lit balconies outside the dining hall and ballroom, the bowls of iced champagne, the tables of food with pleasant women to serve it, were all part of a memory to be stored for future recall. And later in the dimmed ballroom when she and Gilbert began the dance, two tall, handsome people dancing together for the first time in nine years of marriage, Anne felt as if she had awakened in paradise, especially when she caught Paul's sardonic eye across the heads of other couples and watched him make the French gesture of approval with his fingers to his lips.

She danced with her father and her brother and listened to their praise. She danced with neighbors, too, of course, but Anne was not yet lady enough to remember names before she knew the people. She saw Gilbert watching her as she danced with Paul and felt a little wicked when that not-quite-reformed flirt murmured in her ear, "Ah, *chérie*, you still don't know that you are an exciting woman. Your husband knows, though. He is, I think, still a little jealous. If he ever becomes indifferent, we will maybe introduce him to Claude." Grinning wolfishly at her startled response, he whirled her around the floor until a hand landed on his shoulder, and Lord Brownwell reclaimed his property with his own smile of predatory victory.

Anne's memory of the party stopped at that dance with her husband. For a few steps the music guided their feet; but as they neared the open doors leading to the terrace, he led her out to a darkened corner and whispered, "I can dance with every other woman in the room. But not with you. I get you in my arms and it's not dancing I'm thinking of."

Responding with the joy that had been building all night, Anne returned his kiss. A moment later when they separated and smiled at each other like truant children, he mentioned casually, "I returned the two thousand pounds of your dowry to your father."

"Why?"

"Why did you give him back the fifteen thousand your grandfather paid out for my debts?" he countered.

Her eyes burned into his. "Because I didn't want anyone but me to own any part of you."

"No one else ever has, Anne." Her memory stopped right there.

Chapter 21

ONLY one other chapter in that tumultuous three years of her life continued to nag her memory with recriminations despite her oft-repeated self-assurances that she'd had just cause for her attitude. Anne had discovered her own feet of clay—she hated that biblical reference almost as much as she did the Greek Achilles' heel. In one searing revelation her character had been revealed as less than sterling, and only through the wisdom of her husband and Aunt Margaret had she narrowly avoided destroying the happy serenity of all of their lives.

During the aftermath of the housewarming ball when all three of Anne's families had remained at Brownsville for a holiday, her life had been idyllic. With housekeeping reduced to a minimum, since only a few of the guests were dependent upon servants, Marie found she had half a dozen expert helpers in the kitchen led by Lynette and Maude, who excelled in preparing picnic hampers and arranging alfresco meals on the terrace. In the warm spring weather, young Geoffrey Ashton, who knew the recreational delights of the Aire River far better than his oldest sister, acted as guide for the younger guests and children. Each morning he assembled his adventurous troops for a day's outing and marched them to the water barrels when he returned them home dirty and bedraggled hours later. After the first outing, at Maggie's fierce insistence, he had rigged a blanket screen between the two sets of barrels to separate the sexes. The pigtailed eight-year-old had won her first small battle for equality.

At the sheep pens, which Lord Ashton had expressly come to study, he met the several neighbors who had decided to convert to merinos and to the more efficient organization Gilbert had devised, which had earned double the profits in the last two seasons. Since most of the available merinos of England now resided at this farm, stock for these planned conversions would have to come from Spain and France. A startled Lord Gerald Gray and Paul Bouvier were approached by the determined sheep men to supply the ships for transportation. Thus for several days the manor's library became a masculine domain where vacationing men eased the boredom of unaccustomed leisure by transacting new business over glasses of Madeira wine.

Anne was left with a small nucleus of people who had learned the art of conversation. Surpisingly Lady Suzanne sheathed her claws and joined this group. To Anne's amazement, her mother-in-law had taken the time to meet her grandchildren and talk to them.

"My late husband," she murmured thoughtfully, "would have adored all of them. Who would have thought that Gilbert would be the son to produce two like their grandfather in spirit and a namesake who even looks like him?" Not exactly effusive approval, but certainly a far cry from her earlier disavowal of relationship.

Nothing else of moment occurred during those golden days, unless it was the arrival of a sentimental gift from Alan Chadwick and the once again actor, Philip Trent. Mounted on a velvet-covered board were a British Lancers saber inscribed with Lord Brownwell's name and an ebony sword cane engraved with his wife's. Etched into the shiny brass plate below was the legend "Mementos of an Underground Safari into Tartarus." Anne smiled at the inference; only the theatrical mind of Philip Trent would liken the Doncaster coal mines to the hellhole prison of Hades in Greek mythology. Encouraged by the mystified guests, who had not heard the details of the Brownwells' adventure, Lady Margaret told the entire story with dramatic effectiveness and excusable exaggeration. Reaction among the listeners ranged from frowning disapproval on Lord Ashton's part to quiet laughter by Paddy Neill and Paul, and finally to a passionate defense of her parents by Margaret Maude. But it was her husband's comment Anne remembered with a warm glow.

"She saved my life with her courage, and she earned us a fortune with that neatly convoluted mind of hers. Of course, it helps that she's also beautiful and lovable."

From that euphoric height and the excitingly productive months that followed, Anne asked herself in disgust how she could have crashed to the despondent depths she had. Not even the night Gilbert had suddenly stopped in the middle of making love to her was of any lasting consequence.

"Something just kicked me," he accused his wife. "Is it what I'm thinking?" In the dark she'd nodded glumly. Enough, after all, was enough.

"I wish you'd give me a little warning. When is this one due?" He sounded cheerful and happy about the prospect, she thought with only limited tolerance for the male urge to populate the earth.

"Four months," she admitted and was once more packed away in cotton padding or perhaps, in her case, wool fleece and forced to wait patiently for the inevitable. Prepared this time with the midwife Grimes encamped in a nearby room, Anne counted out the days and hours. When the pains finally began, she expected her usual swift delivery; but this child took its time. For eight long hours Anne labored and then produced a tiny dark-haired girl whose face was pretty even in those predawn hours.

As Anne looked at the baby, she cried out, "My God!" as she had with the twins; but this time there was no reverence or joy in her reaction. It isn't fair to reproduce a woman I've never seen and who never wanted to see me, she raged silently, and to force me to love a child who isn't mine or Gil's. Everyone believed that her listlessness and lack of interest in the baby were due to the painful hours of childbirth. Her husband was particularly patient with her even when he undertook the delayed task of naming this new baby.

"What do you think of the name Lynette?" he asked. "Lynette Anne?"

"Lynette is fine, but not Anne. Why don't you use Marie for a middle name? At least that way, she'd be named after two good women. Gil, are you picking that baby up again? You'll spoil her."

"I didn't spoil Harold."

"No, but she's different."

He smiled at his wife and tucked the happy, gurgling infant back into the elaborate small basket bed he'd bought because Harold's old crib had been too large.

"She is that, Anne. She's not like our others."

Anne suppressed the sour words that flooded through her mind. "He'll be calling her Princess before the year is out, and she'll grow up to be a pampered, irresponsible woman everyone forgives because she's so little and so pretty."

The first part of this unpleasant prediction was realized when Lynette was only a month old and her grandfather came to inspect his fourth grandchild. As with the older three, Lord Ashton was enthusiastic in his approval; but with this tiny, perfect child, he was considerably more. He was unmistakably doting.

"Well, look at you with your pretty green eyes and black curls! So tiny and so sweet! You're going to be Grandpapa's little princess, aren't you." He glanced over at the three adults who had been watching him with varying degrees of raised eyebrows. "Your Maggie may be more beautiful, Anne, but this baby is very special," he murmured sentimentally.

His daughter smiled faintly, put her arms around twenty-one-month-old Harold, and hugged him wordlessly. Even Gilbert, who himself tended to dote uncritically on all his children, was taken aback by the fatuous look on his father-in-law's face. It was Elizabeth's comment that gave him the first hint of explanation for his wife's odd attitude toward this child.

"Your father has never forgotten his first love, Anne. But now I'll finally get to see what my old rival looked like."

Anne shrugged with a studied indifference. "Don't be silly, Elizabeth. I just got one of yours by mistake this time."

"Don't I wish it! This one is prettier than either of my girls were. Your mother must have been a beautiful woman, Anne."

"Not as far as I'm concerned," Anne snapped. "For me, she's a faceless nothing; and I'd have preferred she remain that way." That was the first time Gilbert had ever heard his wife refer to her mother, and the bitterness in her voice stunned him. Over the last four years he'd grown to depend on her humorous common sense and cheerful courage. It would never have occurred to him that part of her boundless drive for accomplishment was a form of revenge against the self-centered woman who'd refused to be her mother. Regretfully, he recalled his own cruel words to Anne right after their wedding; and in a flash of understanding, he realized how she'd been the innocent victim of adult cruelty, his own included. But he recalled something else far more critical to this present problem of a unwanted baby. His own foolish mother had destroyed the unity of his boyhood home by adoring him and detesting his brothers. Both her favoritism and his father's resentment had contributed to an unhappy childhood for all three Brownwell sons.

"Not in my own family!" he vowed; and long before the dinner hour an urgent letter to Aunt Margaret was on its way to Grayhaven. He minced no words in expressing his fear that this latest child had alienated Anne. "And in a way, I don't blame her. Lord Ashton acted like a fool about Lynette. Help me if you can, Margaret. I'll admit I'm out of my depth."

Lady Gray's response was characteristic. She arrived the week after the Ashtons' departure with a carriage full of people and a determined expression. Greeted only by Marie at the front door, she took over the duties of hostess and sent Tony out to locate his father.

In the remote room on the third floor that Anne used as her own private office, she heard none of the downstairs commotion. Immersed in work as she always was when emotional problems threatened her composure, she had momentarily repressed her irritation with herself and her father; however, her nagging awareness of Gilbert's growing disapproval was impossible to blunt. For once her acting ability had failed to be convincing. Despite her best efforts to appear the fond mother in front of her father and Elizabeth, her husband had known that she was not and had watched her with increasing concern.

Jarred out of her preoccupation by the imperious sound of her oldest daughter's voice outside the door, Anne's heart speeded up in alarm. Maggie was supposed to be at school.

"Margaret Maude, what are you doing home? Are you and your brother all right?"

"Of course we are, Mama. Papa said you weren't feeling well, so I'm taking my friend Scott to see the new baby. And I want to see if Harold remembers what I taught him the last time."

Who the devil is Scott? Anne wondered impatiently as she smoothed her hair and skirts. And what in the world is Aunt Margaret thinking of to allow nine-year-olds to travel across England with a stranger? Her spoken question, "Is your Uncle Geoffrey with you?" elicited no response from her mercurial daughter, and Anne smiled a little grimly as she hurried down the corridor toward the nursery. Maggie had an annoying habit of not waiting for permission once she had announced her intentions. Inside the large room she found her tall daughter holding Harold's hand as she peeked into the lace-draped basket bed of her baby sister. Anne herself was greeted by a smiling young man resplendently garbed in the uniform of a junior officer of the Royal Navy.

"Your husband gave me permission to accompany Maggie upstairs, Lady Brownwell. I'm Scott Palmer."

Maggie swung around belatedly to complete the introduction.

"I told you already, Mama. Scott is a friend of mine, and we've been driving ever so long to get here."

"Who's we, Maggie?"

"Aunt Margaret, my grandfather—"

Anne frowned. "Your Grandfather Ashton?"

"No, Mama, Grandfather Gray and another lady. Mama, why is the baby all covered up in all that silly lace? Is something the matter with her?"

Unprepared for this blunt, unsentimental question, Anne chuckled. "Nothing is the matter with her."

"Then why is she so small?"

"All babies are small."

"Harold never was."

"Yes, Harold was. Now you take him and your friend Scott downstairs and tell your father I'll be down later."

As she turned to leave, Anne found her way blocked by the young man. To her surprise, he politely changed her instructions. "Do as your mother says, Maggie. She and I will both be down later." Before Anne could protest Scott Palmer's casually presumptive suggestion, he demanded, "Lady Brownwell, I want to talk to you. Is there someplace where we won't disturb Lynette?" Turning back to Maggie, he gave her a playful shove. "Get going, Miss Big Ears, this doesn't concern you."

Anne was amazed when her daughter obeyed this stranger with greater alacrity than she ever obeyed her parents. She discovered minutes later in the nursery sitting room that Scott Palmer was an entirely surprising young man. Without any hesitant preliminaries, he announced bluntly, "I'm your brother, Anne Gray, and Aunt Margaret has already told me that you've never had the foggiest idea I existed."

She felt stupid as she repeated the word. "Brother? I don't understand." And then she did even without his explanation.

"We have the same mother," he informed her defensively.

"How long have you known about me?"

"Since the first summer I spent at Grayhaven ten years ago. Everyone there referred to Anne Gray as if she were ten feet tall and unbeatable. When I asked Aunt Margaret who this Amazon queen was, she told me. So I've followed your career ever since.''

Anne grimaced. "From the English newspapers? You must have an odd impression of me.''

"Mostly from your friends, Anne, and since last year from the twins. They're gorgeous youngsters. Two of my ship-mates were in love with Maggie until she beat them at cricket.''

It was impossible for Anne not to like this younger brother who had quickly recovered from his brief awkwardness and reverted to the handsome, merry-faced man he was.

"Do Maggie and Tony know you're their uncle?''

"Not a chance. Aunt Margaret was a martinet about that. But I'm afraid most of my friends know you're my sister. After that flap two years ago in Birmingham, you were a very famous woman; and I couldn't resist boasting about you.''

"I'd have thought you'd have more important things to talk about aboard ship.''

"Than a lady aristocrat who made a fortune in America and who turned the stuffed shirts of England topsy-turvy and even won the approval of our queen? Not hardly! You're referred to as the invincible Anne by my fellow officers.''

"I can imagine the other adjectives they use," she scoffed dryly, "and if Her Royal Majesty even knows I exist, it's probably as the horrible example.''

"No, Anne, that's one of the reasons I'm here today—to deliver an official summons from Queen Victoria for you and your husband. Incidentally, he's a smasher!''

"And you're a worse liar than I used to be, Scott Palmer.''

"No, I'm not." He grinned at her. "I gave the official invitation to your husband, and he said the same thing. Don't you two ever read the London papers?''

"Not unless there's an article about a new breed of sheep. We're simple farmers.''

"And mill owners and coal mine financiers. In addition to being very much a current news item. Last month the Blake brothers were knighted for their part in cleaning up the coal industry, but they refused to accept the honor unless you and your husband were given equal recognition. Furthermore, your husband is to be presented in court as the outstanding new pioneer in wool production.''

Anne smiled cynically. "I don't know about Gil, but I have no intention of making another spectacle of myself for the enjoyment of the British public, Scott."

His face was serious again. "I'd like you to go, Anne, for a personal reason. If you'll promise to quit using that tongue of yours to slash me to ribbons, I want to explain something and ask for a favor."

"The other lady downstairs is your mother, isn't she?"

"Our mother, Anne."

"No, not mine. Aunt Margaret is the only mother I ever had."

"Lucky you! Now will you listen to me?"

Anne shrugged noncommittally, but her eyes held a resentful glint; she had no intention of being manipulated by this charmingly persuasive flatterer. Daunted a little by her uncompromising attitude, Scott began his explanation.

"I know all about our mother's—" He corrected himself quickly and continued, "My mother's youthful indiscretions and worse, because she told me; but for twenty-five years her life has been blameless. My father's in the diplomatic service, a position our grandfather paid for since my father had no money of his own. Until he was knighted six years ago, he didn't have a title, either, although his family is cluttered with them. I've never met a one of those snobs because they refused to recognize my mother, and they snubbed our grandfather because he'd made his money in trade. But even so, my parents were very happy as long as their diplomatic posts were abroad. Most of the time I stayed here and went to school, and they would come home for holidays. During those years my mother worked as hard as my father did, but four years ago he was appointed secretary to Lord George Clarendon, who is the most important diplomat in England.

That was just about the time you returned from America, Anne, and received the full libelous treatment by the scum who call themselves journalists. No, my mother wasn't smeared in the papers; but she was castigated just the same—by every lord and lady of our gracious realm.

"I'd like to be able to boast that my father resigned his post in outraged fury at the treatment my mother received during every function she attended in London. But he didn't! He's a very ambitious man, and he took the precaution of protecting his own good name by leaving my mother home with Grandfather Gray. Last year, when Victoria appointed Clarendon her foreign minister, Sir Robert Palmer moved into the diplomatic wing of Buckingham Palace along with Lord Clarendon and other members of his staff. But not my mother! Oh, my father still comes to see her when he has nothing better to do, and occasionally he admits I'm alive. But he refuses to jeopardize his position by inviting Mother to join him, and she's miserable. She's worked hard to make him successful for years, and now she's been dumped while he enjoys himself."

In spite of her resolve to remain uninvolved, Anne's resentment against male domination was too firmly entrenched for her to remain completely indifferent. Sir Robert Palmer was like every other ambitious man she'd ever met who demanded that his wife be like Caesar's—above reproach—even if he himself were as loosely moraled as a Jonathan Swift Yahoo. Her angry words were an automatic response in defense of any woman trapped by such a man.

"She's better off without her husband if he's that much of a hypocritical prig."

Scott stared hard at his sister. "Were you, Anne? Better off without your husband?"

Swiftly her anger shifted direction. "You've done a thorough job of research into my private life, haven't you, little brother?"

"Not for any reason other than curiosity and admiration, Anne. But I know how hard you fought for the equality you've won. Unfortunately not everyone is as strong as you are. Just for a minute, forget your bitterness against my mother. Think of her as a person who's being unfairly treated. Your father escaped every bit of scandal; and so have I, because next year I take over the management of Gray's Shipping, and the powerful naval lords want me on their side. As for you, you're respected now and so wealthy no one would dare snub you. Why should my mother be the only person punished for something that happened almost thirty years ago?''

Anne heard the question only dimly; her conscience was shouting another, more damning, more imperative question. Why should an innocent child suffer because its mother was too self-centered to forget her own childhood hurt? She thought of her beautiful little Lynette, who resembled one grandmother just as Margaret Maude did the other, and she cringed in shame. How could she have been so stupid as to condemn a child to a life of being rejected by its mother? Oh, God, she mourned, I'm worse than my own mother was because I'm older and happily married. She felt a sudden intense yearning to cuddle Lynette Marie, to assuage the hurt she'd caused, and to offer her precious baby the love that now gushed from her heart in a painful flood.

Gently she answered her brother's question. ''Your mother shouldn't be, Scott.''

''Then will you sponsor her in court when the queen summons you?''

Anne shook her head with genuine regret. ''No, because I will refuse to go.''

''Not even you can defy the queen; Victoria won't let you. She's already publicly promised the Blakes, and our vain monarch will not allow any subject to embarrass her. You're in a wonderful position to request a favor, especially since Lord Clarendon has already promised me his support in petitioning the queen.''

''How does your father feel?''

Scott smiled cynically. ''Oh, he'll welcome Mother because he likes to be waited on and flattered; and as long as his own unblemished reputation isn't besmirched by her presence at court, he'll strut around like a peacock because she'll be one of the prettiest women there.''

Anne began to laugh. This brother of hers had a raw honesty she respected, and the very outrageousness of his request challenged her imagination. "Have you any idea how the London papers will lampoon your mother and me? Whore and bastard will probably be their kindest words.''

"They wouldn't dare because our puritanical queen would take any criticism at all as a personal affront to her own judgment. Even the lords and ladies will have to be polite in public. Will you do it, Anne?''

Anne sighed in surrender. "If my husband doesn't object, yes, I'll do it.''

"Thanks, Anne. One more favor; my mother doesn't know a thing about what I've asked you to do. She's here to meet you and your children because Aunt Margaret insisted. Not that she isn't proud of you; she's followed your career as closely as I have, and she'd like your permission to know you and your family. She doesn't have many friends.''

Anne felt no great sudden warmth for a woman she'd never seen, just an overwhelming impatience to restore serenity to her own disordered house. She had four children and a husband to weld into a harmonious whole, and she was impatient to hold her youngest and begin the building of a strong bond of love.

"Come on, Scott. Let's take Lynette down to meet the rest of her family.''

Gilbert was waiting alone at the foot of the stairs, his eyes studying her anxiously as she descended with Lynette cuddled in her arms. His own arms encircled the two of them, and his laughter was warm as Anne scolded him.

"Gil Brown, don't you ever let me act like such a fool again, even if you have to slap some sense into me.''

Scott Palmer joined in the relieved humor as his brother-in-law responded, "I wouldn't dare, Anne Gray, you'd slap me back."

The introductions that followed in the gracious drawing room were as easy as that laughter. Anne deposited a contented Lynette in Aunt Margaret's lap and kissed the wrinkled cheek of the only mother she'd ever known. "You've always been there when I needed you. I hope that some day I can be as wise as you are."

Margaret chuckled as she peered down at the wide-eyed infant. "You will be, Anne. After all, I was the one who molded your character, just as you'll do for Lynette."

Pausing to kiss Lord Gerald's forehead and to smile at a fascinated Harold, who was busily investigating his great-grandfather's gold watch fob, Anne found another small piece of the past blended into the future when the old man winked at her. "I've already told Scott," Gerald Gray intoned the jovial words half-seriously, "that if he has any problems building ships, he's to consult with Andrew Grey."

Still flanked by her husband and brother, Anne moved toward the remaining three occupants in the room—her tall handsome twins and a small, still slender, still pretty woman from whose guarded eyes all trace of rebellion had disappeared. Soberly Tony made the introduction. "Mama, I want you to meet my grandmother, Lady Mary Palmer."

Anne inclined her head and extended her hand without condescension or bitterness. "Hello, Lady Mary."

"Hello, Anne. I've enjoyed meeting your lovely children." Although the voice was controlled and gracious, Anne heard the faint tremor and relaxed still more. The distant past was no longer important to her, it had lost its power to hurt.

"Then you'll like the fourth one, too, Lady Mary. She's a very special child."

Abruptly the dramatic events happening at the moment crowded out Anne's memories of that final resolution of her life three months earlier. She and her husband were standing in one of the large, austere reception rooms of Buckingham

Palace awaiting an audience with the queen. Weeks before, the carefully phrased letter Gilbert had written to Lord Clarendon explaining Anne's reluctance to attend court unless an equal courtesy was extended to her mother had achieved its purpose. Mainly because Clarendon was the only man besides her royal husband whom the stubborn queen respected, Victoria had acquiesced and granted the request. As quietly as the circumstances permitted, Lady Mary Palmer had been integrated into the outer fringe of the royal household and now lived there with her husband in a somber apartment reserved for the lesser personages.

On their arrival at the palace, the Brownwells had been officially greeted by the Palmers; and Lady Mary's almost inaudible "Thank you" had been drowned out by Sir Robert's eagerness to impress this rural lord and lady with his own importance in the world of diplomacy. As he was expounding grandiloquently on the favorite Victorian theme of "Where Britain goes, so follows the world," Anne remembered Winchell Rawlings and wondered if she'd done her mother any favor. The prospect of a life monitored by a demanding and opinionated queen sounded as dull as the circumspect existence of a Harvard professor's wife. Eventually Sir Robert spotted more impressive targets for his hosting talents and left the Brownwells to the enjoyable companionship of the Blake brothers. Like Anne and Gilbert, these two recent inductees into the lowest echelon of aristocrats had been ordered to attend this ceremony; they much preferred the greater stimulation of running a productive business.

Waiting now for the rites of royal recognition to begin, Anne studied the other sixty or more people gathered in the hall. Except for the ten agricultural and industrial honorees, the lords and ladies present seemed to be a special contingent of aristocrats whose job it was to fill the empty floor and applaud the queen during dull receptions such as this. The elegant people, ladies in tiaras and satins and lords in oddly assorted medieval garb, chatted easily with each other like the long-time friends they were, largely ignoring the honorees whose one short day of glory could never admit them to this gilded circle of elite favorites.

When the plump queen, rendered plumper still by pregnancy and concealing crinolines, entered the room at the far end where a wooden replica of the throne had been placed, the crowd of regular attendees dipped low in flawless, perfunctory bows and curtsies, followed raggedly by the uninitiated. Momentarily the queen surveyed the audience, nodded to the sober-faced prince consort, and seated herself. The panoply of majesty had begun.

Alone or accompanied by their self-conscious wives, the candidates responded to the sepulchral intonement of their names and paid obeisance to the throne, receiving in return a royal nod and smile. When it came their turn, Lord Brownwell and his Lady Anne, taller than the others and more strikingly handsome, walked shoulder to shoulder to the place of honor. With the careless grace he'd mastered during a misspent youth, Gilbert looked like a seasoned courtier whose deep tan had been acquired on the playing field rather than in the filth of sheep pens. For her unasked-for moment of display, Anne had chosen an ensemble of bold design with a flaring cape anchored beneath the low-cut collar of her dress, a cape that trailed gracefully on the floor more like a queenly train than a garment intended for warmth. As she straightened up from the sweeping curtsy she'd practiced all week, shrewd royal eyes watched her and the royal voice sounded sharply.

"We can see, Lady Brownwell, why you were successful in posing as a man. You have a man's look of courage, but"—Victoria paused and swept Anne's dramatic stance and costume with the merest glint of humor—"your daring, we think, is very much your own, and not, we hope, a permanent affliction."

Subtly reminded of the potential power of royal displeasure, Anne bowed her head and smiled in tribute to a monarch who could control a rebellious subject with such a delicately worded reproof. Still amused by the discerning reprimand, she was more aware of the curious eyes of the audience as she and her husband returned to their alcove. Standing alone after the presentation ended, they had long since ceased listening to the diplomatic Lord Clarendon as he extolled the contributions of the nine men and one woman who had been honorees. His voice had that mellifluous quality which either put listeners to sleep or made them think of things other than his profound words. Gilbert's thoughts were more pleasantly centered on other things as he slipped his hand under Anne's long concealing cape and deliberately cupped one of her buttocks. Imperceptibly she wriggled more comfortably into that exploring hand and kept her eyes straight ahead as her husband whispered into her ear so conveniently close to his mouth.

"I wonder what else our good queen would have said if she'd known that the daring Lady Brownwell does not wear proper underthings and that her husband encourages both that and other lewd behavior?"

"She'd call us what we are," Anne murmured, "a happy pair of reformed bastards she was forced to acknowledge publicly as aristocrats." The sound of their irreverent laughter never quite reached the queen's ears.